CW00550125

Force Of Mind

Second in the Psiclone series

SIMON STANTON

CONTENTS

One

London - Friday, late afternoon

Even out of the city centre, London traffic was dense at this time in the afternoon. The roads were packed with cars, crawling along, an army of commuters each inching their way home. One car made faster progress. The grey Audi A5 had blue lights flashing from behind the front grill, a shrill siren pierced each car's cocoon of talk-radio or music or quiet. Some cars moved aside quickly, perhaps thinking an ambulance was approaching. Others took longer to be persuaded to give way. Even with the lights and sirens, progress was slow, certainly slower than the Audi's occupants would have liked.

The driver focused on the road and the traffic, weaving in between cars, charging through red lights and across junctions, much to the ire of those stuck in the stationary queues. The passenger stared out, pensive, anxious. The passenger looked at the people in the cars, thinking about the lives they must lead, ordinary people living ordinary lives, dealing with ordinary problems. He pondered how ordinary life could go on in such blissful ignorance of the violent forces in its midst. Michael Sanders was all too aware of these forces. The last week had been a battle against them, and he had escaped with his life, but only just.

Three of his former colleagues, all Special Forces soldiers, had reappeared in his life, bent on revenge. They had cut a path of murder and violence through London in their quest to steal fifty billion pounds from the Bank of England, and to kill Michael. He had foiled their plan, but the Three had evaded capture and he was sure they had an escape route planned. He was also sure their anger at him would have reached epic proportions.

His former colleagues were skilled, and Michael had no expectation that the civilian police, nor MI5 nor GCHQ would be able to trace the Three, not before they reached whatever hiding place they were heading for. But Michael had a way of tracking them. Potentially had a way, he corrected himself. If he could get there in time. Michael felt a growing anxiety that his only lead might slip away, but at the moment he clung to the feeling of having the target in his sights and a clear shot. All he had to do was aim steadily, and squeeze the trigger.

Michael and the Three all shared a secret, a secret that had been with them for years, ever since they had been recruited into a secret military experiment. The experiment had left the four of them with powerful telepathic abilities. To begin with it had made them a force beyond all others, soldiers powerful like no others. The ability to communicate mind-to-mind meant that they were immune to the problems which bedevilled radio communications. They could communicate underground, they were immune to all electronic eavesdropping, and they could communicate over almost any distance. Their ability to control other people allowed them to conduct covert surveillance from right inside their target's circle of security. But a problem grew amongst them. Three of the four; Vince

Marshall, Evan Bullock and Julian Singh, became tempted by what they could achieve for themselves, and this had put them on a collision course with the shadowy forces running the project.

Marshall, Bullock and Singh had "parted company" with the Army and had set off to use their powers for their own gain, and now they were back. They had used their abilities to control innocent people and to destroy lives. One of their victims was the Bank of England's IT security manager, Jason Mason, now languishing in a police cell. Mason had been a puppet, telepathically controlled, and unaware he was playing a part in a major theft. But Michael couldn't tell the police this, he could do nothing to help Mason.

During the journey, Michael had tried to connect with Mason telepathically. He had reached out with his mind and found the distinctive sense of Mason's thoughts. Each mind had its own distinct signature. Michael couldn't quite describe it, it wasn't a sound or a smell, but it was a distinctive essence unique to each individual. He let his thoughts join with Mason and what he found was a man in turmoil, the man was a mental wreck. Now that the telepathic link between Mason and the Three had been broken, Mason was alone, confused as to what had happened, why he'd done what he had, and why he was under arrest. Michael had tried to calm him, but Mason was in a world of confusion and disbelief, suspecting that he was hearing voices and going mad. Michael had tried to exert a calming influence on Mason's thoughts, but the man had reacted against it, increasing his mental turmoil. Michael had conceded defeat and withdrawn from the telepathic connection. Now Michael was left with his own thoughts as they swept past cars and lorries. Why had his colleagues come back now? What was their plan? They always had a plan. He'd trained with them and worked with them in Special Forces. He knew how they worked; they were methodical, careful, always with a purpose. They had been a close-knit unit of soldiers who trusted each other, but now they were enemies.

Michael's driver, Eric, had been silent for the whole journey. Like a married couple who'd just had an enormous row, the pair had sat in silence for nearly three quarters of an hour. Michael knew that Eric had questions about what had happened, and deserved answers: Eric had almost been killed too. But now was not the time for Eric's questions. Now Michael had something more important to do.

They finally arrived at their destination, a suburban housing estate in Redhill, Surrey. As ordinary and "normal" as you could imagine, the estate was not the kind of place you'd expect to find the widow of a suspected terrorist. This was an estate of smart, detached houses. Company middle managers lived in houses like these, with a spouse and the stereotypical two point four children, and a dog. This was not what anyone would imagine as a hotbed of far-right extremist violence.

Eric pulled the car slowly into the cul-de-sac. Approaching them, driving out of the cul-de-sac, was a white Ford Focus. Michael and Eric deliberately paid no attention to the car, knowing the covert front-facing camera behind the driver's mirror would capture the car's registration and an image of the driver. These would be uploaded to the MI5 data network and from there the GCHQ computers would trace the car and carry out facial recognition on the driver. Any threat would be conveyed to Michael and Eric without them having to lift a finger, espionage without the effort.

Eric pulled to a halt on the drive of one of the houses and turned off the engine. Michael sat and looked at the house. Eric looked at Michael.

'Are you going in?' asked Eric, 'or are we here just for the view?' Michael still wasn't sure if he appreciated Eric's sense of humour. Eric had proved himself a capable and resourceful field agent, but he had a tendency to bluntness, and a sense of humour that Michael suspected was an acquired taste. Michael was still trying to acquire it.

Michael took a breath, about to explain himself, but Eric got in first. 'And don't tell me you feel guilty about what they did to her husband,' he said. 'That was them, not you, nor me. Sorry, but shit happens, and we need to fix it.'

Michael was silent. His three former colleagues had also taken telepathic control of Gerald Crossley. They'd set him up to appear on the security services' radar as a suspected far-right activist, and had then shot him dead, all to get Michael's attention. Vince Marshall never did consider anyone "innocent," they were either useful or enemy.

'I assume we are here for a reason,' Eric said.

'Yes, we are,' Michael said. 'I'd appreciate your help.' Eric looked at him; he returned the look. 'Your friendly face will help.'

'Did she not like you last time?' asked Eric.

'She was fine when I left,' said Michael, 'I think I put her mind at ease, a bit. Hopefully, we'll get what we need, quickly.' Michael hoped he sounded more confident than he felt. He doubted Joanna Crossley would be helpful, why should she be? The police and security services had treated her more as a criminal than a victim. Michael could have felt sorry for her, but right now he had to put those thoughts to one side. Sorrow wouldn't help find Marshall, Bullock and Singh.

Michael and Eric walked to the front door, and rang the bell. The doorbell was a stereotypical door chime, some electronic rendition of an orchestral piece. They waited. The door opened, and Joanna Crossley stood there, a look of thunder on her face.

***

'What the hell do you want?' she said, her voice venomous. Michael held his ground, he needed her co-operation, even if she resented him or what he represented. He made himself remain neutral, neither being apologetic nor confrontational.

'Mrs Crossley,' Michael said, but she'd already begun to push the door shut. Michael pushed his hand against the door, this was no time for politeness. 'I'm sorry, but we really do need to talk to you.' He stepped forwards and was relieved that she stepped back and allowed them both to enter. As they stepped into the hallway Michael was struck by the pungent smell of air-freshener and disinfectant. Someone had been doing some serious cleaning.

She let them walk into the living room. Photographs adorned the walls, trinkets sat on shelves and mantelpieces. The furniture was smart but simple, all muted colours. Joanne Crossley stood with her arms folded, and showed no sign of suggesting they sit. This was going to be difficult. The redness in her face showed that she'd been crying, but she maintained a defiant posture. She'd found some fight in her since Michael had last met her, and Michael doubted that she'd accept an offer to shake hands. Making physical contact was going to be difficult.

At their last meeting Michael had forged a telepathic link with Joanna Crossley, but had only used it to calm her, he'd not used it to control her. He let his thoughts extend towards her. It still felt strange to feel his own thoughts extending out and meeting the mind of another person. He felt his mind touch the outer barriers of her mind. Her face didn't change. Her spirit was stronger than before. He'd have to find a way to make physical contact again to establish a stronger link.

'Mrs Crossley, I need to examine some of your husband's things. Particularly a book he had,' said Michael.

'I've cleared out a lot of his stuff, I've cleaned up what your lot didn't take away,' she said. 'Anyway, you lot need a search warrant.'

This took Michael by surprise. The book in question had been used as a psychic link between Gerald Crossley and the telepath who had controlled him. Michael had been counting on using that link to discover the location of Julian Singh and the other two. He had no doubt that Singh, Marshall and Bullock would be too focused on their own escape to have yet disconnected themselves from the objects and people they'd used. Crossley's book was the one object Michael knew was a direct and active link to Singh, but it had been an hour since the Three had escaped. It wouldn't be long before the link was lost.

Michael had no choice, and he had no warrant, he'd have to search regardless. He turned for the door to head upstairs, but she moved sharply towards him. In a deft move, Eric had a hand on her shoulder to hold her back. She was caught unawares by this and for a moment hesitated, unsure which of the two men she should remonstrate with first. Michael took his chance. With a gentle movement he took her hand, and let his mind flow strongly into hers, subduing her with a wave of telepathic energy. He had a brief sensation of handling a delicate glass object, something strong yet fragile. He could feel that the slightest push in the wrong direction could shatter it. She was far from as strong as she believed. He let his thoughts soften, a gentle flow of relaxing thought extending through his hand to hers and he felt her relax. He saw the tension leave her shoulders and neck and face.

What Michael hadn't expected was the sudden look of calm that had come over Eric. In that moment Michael realised that he had never tried telepathic control of one person through physical contact of another. For a moment he was tempted to increase the flow of energy, but had to remind himself that time was against them. Experiments would have to wait for later.

'Eric, let go,' he said/thought, it was hard to tell whether he actually spoke the words out loud. Eric dropped his hand from the woman's shoulder, and he frowned at Michael.

Almost (exactly?) like a stage hypnotist leading a subject Michael led her to a chair, and she sat.

'Joanna,' he said out loud. 'Gerald's book about psychics, it's important I see the book.'

In a soft voice, she said, 'I burned it, I burned a lot of his papers, it was important to get rid of them.'

'Why Joanna? Why was it important to get rid of them?' He could feel the confusion in her mind. She didn't know why it was important, she had done it without knowing why. A part of her hadn't wanted to destroy her husband's possessions, but something had compelled her. He fought back the feeling in his own mind, the target was no longer clear in his sights, perhaps he'd missed the chance of a clear shot.

'I had to,' she said, 'he was very clear that I had to get rid of them.'

'Who was clear Joanna?' Michael knew he needn't ask, he knew who had compelled her to clean up her husband's things, to make sure the psychic object was disposed of, but he needed her to think of the person who had compelled her to act. Joanna Crossley's thoughts remained in motion, disjointed, allowing Michael to sense her confusion. There was something there, he could sense it. In her thoughts was something important, but it was like a picture behind frosted glass. He pushed, psychically, and felt the fragility of her thoughts. He could get at that one thought, but it would damage her. He could discover who had influenced her, but she would pay a high price. There was no doubt he was strong enough to smash his way through her mental defences and take whatever memories he wanted, but should he? He let his thoughts recede.

'Why was it important? When did he tell you?' Michael asked. Michael sensed a thought surface in her mind. It wasn't a clear, definite thought it was more like recognising a familiar scent left in the air, but it was unmistakably the impression of another mind, someone else's thought in Joanna Crossley's mind. Somehow, one of the Three had had a telepathic connection with her, as well as with her husband. And if Singh had exercised his telepathic control he would have used a physical object as a kind of transmitter, a psychic relay. The book had been his relay to Gerald Crossley, but if the book was gone how was he maintaining a link with Joanna Crossley?

Michael let go of her hand. Joanna's eyes closed. He stood up and faced Eric.

'I don't suppose there's any chance you're actually going to explain what the bloody hell is going on?' said Eric.

'Yes, I will, but not yet. I need to find something. An object. Something that the police would never suspect was connected to Singh and the others, but something that is out of place.'

'Oh that narrows it down.'

'I need help, not sarcasm,' said Michael. He had to hold himself back, it would be too easy to be sarcastic in return, but he needed Eric's help.

'I will explain, but we need to find this object quickly. Just look around, see if anything looks out of place.'

The two of them looked around. Michael had an idea he might recognise something if he saw it, but he doubted Eric would know what kind of object they were looking for. It would have been useful if Michael had been able to sense objects which had a strong telepathic imprint, but he couldn't. He had no more ability to sense them at a distance than Eric did.

'So it could be anything?' asked Eric. Michael turned round and saw Eric holding the TV remote control. He had to suppress his annoyance.

'No,' said Michael, 'nothing ordinary. Something that you won't handle often.'

They both looked around the room, at the pictures on the wall and the books in the bookcase and the ordinary items of everyday life. Michael looked at the china figurines on the window ledge and held his hand out close to the nearest one and brushed a fingertip against it. He felt nothing, nor from the next one nor from any of them.

'You mean something like this?' said Eric a moment later. He was pointing to a small, souvenir model of an Egyptian pyramid sitting on the mantelpiece next to the photo of Joanna and Gerald Crossley in Florida.

'What makes that out of place?' asked Michael, more to test Eric's reasoning than because he doubted the man's conclusion.

'Lots of holiday photos,' Eric said, looking around the room, and indeed there was a collection of various holiday photos on the walls and in photo frames. 'Holiday souvenir pyramid, but no photos of Egypt.'

Michael looked at the toy pyramid. Eric's reasoning was sound. He hesitated. The chaos and violence of the last few days had started when Michael touched a piece of paper charged with telepathic energy, a psychic calling-card from Julian Singh. He was in no rush to repeat that experience.

Michael reached out and touched the object, and instantly felt the buzz of telepathic energy. There was no choice, if he wanted to find Julian Singh he had to connect with this object. He stilled his mind, almost waiting for whatever would happen. It happened in a rush, he felt the blast of energy, of anger, of fury. Julian Singh was indeed beside himself with rage. Through the telepathic connection, Michael could feel the man seething with anger, struggling to keep the emotion under control. He was fleeing, escaping, but according to a plan, everything had to be done according to a plan, but where were they going? Michael let himself sink deeper into the cesspit of Julian Singh's fury. He had a sense of other people, so no doubt the Three were escaping together. He felt the fury lessen, a sense of satisfaction starting to creep in, because wherever they were going, they were almost there. Almost where? An image came into Michael's mind, a country scene, rolling green fields, a village church sat in the middle of the scene, it's steeple reaching up into a still sky.

Julian Singh's face exploded into Michael's mind and Michael yelped and dropped the pyramid. The world went quiet around him, and the link was broken.

'What was that?' said Eric.

Michael took a moment to collect himself. He bent down and picked up the pyramid. It felt almost cold. The telepathic connection with Singh through the object had been broken, he'd get nothing more from it. He put it back on the mantelpiece. The target was gone. Would there be another chance of a shot now?

Michael looked at Eric. 'There's nothing more we can do here, we need to get back to The Office.'

***

Anna Hendrickson sat in the door of the ambulance and watched with mild disinterest as the police, fire and ambulance crews rushed around her. She sat with a silver space blanket wrapped loosely around her shoulders. No-one seemed to pay her much attention, and she was too lost in her own thoughts to pay much attention to them. At least, she thought they were her own thoughts, but she wasn't completely sure of that.

The last few hours had been rather confusing. She remembered what had happened; she remembered what she did, she just wasn't sure why she'd done it. She remembered being with the Three men who were now being hunted by the police, by MI5, by GCHQ. She remembered helping them hack into the Bank of England's computers, and she remembered being part of trying to transfer a very large amount of money out of the Bank. At the time, it had all seemed perfectly normal. The Three men had been her friends, but of course, they couldn't have been. That didn't make any sense. The more she thought about it, the less sense it made.

She had been with friends, in the communications vehicle. She remembered being in the Battle Bus, the GCHQ communications vehicle, part of an MI5 operation. The details were hazy, but she could remember someone had warned her that she was in danger. She'd left the vehicle, and met one of her friends. No, not a friend. She'd met one of the Three men, and then the vehicle had exploded. She stopped thinking about it, she didn't want to think about the friends who'd been inside the vehicle, the real friends.

This was why she worked in an office. This was why she was an analyst, working with data and computers. She didn't belong in this world, this world of violence and danger. She wanted to go back to her world of analysing data, of being clever. She wanted to go back to the Doughnut, the GCHQ building in Cheltenham, where she knew she would feel safe.

Her thoughts were interrupted when she became aware of a man standing in front of her. He was a big man or seemed so to Anna as she looked up at him. He was in a police combat uniform. The name badge on his breast said 'Halbern' and the circular rank insignia on his shoulder proclaimed him to be a Commander.

'I'm Commander Halbern,' said the man, 'Counter Terrorist Command.'

Anna smiled, or as much of a smile as she could manage.

'When you feel up to it,' he continued, 'we'll need to you to come to a station and give a statement.'

Thoughts jumped up in Anna's mind, too many to contend with all at once. 'I, er, yes, I suppose, I mean, I think I ought...' was about all she could manage.

'You'll need a GCHQ solicitor with you,' said Halbern, more as a statement than question, 'It's being organised.' Halbern gave a brief smile and walked off.

She wasn't yet sure what she could tell anyone, she couldn't remember herself exactly what had happened and when. She did remember that she'd been in a room with computers, and that there had been shooting and explosions. She remembered that Michael Sanders had appeared in his full SAS-style combat outfit. He'd rescued her. Yes, he'd rescued her from the data centre, where the other people had forced her to do things, or persuaded her to do things. And now Michael had left, and so had Eric, now she remembered Eric. They had driven off and everything had calmed down, and now she was sitting in an ambulance, outside the data centre. Thinking things through felt helpful, it felt familiar, like solving a puzzle, she remembered she liked solving puzzles, and she remembered she was very good at it.

Anna looked across at the building she'd been in for most of the previous day, or longer, she wasn't sure. The large, anonymous warehouse-like building showed the scars and damage from the guns and explosives used in the recent battle. The main gate into the building's car park was open, but the pedestrian turnstile was twisted and distorted, the result of an explosion she supposed. Yes, she remembered more clearly now how Michael Sanders had rescued her. She remembered him in his black SAS-style combat outfit, complete with submachine gun and grenades. She remembered the others. She didn't know who they were, the Eastern Europeans. More came back, she remembered the data about them: Petric, Dulic and Vlad, thoroughly nasty men. The more she thought about it, the more keenly she realised she could remember what happened, but not why she had been so willing a part of their plan. She had to know. She had to understand. She wanted to go back to her old job in GCHQ, but she couldn't go back with this confusion in her mind.

Had they drugged her? She didn't feel like she'd been drugged. Had they hypnotised her? Unlikely, she didn't believe hypnosis would be enough to compel her to betray everything she held to be important. So why had she helped them configure their IT to attack the Bank of England? And then it crept into her mind. A thought. A small voice that whispered to her. Her role was to analyse, to use advanced computer systems to analyse data. She'd helped them to use the advanced computer systems inside the building. And she remembered seeing things inside the building which made her wonder what their plans were. The three of them, the Three who had controlled her and tried to steal the money, they were working to a plan. They were very organised, but there were things she'd seen which didn't fit with their plans. The more Anna tried to think about it the more the memory slipped away.

She looked again at the building. Maybe if she went back in she could find what she'd seen, remember why it had seemed so important, and perhaps she could provide some help in the search for the three men. But going back into that building would be like going back into the lion's den. She'd escaped it once, perhaps it would be foolish to go back in, and yet she couldn't escape the feeling that there were answers inside, answers she wouldn't find anywhere else. Anna was not brave, she certainly remembered that. She liked keeping to rules, not breaking them. She had the sudden feeling that what she was experiencing was like sobering up after having been very drunk, not that she got drunk very often. There was one time, at University, but she forced her attention back into the here-and-now, there were things here she needed to pay attention to, not reminiscing. This was like sobering up more quickly; memories came back, physical strength returned, sensible decision making became easier. There was also that period before full sobriety returned when an unexpected degree of bravado was still possible.

Anna slipped the space blanket off her shoulders and started to walk towards the building. The police and the others walked around her as though she was invisible. It all still seemed slightly surreal. But if she got inside she could find answers. She walked through the main gate and down the short drive towards what must be the front door to the building. There were no signs outside the building, nothing to identify the owner, nothing to invite visitors to ring a bell or push a button. This was not a building intended for visitors. The front door was as featureless as the rest of the building. Only the door handle and the very dark smoked glass identified it as being a door of any kind. Anna stood at the door, caught in a moment of indecision. She took in a breath. She'd been brave before, she could be brave again. She reached for the door handle.

A bright sparkle of red laser light dazzled her as it reflected off the door handle. Anna froze, from her recent experiences she recognised a targeting laser. She froze, not moving, not even breathing, but aware of a trembling starting in her legs.

A woman's voice came from behind her. Not immediately behind, but from some distance behind her. 'Step away from the door, Miss,' the voice said.

Anna wasn't sure which way to move. Should she turn around? Should she simply back up?

'Please Miss, step back, away from the door,' said the voice.

Anna extended her arms out to either side, making her hands visible, starting to raise them. She couldn't imagine who would be aiming a gun at her, this wasn't what was supposed to happen.

The voice spoke again. 'I don't need you to raise your arms, Miss. I simply need you to step away from the door. It's booby trapped.'

Anna lowered her arms and turned around. A woman, dressed in police combat fatigues, held a submachine gun pointed towards Anna. Not directly at her, but pointing past her, at the door. The woman, Anna guessed no more than mid-twenties, lowered the weapon. 'I'm sorry,' said the woman, 'but we think the building's full of booby traps, it's not safe to go in. It's best that you come away from the building.'

Anna took a deep breath and exhaled, the trembling in her legs increasing, but to a degree she relaxed. Perhaps being brave really wasn't what she was cut out for. Maybe it was time to go back to Cheltenham, back to analysing data. Perhaps she could find answers there, or perhaps other people could provide her with answers.

Two

The lorry trundled up the drive, a gravel track which led from the main road to the open gates of the farmhouse. It was big, for a farmhouse, though any association with active farming was probably lost decades ago. This was a now a country retreat, more a manor house than a farmhouse, nestled in a small village in the green landscape, a church spire the most defining local landmark. The house was smart, with dark stone walls, smooth slate roof, a manicured lawn at the front. The stone wall and the neatly trimmed thick hedge that encircled the house and the immediate grounds provided privacy and seclusion. The traffic on the main road was out of sight of those in the grounds of the house, and more importantly, those in the grounds and the house were out of sight from the road.

The lorry rolled through the gateway and further up the drive to the yard at the back of the house. Beyond the yard was a large, manicured lawn, ornamental gardens, all the trappings of a country escape for someone rich or famous or powerful. The current occupants were not famous and had gone to extreme lengths to protect their anonymity. They were considerably less rich than they had expected to be, about fifty billion pounds less rich. But they were powerful, more powerful than almost anyone would imagine. The only force that matched their power was their anger. The two men waiting for the lorry's arrival took an involuntary step back. They might not have been able to explain why they stepped back, or what they sensed, but they felt a palpable sense of unease, as though they suspected the lorry contained uncaged wild animals. In a way, it did.

The driver got out of the cab and walked around to the back of the lorry. He flipped open the catch, and the roller shutter clattered upwards. Inside the lorry was a brown BMW Mini, and propped up against the far wall of the inside of the lorry were two motorbikes. Sitting inside the car were three men. No-one said a word. No-one moved. After a pause, the door of the Mini opened. One by one, the three men climbed out of the car. No-one laughed (or even thought of laughing) at the almost comical way the larger of the three had to squeeze himself out of the back of the car, crammed inside the lorry.

The two waiting men stepped forward and placed three hats on the inside ledge of the lorry. A baseball cap, a Panama hat and bowler hat. A ridiculous sight, but still no-one spoke. The three men inside the lorry each put on a hat, jumped down out of the lorry and walked towards the back door of the house.

'This is fucking ridiculous,' said one of the men.

'Shut up,' said one of the others, 'we can't risk any aerial surveillance recognising us, not now.'

One of them looked up slightly, looking down the driveway, to the country landscape and hills and church beyond. He stopped, shaking, fists clenched.

'What?' said one of the other three.

The one who had stopped was shaking, his fists shaking. 'Nooooo,' he said, as though in pain. 'Get out,' he roared. He took in a deep breath and calmed himself, releasing his fists.

'What was that all about?' asked the other.

'Sanders trying to get clever,' said the one who had stopped. 'I've cut him off.'

'Did he get anything?' asked one of the others.

'Only a telepathic punch in the face.'

After a short walk, the three men were inside the house. They took off the hats and dropped them on the floor to be picked up by one of the following men.

The back door of the house opened into a large and well appointed, stylish kitchen. Granite worktops, a stone floor, dark wood fittings. The inside of the house was as smart as the outside.

There was a shattering crash as the biggest of the three punched his fist into one of the cupboard doors.

'Go on,' said one of the others, a slighter built Asian man. 'Smash the place up, I'm sure that'll achieve a lot.'

'I'll smash Sanders,' said the punching man, big, African, broad shouldered. 'I want to see his eyes when I cut his throat out.'

'Join the queue,' said the third man, blond, also solidly built.

The black man looked at their followers, all standing there not knowing where to look. 'You lot, fuck off,' he shouted at them. Without a word they turned and exited the house, shutting the door behind them.

The black man, Vince Marshall, turned to the Asian man, Julian Singh. 'Right,' he said to Singh, 'how soon can you find Sanders?' Marshall was struggling to keep his anger under control. He had a growing urge to bring in their three pet "minders" and spend a cathartic hour dismembering them, but they were too valuable to waste like that.

'No problem. And then what? Do you think you can just waltz back into town and have a word with him?' Singh's words were dripping with sarcasm. Marshall was very tempted to do just that, and damn the risks and consequences. Every moment of his experience and training had been about being prepared, having the advantage through intelligence and stealth, but now he simply wanted to charge back to the city and do as much damage as he could.

'There's no chance we can get back into the city,' said the blond man, Evan Bullock. 'The police will be everywhere. We need to leave, now.'

'I'm not leaving without Sanders' eyes as souvenirs,' snarled Marshall. He clenched his fists again, ready to punch another door.

Bullock opened the refrigerator and pulled out a bottle of beer. He opened the bottle and drank half of it in one go.

'Everyone is going to be looking for us,' said Bullock, 'police, MI5, port authorities, everyone.' He gripped the bottle even tighter.

'He's right,' said Singh, 'their surveillance is going to be total. We can get out, but we have to leave now.'

'No,' shouted Marshall, 'not after what he did. I want him dead, and I want her dead.'

'Sorry,' said Singh, 'but I'm not prepared to go on a suicide mission just to satisfy your bloodlust.'

Marshall had to bite his tongue, literally, to stop himself from snapping that Singh should consider going on just such a suicide mission.

'The plan's ruined, we can't succeed now, we have no choice, we need to get back to Hong Kong,' said Bullock.

Marshall walked to the refrigerator, then back across the kitchen to the sink, then back to the refrigerator, and finally got himself a beer. He snapped the top off and threw it across the room, then drained the bottle in one go. It seemed to calm him to a degree. He wanted to get revenge on Sanders, now, without waiting. But he couldn't, he knew he couldn't. He forced his anger back into its mental cage. There would be a time when he could let it out, it would have its day and he would have his revenge.

'There are still loose ends to tidy up,' said Marshall. 'We need to make sure this lot,' he gestured to the window and the men outside, 'aren't left around.'

'What about the girl?' asked Bullock. 'You had a strong connection with her, probably still do.'

'Yeah,' said Marshall, 'but she didn't know anything. She was useful, but I made sure she never knew why she was doing anything.

'Mason,' said Singh. The others looked at him. 'Apart from the ones here, there's no-one else who can identify us and locate us, apart from Mason.'

'So what do we do about him? asked Bullock. 'We can't go and kill him, unless you can use your link to melt his brain or something.'

'No, and I don't think I can make him kill himself, the link doesn't work like that,' said Singh.

All three of them, even after all this time, were still only just getting used to being telepathic. None of them had a full understanding of how the psychic ability worked, of what they could and couldn't do. The one aspect of it that still disappointed Marshall was not being able to kill remotely, not even being able to force someone to commit suicide. Other aspects of the telepathy were very useful, like being able to dominate and control people, such as their compliant bodyguards. Despite what they first thought would happen, the three of them still used normal speaking voices for communication. Somehow, while it was extremely useful in certain situations, speaking telepathically just felt too personal a connection to be used for trivial conversation.

'So what does he know?' said Marshall.

'He knows about our interest in the company's IT defences,' said Singh, 'he knows what we had set up at the data centre, he knows we want to get into their network centre. He knows too much.'

'Then we have to kill him,' said Marshall.

'How? said Bullock, his voice louder. 'He's probably locked up in a police cell.'

The two of them talked louder, their voices becoming shouts, each as determined as the other that they were right about what needed to be done.

Marshall took in a deep breath, obviously about to shout even louder, and stopped. He stared at Julian Singh, who was leaning back against the worktop, a broad grin on his face. The three of them had had their fair share of disagreements, but had never used violence on each other, but Marshall was very quickly coming to the point where he might change that.

'What the fuck are you smiling about?' hissed Marshall.

'We can still do it,' said Singh, 'we can still get what we need.' His voice had become calmer, losing the anger he had demonstrated only moments previously.

'How? We've lost everything,' shouted Bullock.

'No, we haven't,' said Singh, more calm and rational. 'A lot of the computer stuff we need is here, it was never all at the data centre.'

'But we need access to the company,' said Marshall, 'the money would have bought us access, quiet, no fuss.' He stared at Singh. He didn't know what Singh was thinking, but if Singh said they could still get what they came for, then it was because he'd thought through the problems and found a way.

'Yes, that bit's more of a problem, but we still have a way into the company,' said Singh, still grinning.

The other two looked at each other and then at Singh, who was enjoying the moment.

'Mason,' he said, 'Mason is our way into the company. All we need to do is rescue him.'

***

It was early evening when Michael and Eric got back to Thames House. Often referred to as 'The Office' by its occupants, it was an imposing building on the north bank of the Thames. As they approached the security turnstiles in the entrance lobby Michael looked around. He was always curious but could never spot the concealed cameras. He knew, or had been told, that the security cameras were linked to an artificial intelligence system which identified each authorised person by their gait, stride length, body posture, typical pace, as well as voice recognition by hidden microphones. Their ID badges were almost redundant as a security measure, now as much a fashion accessory as anything.

The building looked old fashioned from the outside, and some of the offices still had a traditional look about them. Other areas of the building belonged firmly in the twenty-first century. They reached the Operations Directorate on the first floor, a collection of meeting rooms, open plan offices and state-of-the-art command-and-control rooms from which field operations were directed. Michael had called ahead and had a meeting room reserved for them. On this Friday evening the open-plan office space was almost as busy as during the working day. As they approached the meeting room the Head appeared from an office.

Michael gestured to Eric to carry on ahead of him. The MI5 Head of Section, referred to as Ma'am or (not to her face) just the Head, was a grey-haired woman with a permanent look of determination.

'Not quite the outcome we were hoping for,' said the Head. As Michael expected, there was no expression of satisfaction that Michael was still alive, nothing approaching compassion. Michael was about to reply, but the Head spoke first. 'Did you get anything from the Crossley woman?'

'She didn't know much, and she was fragile,' said Michael.

'I don't care,' said the Head, 'did you get anything useful?'

Michael fought back the flash of anger. The lack of empathy, especially for innocent victims, was not a characteristic he found appealing in the woman. 'Not much, an image, might be useful,' said Michael. He was about to ask her something, but she huffed and walked off. Apparently the conversation was at an end.

He had to admit, he had no plan for finding the Three, no plan at all. Even if desperate situations when he and Marshall and the others had been a Special Forces unit together, they always had a plan, they always had some idea of the way forward. Now he just felt that every door was being closed, every way forward was being blocked. Perhaps they needed a plan to deal with the inevitable fallout of the Three succeeding in their plan, whatever that might be. He dismissed the thought immediately. His aim, his only aim, was stopping the Three. He'd never in his life entered a race without the intention of winning, not even cross-country running at school, up against the county champion, his only aim then was to win. It was the same now.

Michael walked into the meeting room and closed the door. Anna and Eric sat on the other side of the table. Michael had no idea how he was going to do this, no idea how much he should tell them. Without anyone intending it, both had become caught up in Michael's battle with his past and both were nearly killed because of it. Certainly, they had the right to know the truth, but not the whole truth, he couldn't afford to share the whole truth, even if he'd known it, even if the Head had shared it with him. This whole thing was a mess of shadows caught up in secrets hiding in dark corners. He couldn't tell them too much, that would be a risk too far.

Michael sat down at the table opposite Anna and Eric.

'Okay,' he said, readying himself. 'A lot's happened, some of it hard to explain.'

'That's an understatement,' said Eric.

'So I'll explain what I can,' said Michael. 'Here goes. This is going to sound strange,' he stopped himself. Strange didn't begin to describe what he was about to tell them.

'I've got a pretty good sense of what's strange and what's normal,' said Eric, 'and right now my weird-as-shit meter is going off the scale.'

Michael began. 'I'll tell you as much as I can. I can't, and won't tell you everything, and I'll explain why that is.' He paused, and thought that this is what it must be like when someone confessed to having an affair, or a criminal past. He'd never actually thought how he'd explain things to Anna and Eric, what the "right" way would be. Perhaps there wasn't a "right" way, perhaps he should just say it. Or perhaps he should make up some story to explain things, keep Anna and Eric at a distance. Marshall and the others were his problem to sort out, he might be doing Anna and Eric a favour by shutting them out, now, before they got involved any deeper in this battle, before they got killed. Michael realised very quickly that he had no idea what alternative explanation he could possibly give.

'Four years ago,' he began, 'my Special Forces unit was recruited into an experiment, to test a drug which was supposed to increase our stamina and resilience. It didn't, but it did make the four of us telepathic.' He looked at Anna and Eric, waiting for their response. The two of them looked at each other, and then back to Michael. He waited for a response; a laugh or a denial or a question, but they both just stared at him.

Finally, Anna spoke. 'I thought we didn't do experiments on people like that?'

'The experiment was all above board,' said Michael. 'It was overseen by doctors, it had been lab' tested first, but it seems no-one had noticed this particular side effect.'

'So now you're a wizard who can tell the future and stuff?' said Eric, with a more than slightly mocking tone. This was more like the response Michael had expected.

'No, not a wizard, and I can't tell the future. But if I touch someone I can establish a telepathic link with them, and I can use that to control them, like I did with Joanna Crossley.' He waited for Eric to join the dots. 'That's what you felt when you had your hand on her shoulder.'

Eric stared into space for a moment, remembering what he'd felt, trying to make sense of what had happened and what Michael was now telling them. 'So you touched her and used your magic powers to control her, but you also got me?' he said, mocking just a little.

'Not magic, but yes, I did control her, and yes I did get you, sorry.'

Michael looked at Anna. 'That's how Marshall was able to make you help him, why it seemed that helping him was such a normal thing to do.'

'I was under his spell?' she said.

'Please,' said Michael, 'stop with the magic references.' His exasperation was becoming apparent. 'The four of us have telepathic abilities. We can communicate with each other telepathically and we can with other people once we've made a physical connection.'

Eric took in a breath, obviously about to say something flippant. Michael shot him a look as if to say "don't even think it."

'So they had me under their telepathic control?' asked Anna.

'Yes.'

'And Jason Mason?'

'Yes.'

'And they can communicate with you?'

'No,' said Michael. After we parted company we each made sure that I can't connect with them, and they can't connect with me.'

'So what about Mason?' asked Eric.

'At the moment there's nothing we can do,' said Michael. 'The police will have him and there's nothing we can tell them about why he cooperated with Marshall.'

'But they'll arrest him,' said Anna, 'they'll charge him, they'll think he was an accomplice.'

'Yes, they probably will. But there's nothing we can do, unless you're suggesting we go to the police and explain that the three criminals they're looking for are telepathic and were able to remotely control people against their will?'

There was an uncomfortable silence, which went on for too long.

'Well?' said Michael, 'say something.'

Anna and Eric both opened and closed their mouths, looked around, breathed in, and then out, trying to find words to express whatever it was they were feeling.

'It's all a very big claim,' said Anna.

'That's not how I'd phrase it,' said Eric. 'Care to give us a demonstration?'

'No, I wouldn't. But I do need to do something.' He looked at Anna. 'Anna. Vince Marshall formed a strong telepathic connection with you. If you relax, let your mind form an image of him, you'll sense what I mean.'

Anna looked at Michael, then at Eric, as if to say "okay, why not?"

She closed her eyes, and Michael could see her face relax slightly. In an instant her eyes shot open, she gasped and tried to stagger backwards, struggling as the chair prevented her. She clambered out of the chair and backed up to the far corner of the room. Eric was on his feet, trying to work out if she was fitting, or panicking, or faking.

'What?' said Eric, 'what is it?'

'I can feel him,' said Anna, sounding scared. 'I can feel his mind. Oh my God, I can feel his mind inside mine.'

Michael was the only one remaining completely calm. Eric seemed to have braced himself, ready for action, but without knowing what he could do.

'Sit down, Anna, and I can teach you to disconnect yourself from him. I can teach you how to protect yourself so he can't reach you.'

It took half an hour of coaching by Michael to get Anna to the point where she was once again calm. He talked her through the mental exercise of taking the image of Marshall and moving it away in her mind's eye, shrinking it and making it distant. She described how it was strange that she could do it with an image of anyone else, and it was just moving pictures in her imagination, but with Marshall, she felt she was moving something physical. Michael moved on to talking her through creating the idea of a glass wall in her imagination, impervious to thoughts she didn't want. Through all this, Eric sat and watched, slightly bemused. Michael wasn't sure how much Eric believed of all this, if any. It was then he started to wonder how much they could really be a team. Anna and Eric were skilled and focused, he couldn't deny that. They had skin in the game now, but they weren't on his level. Maybe this was still just him against the Three.

'So,' said Eric, when Michael had finished "fixing" Anna (as Eric had called it.) 'After this miracle drug turned you into superheroes, what happened next? I'm guessing this didn't have a happy ending.'

'There were four of us,' said Michael, 'myself, Vince Marshall, Evan Bullock and Julian Singh. The telepathy was definitely an asset when it came to undercover surveillance work.'

'I can imagine,' said Eric. 'All you'd need to be unstoppable would be invisibility.'

'And that's how Marshall and the others started to see it,' said Michael. 'They started to see the opportunities for personal gain.'

'Ah,' said Anna, 'they went rogue.'

'That's one way of putting it,' said Michael. 'They started undermining missions for their own future gain. I think they thought no-one knew, but someone did know, and whoever it was decided that having a group of telepathic soldiers had become more of a risk than an asset. We were sent to Afghanistan on what we were told was a surveillance mission. In fact, it was to get us to a place where a group of killers could get rid of us.'

'And would this be the same group that did for our three Serbian friends?' asked Eric.

'No. The four sent after us in Afghanistan were killed, by Marshall and the others, but they were almost certainly sent by the same person.'

'So how did you end up in MI5 and the others end up trying to rob banks?' asked Anna.

'Vince and the others didn't react well to someone trying to kill them,' said Michael, 'they went off threatening revenge. I came back to make sure that if they ever appeared again in this country there would be someone who had a chance of stopping them.'

'I'm guessing it didn't all work out according to plan,' said Eric, 'what with them nearly killing us and managing to kill a whole load of police.'

'They've become more powerful than I realised,' said Michael.

'And I assume they'll be coming back,' said Anna.

'I somehow doubt that they'll give up and go home, wherever they call home these days,' said Michael. 'I don't know where they are or what they'll try and do next, but I've no doubt they'll be back, and soon.'

'So why not create more telepathic soldiers?' asked Eric.

'And there's the problem,' said Michael. 'That's why I can't tell you anymore, that's why you can't share any of this, with anyone. This whole thing has to be kept as secret as possible. Imagine what would happen if the Americans or the Russians or the Chinese got the slightest hint that we had a quick and easy way of making genuine telepathic soldiers.' He let the idea hang in the air for a moment.

Anna spoke first. 'I think they'd probably want to either stop it, or take it for themselves.'

'Exactly,' said Michael. 'And if they did then anyone and everyone involved in the project would be in immediate danger. The less anyone knows, the better. So now only the Head and the three of us know about it.'

'And whoever sent the killers to get rid of the Serbs,' said Eric.

'So what do we do next?' asked Anna, obviously trying not to dwell on Eric's observation.

'You need to go back to GCHQ,' said Michael, at which Anna smiled. 'We'll need as much surveillance power applied to this as possible. The police will be looking for the Three, but as criminals, they won't have a clue what they're capable of. MI5 will have an interest from a counter-terrorist point of view, but only we'll know what we're really looking for.'

'So what do we do?' asked Eric.

'I'd like you to take Anna back to Cheltenham. Then you and I need to go and trace their escape route, see how much of their trail we can follow.'

Michael didn't volunteer an explanation of what he'd do. He wasn't sure what his next step was, but whatever it was, it would be his alone.

***

Michael left Anna and Eric to make their plans to get Anna back to Cheltenham. He walked down the corridor, looking around to see if he could find the Head. Somehow he doubted she'd have gone home yet. She wasn't in her office nor in the open-plan area of the first floor. Michael was in two minds about discussing certain topics with the Head. He still hadn't decided if she was an ally or a threat, or perhaps both. He had no doubt that she knew much more about the Psiclone project than she had ever let on, but he wondered if she was a driving force in the project or just another cog in a much larger machine.

At one point Michael had the bizarre thought that he would have felt more confident if he had been inching down the corridor, gun in hand, looking for an armed opponent than he was looking for a supposed-colleague. Offices and politics were not his battleground. His experience was in firearms, in combat, in fighting. When the four of them had been together they had been a formidable force. Michael had valued his time with his colleagues, but he had to stop and remind himself of recent events. They were friends no more. A line had been crossed a long time ago, now they were enemies and no doubt he would face them again, with gun in hand.

He found her, of all places, at the coffee machine. The expression on her face showed she had the same opinion of the coffee as most others.

'The three of you have a plan to find them?' she said, before Michael could chip in with any sarcastic comment about the machine generated coffee.

'We have actions,' Michael said, trying to divulge as little as possible. 'They'll have covered their tracks well, but there's a lot we can do to uncover them. To paraphrase someone, they have to be lucky all the time, we only need to get lucky once.'

'I'd expect a better strategy than "luck,"' said the Head.

Almost before he could stop himself, the words had escaped from his mouth. 'At the moment, luck is the only strategy we've got.'

'You need to find them, before the body count gets any higher,' she said, the softness of her voice emphasising her point.

'I'm well aware of that, but I might have a better chance if I didn't have one hand tied behind my back.'

'You know full well why I can't give you any more resources.'

'It's more than that,' he said. 'It would help if I knew who the real enemy is.'

She studied him for a moment before answering. 'You know who the enemy is, it's your former colleagues. Find them, and stop them.'

Michael thought the Head acted as if it was all so clear, all so simple, but he found himself more uncertain than ever of where he stood. He was more uncertain who he could trust, where the real danger lay. Soldiering, by comparison, had been easy. The enemy was always clear, even in covert operations against insurgents there was a clear "us" and "them." Perhaps he wasn't cut out to be a spy after all. MI5 had seemed a natural home for him after Afghanistan, after Marshall and the others had gone their own way. His agreement had been clear; if Marshall and the others ever reappeared he was to find them and stop them, and in the meantime working as an MI5 field agent would provide a suitable cover. But now it was less clear who he had made an agreement with.

'So who sent the kill-squad in Afghanistan? Who sent the soldiers who killed the Serbs, and almost killed me and Eric? Who am I really fighting?'

'Mr Sanders,' the Head said, even more slowly for even more emphasis. 'I work for MI5, I don't send assassins anywhere to kill anyone, and if I did then I doubt we'd be standing here debating it.'

Now that she put it like that, the idea of the Head being behind the team of killers did seem less logical, but in Michael's mind it still left a very big unanswered question.

'But who?' he began.

'I've told you as much as I can,' she said, 'but we all take orders from someone. I warn you, any good skier knows that going off piste can be dangerous, you never know what hazards you'll encounter. Stay focused on your mission.'

She left Michael alone to consider her meaning, which he found was crystal clear.

***

The three of them stood in the kitchen of the farmhouse. Marshall and Bullock stared at Singh, expressions of disbelief on their faces.

'Are you completely fucking mad?' asked Marshall, speaking slowly, to emphasise his meaning. His voice might have calmed but the anger was still burning in his eyes.

'Not at all,' said Singh, his voice calm and measured. 'It will be risky.'

'Risky?' exclaimed Bullock. 'You do realise that virtually every police officer and all of MI5 and GCHQ are looking for us,' he said waving his arms to add emphasis. Bullock had never been the most subtle of people. Marshall had sometimes doubted Bullock's intelligence. The man was skilled with weapons and was a fine sniper, but either didn't grasp the finer points or didn't value them; it amounted to the same thing.

'Forget it,' said Marshall, sounding as final as he could. 'I only need one thing, I need to kill Sanders.' This one thought had grown stronger in his mind ever since they started their escape from the data centre. He still wasn't sure how and when Sanders had sabotaged their plans, and by now was past caring. His sole thought now was of revenge.

'There's no chance,' said Bullock. 'He's too well protected.'

'I'm the bait, he'll come for me, you know he will, then you get him with the rifle. Easy,' said Marshall to Bullock. All it took was some balls. Perhaps Bullock was losing his nerve.

'No chance,' said Bullock. 'There's no way I'm going anywhere near the city, it's suicide.'

Marshall stared at him, the anger almost crackling in the air around him. Marshall could be menacing even when he wasn't trying, but now he seemed to manifest all the rage in the world. Bullock stared at him. Neither were going to back down.

'You want Sanders dead as much as I do,' said Marshall.

'We all want him dead,' said Singh, still the only measured voice in the room.

'Then do your bit,' snapped Marshall, 'get him out into the open, he can't fight all three of us.'

'Bullock's right,' said Singh, 'it would be suicide.'

'I don't care,' screamed Marshall. He slammed the beer bottle down on the granite work surface. They were all surprised that neither broke.

'But I do,' said Singh, his voice still calm, even against Marshall's rantings. 'I'm not prepared to give up and get killed in some vain attempt at revenge.'

'They got us out,' shouted Bullock, gesturing at the men outside in the courtyard. 'They can't do it again.'

'Yes, they can,' said Marshall. The plan was becoming clear in his mind. He at least had the drive and the clarity to achieve one last victory. He knew that if it came to a battle against Sanders, one-on-one, Marshall would win.

'How? We've no plan, we've no resources in place, one traffic camera catches us and we're dead. One mistake and we're finished.'

'I'll take that chance.'

41

'I won't,' shouted Bullock, trying to match Marshall's fury, and failing. 'We need to get back to Hong Kong, we're not done yet, but we will be if we go back into the city.'

Bullock turned to Singh, but Singh had left the room. 'Great, now he's pissed off.'

'If we leave now,' said Marshall, turning down the anger, 'we won't get another chance, the door will shut behind us.' He had never been much of a negotiator, but if he could persuade Bullock to join in he'd at least have a better chance of killing Sanders.

'There will be other targets,' said Bullock, 'and we can't go for them if we're dead, and we will be dead if we try going after Sanders.'

They stared at each other, until Bullock turned away, staring out of the window into the courtyard and the gardens beyond. He took a final drink from the bottle and placed it down on the worktop, so carefully, as though it were the most fragile thing in the world.

'I want Sanders dead as much as you do,' he said. 'We all want to tie him down and take our time at cutting him up into little pieces. But the surveillance around London will be total. Even if we kill him, they'd have a battalion of troops on the ground faster than you could say "shoot me."'

'I'm not prepared to give up and run away,' said Marshall, his voice now so quiet. 'I never have done, and I'm not going to start now. He hung us out to dry once before. He's got a lot to answer for. He's got a lot of pain coming his way.'

'He has, but I'm not going to do any Butch Cassidy act,' said Bullock.

'Gentlemen,' said Singh.

Marshall and Bullock turned around to see Singh walking back into the kitchen, carrying an open and active laptop computer in one hand. He placed the laptop on one of the worktops and turned it so that Marshall and Bullock could both see the screen.

'I have something to show you,' he said and gestured at the screen.

Neither of the other two moved, Marshall at least had no interest in any more of Singh's cleverness with computers. Their plan had depended on Singh out-manoeuvring the computer experts of MI5 and GCHQ and the Bank of England, and now that plan lay crushed and ruined. Singh stood silently beside the laptop, the image clear for Bullock and Marshall to see. Eventually they did look at the screen.

'Who's that?' asked Bullock.

'That, is Jason Mason, languishing in a police cell,' said Singh.

Bullock and Singh stared at the image on the laptop. It showed the plain and featureless cell. A single horizontal padded surface functioning as a bed, a toilet just out of sight. A figure lay on the bed, curled in a foetal position, arms held in tight. The sharp business suit looked incomplete without the shoes, the trousers slightly loose without the belt, the shirt open at the neck after the tie was taken. After a moment he moved, the figure raised a hand to his face and wiped his nose.

'Is that live?' asked Bullock.

'Oh yes,' said Singh, almost sounding triumphant. 'That is Mr Mason, safe and sound in a police cell.'

'How?' asked Marshall.

'We still have the holes in their firewall that Mr Browning created for us, so we still have access to their surveillance feeds,' explained Singh.

'How long's that going to last?' asked Marshall. Despite his anger and desire for vengeance he could still recognise an opportunity that was worthy of consideration.

'Long enough, Browning was very good. They'll find it eventually, of course. But we have a window of opportunity. We have a chance to get at Mason, and he's our way into the company.'

'So you can hack in and order them to move him, yes?' asked Bullock.

'No,' said Singh, 'can't do that. But we can still plant things into their systems.'

'So what are you proposing?' asked Marshall. Singh looked at him.

Perhaps there was a chance, maybe just a chance that their plans could be salvaged. Singh was good with weapons and with knives and in hand-to-hand, but he was best at using technology as a weapon. If there was a chance to deliver on their original plan then it had to be considered. After all, killing Sanders had been part of their original plan. If it could be done then Bullock would go along. Bullock was good at what he did, and he was tough and independent, but ultimately would follow Marshall's lead.

'I have a strong enough connection with Mason. I can make him confess enough information to convince them he's valuable. We can use the network access to plant enough clues to convince them that Mason is a threat. Then they'll move him to somewhere more secure.'

'And we take him while he's being moved?' said Marshall.

'Yes, that's when he's vulnerable.'

'What about Sanders? He must have had a connection with Mason.'

'Mine's stronger. If I start now, I can block Sanders from getting into Mason's mind. He won't get to play the same trick twice.'

Marshall leant back against the work surface, considering the implications of Singh's suggestion, working through scenarios and options. They'd lost a lot of their resources when they'd fled the data centre. They'd had to leave a lot of their weaponry behind, but perhaps there were other ways.

'So what happens once we've got Mason?' asked Bullock. Marshall was already five steps of the plan further ahead.

'He has connections with the company, he configured their servers for the Bank of England, so he can get us an introduction.'

'Can he get us inside?' asked Marshall.

'Probably not, but he can get me close enough to someone who can. I only need access for a few minutes, from there I'll have all the control I need, then we'll be ready to take what we came for.'

Marshall stared at Singh, his eyes not betraying his thoughts, but no doubt weighing up the options.

'Once we've got that,' said Marshall, 'Sanders will be ours to take apart, piece by piece, then we get to ride off into the sunset, happy as Larry.'

Marshall looked at Bullock.

'Looks like we'll all get what we want. Okay, what's first?'

Three

London - Saturday morning

Bullock had never considered London to be
hostile territory before, but now he felt like he did the
time they'd crept over the border into Iraq. Danger
was all around, unseen, hidden by anonymity. His
companion drove the car. The darkened windows
provided some protection, but he knew that if his face
was captured by a single traffic camera it could spell
disaster. The baseball cap and sunglasses were an
almost comical attempt at disguise, but they had to be
enough, anything to make the massive computer
systems of GCHQ take longer to recognise him.
They'd driven into the outskirts of London an hour
ago, driving deliberately past traffic cameras, speed
cameras, a police station bristling with CCTV, waiting
to see if there was any response. They had escape
routes ready if police or security services made an
appearance, but none did. So they pressed on.

The man driving the car made no attempt at
conversation. Bullock still wasn't sure how far he
trusted these "consultants," but he had to admit,
without their help he, Marshall and Singh would never
have escaped from the data centre. The man and his
three colleagues were from a small private security
firm. They provided a discreet, complete and no-

questions-asked security service. With the addition of an enormous amount of telepathic control of them and their boss, Bullock and his colleagues had three "minders," who would quite literally walk over broken glass for their employers. The men were useful. The security services had no reason to link Bullock and friends to these people, so the minders could walk out in the open, with no fear of being recognised. And the biggest benefit of telepathic control? No technology in the world could hack it or intercept it.

'Are you there yet?' came Marshall's voice into Bullock's mind. He maintained control, there was never any warning when a telepathic voice would come into his awareness, it would always just appear. It was almost like he could hear Marshall next to him talking to him, and almost like a remembered voice. It was fine Marshall being there in spirit, but it was Bullock who was there physically, and if anything went wrong, powerfully telepathic he may be, he couldn't just "teleport" himself out. He was the one in the firing line. He relished the idea of a firefight with police or security forces, but only if he had a planned escape route.

'Close, five minutes,' Bullock thought/said. He watched the traffic as they turned off the main road and onto the Isle of Dogs, that curious hump of land made by the distinctive bump in the River Thames. Anonymous houses and shops passed them by. The traffic was light, enough traffic so they didn't stand out but not too much to trap them should they need to make a rapid exit. Bullock watched every side road, looked at every other vehicle. It was a long way from here to safety, out of the Capital. A long way along busy roads. Escape would take time, time for the security forces to get extra men and guns in place ahead of him, and they would have helicopters and personnel carriers full of armed police. The more he thought about it, the more he wondered if this was worth the risk. Singh hadn't been certain that Mason could actually get them what they needed, this all seemed a very long way from the safety and stealth of their original plan. Steal fifty billion pounds from the Bank of England. While the economy starts to collapse the money would have bought them easy access to the company, and from there they would have been able to walk in and take what they wanted. But now, here he was, head firmly in the lion's mouth.

They continued down the Manchester Road, ahead of them a slow driver dawdled along the road. Bullock hated slow drivers, but this one was a blessing. With cars parked on either side of the road, it wasn't safe to try and pass the slow driver, so Bullock and his driver had to be patient and drive slowly, which suited Bullock perfectly. He had the chance to look at what he needed to without looking suspicious. The police station was a modern red brick building. It could have been the offices of a computer company, except outside was an old fashioned blue Police street lamp. As they crawled past, Bullock looked down the side road, down the side of the police station. There was a heavy grey gate for pedestrian access and a little beyond that a larger gate for vehicle access. As police stations went it was unremarkable. At the front of the building, steps led up to the front doors, the Metropolitan Police crest on the wall above the doors. And soon enough they were past it.

'Why are they holding him here?' Bullock thought.

'Singh says Limehouse was full, yuppies brawling over who spilt the champagne. This is the nearest police station.' Marshall's voice was clear in his head.

'This won't work,' thought Bullock.

'We're only after one man,' said Marshall's voice.

'Yes, but there's no obvious ambush. As soon as they leave the police station they can go left or right, fifty-fifty decision, we can't cover both roads. There's nowhere on the route that's quiet, both routes soon hit main roads, there's nowhere to do this.' Bullock's scepticism was clear even through his telepathic voice.

'Then we'll have to make them go the way we want,' said Marshall.

'The road's too big to block, we don't have the resources,' said Bullock. 'There's no way to do that and stay out of sight.' An ambush required a few basic elements, whether it was in a jungle or in a city. There had to be somewhere to trap the target, somewhere from which the target had no easy escape and could find no easy cover. There also had to be a clear exit path after the ambush, there was no point springing an ambush only to become the target of someone else's trap, and these streets had all the makings of a trap.

'If they arrest Mason and charge him then we'll have to get him by force,' said Marshall, 'but they might not. If they don't charge him they'll release him, and then we simply have him come to us, quiet and easy.'

Bullock looked to the right. The trees to the right of the Docklands Light Railway station were the southern edge of Millwall Park, which looked distinctly like the sports field where he'd shot Crossley, the event that had started all of this.

'We need to turn around,' he said (or thought) to the driver. He was never sure if these orders came out as spoken words, but presently the driver turned right, followed the road round, and in a couple of turns was back on the main road heading back towards the police station.

Bullock had an idea. He gave an instruction to the driver, then spoke telepathically to Marshall. 'I'm going to have a look at the back of the police station.'

'Why? They wouldn't come out that way.'

'I just want to see what's there, see if there's any advantage we can use.'

The driver turned right off the main road, down a leafy residential road. At the end was a T-junction with a pub on the right-hand corner. To the right the road was lined with new apartment blocks, to the left was a line of not-quite-so-modern two storey apartments.

What he saw in front of them made him have the driver stop the car. He'd probably seen it on the maps when they first looked at the area, but hadn't realised the opportunity, proving that there was no substitute for getting out into the field and seeing the field of battle in person. Now that he looked at it, it was so obvious. His thinking must have been apparent to Marshall, even if he hadn't vocalised it.

'What?' asked Marshall. 'What's going on?'

'There is a way,' said Bullock. 'The dock, down on to the Thames.'

There was a pause, probably Marshall using a laptop to pull up the maps of the area. Marshall wasn't the greatest with technology, he had many strengths, but computers wasn't one of them.

'So what are you thinking?' said Marshall.

Bullock thought about making some quip about why didn't he read his mind, but thought better of it. 'Hit them as soon as they leave the police station, maximum force so no-one gets chance to use a radio. Mason comes with us, one short boat ride across the Thames.'

'Oh yes,' said Marshall, sounding triumphant. 'On the other side is Greenwich, it's a maze of residential roads. Hang on.'

There was a pause, then Singh's voice joined the psychic conversation. Computers were Singh's strength. 'There's little CCTV there,' he said. 'Few traffic cameras, most of the private CCTV is inaccessible by GCHQ. We can change vehicles, use side roads and residential roads for a couple of miles, they won't be able to track us for miles.'

'Okay,' said Marshall. 'If they do decide to move Mason we need to be ready. Bullock, get back here, we've got a lot to do.'

***

Even on Saturday morning Thames House was busy. Busy people occupied most of the desks, filling the open-plan office area with a hum of conversations and discussions. Michael had found a free desk and had logged on to the computer. He wanted to check on the progress of the police hunt for the Three. It seemed most were referring to them as Marshall, Bullock and Singh, or "the criminals" or "the fugitives." Michael had become used to calling them "the Three."

As he suspected, the police forensics team had found little usable evidence from the data centre, nothing that was helping them find the Three. The data centre itself was still off limits until the Army had disposed of the booby traps and made it safe, and for some reason, they seemed to be taking their time. The police effort was focused on finding the three men responsible for the killing of Gerald Crossley and the murder of a dozen officers in a gun and bomb attack. The hunt seemed unconnected to the attempted theft of fifty billion pounds through the Bank of England's computer system. Michael did some more digging and found that the theft was being investigated by the

Serious Fraud Office, and it was they who were holding Jason Mason for questioning.

Michael was due to be interviewed by the police at some point later, Eric would be too after he returned from taking Anna back to Cheltenham. This was hampering Michael from getting back to the data centre and trying to pick up the Three's trail, or from seeing Jason Mason. He was sure Mason knew more about the Three's plans and had a stronger connection to them than Michael had yet discovered. He was the most substantial lead they had, and Michael couldn't get at him. He felt his frustration growing. Time was not on his side.

Michael found the contact details for the officer leading the SFO investigation and called him. It took a moment to establish his identity and for the man to verify him as an MI5 officer.

'I'm sorry Mr Smith,' said Detective Inspector Hart, making it clear that he didn't for a moment believe the name "Smith" and that he was disappointed his caller hadn't chosen a more original alias. 'But Mason is a key suspect in a major crime. I cannot allow him to be interviewed by anyone outside the Force until I decide if we're going to charge him.'

'DI Hart,' said Michael, 'Mason is also a key witness in another matter. I hate to use the phrase, but it is quite appropriate, this is a matter of national security, and it's urgent that I speak with Mason, even if it's brief.'

'No,' said Hart, 'it's out of the question. Not until I've decided if we're going to charge him.'

'And when will that be?'

'Later today, our twenty-four hours are up at about four o'clock.'

Michael ended the call. He obviously wasn't going to get anywhere with Detective Inspector Hart. For a moment he considered calling Commander

Halbern, the man who had led the operation which the Three had ambushed, and then led the armed assault on the data centre, but only after the Three had fled. He decided against it. Halbern wasn't his biggest fan, and Michael wasn't going to try and explain how he believed Mason was connected with the Three. Another door was now shut.

Instead, he called the Head.

'I need to speak to Jason Mason,' he explained

'So go and speak to him,' she said, as though it was the simplest thing in the world.

'I can't, he's being held by the police in connection with attempted fraud. They won't let me see him. I need MI5 authorisation to over-rule the investigating officer.'

'That would be easy,' she said, 'if you were part of an official investigation. But you're not, so I can't give you any official MI5 authorisation. You'll have to find your own way.'

She ended the call, and so closed yet another door. Sometimes he wondered whose side she was on, but knowing that would require knowing what the sides were, and that was something he still didn't know. It was tempting to think that he could go to the police station and use his ability to control people telepathically to get access to Mason. But it wouldn't be possible. He'd never be able to establish sufficient control over enough people to make it happen before someone alerted Hart, who would undoubtedly stop him.

If he couldn't get physical access to Mason, which was his preference, he'd have to try and connect with Mason telepathically. In his last meeting with Mason, Michael had established a strong connection with the man, enough to confuse him and prevent him from following Singh's telepathic orders to transfer the fifty billion pounds out of the Bank of England's IT system. But Mason was currently an emotional mess, and getting anything out of him, especially remotely, could be difficult. But Michael had no choice.

He logged off the computer and found an unoccupied meeting room. He closed the door and lowered the blinds on the internal window. Michael sat in the chair and closed his eyes. Making a telepathic connection with someone was a strange experience. Each mind had a unique signature, something recognisable, a kind of mental scent, or something like the way in which each person's voice is unique. Michael brought to mind the unique sense of Jason Mason's mind and felt his thoughts reach out for a connection.

Michael was waiting to sense the anxiety and fear from Mason's mind. He got a sense of Mason, that unique sense that identified Mason's mind, but Michael was surprised. It was just like walking into someone's house, expecting it to be untidy, a complete mess, and instead walking into a clean and tidy and well presented home. Michael felt Mason's thoughts, and they were calm and relaxed. The fear and anxiety were gone. Instead, he was peaceful, and this worried Michael. Mason hadn't struck him as the kind of person who could control his thoughts so effectively. In fact, the fear and anxiety he had sensed last time were proof that Mason couldn't, so how had he been able to calm himself?

Michael let the connection strengthen, without saying anything, acting almost as a bystander, watching the scene in front of him. It was almost voyeuristic, but Mason knew that Michael was there, it wasn't possible to connect to another person without their knowing about it. He sensed Mason's thoughts drift. He sensed images, words. Office scenes, perhaps from where Mason had worked, or visited, the faces of people, again possibly work colleagues. Words drifted in and out. The image of a leather bound diary, his Xbox, the inside of a police cell, a feeling of calm and of waiting, his Xbox again.

'Hello Michael,' came Mason's voice. Mason, it seemed, was now rather more comfortable with the idea of another person's thoughts being in his mind.

'Hello Jason,' said Michael. 'How are you now?'

'I feel better, but I have to confess I'm not sure what I'm doing here.'

'I'm afraid you're in a police cell,' said Michael.

'Yes,' said Mason, 'I know where I am, but I'm not completely clear about why I'm here.'

'What do you remember?' Michael asked.

'Everything, but I'm not sure why I did some of the things I did, it's all a little hard to rationalise.'

Michael was becoming more suspicious. Mason was not only calm, he was too calm. Michael had not sensed this level of self-control when he last connected with Mason. It could only mean that one of the Three, probably Singh, had been connected with Mason. If that was the case, Mason was a definite lead to finding the Three.

'Jason, do you remember Julian?' He wasn't sure if Mason had ever known Singh by name, but if Singh had had such a strong control over Mason then his name may have become known.

'Oh yes,' said Mason, as though it was obvious that he knew Julian Singh. 'I'm not sure where we met, but I feel I know him well.'

'Has Julian asked you to do anything?'

'Not today, he simply wanted to wish me well, to make sure that I was alright, and to tell me that everything was going to be okay.'

'Did he say how everything was going to be okay?'

It came without warning, like being pushed from behind. An enormous mental surge, a darkness that suddenly engulfed everything, and Michael had a feeling like he was being pushed out, expelled. He felt the connection with Mason starting to disappear, and before it faded, he caught the unmistakable sense of Julian Singh.

Michael opened his eyes. He fought the urge to swear loudly. The feeling grew that this was a game of one-against-three with the referee biased heavily towards the three.

He looked around the empty meeting room. 'Welcome to the team,' he said to no-one. For a brief moment a feeling came over him, a familiar feeling, but not a pleasant feeling. For a second he had the sense of being behind enemy lines. He focused his mind back on what had just happened.

His connection with Mason was gone, permanently, Singh had seen to that. It proved two things, Michael thought. First, the Three were still very much active, and second, they still considered Mason to be important. Asset or threat? Michael couldn't tell, but it was now more important than ever that he get physical access to Mason, whatever it took.

***

Anna approached the entrance to the Doughnut with a mixture of trepidation and relief. The sheer scale of the building never failed to impress her, the huge glass sides of the circular building (hence its name) curved away to either side. She walked through one of the revolving doors and into the entrance foyer. She had no doubt that surveillance and verification started even before this point, but she never spent too long thinking about it, this was where she worked, this was where she was meant to be. As the main location of the Government Communications Headquarters (GCHQ), the building was home to the armies of data analysts, security specialists, cryptographers, mathematicians and all manner of computer and IT experts. Between them, they intercepted an almost unimaginable quantity of communications data and other intelligence, analysed it, sifted through it, identified threats to national security and identified those who would threaten the nation.

Once past the ID scanners and turnstiles Anna walked down the broad avenue between the inner and outer buildings to the office area she worked in. She smiled at the occasional familiar face, but no-one it seemed noticed that she'd been absent for a few days, nor thought it remarkable she was back. Why would they? Her activities had been secret, and almost everything that happened in GCHQ was secret in some way or other. She pushed through the heavy glass doors into the open plan office area. Dozens of people sat at desks, staring at multiple computer screens, a few engaging in conversations, some on telephone conference calls or video calls. Signs hung from the ceiling at various points indicating which team sat where. Anna found her desk, almost exactly as she'd left it, and sat down.

Stuck to the keyboard was a single yellow sticky note, with a smiley face on it. She had no doubt that Kingston had left it. The desk next to hers was so far vacant. Her co-worker, Kingston Smith, hadn't arrived yet. She liked Kingston, they worked well together, and she realised that she had missed him, even though she was the one who'd been away, and only for a few days, and had been too busy nearly being killed to think about it. The last few days were already starting to feel like a dream, something that didn't really happen. Eric had driven her back to Cheltenham early that morning. She'd enjoyed his company, and they'd talked about a lot of things, but nothing about recent events. She couldn't now remember what they had talked about, nothing important, all of it fun.

'Hello trouble,' said a voice from behind.

She turned around, and Kingston Smith was walking to his desk. For a moment she had an urge to get up and hug him, but she didn't. She smiled a huge warm smile at him, and he returned the same.

'Nice to see you're back,' said Kingston.

'Nice to be back,' she said, not really sure what else to say. A lightly flippant remark or mild sarcasm was their usual level of humour, yet today that seemed a little out of place.

'It seems everyone's chasing your bad guys,' said Kingston, switching on his screens and logging into his computer.

Anna started setting up her workstation. 'Yes, they certainly seemed to have caused some trouble,' she said.

'You won't have met Maria yet, will you?' said Kingston.

'Maria?'

'Our new team leader.'

Anna looked over the divider at the desk immediately opposite hers. The seat was pushed up to the desk, which was clear of any personal items, it was a desk clearly unoccupied. It had previously been occupied by Wayne Browning, their team leader, but Browning had been killed by Evan Bullock and Julian Singh. Thoughts started to swirl in Anna's mind of all the people who'd died recently, but she pushed the thoughts away. She knew she couldn't afford to dwell on them, not here, not now.

'No, not come across her before,' she said.

As the various windows opened on her multiple screens and programs came online, Anna pondered exactly what it was she needed to do. Finding the Three would be a challenge. She realised she'd picked up Michael's habit of calling them "the Three," but she couldn't think of a better name. She wasn't sure where to start, either logically or geographically. She doubted they would oblige and stand in front of a surveillance camera. No doubt they would take measures to avoid appearing on any kind of CCTV, or use any traceable electronic communications. Whatever psychic abilities they or Michael had, Anna doubted she could trace a telepathic communication.

'Anna Hendrickson?' came a voice, jerking Anna out of her musings.

Anna turned around and assumed that the young lady standing there was the new team leader.

'I'm Maria Cho,' said Maria Cho.

Anna's first impression was that Maria was dressed smartly, slightly conservatively, but with just a slight hint of Goth. She wasn't sure if it was the darkness of everything Maria was wearing or the distinct purple streak in her hair. Maria offered her hand, and Anna shook it.

'Sorry we haven't had time for a proper introduction,' said Maria, 'but as you can imagine things are a bit busy here at the moment.'

'Yes, I can imagine,' said Anna, suppressing a smile and resisting the urge to shoot a glance at Kingston.

'Good, well there's plenty for you to do,' said Maria. Anna struggled to keep from saying something along the lines of "you don't know the half of it." There was certainly plenty to do. Ideas were already forming in Anna's mind about how to start a wide search for signs of the Three.

Maria, however, had other ideas. 'I need you to work with Tech Services on finding and fixing the holes in our firewalls.'

Anna stared at Maria, not sure how to respond.

'I'll need an update by noon,' said Maria, 'we've got some serious gaps in our outer defences, they need closing as soon as possible.' With that, she walked off lifting her mobile phone to her ear. Anna sat in silence for a moment. She knew that Wayne Browning had created openings in the GCHQ firewalls, but that was while under the telepathic control of Julian Singh. She wasn't sure what else Singh had managed to do, and no doubt there were serious gaps in their defences, but this was not what she needed to be spending her time doing.

'She's a bit of task-master,' said Kingston. 'A word to the wise, have an update ready for her.' He turned back to his own screens.

Kingston focused on his screens, leaving Anna to ponder her new situation. Dealing with "assertive" characters was not something Anna enjoyed. She had enjoyed the debating society at University, and arguing the finer points of mathematical theory in tutorials, but there all were equals. Here, team leaders and senior analysts were superiors, arguing with them was a different game. Wayne had been easy to work with. He'd been a bit of task-master, and a bit of a micro-manager, but he'd been fair, Anna had always been able to discuss priorities with him. Her first impression was that Maria Cho was not someone who discussed priorities. This was a problem. Anna had no doubt that her priorities were going to be very different from Cho's.

Anna opened up a window on one of her screens and looked for the relevant information about the work being done by the Technical Services and

Support Team, usually known as Tech Services. She read the details, and started thinking how she could add to what they were doing, which of their problems she could solve. This is what she did, solve problems.

She'd always enjoyed solving problems, particularly math's problems, ever since her father had given her a book of math's puzzles. She'd taken it away and started working on the first chapter of puzzles and problems, intrigued by them, but infuriated by them, by their complexity, which defeated her. She'd eventually given in to her curiosity, and looked in the back of the book for the answers. From there she'd used the answers to the first three chapters' questions and worked backwards, discovering how to answer the problems. When she'd announced to her parents that she'd done the first three chapters they were delighted, and her father had challenged her to show him how she'd do the problems from the fourth chapter. She both delighted and surprised herself to find that the answers came easily, and from there her path was set. School, Oxford University, GCHQ, a star pupil, a rising star amongst the analysts. Wayne Browning, annoying though he was, had shown her how the organisation worked, beyond just the day-to-day work on problem solving.

Browning. Her reminiscing stopped as it collided with the memories of recent events, and the brutality of the real world. Her world had changed, at least for a time, for the time she was captive of the Three, and now they were still at large, and Anna had an inside track on finding them. This was a problem she was uniquely qualified to solve.

'Kingston?' she said, keeping her voice down. 'I can't spend time on this firewall stuff.'

'Why not?' he said, without looking up from his work.

Anna paused. She knew little enough about Michael and his past and what happened with him and the three others, but even so she couldn't share any of it.

'There are just some other things I need to do,' was all she could think to say.

'Not sure Maria would be sympathetic to that,' said Kingston. 'I'm running pattern analyses on the police evidence. Not exactly thrilling, but these three killed a dozen police. I'd like to think I can help catch them.'

'They killed Wayne, too,' said Anna, before she could stop herself.

Kingston turned sharply to face her. She couldn't read his face. He was struggling to find words.

'I'm sorry,' she said, 'they hadn't told you.'

Kingston shook his head slowly.

'I can't say anything, but there are things I need to do to find them, and closing holes in the firewall isn't part of it.'

'Were you with him?' Kingston asked, his voice more subdued than before.

'No.'

'Were you with that Sanders character?'

'Michael's on our side, he really is, but I can't say any more.'

'You know more about them than I do, don't you?' asked Kingston.

'That would be a reasonable assumption,' Anna said, wondering how to answer questions without answering them, hoping that Kingston would catch on. He was smart, he was very smart, she hoped he'd ask the right questions. If he did, she could answer him obliquely, hint strongly enough without being guilty of saying something she shouldn't. Kingston stared at her, perhaps wrestling with his own thoughts about who he should trust, where his loyalties should lie.

'Then I could imagine that you have insights into finding them that others might not have,' Kingston said, just the hint of a smile creeping across his face.

'That would be a good thing to imagine,' she said.

'And if anyone had such insights, it might be beneficial if they had support in following those insights.'

'It certainly might.'

Kingston stared at the floor for a moment. 'There are automated alerts we could set up, facial recognition traps, social media deep dives,' he suggested.

'They would all help,' said Anna, 'if they were set up to look for the right things. But it would take time.'

'Two people could start setting them up,' said Kingston, 'as well as making some progress on firewalls and pattern analyses.'

Anna smiled at her knight in shining armour, and they got to work.

Four

Marshall sat on a stool at the workbench in the farmhouse kitchen. Bullock was on his way back from London, and so far there had been no indication that he'd been identified while out and about. Marshall had a laptop open in front of him and was making notes, sketching diagrams of the roads on each side of the Thames. He knew he'd need Singh's input to identify where there were dangers from CCTV cameras which might identify them. Part of the trick was knowing which cameras GCHQ could tap into and which they couldn't. The other key decision was how much use to make of their security consultants. Unlike the Serbs these three weren't mercenaries, they weren't naturally inclined to happily kill anything that moved. With sufficient telepathic control, they could be commanded to fight, but it would take more effort. They were useful, very useful as dogs' bodies, as gophers, as messengers and remote eyes and ears, but when the shooting started Marshall wanted to focus only on what he needed to do, he wasn't sure he could afford the distraction of also trying to play puppet master. Perhaps they could yet exert a greater influence over the men, even to the point where they could be commanded to simply fight, and then left to get on with it.

He could hear Singh in the other room, tapping away on his own laptop. Other than the sound of keyboards tapping, the house was quiet.

'Bastards,' came the shout from Singh in the other room, puncturing the silence.

'Now what?' asked Marshall, not sounding too concerned. Singh wandered in, a scowl written across his face.

'Courtesy of GCHQ I'm keeping an eye on their record of interviewing Mason. Looks like they're going to charge him.'

Marshall breathed in and sat up. 'Game on then,' he said.

'Problem is,' said Singh, 'they're going to charge him with fraud and false accounting, looks like they're going to keep him at Canary Wharf for the time being.'

Marshall was silent as he digested the news. 'That's not so good,' he said finally. 'What happens then?'

'No idea,' said Singh, 'they might release him on bail, or move him, but that could take days.'

This wasn't what Marshall had in mind. He preferred to move quickly. Hit hard, hit fast, that was how he preferred things. Sitting around waiting to see what someone else was going to do wasn't his natural approach. He had thought about hitting the police station itself. They had the firepower, there was little doubt they could get in and retrieve Mason, and he had no problem with how many more police officers they'd kill. What he couldn't be certain of was getting out in time and avoiding detection during their escape.

'We need Mason outside that police station,' said Marshall.

'I know,' said Singh, who leant back against the refrigerator.

Marshall stared at him. 'Well?'

'Well what?' said Singh, indignant. 'I don't have a magic answer.'

'You've got all the IT, you've hacked their systems, find some way of persuading them to move him. You said you could plant evidence, make them think he's a threat. Make them worried, make them move him.'

Singh's eyes narrowed, no doubt as he thought through options and possibilities, and then he smiled a little.

'If we make them think that he's connected with armed terrorists and that there's a possibility they'll either try and liberate him, or kill him,' Singh's voice trailed off.

'Yes?'

'Then they're more likely to want to move him to a more secure location. Probably Paddington Green.'

'So how do we do that, then?' asked Marshall. Sometimes it was like pulling teeth getting people to explain a plan.

'If Mr Mason were to make a confession, give up a couple of names, a few details that showed he was in league with us, then they'd take it seriously.'

'Would they take it seriously enough?'

'No, they'd look into it, while they held him at Canary Wharf. But if they also had evidence that we were targeting him, that would spur them into action.'

'And do they have this evidence?'

'Not yet,' said Singh, grinning. 'But they will in about half an hour. They'll find a record in their evidence system of a text message, confirmed as being from you, mentioning Mason. Tangible evidence that there's a material threat to him.'

'And is Mason ready for what we're going to do?' This was Marshall's other big concern. His greatest worry was that when it came to the crunch,

Mason would panic, or curl up in a ball and refuse to move. Marshall doubted they'd have the time or the energy to try and carry Mason.

'No, but he will be. I already caught Sanders trying to have a psychic one-to-one with Mason, so I kicked him out.'

'Good.'

'Mason's a lot calmer now. I'll spend more time with him this afternoon. Then he'll be ready to make his confession.'

'There's no way of having Mason play nice so they release him on bail?' Marshall had hoped to avoid a direct confrontation. He had no problem with the idea of an armed assault, but the risks were huge. If there was a chance of acquiring Mason quietly, it would be a lot better for them.

'No, there's nothing he can say that's going to make them let him walk out.'

'Right, as soon as Bullock gets back we'll go over the plan. Then we'll get our pet minders to go and get things ready.'

Marshall looked out of the window. This was all far riskier than they'd planned for, but at least they were back on the offensive. Once they had Mason, they could start to get their original plan back on track. Marshall allowed himself a small smile as he began to think that their end goal might be in reach after all.

***

Croydon - Saturday afternoon

The grey Audi was parked on the road outside the data centre. Eric sat in the car, while Michael paced up and down the pavement, his phone pressed to his ear. As soon as Eric had returned from chauffeuring Anna back to Cheltenham, Michael had been keen to get to the data centre. Being denied permission to interview Mason had complicated things, but now that his telepathic access had been cut off Michael had few options left.

Any tangible evidence they might have about what the Three were doing, what they were planning next, was probably inside the data centre. A monolithic, totally anonymous grey industrial warehouse building, the data centre had been "borrowed" by the Three from an insurance company, no doubt at the cost of the life of whichever director they had taken control of.

The front gate and the remains of the pedestrian turnstile were wrapped up in blue and white police tape. Various criss-crosses of yellow tape adorned the front door of the building. Remarkably, there was no physical police presence. No constable on sentry duty.

Michael was taking bigger and bigger strides as his frustration grew. He might not be on Commander Halbern's Christmas card list, but if he wanted to keep his and Eric's activities as low key as possible, he'd at least need to warn Halbern of what they intended. So far, Halbern had proved difficult to get hold of, and Michael felt he'd been fobbed off onto one of Halbern's lackeys.

'The Commander has made it quite clear to me, so I'm making it quite clear to you,' said the lacky, 'that the building is still a crime scene and is therefore off limits.'

'And I'm part of the operation to apprehend the people who did it and to stop them doing any more damage and killing any more police officers,' said Michael, sounding a little more frustrated than he'd intended.

'We're all working on that, but the building remains off limits. Never mind the crime scene aspect we also suspect it's booby trapped, so until Army Bomb Disposal finish with it you're ordered to stay out.'

'I'll remind you,' said Michael, 'that I don't take orders from you.'

'Then I'll make it clear, as a matter of record I'm denying you permission to access the building. Is that clear?'

Michael paused. The "matter of record" bit could make things difficult. 'Yes, that's clear.'

Michael ended the call and swore loudly. He stopped walking, and stood for a moment thinking.

Don't run too fast. It was the worst advice his mother had ever given him, and the best. At school he'd loved cross-country running, the challenge of beating the competition with nothing but his own determination. Running too fast was folly, over a longer distance he'd learnt he ran out of strength. But sometimes there was no other strategy than to risk it all and run too fast. Win or die, sometimes going too far or too fast was the only option.

He walked back to the passenger side of the car and got in.

'So, how did that go?' asked Eric. Michael suspected that Eric had heard the swearing.

'Fine, we're good to go,' said Michael, putting a big smile on his face.

'Liar,' said Eric.

'Yeah, some oik said we don't have permission and had to stay out.'

'So, do we go in the front door or the back door?' asked Eric.

Michael thought for a moment. 'Let's have a look at the front door, but I suspect Marshall will have left a few surprises.'

'Thought as much,' said Eric.

Michael phoned Anna. It would be a big help to have her expertise with them, even if only virtually. Someone else answered her phone, identifying himself as Mr Smith. Michael wondered if that really was the man's name, and for a moment was amused by the coincidence of the alias he used and this man's (probably) genuine name. He left a brief message and hung up.

They collected some equipment from the back of the car, various bits of kit useful in detecting and neutralising explosives and for negating various forms of lock.

As they were pushing various devices into their pockets, Michael's phone rang.

'It's Anna,' said Anna, sounding like she was trying to talk quietly.

'Hello,' said Michael. 'I was hoping you could keep an eye on us?'

'Why? What are you doing?' she asked.

'Eric and I are going into the data centre.'

'Oh no,' said Anna, surprised. She composed herself. 'That's a bad idea, there are booby traps.'

Michael and Eric looked at each other.

'Yes, I'm sure there are. We'll be careful. Can you help us?'

There was a pause. 'I'll try. Do you have a camera you can take with you?'

Under Anna's direction, Eric and Michael selected a body-cam each which they clipped to their lapels, and selected various other items of equipment which Anna felt "might come in useful." Anna confirmed that she could communicate with both of them via their earpieces and receive the feed from their cameras. The communications all linked to the car's communications system, which boosted the signal and connected them to the GCHQ secure network.

The two of them squeezed through the wreckage of the turnstile and walked to the front door of the building. Eric pulled a palm-sized device from his pocket and waved it slowly around the edge of the door.

'Seems there's still power to the burglar alarm,' he said. 'Neat trick, given somebody blew up the power supply to the building.' He grinned at Michael.

Anna's voice came through each earpiece. 'The police have logged booby traps on the front door, the rear fire escape, the trap door in the loading bay, and door into the server room.'

'I think there's one door which should be okay,' said Michael. They walked down the side of the building, almost to the end. A large wooden panel, six-foot square, had been bolted to the side of the building, with black soot marks stretching out from under the wood and creeping across the grey exterior. The main feature of the wooden panel was a door, padlocked shut, securing the building from unauthorised access. The original door had been destroyed during Michael's first visit when he had shot out the lock and then used a grenade to deter his pursuers. At least they could be confident that the grenade had also taken care of any booby traps.

Eric pulled a set of skeleton keys from another pocket and made short work of the padlock. They each switched on a torch, pulled open the door, and stepped inside.

They picked their way through the wreckage of the first two rooms. Then came the door which led to the loading bay. Eric used his detecting device and scanned the door and its surrounding.

'Looks okay,' he said.

'That's reassuring,' said Michael.

'Well, I'm assuming that in your last meeting with them, they were in a hurry.'

'You could say that.'

'So they didn't have time to stop and set up trip wires,' said Eric.

'Nope, the building's just as they left it.'

'So the only surprises are ones they set, like the trap door, or ones that switched themselves on after they left, and that takes power, and I don't detect any power.'

Eric's reasoning was sound, thought Michael.

'Good,' said Michael. 'Since it's your assumption, you can go first.' He thought it was probably a good job he couldn't clearly see Eric's expression.

'You can't use your woo-woo powers to detect booby-traps, I suppose?' asked Eric. Michael didn't reply.

Eric took hold of the door knob, twisted, and pushed the door open. They both paused for a moment.

'Assuming that didn't start any kind of countdown, we should be okay,' said Eric.

'Too many assumptions and shoulds for my liking.'

He half expected a comment from Anna, but there was silence in his earpiece.

They stepped through the door into the darkness of the loading bay.

The room was big and dark. This was the room where, when the building was a data centre, trucks would arrive and unload pallets of computer equipment, heavy-duty power distribution equipment, office equipment, vending machines and the like. As they swung their torches around they could see the Black BMW X5 sitting in the centre of the room. In the floor under the vehicle was the service hatch through which Marshall, Bullock and Singh had escaped, setting booby traps as they went. Michael and Eric had no intention of exploring that route.

Around the outside of the room were workbenches, strewn with an odd assortment of handguns, submachine guns, grenades and other armaments. There was a sofa positioned in front of a large flat-screen TV, beer cans still sitting on the floor. It was like coming back into a house after the party had finished. There were memories of the energy and activity that used to be here. A battlefield the morning after the battle was always a strange and eerie place. Michael had seen battlefields the day after, often characterised by scattered body parts. He caught a glimpse in the half light of Eric's face, and reckoned Eric too had seen the aftermath of war.

'Not sure there's much here,' said Eric. Michael agreed but said nothing. There was nothing here that looked like any kind of personal item, nothing he could connect with and establish a telepathic connection with its owner. He doubted the armaments themselves would yield any clues, but no doubt the police would chase down any such clues when they were finally allowed in.

'They did most of their work in the office area to the left,' came Anna's voice through the earpieces, 'but I'd like to see inside the main server room.'

'Why? What's in there?' asked Michael.

'Oh, I don't know, servers maybe,' said Anna. 'If I can get details of the servers they were using I might be able to try and track any Internet traffic.'

Michael recalled the layout of the building from the schematics. The loading bay led into the main room in the building, the even bigger space destined to hold the racks of servers and mainframe computers for the insurance company.

'Anna,' Michael said, 'any police reports of booby traps between here and the server room?'

'Yes, lots,' she said, 'but I'm afraid not much detail. They may as well just have written: "here be dragons."' Michael couldn't see Eric's grin.

Michael and Eric made their way to the door to the main server room. There were two doors, a large roller shutter which would have been used for moving large items of equipment in and out of the loading bay, and a single door. Eric shone his torch at a small grey item taped to the door next to the handle of the door.

'I'd guess that's a motion triggered explosive,' he said. 'Probably a surprise for anyone who came through the front door and coming to the back.'

Michael held both the torches to give Eric enough light while he disarmed the device and pulled it away from the door. It was a simple device but would have been horribly effective if anyone had opened the door from the other side. The device consisted of a block of plastic explosive, and on the back was the motion sensor circuit and the electronics which switched it on, probably in response to some remote control carried by the Three as they escaped.

They opened the door and walked into the server room. It was cavernous, making up probably half the internal space of the building. Huge, but strangely empty. The insurance company had never had a chance to occupy the building before Marshall and friends had "borrowed" it. In the middle of the room were three racks of equipment. Each rack was a metal cage, six feet high, three feet square. Michael and Eric approached, taking their time, making sure Anna could get a good view from the body cameras. The first rack was grey or appeared to be grey in the light of the LED torches.

Under Anna's instruction, Michael opened the front door of the cage. Inside were servers, each was flat and roughly square, a high-performance computer lacking the familiar screen and keyboard of a desktop PC. Michael got to work, following Anna's directions, using a device he'd brought with him. To all intents and purposes, it looked like a regular external hard disk drive, but Michael suspected there was a lot more to it. He plugged the device's USB cable into the socket in the front of one of the servers and let the device do its thing.

As he worked, Eric walked off, exploring more of the data centre. Michael listened as he occasionally asked if a particular door held any particular threat, none did. Michael's device beeped, and he plugged it into the next server. It was slow and laborious, but he knew that the more data Anna had the more she'd be able to try and trace the Three. He finished with the first rack and moved onto the second. Eric continued his slow and methodical sweep of the rest of the building.

Marshall and the others had almost succeeded in bringing down the Bank of England, not with guns but with keyboards. Cyber-warfare was a part of the future, the likes of Julian Singh were the Special Forces of the future, but as Michael looked around the data centre he thought about the guns in the loading bay, and the dead police officers. Singh wasn't the whole of the future. There would still be people like Vince Marshall, and people like Marshall needed to be stopped.

As he finished the final server, Michael looked at the third rack. It was black, and looked to be more solid than the first two, and in its own way it looked more menacing. There was no manufacturer name on the front of the rack, and the door was obviously locked. Not locked with a small lock meant simply as a "please don't open this" message, but a hefty "thou shalt not enter" kind of lock.

'Oh,' said Anna, with a note of surprise. 'I didn't see that coming.'

'Why? What is it?' asked Michael.

'It's an exVoxx server.'

'XBox? What is it with you people and computer games?'

'What do you mean "you people"?' She sounded truly indignant.

'Sorry, but Mason was thinking about his XBox as well.'

'How do you know what he was thinking?' Anna obviously realised what she'd said. 'Oh, of course.'

Michael was about to ask another flippant question when Anna spoke first. 'No, not X-Box,' she said, stressing the B. This is an exVoxx server.' She stressed the V.

'Don't follow you,' said Michael. 'What's an exVoxx server?'

'It's a system that protects an IT network from outside intrusion, it encrypts all incoming and outgoing communications, it recognises and defeats hacking attacks, and it's only used by government and military systems.'

'So, our boys had access to military grade IT,' said Michael. 'That fits with the level of the other equipment they had.'

'That's not the best bit,' said Anna, determined to explain more about the IT system. 'exVoxx servers can coordinate with each other. If you try and hack one, they'll link with each other and hack back, to disable whichever system tried to attack them.'

'Cool,' said Eric over the earpiece, Michael could see him walking back. 'Computers that fight back.'

'They'd have needed this to hack the Bank of England's systems,' said Anna. 'And Jason Mason was the Bank's key specialist in exVoxx systems.'

'And they're still interested in Mr Mason,' said Michael. 'So they are planning something.'

'Something that probably involves hacking a government or military system,' said Anna.

'One more thing,' said Eric. 'I can't find any beds.'

Michael looked at him, and imagined Anna would have, had she been there. There was a moment's silence as they each tried to think of the best, and wittiest response.

'I'm serious,' said Eric. 'No beds, no cooking equipment. They never lived here. This never was their base of operations.'

Michael sighed and realised they'd all assumed (but never checked) that the Three had based themselves in the data centre. But they hadn't, they had always had another location. A case of so near, yet so far.

'So we never really found them in the first place,' said Anna.

'Back to square one,' said Eric.

'No,' said Michael. 'They led us on a song and dance, but we never left square one.'

Five

The farmhouse - Sunday morning

The drizzle fell from a dull grey sky and speckled the windows. Marshall sat in the easy chair in the living room of the farmhouse. Singh sat opposite him, laptop open on the coffee table between them, tapping at the keyboard, pausing now and then to sigh or smile. Marshall never found someone else working on a computer to be much of a spectator sport.

Even less entertaining was watching someone else in telepathic contact with another. Singh had spent the previous hour in psychic connection with Mason. He'd hardly moved or spoken for the whole time. Marshall had exchanged barely a dozen words with him. He had no doubt that now, or very soon, Mason would be ready for them to rescue him. He wouldn't panic if there were gunfire (when there was gunfire,) and he wouldn't hesitate to come to Marshall and Bullock (who would carry out the assault.)

Marshall looked out of the window at the drizzle, glad he was inside. He had no dislike of rain and more often than not he preferred to be outside, it felt less constrained. But at this moment he needed to be inside and quiet, able to get the plan completely straight in his mind. They'd be outside soon enough. Bullock was out, making arrangements, ensuring that assets were in place. It was dangerous, every time they stepped outside they risked inadvertently looking into a camera and being recognised by the all-seeing Leviathan of the GCHQ surveillance system. Every time Singh went online there was a chance that somehow or other, GCHQ would detect their activity and trace them. They had to take risks, the prize they sought was worth the risks, but they had to be calculated risks.

'How's it going?' Marshall asked, unable to watch in silence any longer.

Singh looked up. 'Mason's ready. He'll make his confession, give up some names.'

Marshall coughed. 'Yeah, my name.'

'No pain, no gain,' said Singh with a smirk. 'As soon as the police hear that they'll connect him to the search for us.'

'So when will they move him?'

'We need them to think that he's a security risk, otherwise they won't.'

'So?' said Marshall with exasperation. Sometimes Singh was too keen to explain his genius, other times getting him to explain things was like getting blood out of the proverbial stone.

'Wouldn't it be convenient?' said Singh, 'if the police had a record of a voicemail from Bullock giving an instruction to someone to find Mason and kill him no matter what it took, a voicemail found on a phone dropped as we left the data centre.'

'Then they'd put two and two together, assume Mason had genuine information and was at risk, and they'd move him to a secure location,' said Marshall. 'Assuming they don't wonder why they never picked up on the voicemail sooner.'

'They miss bits of evidence all the time. By the time they look into it, we'll have finished.'

'Great, so how do we get them to find such a voicemail?' asked Marshall.

'I just need to get into their HOLMES system and fake an evidence record. I've already faked one that says images of Canary Wharf police station were found on a computer retrieved from the data centre. Given the number of guns we left there, they should get the message that there's some serious trouble coming their way.'

Singh frowned and leant closer to the laptop, something having caught his attention.

'What?' said Marshall.

'GCHQ are obviously closing all the gaps that Browning left for us, I just got cut off.'

Marshall thought of things he could say, but he bit his lip. Singh was skilled and focused, he knew what he needed to do, and he knew how to do it. He watched as Singh tapped away on the keyboard, and mused that ten years ago no-one in Special Forces needed to know how to type. Now, Singh's skills were invaluable in surveillance and ambush operations.

'Damn,' Singh hissed.

'What?' asked Marshall.

'They closed another hole in their firewall.'

'Is that a problem?'

'They're close to shutting us out completely.' Singh's eyes narrowed as he concentrated on his screen, and his fingers danced over the keyboard. 'They're working hard to undo all Mr Browning's good work.'

'And if they shut you out completely?'

'Then we're screwed, basically.'

Singh paused. He stopped typing and smiled slightly.

He typed some more. 'Browning left one way in that will take them longest to find.'

'But...?'

'As soon as I use it, there's more chance they'll see it's there. It's time to play our final card.'

Marshall couldn't help but lean forward as if watching the game closer, even though he couldn't see the screen and wouldn't have understood it even if he could.

Singh pressed a key on the laptop with a flourish and sat back in the chair, hands behind his head.

'Done, one faked evidence record. As I said, by the time they look into it and realise they can't actually find the phone, we'll already have Mason.'

***

The morning sunshine filtered through the windows of the Doughnut's outer office area. The windows were slightly tinted (to thwart anyone who might try to see in with a telescope,) and double glazed (for heat efficiency, but also to prevent laser microphones picking up conversations from inside,) but the light streamed in and lit the dark brown carpets. Many of the desks were occupied. Anna looked around and thought how many more people there were than was usual for a Sunday morning. Most were in casual clothes; the dress code was relaxed at weekends. Many of the people here would be supporting the hunt for the three criminal suspects, especially since the three were implicated in the murder of Wayne Browning. Wayne's killing had made this a personal matter for many of them. They would be professional, methodical, logical, but there was an extra drive. Anna thought it was a pity that so much effort would yield so little result, but she took consolation in knowing that she had her own insights into finding the Three.

Her consolation, however, was diminished by her frustration. Maria Cho, the new team leader, was insistent that Anna worked with the Technical Services team identifying, and closing, the openings Wayne Browning had left in the GCHQ computer network's defences. She knew that closing the openings was imperative, to prevent Singh and the others from taking advantage of GCHQ's intelligence systems, but she also thought that Tech Services could do it just as well without her. Every minute she worked on network issues was a minute she wasn't actively hunting for the Three.

Anna, thanks to Michael's and Eric's escapade in the data centre, now knew that the Three had used their own exVoxx servers in their attempt to steal from the Bank of England. On one of her screens, Anna had opened a window and was running a trace program searching for network logs which might hold records of the Internet traffic from the data centre to the Bank of England. If she could find any evidence she might find some electronic fingerprint, and from there she could search wider for any more recent instances of the fingerprint.

She turned to ask Kingston something and saw that he was looking across at her screen.

'Cho's going to be cross if she catches you doing that,' he said.

'She's only a team leader, not the Wicked Witch of the West,' said Anna, not sounding convinced.

'Of that, I am not so sure,' said Kingston.

He was dressed today in jeans, but smart jeans, and a red shirt and waistcoat. Anna didn't think she'd ever seen Kingston actually dress "down," he was either smart or stylish, but never casual.

'I need to try and find some kind of lead on these three,' said Anna. 'I've got data I need to analyse.' She was referring to the data Michael had harvested from each of the servers in the data centre. Before they left the Three must have triggered some kind of clean-up protocol. The servers had run programs which erased most of the data on their hard drives. Fortunately, some fragments of data had remained, as had each server's basic information such as its unique machine identification number, the unique Internet address hard coded into each of the network circuits. It wasn't much data, but it was certainly enough to base a search on, if only she could devote some uninterrupted time to it.

'She's wandering around somewhere,' said Kingston, 'watch your back.'

There was the soft warbling of Anna's mobile phone. She looked at the display, it was Michael calling. Anna locked her screens and walked away from the desk as she answered the call.

'Hello,' said Michael in a cheery voice.

'Hi,' said Anna, looking around to make sure that Cho was nowhere near.

'How's life back in sunny Cheltenham?' he asked.

'Actually, it's sunny.'

'Good, good.' Michael turned back to his serious voice, perhaps losing interest in trying to make small talk. 'Any luck with what we got from the data centre?'

'No,' said Anna, leaning into a space between a coat rack and a snack vending machine. 'It's difficult getting time to focus on it.'

'We need to get some kind of lead,' said Michael, stating what Anna took to be the "bleedin' obvious."

'Yes, I sort of know that, but Maria…'

'They can't have run an operation like that and not left a trace, we need to find it. Don't just focus on the technology, look at the people as well.'

'What people?' Anna hadn't thought of the people side of the operation. All she knew was that Marshall, Bullock and Singh had been involved, and she didn't have any particular lead on them personally.

'Anyone, they didn't do this alone, they didn't magic that data centre out of thin air.'

'No, I thought...' but then Anna realised she hadn't thought how they came to have occupied the building. 'No, they obviously took it from someone,' she said.

'Yes, find out who, find any other leads.'

'Well, whoever they got it from, it must have been a significant business, which would mean lots of people, which would mean lots of phone and email records to dig into.' Anna started churning over in her mind all the leads she could start to pursue, if she could escape Cho's attention for long enough.

'Good,' said Michael, 'what else?'

'Well you got us some details of the servers, they must have bought them from someone, and that someone must sell to other people as well.'

'Excellent,' said Michael. 'As many ways of digging as you can, lots of people must have provided them with equipment and resources, even if they didn't realise it. Their operation was well planned and well put together. They'd have been able to get people to co-operate without them knowing it, so there may be connections that aren't obvious, that other people wouldn't think to look for.'

'So was their escape plan,' said Anna in a moment of epiphany. 'Whoever provided resources for their plan might also have provided resources for the escape, or for wherever they're hiding now.'

'Brilliant,' said Michael, 'I'll leave it with you.'

'What are you and Eric doing today?' Anna asked before she could stop herself.

It was Michael's turn to pause for a moment. 'Ur, we were going to go back to the data centre, see if there's anything about their escape route we can pick up, then we've got to enjoy the thrills of giving police statements.'

'Oh, okay, doesn't sound like fun.' Anna looked around again, making sure Cho had not crept up on her. 'This isn't going to be easy, doing all this digging into people and their communications. It's all going to take a lot of computing power. Someone's going to notice.'

'Sorry, I can't help with that.' There was a pause. 'I need you to do something else, and I need you to keep it strictly between us.'

Anna had a suspicion she wasn't going to like whatever Michael was about to suggest. This was already an "off the radar" activity in a classified operation inside the secrecy of the security services, and now Michael was talking about something even more clandestine.

'Can you investigate someone's mobile phone communications?' asked Michael.

Anna was taken aback. 'Yes, of course, it's what we do.'

'Even if the mobile phone is a secure phone on an encrypted network?'

'That can be more challenging, but again, it's what we do.' Anna paused, trying to control her enthusiasm before she volunteered for something she'd regret. 'Why? Whose phone do you want me to look at?' And as soon as she'd asked she wished she hadn't.

'I need you to investigate the Head's phone,' said Michael. 'Some time before the Three escaped she must have made a call about that squad of soldiers called in to kill the Three. I need to find out who she spoke to.'

'That could be dangerous,' said Anna. 'If she got wind that we're digging into her affairs...' She didn't complete the sentence.

'Then you'll have to be careful,' said Michael, and hung up.

***

Michael stood at the window in Thames House, staring at the rain splattered London skyline. Rain or shine, he'd rather be outside, doing something, doing anything other than sitting here achieving nothing.

He'd made another and final attempt to secure permission to interview Jason Mason, and again the police had very firmly shut the door on him. So much for inter-agency cooperation. To make matters worse, he and Eric had received very official orders to attend a police interview and give statements about the events at the data centre. Between the police and the MI5 legal representatives, the interview would likely be a long and tedious affair, depriving him of yet more time to actually do something.

The more he thought about it, the stronger his conclusion that Mason was the only tangible lead he had. Anna may discover something in her analyses, in fact, Michael was sure she would, but for the moment Mason was the only physical entity he could work with. He needed to bring more pressure to bear. He had been reluctant to contact the Head. The less he had to rely on her help the better. Understanding which side someone was on should have been a black and white affair, yet it rarely was. More often it was shades of grey, and Michael wasn't sure in which grey and gloomy corner the Head really stood. He knew that he certainly didn't trust her. He knew that logically it couldn't have been her that called in the squad to kill the Three, but a part of him didn't trust her on that, a part of him still believed she was part of that decision making.

He used the desk phone and called her office. He couldn't tell if or when the system redirected his call to her mobile, but he hadn't expected her to be sitting behind her desk. When she answered he could hear conversations in the background, voices amplified over loudspeakers. No doubt she was in one of the command and control rooms directing some aspect of the operation.

'Progress?' she asked with a sharp voice. Ouch.

'Some,' he said, determined to give as little away as possible. 'The police are still blocking access to Mason.'

'So?'

'So I need some support, there's only so much I can achieve with absolutely zero resources,' said Michael, more sharply than he intended.

'I told you, I can't give you any official authorisation to see Mason, you have to find another way.' The Head ended the call. Michael resisted the temptation to slam the receiver down and worked even harder to avoid swearing out loud. He hated being cooped up in an office. He hated being cooped up in an open plan office even more, no opportunity to swear properly.

He looked around and noted that no-one was paying him any attention so he found a clear desk in the corner of the office. He sat in the chair and relaxed, closed his eyes for a moment and let his mind reach out. He recalled the distinctive mental sense that he would recognise as Jason Mason, almost calling it in a silent kind of way, not quite inside his head and only sort of outside his own head. His psychic call was met with silence. He waited, holding in mind his intention, his desire to connect with Mason. It was like calling someone's name but in a silent and non-verbal way, it was a strange experience, but even stranger was the silence. He didn't get the sensation he got when he tried to connect with someone who was dead. This was more like trying to talk to someone who was deliberately ignoring him.

Michael brought to mind the distinctive tone of Julian Singh's mind, holding it in his thoughts alongside the tone of Mason's mind, almost like calling them both at the same time. He waited, sensing something was there, like waving his hand through fog, it was there but just slightly untouchable. Then it came to him. He had the sensation of standing outside a building, like standing in the dark night time car park of an old shuttered building. He could almost sense the ramshackle house in front of him, wrapped in darkness. It was a metaphor in Mason's mind, it was how he was creating a barrier against Michael's telepathic connection. The house had the mental taste/smell/sensation of Julian Singh all over it.

He opened his eyes sharply and stared ahead. The house had had a sense about it like he knew it would be dangerous to go in yet he was fascinated to see inside. The suspicion had occurred to him that Singh might have laid a telepathic trap, some kind of psychic assault that would be sprung on him had he tried to force his way into the house, into Mason's mind. He didn't know if such a thing was even possible, but it made him think that perhaps Singh (and the others?) had become more skilled in their use of telepathy.

Michael sat back in the chair and let himself relax, letting go of the telepathic effort of making contact. He focused on the desk in front of him, at the grain of the fake wood, the surround of the computer screen, of the dust in between the keys of the computer keyboard. He found such details useful in bringing his mind back fully into the present, into the material world, a world of dead ends.

He had no doubt that his enemy had options and plans and were working hard to advance those plans. It was clear what he needed to do. All other avenues had been closed. First thing in the morning he and Eric would have to go and see Mason, visit him physically, and use whatever persuasive means he needed to get access.

***

Anna and Kingston worked together at her desk staring at one of the screens. A window on the screen showed a scrolling list of cryptic computer information. She'd managed to enlist Kingston's help in completing some of the work she'd been assigned, and Kingston had welcomed the break from trawling through records of police evidence. The two of them stared at the screen, knowing that something wasn't right but unable to explain exactly what or why.

'So, run that by me again,' said Kingston.

'We know that Wayne Browning opened up some gaps in our IT defences, which Singh and friends were using to access our own surveillance data,' said Anna, using the chance to explain it out loud as a way of getting her own thinking straight. 'Some of the gaps were easy to find, we've closed them. But Wayne was good. He also set up some ways for Singh to basically knock on our IT door and a hijacked server would open it up for him, then close it when he'd finished.'

'Which he did by using one of their own exVoxx servers,' said Kingston.

'Yes, but we found all the servers Wayne programmed, and we've deleted all the virus programs he installed, our system should be clean.'

'Only it's not,' said Kingston, nodding at the screen.

It was not. The screen showed a log of computer activity which they had identified as being surveillance data being sent outside their network to an unknown destination. What perplexed Anna and Kingston was that the activity had continued after they had closed the final hole in their IT defences.

'Every time I try and find which server is being used to send this data outside the network it stops, then later it starts again somewhere else. Someone has been very sneaky,' said Anna. She felt a thrill of finding a bigger and more challenging problem to work on. This is what she did best, this is what she enjoyed. From her earliest childhood she'd enjoyed puzzles and games and quizzes. She loved the challenge, the blend of the logical and the creative, and the slightly naughty thrill of working on things that were Top Secret.

Every now and again they'd each look round to make sure that Maria Cho was nowhere in sight. Cho had wandered over a few times during the morning, checking on how things were going. Her random presence was annoying and had prevented Anna making any real progress either analysing the information Michael had retrieved from the data centre or thinking how she might go about analysing the Head's private communications, without getting caught.

'It's like looking in a dark room for a black cat that isn't there,' said Kingston.

'Only the cat is there, we've heard it purring.'

'So we either turn the light on, or we set a trap for it.'

'Hmmm,' said Anna. 'Not sure, metaphorically speaking, we have a light we can turn on in this instance. What kind of trap could we set?'

Kingston leant closer to the screen.

'Oh,' he said. 'That's curious. I recognise that sequence of time stamps.'

He pointed at the screen, indicating a column of information showing exactly when certain computer events had taken place.

He wheeled his chair back to his desk and clicked with his mouse a few times.

'Now either that's a very big coincidence,' he said, 'or what you've got on your screen is a trace of somebody accessing these items of police evidence. I was looking at these earlier, the times these evidence records were last accessed matches exactly that sequence of data being sent outside our network.'

'So we've found the cat's paw prints,' said Anna. 'We know where it's been, we just don't know where it is now.'

'Maybe we can find out where it's going to be next,' said Kingston.

'I tried, different servers seem to be involved at different times.' Anna stopped, eyes widening as an idea occurred, a real light-bulb moment. 'It's a single-instance self-replicating virus,' she said. 'It makes a single copy of itself on another server, then deletes the original copy, it basically moves from one server to another, that's why we've never pinned down the one server involved.'

'So we know it's moving, and we know we can identify it,' said Kingston, 'we can get the network routing data based on the instances we've seen.'

They both got to work, putting together the bits of information they had, crafting a custom-made anti-virus routine, which would sit in wait.

Maria's voice took them both by surprise. She'd approached from behind. 'You two seem busy,' she said. They both turned around, trying hard not to look like naughty school kids caught looking up rude words in the dictionary.

'Yes,' said Anna. 'We've closed the last firewall breach, Kingston was just helping me identify some server activity. I wanted to make sure we hadn't missed anything.'

'Good,' said Maria, 'though I doubt Tech Services would have missed anything. When you've done come and find me, I've something else I need you to do.' She walked off before Anna could protest.

Anna turned back to her screens and saw a message appear at the bottom of the scrolling information, which had stopped scrolling.

'Done it,' she said, smiling at Kingston. 'Found the virus and deleted it.'

'Cool,' he smiled back at her.

'That's shut the Three out for good, let's hope they didn't find whatever they were looking for.'

'Hope so,' said Kingston, 'let's hope that's stopped whatever they're planning.'

Six

London - Monday morning

The Isle of Dogs wasn't a true island, it was an almost-island bordered on three sides by the largest meander in the River Thames. The Northern part of the area was dominated by the towers of Canary Wharf, but much of it was housing and schools and looked as ordinary as many other suburbs of London. Michael was glad it had stopped raining, but the sky was still grey and overcast, almost as grey as Eric's Audi. They cruised down the Manchester Road, the main road that followed the outer contour of the Isle of Dogs, past shops and houses and schools and churches. The traffic was moderate for a Monday morning. Trees lined each side of the road, more on the left than the right, giving a pleasant green break from the grey concrete of many of the buildings.

Eric seemed to drive without the aid of the sat' nav', making Michael wonder if, as part of his MI5 training, Eric had done The Knowledge, the famous feat of memory undertaken by London taxi drivers. To be fair, Canary Wharf police station wasn't hard to find; follow the main road into the Isle of Dogs, drive along it, and the police station is on the left. The main road continued on, curving to the right until it rejoined "the mainland" as Michael thought of it, and the chaos of London traffic.

Sunday had been a complete waste of time, as he had half expected. The process of giving a statement to the police, at least one that the MI5 legal counsel was happy with, had been a tortuous affair. In the end, his statement did little more than admit that he had been there, discharged his weapon an unknown number of times whilst trying to apprehend persons known to present a threat to national security who had subsequently evaded capture. Eric at least had had the chance to return to the data centre and scout around the outside, examining the exit the Three had made from the service tunnel, but the trail had gone cold. The Three had been meticulous in their planning and between them and the police there were no clues left to be found. Michael doubted very much that there would have been any material object he could have connected with telepathically.

All of this left Jason Mason as their sole remaining potential lead to the whereabouts and activities of the Three. Michael and Eric had discussed briefly during their journey how they would attempt to gain access to Mason, but other than concluding that Eric would effect some kind of distraction while Michael used his "Vulcan mind meld thing" they agreed they had no workable plan and would simply improvise. Michael couldn't help think of the adage, "Fail to plan and you plan to fail." He didn't voice this out loud.

He had spoken to Anna briefly that morning. Apparently some woman named Maria had been causing Anna problems but was, for the moment, absent. Anna's voice came over Michael's and Eric's earpieces.

'The police station is about half a mile on the left,' said Anna. 'I've checked, they've arrested him and charged him with just about everything they can think of.'

'Okay,' said Michael, 'I'm hoping I won't need long with him.'

'That's good,' came Anna's voice, 'they're planning to move him to Paddington Green.'

'Why?' asked Michael.

'It seems he admitted to working with Marshall, and the police found a voicemail linked to Bullock saying they were planning on getting Mason. The police view him as being in physical danger and want him in a secure location. Nearest one is Paddington.'

'When are they moving him?' asked Eric.

'Not sure,' said Anna, 'I can't tell from the records, but probably soon.'

'Nearly there,' said Eric.

As they approached, they could see the road on the left between the trees which led to the vehicle access to the rear of the police station. The station itself was a red brick building on the left. Modern, fairly smart, plain, a contrast to the old-fashioned police street lamp on the pavement outside. Eric slowed and indicated left.

It took only a moment for them to realise what they were seeing. A police car had exited the rear of the police station, and no sooner had it joined the road than a silver Ford Mondeo had slid to a halt across the road blocking its path. As Eric braked hard, two men were already leaving the Mondeo and heading for the police car. They could see the men wore ski masks, hiding their faces, submachine guns raised as they approached the police car, the two men shouting orders at two police officers in the car.

Michael felt a flare of anger, and was about to open the car door. Eric leant hard on the centre of the steering column, and the blare of the car's horn cut through the morning quiet and echoed off the surrounding buildings. In a single movement the two armed men turned and fired, Michael and Eric ducked as the bullets shattered the windscreen. Their cursing was muffled by the banging and cracking as the bullets hit the car's bodywork. No sound of gunfire, their weapons were silenced. Contrary to popular myth, MI5 vehicles were not clad in bulletproof materials, impervious to all weapons, but the few Kevlar panels in the car's body did protect them from most of the bullets. Eric slammed the gears into reverse and stuck his foot hard on the accelerator. Driving blind the car launched backwards. There was the blare of another car horn and a bone-jarring bang as they collided with another vehicle.

'Shit,' shouted Eric.

They quickly exited the car, Michael shouting at the occupants of the car they'd hit to stay still and not move. The elderly couple in the small Honda looked shocked and did exactly as they were told. Fortunately, the Honda had rolled backwards and Eric was able to open the boot, he and Michael retrieved a pistol each.

'Let's go,' said Michael, but as slammed the boot lid it simply bounced open again, the collision having bent the rear of the car.

'Shit,' said Eric, again. 'You'll have to go,' shouted Eric. Michael was about to protest, but Eric gestured to the small arsenal in the rear of the car. 'I can't leave this open.'

'Shit,' said Michael. He set off running towards the police station, keeping low, moving left to use the trees as cover. He could already hear shouts and cries from the nearest bystanders, now realising that what they were witnessing was murder. The front two doors of the police car were open. Michael could see the driver lying in the road, motionless, blood pooling around the head. No doubt the accompanying officer was also lying dead on the other side. The rear driver's side passenger door was open, and the car was empty. Michael could see a police officer lying on the ground outside the front entrance to the station, and another was trying to get to her colleague, shouting to those inside for help.

'Get inside,' he shouted at the officer, 'and call for armed support.'

Anger and fear roared inside him in equal measure. He wanted to hurt Marshall and the others, hurt them as much as he could, but he had no inclination to walk into anyone's line of fire. He could feel his stomach tightening and he had the urge to do the easy thing, to take cover, to wait for armed support, but he forced himself on, this was his fight.

He could see three men further down the side road, almost at the end, walking as though they hadn't a care in the world, except two of them were carrying submachine guns.

It was only then that he realised Anna was shouting in his ear and Eric was trying to tell her what had happened and to alert CO19, the Met' Police anti-terrorist command.

'Two of them,' shouted Michael, 'don't know which two, but I bet Marshall's one of them. They've taken Mason, on foot, heading down Glenworth Avenue.' Michael moved forward, moving as quickly as he could in a semi-crouched position. He heard screaming behind him, possibly a member of the public had gone to help and then realised that people had been shot, probably killed. He had to reach Marshall before more were killed. He reached the end of the road and looked right. The three men looked to be walking more quickly. He recognised one of them as Mason, who seemed to be walking with the other two, not being dragged or manhandled, no doubt now telepathically subdued and controlled. Further along the road was a pub, another road branched to the right.

'What's down this road, Anna?' Michael asked.

'Right is back up to the main road, straight on goes past some gardens, and left is the Newcastle Draw Dock.'

'What's that?'

'If they've a boat, an easy way across the Thames.'

Michael had the sense that things were going from very bad to very much worse, and he had little time left to do anything about it. The Three men had indeed taken the left turn into the pedestrian area and had disappeared from sight. Michael ran faster, but his heart sank when he heard the throaty roar of an outboard motorboat engine. He ran left towards the Dock and had to throw himself backwards as he caught sight of Marshall standing there, gun raised. He heard the hissing of the silenced automatic weapon firing, glass breaking as the bullets landed somewhere behind him. He scrambled backwards to take cover behind one of the large bollards which kept vehicle traffic off the Dock, instinctively curling up and making himself as small as possible. He thought about firing towards the boat but then thought better of it, he was as likely to hit Mason as anyone. When he looked out from behind the bollard the inflatable motorboat was already bouncing across the choppy Thames towards the other side.

'What's on the other side?' he asked, not expecting an encouraging answer.

'Greenwich,' said Anna. 'Lots of residential areas, little CCTV I can get at. I can't find many police patrol vehicles in that area, and the only available helicopter's on the other side of the city.'

Michael sat down on the bollard, making sure his pistol was safe, and tucked it into the waistband of his trousers, out of sight. There would be all hell to pay for this, he had no doubt. Halbern would no doubt be apoplectic that Michael must have had evidence he hadn't shared and now more police officers were dead. The Head, no doubt, would be screaming blue murder because instead of being off the radar this had become as public as it was possible to get, and the Three now had custody of Mason and all his knowledge of the exVoxx system.

He took out his phone. It would only be a matter of moments before it starting ringing.

***

Michael was alone in the conference room, alone with his anger and frustration. He was back in Thames House far sooner than he had planned. The day had not gone well, and he didn't think it was going to go any better from here. His first plan had been to examine the car that Marshall and Bullock (it had looked more like Bullock than Singh) had used to ambush the police car. There was a slight chance that someone had left some kind of psychic imprint he could use. But that plan was closed off very quickly. The police had arrived, followed by a tactical unit of armed police, then SO19 officers, then the press. The area had been cordoned off, but Michael could see television and radio outside broadcast units setting up just outside the police lines. As soon as the police had confirmed his identity he'd been taken inside the police station, out of sight of the media. In his brief conversation with the Head (hardly a conversation, she'd spoken, and he'd listened) she'd made it very clear that he was expected back at Thames House and that other MI5 officers would escort him.

So instead of continuing the pursuit for the Three, here he sat, waiting for his telling-off from the headmistress. The door opened and in she walked, closing the door behind her. She didn't shout or do anything melodramatic, but Michael thought it might have been easier if she had.

'I believe Commander Halbern would like a word,' she said. She dialled numbers on the conference call phone, and after ringing only once the phone was answered, Halbern's voice coming through the loudspeakers secluded around the room, making him sound omnipresent. Commander Halbern was with the Metropolitan Police anti-terrorist command, SO15. It was his officers who had borne the heaviest casualties in the previous encounters with Marshall and the others.

'Mr Smith,' Halbern said in a very matter-of-fact way. 'Three police officers are dead, two are injured, several more are traumatised, and several members of the public are in varying states of shock having been shot at. You will of course, again, be required to give a statement to the police, but I would like very much to know what you were doing at Canary Wharf police station, especially as you were explicitly denied permission to see Mason.'

Michael paused, he wasn't certain how to explain any of what had happened. 'Sir,' he began, politeness was often a good measure. 'I think there's little doubt that it was Marshall and one of the other two, probably Bullock, who attacked your officers and abducted Mason.'

'Abducted?' snorted Halbern. 'The CCTV is clear, he got out of the car and walked off with them. There was no abduction.' His voice was getting progressively louder. 'Mason had confessed to working with the three criminals we are searching for. Intelligence shows that they were planning an action on or involving Mason, and at the exact moment they launch this armed action you show up. And what happens next? Another shoot-out. You were also denied permission to go back into the data centre, yet you went anyway.' The Head shot an angry glance at Michael, she obviously didn't know he'd been back to the data centre.

Halbern continued, 'I want to know what other intelligence you're holding back?'

Michael was painfully aware of the Head's stare boring into him. She was still standing, arms folded, face impassive.

'I had no intelligence that they were planning any kind of armed attack,' said Michael. He heard Halbern snort again, not believing him.

'I'll be lodging a formal complaint through the Chief Constable's office,' said Halbern. 'Every time you turn up people get killed, and we're no closer to catching these men, now more of my colleagues have got more families to go and visit, to tell them their loved one isn't coming home. Do me a favour, stay out of this operation. Just stay away.' The line went dead.

'I've had analysts review the media coverage,' said the Head. 'As far as we can see you and your driver weren't filmed.'

Michael had wondered what had happened to Eric. He imagined that Eric was currently experiencing his own "debriefing," no doubt having a strip torn off him for getting the Audi wrecked.

'I asked you for help in getting to see Mason,' said Michael, making an effort to remain calm.

'And I told you, again, that your activity has to be completely unofficial.'

Michael stood up sharply. 'And this is what happens when you want fucking miracles,' Michael said, almost shouting. 'I could have prevented this, but no, you wanted to keep your distance, you don't want this off the radar, you just want to make sure that you're not connected with it.'

'Yes, I do want that, Agent Sanders,' said the Head, raising her voice. 'And I'll remind you that it is still unacceptable to shout at a superior officer. I do not want to be connected with this because I am scrutinised by even more senior officials, and I don't want them to be able to find anything because there are people who will bring hell down upon us if they find out what's happening.'

'Who? What people?' demanded Michael.

'Don't ask,' she said. 'You deal with me and no-one else. None of us has a choice. We have to stop these three, and we can't do it through any official channel.'

'We,' said Michael in a mocking tone. 'You mean me.'

'Yes, that was the deal, that was what we agreed when you came back. You're only alive because certain people believe you can find the other three, but those people will be very quickly losing that belief, and if they do then we're all in trouble.'

There was a silence between them.

She spoke first. 'I hope you have some other line of enquiry or some way of establishing a connection with Mason?'

'No, Mason's closed off. We have some data from the equipment in the warehouse. GCHQ are analysing it.'

'Whatever these three are doing,' said the Head, 'they have a plan. They know what they're doing and how they're going to do it. We don't seem to have very much at all. I hope you at least have some kind of plan. Work quickly, Sanders. Time is running out.'

She left the room and closed the door behind her, leaving Michael to his thoughts.

Michael thought of calling Anna and impressing on her how important it was that she find something quickly, but he resisted the temptation. He had no doubt that she realised how important it was. Finding the Three was important to her personally. He hoped that she would find something, and again he reminded himself that hope was not a strategy. So far, though, it seemed it really was the only strategy they had.

***

Maria Cho had been true to her word. No sooner had Anna finished her work with Kingston than Maria had assigned Anna to the task of running facial recognition scans of a mountain of CCTV imagery taken from around the site of the data centre on the day the Three evaded capture. Anna's heart had sank when she realised how much time it would take, and for the first time in a long time she felt that her work would make no difference.

As soon as Cho had gone Kingston and Anna had swapped comments, agreeing that it would be more productive to analyse the CCTV from Mason's kidnapping, but there were procedures and processes to be followed. Anna had suggested they could assist with analysing the kidnapping CCTV, but Maria had made it clear that the police were taking care of that themselves and had no need of assistance from GCHQ.

Maria Cho had taken up residence at what had been Wayne Browning's desk, opposite Anna, and Anna felt a sense of claustrophobia closing in. Cho had a habit of getting up and coming around to Anna's and Kingston's desks to see what they were doing and what progress they were making. This was making it difficult for Anna to run any large-scale analysis of the information Michael had retrieved from the data centre or do any digging into the Head's private communications, not that she knew what she was looking for.

Anna selected a series of video files and prepared them for the next batch of analysis. In a separate window, she had a spreadsheet of information gleaned from the servers in the data centre, and in a window next to that another spreadsheet of names and identities of people associated with the data centre and the insurance company which owned it. She had the analysis programs lined up and ready to run. All she needed was some time without moment-to-moment micromanaging.

A thought kept creeping back into Anna's mind, like a mental itch she couldn't scratch. She knew that getting leads on the Three was important. After the telepathic control they had wielded over her, she knew that better than most. But what troubled her was Michael's account of the soldiers who had been sent to kill the Three and who had ended up killing the three Serbian mercenaries. They had also come close to killing Michael and Eric. They had been working on someone's orders. Michael needed to know whom, and Anna was beginning to think that perhaps that was the higher of her two priorities.

'Kingston,' she said, standing up. 'I'm going to get a coffee, do you want to come with me?' She looked at him with her hardest "yes, you do want to come with me" stare. He got the hint and stood.

'Maria, do you want anything bringing back? No? Okay.' She walked off towards the doors out of the office area, Kingston trotting to catch up with her.

Once they were into the wide and bright avenue of the hallway between inner and outer buildings of the Doughnut, Anna explained her dilemma.

'I need to run some analyses,' she said. 'We've got some data on the Three that no-one else has.' Before Kingston could speak she said 'no, I can't explain what data or where we got it. But Michael's got inside information on these Three. I need to run it through some filters, but I've got to do it without Maria sticking her nose in.'

'That could be awkward,' said Kingston, 'she likes sticking her nose in.'

They swapped ideas as they walked, more and more outlandish ideas about how to distract Maria Cho while Anna ran her analyses. They quickly discounted the most extreme ideas, such as Kingston collapsing or having a fit, or setting off the fire alarm, or even Kingston asking to talk to Cho about some deeply personal issue (Kingston didn't think he could do that and keep a straight face.)

When they reached the wide open space of the restaurant area, Kingston had his own light-bulb moment.

'Parson's Rule,' he said.

Anna looked at him. 'Yes, I'm sure they do,' she said.

'No, ' he said, 'Parson's Rule of Discrete Point Separation.'

'Never heard of it,' Anna said

'I was reading about it, it's a paper that's only just been published, but I might be able to sort of explain how I could use it to find patterns in the police evidence logs.'

'Not sure how that helps our cause,' said Anna.

'Because I'd need to take Cho and go and discuss the idea with McAdams.'

'Oooh, clever,' said Anna. Andrew McAdams was the department's senior theoretical data analyst, a mathematician who specialised in finding and applying mathematical theories to the task of analysing enormous quantities of data and finding meaningful patterns. McAdams was also known for his ability to talk, endlessly, about almost anything. Getting caught in a conversation with McAdams was like getting caught in a time warp; hours could pass without the victim realising it. For the purpose of distraction it sounded like a workable plan.

They bought the coffees and wasted no time in returning to the department. Anna went straight back to her desk. Kingston stopped next to Cho. He cleared his throat to attract her attention.

'Hello,' she said, looking up.

'I had an idea,' said Kingston, 'about using a new math theorem to sort the police evidence, meaningful data from noise.'

'Yes, sounds good,' said Cho. Anna listened without looking. She wasn't sure of Cho's background. She wasn't sure if Cho was savvy enough with the mathematical side of the department's role.

'I need to talk it through with McAdams, and you, to see if it's worth doing,' said Kingston.

Maria sighed. 'Must we?' She was obviously also aware of McAdams' reputation for talking.

'Yes, please,' said Kingston, 'might be worth applying resources to, might not.'

Maria paused, then locked her computer and got up. She and Kingston walked off towards the other end of the floor where McAdams had a small office, one of the few in the department who had an office of his own. Anna noticed that Kingston was walking more slowly than usual, but she would still need to work quickly.

The plan would fail at the first hurdle if there were any chance the Head would be alerted to someone digging into her personal communications. Anna checked the Head's calendar, but could only see that she had no meeting in the diary at the current time. Anna opened up another program which quietly probed the Head's phone number. It was inactive and had been for over a quarter of an hour.

Anna began running a series of programs which checked various cell phone providers' logs, records of mobile phone traffic, IP traces, and more, all in the hour or so before the Three had made their escape from the data centre. The Head seemed to spend a large proportion of her time on the phone, but so far there was nothing suspicious. Most of the calls were to other MI5 internal extensions, MI5 company mobile phones, some external numbers (all listed and verified,) and a considerable amount of traffic to and from the MI5 email servers.

She looked up and saw Kingston and Maria walking back, Kingston still walking dead slow but Cho was trying to walk more quickly back to her desk.

One last chance. Anna called up a program she hadn't used in a while, a dead packet trace. The program examined a cell phone to detect any communications which had no source and no destination, a technique sometimes used by people routing phone calls through the so-called "dark web." And there it was, one call which had no originating phone number. The call appeared in the data-stream from a seemingly non-existent source, and the communication back again had no destination logged, it had just disappeared. Yet there it was, a phone call which had taken place.

Anna could hear Kingston and Cho talking as they approached. She tapped a few more keys, trying to dig deeper and find where the call had originated. A single item of data was listed, the route the phone call used to exit the MI5 secure network. Anna double checked, to make sure she was seeing what she thought she was seeing, then closed the windows. She tapped a key and brought back onto her screen the list of CCTV video files she had been analysing.

Kingston sat down. 'Dead end,' he said. 'McAdams had seen the theory, not applicable.'

'Okay,' said Anna, 'not a problem.' She smiled enough to signal to Kingston that her mission had been accomplished.

'I just need the loo,' said Anna, standing up and taking her handbag with her, 'Back in a minute.'

As soon as she was out of the office area, she used her mobile phone to call Michael.

He obviously recognised her number. 'Hello Anna,' he said as he answered. 'Any progress? On anything?'

'Yes,' she said, not sounding enthusiastic. 'I did find something. You wanted me to look at some phone calls.' She didn't say any more, she wasn't sure how much she wanted to say, not explicitly.

'Yes, I did. Anything worth mentioning?'

'I found one call, it came from a non-existent source, untraceable. Except…'

'Except what?'

'I could identify the channel it came through.'

'And?' asked Michael, sounding a little impatient.

'It came through an internal dark-channel. It came from inside MI5.'

Seven

Anna looked at the clock on her computer screen and realised she'd worked into the afternoon without a lunch break. She wasn't sure she could remember Maria or Kingston taking a break either. Possibly few on the floor had. Everyone's work had taken on a more personal edge. The occasional email summarising progress in analysing the CCTV video had kept Cho satisfied, and on her side of the desk, Anna had fallen into a routine of scheduling various programs to analyse video and then setting up some of the analysis she had planned based on the information from the data centre. She'd come to the conclusion that Maria didn't know quite how effective Anna could be, so couldn't judge that her current progress wasn't her full output. But Anna had a dilemma.

Several times she'd come close to typing in EXECUTE, and setting the various search programs running. As soon as she did the massive computer systems in GCHQ (actually located somewhere else, a location kept secret even from most of the GCHQ staff) would start digging into people's phone records, bank accounts, email accounts, social media lives, employment records, tax records, and more. The systems would harvest vast amounts of data and would look for patterns and exceptions to patterns and anomalies, and would identify anyone who was doing something they shouldn't be, or wasn't expected to be doing. It would be analysis on a vast scale, far larger than any human analysts could achieve. No need for anyone to steam open envelopes or listen in to telephone calls or follow in an unmarked car; it could all be done at the touch of a button. Privacy could be suspended with a keystroke.

Anna's dilemma was that such activity would consume large amounts of computing power, and all usage was logged. All such activity should be approved beforehand, and Anna had no such approval. It wouldn't be long before Maria Cho would be made aware of what Anna was doing, and that would be a problem. Anna would have to explain (try to explain) why she was carrying out unauthorised deep searches, she would have to explain where the data had come from, she would have to explain why she wasn't doing the work she had been assigned to. And she had explanations for none of this. She continued to hesitate. This was not what she had signed up for.

Anna flicked back to the screen of CCTV footage. The program showed that it had run facial recognition on the files and no-one had been identified who appeared on any watch-lists. This was what she was supposed to be doing. This was her job, and she rather liked her job. Her experiences in the Battle Bus and in the data centre were now just memories. She looked around the open space of the GCHQ office. This was her reality. This was her here-and-now.

'Thought you might want to know,' said Cho, looking up and over the divide between the desks, addressing Anna and Kingston. 'The police have issued a warrant for Jason Mason's arrest, they now also want to talk to him in connection with Wayne Browning's murder.' Maria disappeared again behind the divide, going back to her work.

Neither Anna nor Kingston said anything, each thinking their own thoughts, their own memories of Wayne, of what they knew of what happened to him. And now another innocent life was at risk. Maria had told them that the police had reviewed the CCTV of the so-called kidnapping, of how it showed Mason apparently getting out of the car and walking, unescorted, with the two armed attackers. Anna thought how she had also done exactly what Vince Marshall had wanted her to do, how it had seemed the most natural thing in the world. Her throat tightened as she thought of what they would have done to her once she had finished doing everything they wanted. Jason Mason was not a willing accomplice. He was another puppet, controlled by whatever force or power the Three had.

Finding them suddenly became more important. They had to be found before Mason finished doing whatever it was they needed him to do. Anna was sure he would be alive only so long as he was useful. The time to find them was running out, Anna's time to find them was running out. It was a very strange feeling to realise that she was one of the very few people who could save someone's life. Not in an abstract sense, but in a very real stop-them-from-being-shot-in-the-head-very-soon sense.

EXECUTE. She was committed.

***

Amongst the various windows open on her screens, Anna had one small screen which showed the results of all the deep searches she had set running. Every once in a while another line of text would appear, another anomaly detected by the systems, another person whose jigsaw of social interactions had an ill-fitting piece.

She heard a desk phone ring and heard Cho's voice answer it. Cho said little, only the occasional Yes or No, but Anna heard the tone. The first Yes was light and casual, the second Yes was a little more formal, the first No dropped in tone, the second No had the rising tone of a question, and the final No sounded defensive. She heard Cho replace the receiver, and saw her face appear as she stood up. Cho had not been a tall person, but now she appeared to be tall.

'Anna?' said Cho, 'are you running a catalogue of deep searches?' Her tone had all the qualities of a school teacher asking a school child "did you break this window" knowing full well the child did and simply wanting to know if the child was going to be foolish enough to try and deny it.

Anna took her hands away from the keyboard and sat back slightly. 'Yes,' she said. 'I am.'

'I didn't authorise any of this, and it's not what you're assigned to,' said Cho, not quite making it a question.

'I know,' said Anna, honestly not knowing what else she could say.

'I don't know what to say, Anna,' said Cho, walking round to stand in front of Anna. Anna said nothing. 'Can you explain it?' she asked.

Anna thought what she could say, what she might say. 'No,' was all she could think of saying.

'Anna, this is very serious,' said Cho. 'This is a very serious breach of Data Protection, of Operating Procedure. Is this some personal activity you're undertaking?'

'No,' said Anna. 'I can't explain it, I'm not allowed to.' That sounded terrible, she thought, once she'd said it out loud.

'Can't explain it?' said Cho, disbelieving. 'I think I need to consult someone about this.' Cho walked away. Anna felt a little sick.

She looked at one window of information on one of her screens. It showed the only possible positive in a world of mounting negatives. She hoped some good could be done with what she'd found.

'If anyone asks,' said Anna to Kingston, 'you didn't hear any of this.' She picked up the telephone headset and put it on, and dialled Michael's mobile number. He answered almost immediately.

'I found something you might be interested in,' she said, sounding more work-like than she thought she might.

'That would be the first bit of good news I've had today,' said Michael.

'They'd managed to wipe almost everything from the servers in the data centre, but there were some bits. I've traced the servers themselves, looked at where they came from, then looked at the people there and what they're doing, particularly anyone who's doing anything they shouldn't be. It seems one person at the company who supplied one of the servers is running his own porn' website from his employer's IT systems, and I bet they don't know about it. There's someone who works at an IT consultancy who designed part of the data centre. He works on government contracts, but most of his qualifications are forged.'

'Okay,' said Michael. 'Interesting, but I'm not sure it gets us very far.'

'No,' said Anna, 'but there's one more interesting thing. Two of the servers were sold to the insurance company who owns the data centre. They were sold by a specialist IT company, one employee of whom also sells "surplus stock" on the side.'

'Still not sure any of those are a tangible lead,' said Michael.

'No, but the wheeler-dealer also sold one other server to a company that doesn't exist, a company whose invisibility is just a little too perfect.'

'Okay, that's a lead,' said Michael, sounding a little more positive. 'I think the police might like to have a word with whoever's running the porn site, the relevant department might like to ask the consultant about his qualifications, and I'd like to have a quiet word with whoever sold those servers on the side.'

Anna recognised Michael's code of "having a quiet word" as using whatever telepathy he had to question someone.

'Michael?' Anna asked. 'I've also got a small problem here. I might need your help.'

Eight

The farmhouse - Monday afternoon

Each of them looked at the others in turn. Marshall, Bullock and Singh stood in the lounge in the farmhouse, Jason Mason sitting on a kitchen stool in the middle of them. Marshall and Bullock were sipping beers, still coming down from the high of the direct action. They'd all craved some simple violence to vent their anger at recent events. The two of them had got their wish, only Singh was still sitting managing his pent up anger, and now he looked at Mason like a cat looking at a cornered mouse. Mason was sitting with his eyes almost closed, looking like he was on the edge of sleep.

In the garden one of their security "consultants" walked across the grass, making a slow and deliberate circuit around the house. To a casual observer, had there been one, the man would have looked like he was inspecting the garden and the flower beds. His casual clothes were in keeping, his firearm out of sight.

Singh nodded in the direction of the man outside. 'I don't think our ginger friend can be seen in public again.'

Marshall smiled. 'It's okay, another couple of days and none of them will be seen in public again.'

Marshall looked at Mason. 'You're sure this is going to work?' he said to Singh.

'I can't be one hundred per cent sure, no,' said Singh, 'but this is our best chance, our only chance of getting into the company.'

'I still don't see why we need him,' said Bullock.

'Because he can get us access to their network, no-one else can get that. And without access to the network we can't get access to the company.'

'Nope,' said Bullock, 'still don't get it. Why don't we just find a tame scientist, control them, and get them to get us in?'

'What we want is protected, and there's only one person who can tell us where it is and help us get it, and we can't get in without getting into their company network, and we can't do any of that without the network access that Mr Mason can provide us,' said Singh.

Bullock sighed, obviously not convinced or not understanding. They all looked at Mason again.

'Right,' said Marshall, looking across at Singh. 'Do it. But you're going to be the one who goes to the company.'

'It has to be me,' said Singh, 'even if either of you got into their network room you wouldn't know what to do.'

'Fine,' said Marshall, 'but just so we're clear. If this goes tits-up, we won't hang around here. We'll be gone.'

'Your support is so comforting,' said Singh with a distinctly sarcastic tone. He sat down in one of the chairs and closed his eyes. Singh took in a slow and deep breath, and the other two watched him relax.

A moment later, Jason Mason opened his eyes. Marshall handed him a mobile phone. Without hesitation, Mason dialled a number and waited for his call to be answered.

'Phillip, good afternoon,' Mason said in a cheery and friendly way. 'I was wondering if you had a moment.' Mason seemed completely oblivious to his surroundings or the people standing over him. He acted as though everything was normal. Marshall and Bullock looked at each other, and smiled.

There was a pause. The others couldn't hear what was being said by whomever Mason had called. They could see the frown creeping across Singh's face.

'Yes, yes there was a bit of trouble, I'm not surprised you heard a bit about it.' Another pause. 'No, none of us were caught up directly, but the police did want to talk to some of us, quite a nuisance, but probably all done and dusted now.' Another pause. 'No, not in the office today, working from home.'

There was some more talk from the other person. Singh continued to frown.

'Yes,' said Mason, 'different phone number. Had to get a new phone, my old one died, so new phone number and everything. Listen, I need to ask a favour. We've got a visitor, from the Egyptian government. Very informal, very off-the-record, but would be a great help if I could bring him over and let him have a chat with you, they're interested to see if there's anything you could do to help them.'

Marshall and Bullock both looked at Singh. This was it. This was crunch-time. Singh shook his head slowly.

'No, not an official enquiry, just an informal chat. Problem is, he flies home tomorrow, would be a great help if you could spare us a few minutes today. I'll be there as well, I'll vouch for him.'

They saw the muscles in Singh's jaw tighten, almost as though he was about to speak, which in a way he was, speaking by proxy. The conversation was really between Singh and the other person, with Mason simply voicing the words as instructed.

'I understand,' said Mason, agreeing with whatever the other person had said. 'I know it's short notice. We don't need access to anywhere, he's not expecting to be shown the offices or anything, just a seat in a meeting room to have a chat. I wouldn't ask if it wasn't important.'

Singh shook his head slowly, the conversation obviously not going the way he had planned. But then he stopped moving, tilted his head slightly, as though looking around an object in front of him.

'Is there somewhere nearby we could meet?' suggested Mason. 'We'd be happy to meet away from the office if you'd rather.'

Again, Bullock and Marshall looked at Singh, trying to read something from his face. Singh smiled slightly.

'That would be great, many thanks Phillip. We'll see you later.' Mason pressed the key on the phone and ended the call. His eyes closed and his shoulders dropped, as though he'd gone back to sleep. Marshall took the phone from his hand and placed it on the table.

'Well?' asked Bullock.

Singh had opened his eyes and sat forward. 'It seems word has got out that Mr Mason has been involved in something untoward.'

'But you're in, yes?' asked Marshall.

'Close enough, we'll meet Phillip Harris in the coffee bar around the corner from the exVoxx offices. Once I have a chat with him Mr Harris will be far more agreeable to getting me a visitor's pass to the office and showing me their network room. That's all I'll need.'

'So who is this Phillip Harris?' asked Bullock.

'Works in the sales team in exVoxx. Normally happy to talk to potential new clients, but our Mr Mason's a little out of favour at the moment.'

'So what about security?' asked Marshall.

'I'll take one of them,' said Singh, gesturing out of the window, 'I'll keep down until we're close to the office. I'm not worried about getting there. My concern is any cameras around the office park. Most will be on private circuits, GCHQ won't be able to hack them, but given who else is on that park there might be some cameras they can access. That's the risk.'

'If we've got Mason, won't they be keeping an eye on exVoxx?' asked Bullock.

'No, they're more likely expecting us to try and hack someone else's network. Mason doesn't work for exVoxx, and it's only one system he's involved with or knows about.'

'So hack their system, make sure they can't see anything,' Bullock suggested.

'Unfortunately, GCHQ have now found and closed all our ways into their network. This is just one of those "let's take a risk" moments.'

'You'd better get going then,' said Marshall. 'But like I said, if you are spotted, we won't be here waiting for anyone.'

Singh pulled out a memory stick from his trouser pocket. 'All I need is a few minutes in their network room,' he said, 'once I plug this into one of their servers we'll have everything we need, and we'll be as safe as houses.'

***

Michael had finally got hold of Eric and established that he was still mobile. He'd asked Eric to pick him up from the front of Thames House. Michael stood on the pavement looking left and right, but there was no sign of Eric and the Audi. He was about to ring Eric when a blue Ford Focus pulled up in front of him and the passenger window slid down. Eric peered out from the driver's seat. Michael hesitated for a moment and then got into the car. They set off.

Michael turned to Eric to ask him about the car.

'Don't ask,' said Eric. There had obviously been consequences for Eric from the morning's incident. He doubted they'd heard the last of it, there would be further repercussions. MI5 worked according to procedure, it was methodical, it didn't appreciate spontaneous and unplanned actions, especially when they went wrong. Michael wondered if the fixation on procedure would be their downfall. Marshall and the others certainly wouldn't be worrying about procedure, they would do whatever they needed to do, whenever they needed to do it. Michael was certain there were those who wouldn't mind if the world ended, just provided the proper forms had been completed first.

Michael pressed his earpiece to activate it. Nothing happened.

'Won't work,' said Eric. 'Car's got no comms system.'

'Does it have anything useful?' Michael asked.

'Wheels and an engine, that's about it. I've got some stuff on the back seat.'

'So no interesting toys then?'

'No interesting toys, but it does have sat' nav' and air conditioning.'

'You mean it's not got any field equipment at all?' Michael couldn't quite believe that a field support agent, supporting a search for armed individuals, would be given a vehicle with absolutely no technical or ordnance resources.

'Not quite, I made sure it's got a first aid kit and a small arms case, two pistols and a few dozen rounds, so I hope you're not planning on taking on the British Army any time soon.'

Michael gave their destination to Eric, and removed his earpiece, placing it in its protective case and slipping it back into a pocket. As Eric drove East away from the city centre Michael tried to get hold of Anna on his phone. It seemed Anna was also having a spot of bother and couldn't talk to him at the moment. He texted her to let her know he and Eric were going to talk to the man who sold the servers to the non-existent company, and that he would appreciate any support she could give. He rummaged through the kit Eric had on the back seat. Eric had kept some of the devices they'd used in the data centre, perhaps suspecting that their leads would centre around computers and IT equipment. There were no firearms, no advanced communications devices, no Kevlar vests.

The car did at least have a sat' nav', which was useful as Eric confessed he wasn't too familiar with this part of town. The electronic voice directed them off the A13 and into the maze of grey industrial and office units. This part of Rainham was uninspiring, functional and in no way pretty. The industrial units were mostly occupied, but not well looked after. The office units were either completely plain and anonymous or looked like they'd been designed by a 1970s architect more focused on winning an award than designing a useable building. They pulled into the car park of one of the single-story plain units. It had offices at the front and a small warehouse area at the rear. The small and grubby sign next to the door announced that this was the home of "Rainham IT Services." The windows either side of the door were dull, darkened slightly by the inlaid metal mesh and a layer of grime, the windows were in need of a clean as much as the rest of the building.

'They pick the nicest parts of town,' said Eric.

'Yes, people with no reputation to lose and not enough cash to afford mistakes,' said Michael.

'So what's the plan?' asked Eric. 'You going to use your superpowers to suck his brain dry?'

'Something like that,' said Michael, not sure he could be bothered at this moment to try and explain to Eric how telepathic control worked, and how it didn't work. He certainly didn't want to confess to not having a plan. Michael still felt like he was groping around in the dark, trying to find anything to get a hold of that might be a lead to finding Marshall and the others.

Eric pulled the handle of the front door and it opened, security obviously not being high on anyone's agenda. They walked into the front of the office area. Two desks formed a kind of reception area. Some portable screens set behind them separated this from the office area behind. Michael could see a half-dozen desks in the office area, most occupied, people chatting on phones or to each other. The carpet was a decade old orange, stains and holes showed that no-one had paid it attention in years. There were holes in some of the ceiling tiles, most of the bare strip lights worked. The two desks were slightly different heights giving the reception area an odd lop-sided look. A young woman sat at one of the two desks, beckoning to Michael and Eric to wait as she finished her phone call, which seemed to involve her saying "yeah" and "okay" and "no problem" several times. Michael looked around, and wasn't sure the person on the other end would have been convinced that there was "no problem."

'Hello, how may I help you?' the young woman asked in her very best office-receptionist voice.

Michael and Eric flashed their ID badges at her in a look-at-this-but-not-too-closely flourish, without giving her time to read any detail.

'I'm DI Halbern, Thames Valley Police,' said Michael. 'We'd like to speak to Roger Foreman.'

'Oh, is he in trouble?' the young woman asked.

'We'd just like a quick word,' said Eric. 'Is he here?'

The young woman turned to the screen behind her and squealed in a voice that could cut through concrete. 'Javid, is Rog' still 'ere?'

'Nah, gone for lunch,' someone shouted from the back of the office area.

'You just missed him.' She looked past them, through the window. 'There he is,' she said, nodding towards the car park. Michael and Eric both turned to look out to the car park. A large man was walking away from the building towards a line of cars in the car park.

They both smiled at the young woman as they moved quickly out of the office. Not wanting to scare anyone, or draw attention, they each avoided running, but walked as quickly as they could.

As soon as they'd closed the gap, Michael said 'Mr Foreman, may I have a word?'

Roger Foreman had obviously heard because he stopped and turned around. 'Who are you?' was his obvious response.

Michael and Eric did the badge-waving manoeuvre.

'We'd just like to ask a couple of questions if you've got a moment, won't take long,' said Michael.

'You're not in trouble, we just need help following up a lead,' said Eric.

'Okay, but who are you?' said Roger Foreman, not sounding convinced.

'Oh, sorry, I'm DI Halbern, Thames Valley Police,' said Michael, extending his hand in a friendly gesture.

Almost as an automatic response Roger Foreman accepted Michael's handshake, exactly as Michael hoped he would. As his fingers closed around Roger Foreman's hand, Michael sent a wave of telepathic energy through the handshake, a surge of calming and relaxing thought expanded through the large man, and he exhaled slowly, his shoulders dropping slightly.

'That's fine, Roger,' said Michael. 'Just a couple of easy questions, about some servers you sold, to Cardiff Technology Services.' Michael let the thought rest in Foreman's mind for a moment, having asked the question verbally and psychically. Michael waited, expecting an answer, but Foreman just stared at him. There was no mental response, either. Michael felt like he was shouting into an empty void, and had the unnerving feeling that it was similar to his experience of connecting with Gerald Crossley, just before Crossley had surprised him with a strong and painful punch. Michael was on edge; he wasn't going to get caught a second time like that. But there was no punch. There was no response of any kind.

Michael relaxed his own mind. Instead of thinking of the question, or the answer he wanted, he just let himself sense the quality of the connection. And then it came to him. Like hearing a noise in the background and then recognising it as a familiar tune, the note of Vince Marshall's influence. Roger Foreman had been under telepathic control before and had been coached in creating a psychic defence. At least it was confirmation they were on the right track, the groping had led somewhere.

'Is there a problem?' asked Eric.

'He's definitely been in contact with our three friends,' said Michael, 'and they've created a psychic barrier. I need to push harder.'

'Well get pushing, it looks a bit odd, you standing there holding his hand.'

It was tempting, to just overpower the man's psychic defences, power through whatever barrier Marshall had left in place, but that would be the psychic equivalent of kicking the front door in and smashing up a home. Michael hoped it hadn't come to that, not yet. He let go of the man's hand, the telepathic link was now well established. He pushed harder, it felt like pushing harder, or thinking harder. He came up against the mental form of a glass barrier. He could sense thoughts beyond it, but they were hazy, indistinct. He caught flashes of images, of computer equipment, a car, then everything darkened and became more blurred, too blurred to see. Michael pushed harder still, and had the sense like he had a tight grip around a wine glass and he was squeezing. Sooner or later he could shatter the glass. He became aware of Foreman shaking slightly, and sweating, and Michael suddenly wondered if it was possible to induce a heart attack telepathically. He dismissed the thought. He didn't want Foreman picking up on that idea. Instead, he focused more closely on the images beyond the glass, images of a desktop computer, in the office they'd just been in, a spreadsheet of details.

With a deep breath and a sigh Michael opened his eyes.

'Roger has some files on his computer in the office, he's going to show us, aren't you?' said Michael.

'Yes, no problem,' said Roger, slightly dazed, and started to walk back towards the front door of the office.

As they started to follow him, Michael said to Eric, 'get the kit from the car, and see if you can get hold of Anna, ask her what we need to do to get the right files off Foreman's computer.' Eric peeled off and marched back to the Focus.

Foreman walked into the office, and Michael followed. He headed to the left, around the screens and into the office space. He walked up to a vacant desk and unlocked his computer with his password. Michael watched him, aware of the attention they were now getting from the others in the office.

'Excuse me, what's happening here?' asked a middle-aged man. Michael guessed he was Middle-Eastern, but couldn't be more precise. The man was standing at the far side of the office, talking to one of the other staff. He started towards Michael and Foreman.

Michael waved his badge and put it back in his pocket. 'Police, Mr Foreman is just helping answer a couple of questions.'

'It's okay,' said Foreman, 'it's just something they wanted to look at.'

Eric appeared, holding something small in one hand.

Javid came over. 'I'm sorry, I didn't catch your name,' he said looking directly at Michael. Michael stepped back a moment, keeping eye contact with the man.

'I'm Detective Inspector Harper,' said Michael. 'Mr Foreman has been helping answer a few questions in support of an ongoing investigation. I'm afraid I can't be any more specific than that, but he has been a great help to us, and I'm sorry for having had to interrupt him at work, and for interrupting you and your staff.' Michael kept eye contact with Javid but registered in his peripheral vision what was happening behind him.

Javid, unfortunately, didn't seem to be convinced.

'You can't just walk in and start questioning people,' he said, 'and you certainly can't start messing with their computers.' He turned around, to see Foreman and Eric standing there, looking at him, both with arms folded.

'I don't think we need to trouble these people any longer,' said Eric.

'Well, in that case, good afternoon to you,' said Michael, and without hurrying too much he and Eric made for the door. As Michael had hoped, Javid's first action was to question foreman, and perhaps look at the man's computer, before trying to confront Michael and Eric. With luck, he thought, they'd be back in the car and on their way before Javid got that far. As they left the building, they could hear Javid's questioning and accusations of Foreman getting louder and more heated.

Once in the car, with the office receding behind them, Michael felt it safe to ask. 'Did we get what we needed?'

'No idea,' said Eric. 'But Anna said to plug that thing into the computer and she'd retrieve the files. Thing plugged, files got.'

Michael wasn't sure he felt satisfied. He was back in the realm of waiting for someone to analyse some data and tell him something useful.

'What did you get from your brain-drain?' asked Eric.

'Not much. He'd definitely been used by Marshall, but he'd put in place mental blocks to stop me getting too much. I got some images, some bits and pieces, don't know if they'll be useful. We'll have to see what Anna gets off Mr Foreman's computer.'

'She'll save the day,' said Eric. 'She always does.'

***

Anna knew she was in trouble, mainly because Maria Cho had made it plain that she was. Cho had been quite patronising in saying how she understood that Anna had been through a lot, and probably felt the need to help in the search for the Three. She also made it clear that she viewed Anna's instigation of the deep searches as being a serious breach of protocol and would have to be reported. Anna had been relieved that Eric's call had come while Maria had been away from her desk. She was glad that he and Michael had been able to follow up the lead with Roger Foreman. Getting access to the man's machine was easy, all she needed was for Eric or Michael to plug a particular device into the machine, the device would copy a virus-like program onto the machine, which would then give Anna unrestricted access to the computer. The only problem would have been if the computer in question wasn't connected to the Internet, but she reasoned if it wasn't then the man wouldn't have been able to carry on his part-time business of selling dodgy servers on Dark Web sites. People called it the Dark Web, websites not accessible to most home-users, websites which typically sold all manner of illicit and illegal materials and services. To GCHQ, it wasn't Dark, there was just so much of it the problem was knowing where to look and then tying any illegal activity back to real named individuals who could be prosecuted.

Fortunately, prosecution wasn't the goal here. Anna simply wanted to look through the man's hard drive and find any records of the machines he'd sold to the non-existent company. If Anna could find any details which identified the individual servers, and if those were the servers that Julian Singh was using in

130

wherever-they-were-hiding, then she could start looking for Internet traffic with the right telltale signs, and maybe she could then trace it back to where they were hiding. It was a bit of a long shot, but from reading the progress reports of the police investigation into the Three she had more chance of making progress than they did.

Every so often she looked up, to make sure that Cho was still absent, and carried on trawling through the files on Foreman's hard drive. Anna was supposed to be analysing emails, tagging keywords and flagging the messages for later analysis, something completely unconnected with the search for the Three. As before, Anna had been able to do enough to keep Cho satisfied the next time she came checking. In the meantime, she'd found several files which looked likely candidates and had already set in motion the programs to crack the passwords protecting the files. Michael had also told her about some of the images he'd seen during his telepathic connection with Foreman. A blue saloon car, a man with ginger hair, too vague to search for but they were details which might be useful at some point later.

She needed to spend as much time as she could looking through Foreman's hard drive, sooner or later he'd likely switch off when he went home. She needn't have worried. Anna soon came to the conclusion that she'd found all the files she needed. She sent the appropriate message to the virus on Foreman's machine, which promptly deleted itself. Foreman and his employers would never know their security had been compromised.

Anna looked around the office. A few more desks were vacant as people had started leaving for the day. Although it was big and spacious and open plan, she began to feel constrained by the place. If Eric had needed any more help, she realised, she probably wouldn't have been able to give it. If Michael or Eric got into a difficult situation and needed surveillance and intelligence support, she wouldn't be able to help them if Cho was around. There was a chance, a very real chance, that worse could happen. If she was put on other duties she might not have access to any surveillance resources. If she were suspended, she wouldn't have access to anything.

For the moment, she had no choice. Head down, do enough to keep Cho off her back, and hope that nothing else bad happens.

***

Once Michael and Eric had rejoined the main road it was heading into rush hour, and the traffic was getting heavier. As they approached a set of traffic lights the cars closed in from each side. The traffic slowed in front, and in the mirror, Michael could see the stationary traffic behind. He thought the situation pretty much summed up their progress so far - stalled.

'I suppose this doesn't have any lights or sirens either?' said Michael.

'Nope,' Eric replied. 'This car has no interesting toys at all.'

Michael pondered this. They needed more force, more push, the ability to make more noise and make people do what they wanted. In every way they needed this they were denied.

'So what happened with you and Foreman?' Eric asked. 'I'm guessing you didn't suck his brain dry?'

'No, no sucking brains dry. That's not quite how it works.'

'Care to explain?'

Michael pondered again. How much to say? How much to reveal? The more people knew, the more danger they could be in. In secrecy, there was safety, for the moment.

'Truth is, we don't know much about how this works. It's all been kept so secret that I don't know if anyone's researched it. If they have they certainly haven't told us, they haven't told me how it works.'

'But you can read minds?' asked Eric.

'Yes. Once I've had direct physical contact and established a connection I can read someone's mind. I can't suck their brain dry, but I can pick up on individual thoughts. But Foreman had been prepared.'

'How do you mean?'

'Marshall had set up barriers, to stop me probing any deeper into Foreman's mind.'

'You said you needed to push harder.'

'Yes,' said Michael. 'I could have pushed harder, used more mental energy and broken through the barrier that Marshall put in place.'

'So why didn't you? If that gets us the information we need to find them?'

'Because pushing hard enough to break through the barrier could have damaged Foreman, it would be no different from physically beating him. If we're going to do that, we may as well just go all the way and torture people whenever we wanted. We'd be no better than Marshall.'

'So he'd have pushed?' asked Eric. Michael was no longer sure if Eric was just questioning, or if he seriously believed Michael should have pushed harder regardless of the consequences for Foreman.

'Oh yes, Marshall would have pushed.' The car started moving again as Eric followed the line of traffic but soon came to a halt again at the next set of traffic lights.

'It hurts,' said Michael. 'Pushing hard enough to hurt another mind hurts me, hurts whoever's doing the pushing. Deliberately damaging another mind when directly connected to that mind must be agony. The problem is, Vince Marshall enjoys pain. He enjoys inflicting pain, and he enjoys pushing himself to experience pain. It made him an exceptional soldier. He'd push himself harder and further than anyone else I've met. No-one, not even in Special Forces could push themselves like he could.'

'But?' said Eric.

'But this is the most direct experience of inflicting pain and experiencing pain. He's an artist of pain, and he's found his instrument of choice. Imagine how dangerous that makes him.'

'How dangerous does that make you?' asked Eric. Michael had no answer. For a long moment he sat in silence. He'd never thought about it that way. It made him effective, it made him more capable, it made him more able to complete his mission. He'd never thought of it making him dangerous. 'I don't get it,' Eric continued. 'We're at war with these people and you have a secret weapon. The rest of us have bows-and-arrows and you have a nuclear bomb, but you won't use it. Why not? For God's sake people are being killed. If you have to hurt one more person to stop them, just do it.' Michael was taken aback by the rising tone and anger in Eric's voice.

'Because I'm not them, I'm not like them,' was all Michael could think to say.

'Bullshit,' snapped Eric. 'You and they were in the same unit. This isn't the time to get all judgemental. You're not them, but you are like them.'

'I made them,' Michael shouted. Eric fell silent. 'I made them,' Michael said again, his voice softer. 'I took the decision to have my unit involved in that experiment. It was my decision that led to them becoming what they are. It was my decision to give a sadist like Marshall the power to torture people's minds.'

134

'So you knew this drug would make you psychic?' asked Eric.

'No, none of us knew that's what would happen. It seemed like a quick fix to a problem, a shortcut, but it wasn't. I should have asked more questions before agreeing.'

'I don't recall soldiers asking many questions before obeying orders, even in secret experiments.'

'That doesn't change the fact that I'm partly responsible for Marshall and the others being able to do what they do. That's why I have to stop them. That's why I can't risk starting down the same path they did.'

'Frightened you won't resist temptation?' asked Eric, his voice deadly serious.

Michael turned to look at Eric. 'In all honesty? Yes. That's exactly what I'm afraid of.'

'So however it happened, Marshall ended up with this power. What's he going to do with it now?'

'I don't know,' said Michael. 'But it will be big, their attack on the Bank of England showed us that. They're missing the fifty billion they tried to steal, so they're finding other ways of getting what they want, and it's going to involve attacking something protected by this exVoxx system. That's why they've got Mason.'

'And I don't fancy Mason's chances once they've finished what they're doing,' said Eric.

'So we'd better hope that Anna's making progress with whatever you got off Foreman's computer.'

They both watched in frustration as the traffic light turned to green, and all the traffic continued to sit there, motionless.

***

Anna stared at her screens, flitting from one window to another, one program to another, making sure that she was making enough progress with the CCTV analysis to keep Cho happy, but also making sure that the programs she had set running were working on the data from Foreman's computer. She'd managed to access some of the files, spreadsheets and documents, and had a few fragments of information about the servers Foreman had sold to this non-existent company.

It was still only an assumption that this fictitious purchaser was connected with the Three, but Anna felt certain it was. The fictitious company's cover was a little too good. Money appeared from, and disappeared into online payment accounts which disappeared immediately after the transactions, leaving no trace at all. It was like the difference between someone giving a room a good clean and forensically sterilising it. Foreman had sold the servers to someone with a serious ability to cover their tracks, and the timing fitted, the equipment was sold only a month before the Three had attacked the Bank of England, almost exactly when they must have occupied the data centre.

She looked at one window on her screen. A trace program was looking across the Internet for the telltale digital fingerprints of one of the servers. If Singh used that machine Anna hoped she could detect it, but it was a big "if." Singh might have the machine as a backup, a spare. He might have reprogrammed its identifying details, it might be used so infrequently that she would never detect it amid the noise of the Internet traffic. But she had to keep trying. It was only a matter of time.

'Anna.' It was Cho. Anna had been so engrossed she hadn't notice Cho walk up to her desk.

Anna looked up, feigning a pleasant surprise. 'Oh, hello Maria.'

'Can we talk, please?' asked Cho. 'In private.'

Cho led the way, and Anna gave a forlorn look at Kingston before she followed. Kingston gave the slightest shrug of his shoulders, and the look on his face was clear, "I'm sorry, I can't help."

They walked out of the main office area and a short way down the corridor then into another work area. It was quieter, set out with small booths, groups of three and four chairs round small tables, an area for ad hoc meetings, one-to-ones, informal chats. Anna wasn't sure whether to be worried or not. No-one from HR was here, no senior managers, maybe Cho was going to be encouraging or supportive. Anna decided that worrying was appropriate, Cho had not shown any sign so far of being supportive, and Anna couldn't believe she was about to start now. They sat in a couple of chairs either side of a small green table at the far end of the area. It was an internal room, no windows to the outside, only artificial light.

Cho spoke first, of course.

'Anna,' she said, in her most understanding and empathetic voice, 'I do understand that you've been through a lot recently and that you have a very personal motivation for wanting to find the people who detained you.' Anna thought "detained" was an interesting way of understating what the Three had done, but then Cho actually had no idea what they'd done.

Cho continued. 'But we need to make sure that the right people are working on the right problems, and contributing their best.' Anna wasn't sure she liked where this might be going. She took a breath to speak, but Cho was too quick. 'And so I've assigned you to the project reviewing the configuration of our firewalls.'

In her head Anna said 'that's an interesting approach to addressing my concerns, and I would have a lot to contribute to that project, however, I have a particular insight into the three criminals in question and the best use of my considerable talents is to allow me to continue the analysis of key data that only I can do.'

Unfortunately, it came out as: 'Uh?'

'Yes,' said Cho, 'it is a big change, but it's a key project, and you have unique skills and experiences in that area. You'll start this afternoon, there's a meeting in half an hour that you can join, the project leader will get you up to speed.'

Anna tried to form words and voice an objection, but the competing thoughts in her head just collided with each other. She wanted to tell Cho about the data that Michael had got from Foreman, but she couldn't talk about how Michael had obtained the information. Never mind the fact that Eric's (and Anna's) use of the data capture device was probably illegal, she'd never be able to answer questions about how Michael got the device installed or how he had questioned Foreman. She wanted to tell Cho that Mason wasn't an accomplice of the Three, but a prisoner, a puppet, whose life was in imminent danger.

'We need to find Mason,' she began to say.

'The police are searching for him,' said Cho, in an ever so patronising way. 'He won't evade them for long. Anna, you're safe here, they can't get you here.' Anna stopped. In all her thinking about finding the Three and now finding Mason, she'd never considered that they might come after her again. Would they want her again? It wasn't impossible, now that Cho mentioned it. They had wanted Anna for her particular skills, skills which complemented those of Jason Mason. They had Mason. Would they now risk exposure by trying to recapture her?

'They got Wayne,' she said, quietly, still trying to think through the possibilities. 'I need to help find them. I need to help stop them.'

'Anna, you know at least as much as Mason, if not more, about the Bank's security systems and firewalls. They kidnapped you once, but they won't be able to get you again, not here, you're safe here.'

Safe? No, she wasn't safe here. She wasn't safe anywhere, not so long as Marshall and the others were still at large. Cho had no idea how dangerous these people were. How could she?

'I know you feel responsible for finding them,' said Cho, continuing in her oh-so-patronising tone, 'but this isn't your fight. Take a few moments. Think about the firewall project. We can talk again if you want.'

Cho reached across the table and gave Anna's hand a gentle squeeze in a gesture completely devoid of caring. Cho got up and left Anna alone.

She was right. It wasn't Anna's fight. But something inside nagged at Anna's consciousness. It was her fight. She didn't know how, or why. But somehow, for some reason, this was her fight. It was like a name she knew but couldn't quite bring to mind, it teased her, taunted her. The thought was there, just out of reach. For some reason, Anna knew that this was her fight. More than just because they'd kidnapped her. It went beyond their using her as part of their plans. It was more than the thought that they would have killed her once they'd finished with her. But she couldn't put it into words. For some unspeakable reason she was a part of this, and she had to be a part of finishing it, no matter what it took.

Nine

Half an hour later Anna found herself in a meeting room, sitting at a table with a half dozen other people, notebook open on the table in front of her, handbag on the floor by her chair. She had never felt more out of place, like being a stranger in her own home. The Doughnut had always felt like home, it had felt like the place where she belonged, but now it didn't feel like the place she wanted to be. No, she did want to be here, but she needed to be somewhere else.

The discussion started on the topic of firewalls and computer defences, but of course quickly moved to a discussion of weaknesses and how they could be exploited, and that led naturally to a recap of what happened recently at the Bank of England.

'Difficult to prevent,' someone said, 'a system being compromised from the inside. Wouldn't want to be in Mason's shoes when the police get hold of him.'

Anna could feel a pressure rising inside her. She tried to focus on the conversation, but her thoughts were elsewhere. How could she get time at her desk to run the analyses to help Michael? How could she help find Mason? She felt the room was very slightly smaller than it had been at the start of the meeting.

But Cho had been right. The Three had gone to a lot of trouble to kidnap Anna for her skills. They had killed other people to abduct her and keep her abduction secret. She did know more than Mason, why wouldn't they try and target her if she was somewhere accessible. Here, in Cheltenham, she was safe. Safe, and helpless. No, not helpless. There was a lot she could do to help, if she was allowed to, but Cho seemed determined to keep Anna away from the search operation. But something else still tugged at her, a mental itch she just couldn't quite reach to scratch. The more she thought about it, the more afraid she felt. The idea that had crept into her mind was almost terrifying. It would require being brave, and Anna was not brave. She could be creative, inventive, sneaky even. At times she could be confident, and had (on occasion) even managed to be self-assured, but never brave. She felt most comfortable when she was part of the team, when she had the support of others. It had always been this way, at school, in University, she had always been one of the team, supporting others and supported by them. She had never been one of those individuals who could go it alone, strike out on their own, lead from the front.

But she had, once, left the many to follow her own path. Three of them had been head-hunted from University by one of the big City consulting firms. They joked they would have been the Three Musketeers of the consulting world. It had been an exciting prospect, and a comforting one, yet Anna had (at the last minute) chosen to accept an alternative offer. She left her friends, and while they moved to the bright lights of London, she moved to Cheltenham, and the secretive world of GCHQ. She felt a sense of deja-vu. Here, again, the team was not where she needed to be. All she needed was to make one decision, take one action, and to change everything.

Anna realised she had been lost in her own thoughts and had no idea what the rest of the team were talking about. She stood up, picked up her handbag, mumbled an excuse and left the meeting room. As soon as she was a few paces down the corridor, and sure she was out of hearing range of those in the meeting room, she took out her mobile phone. For what seemed like ages she stared at it, almost unable to believe what she was contemplating doing. After only a few moments she realised her hand was trembling slightly. She took a deep breath and made a conscious effort to relax, then selected a phone number she had never expected to use and dialled it.

To her relief (and terror) the call was answered quickly.

'Yes?' said the brusque female voice.

'Hello,' said Anna, 'this is Anna Hendrickson, GCHQ. Is that Mrs Head?' Anna regretted saying that the moment the words had left her mouth.

She thought she heard the Head almost laugh. 'Yes, Miss Hendrickson, it is. Can I help you?'

Help? No, Anna didn't need help. Anna needed her head examining. What she was thinking was ridiculous, but in a bizarre way it was the only thing Anna could think of doing that made any sense. That thought, however, didn't quell the anxiety rising inside her. She hadn't felt this nervous since she'd confronted her GCHQ manager and argued that even though she was only a junior analyst she was more than capable of handling a senior analyst role and should be promoted. She'd won that argument.

'I need your help, I need your authorisation, I need you to over-rule my team leader,' said Anna.

'With what, Miss Hendrickson?'

'I need to move to the London office.'

***

The blue Honda Accord pulled into the car park and came to a halt in one of the marked parking bays. The whiteness of the paint marking the bays illustrated how new the place was. The grass verges had only recently been laid, the asphalt of the car park was still a clean dark black. All the office buildings were the most modern and imposing designs. Set in the countryside, yet conveniently close to the Capital, this was a centre of hi-tech innovation. Every building said Modern.

Julian Singh was glad that it had stopped raining, he didn't like the rain. It was brighter now, he liked that. The driver, a man of medium height and medium build and only slightly ginger hair, sat still in the driver's seat. Singh had wondered if telepathic control, taken beyond a certain level, could permanently subdue an individual's personality, but had then decided he didn't care. The man was useful and would go the way of all useful men once finished with.

Mason sat silently in the back of the car. The tinted windows helped hide them from traffic cameras, Singh's baseball cap and sunglasses were almost juvenile but were effective, and fortunately now more in keeping with the weather. He looked around at the cameras mounted on virtually every corner of every building and every lamp post. He knew some of the cameras were empty boxes, there to make the site look even more secure, but most of the cameras were fully working. He just couldn't be sure how much access GCHQ would have to them. If he was unlucky then GCHQ would have real-time access to the cameras and would be running facial and postural recognition algorithms on the video feeds, and would recognise himself and Mason almost as soon as they stepped outside the car. If that happened, he would expect the first armed police to arrive in no more than ten minutes, followed by an entire battalion of soldiers no more than ten minutes beyond that. Even before they arrived any escape route would already be sealed off, and he would be trapped. This was what they called a do-or-die manoeuvre.

His psychic instruction to Mason was a simple one: 'Follow me.'

He opened the car door and got out, Mason getting out of the rear of the car. They walked towards the cafe on the far side of a small bridge spanning an ornamental pond. He was committed.

There were few people walking about. He imagined that the place was probably busier at lunchtime, particularly in good weather, but in the middle of the afternoon most were back at their desks, beavering away at whatever they did, convincing themselves they were making a difference.

His sense of his link to Mason was like having a dog on a leash. Most of the time the connection was slack, but still there. If he sensed his pet was moving too far, he could pull it back in. If his pet's attention was caught by something he'd feel the tug through the leash. As they walked into the cafe, he felt the tug through the mental connection. Mason had recognised Harris. He relaxed his grip on the mental tether, allowing Mason to act more naturally.

'Phillip,' said Mason, smiling.

Phillip Harris was a tall and wiry individual, smartly dressed in a dark business suit, a takeaway coffee cup in one hand and a notebook and mobile phone threatening to break free from his other. He nodded his acknowledgement to Mason and then motioned towards a table. Most were vacant. Only a few other people were sitting drinking and talking. The three of them sat down. Singh noted the discreet CCTV cameras in each corner of the room, all wireless devices, easy to hack by anyone who had the resources, and reason.

'Sorry to be awkward,' Harris said, 'but after recent events they've tightened up on security, no visitors in the office unless the Head of Security approves, and they've locked down the server rooms.'

'Not a problem,' said Mason cheerfully, 'just glad you could spare us a few minutes.'

'Only a few, I need to be back in ten minutes. Why the hurry? What's this about? I thought you'd be tied up in Old Lady meetings after all the goings-on.'

Singh eyed the man in front of him, his coffee cup still in one hand, fiddling with his mobile phone in the other, presenting little opportunity for a natural looking gesture that would involve direct physical contact. He recognised the Old Lady reference as meaning the Bank of England, the Old Lady of Threadneedle Street, and Harris' suspicions about Mason were a problem to be overcome. What worried him, however, was news that exVoxx had locked down their server rooms. Singh's plan depended on getting into one of the main server rooms.

He was half aware of Mason offering some platitudes about his colleague (Singh) having an interest in enhancing the security of his government's financial systems, or some such. Without staring he watched Harris. The man was unlikely to respond to any friendly gesture from Singh, and was very soon likely to make his excuses and leave, and that would be the end of his one and only chance to get inside the exVoxx facility. Singh felt himself tighten his grip on the psychic leash and pull Mason ever so slightly closer to him. He let Mason burble on for a few moments longer. He judged Harris would give him that long. Singh felt his mind expand through the link into Mason. He hated Mason's mind, it was dull and uninteresting, like a really boring museum with nothing to do or see, and ever so slightly neglected, but he let his own thoughts expand and flow into Mason's. He had the strange sensation of seeing Harris simultaneously from his own point of view and from Mason's. He focused. This was a one-time opportunity. He thought for a moment it was like trying to kill someone quietly, there was always the chance they'd make an involuntary cry, but sometimes you just had to take the chance. Singh formed the words, formed the intentions, and Mason voiced them.

'Phillip, I know things are a bit up in the air at the moment,' said Mason, 'but I do appreciate you doing this favour for me.' Mason offered his hand to Harris to shake.

Harris considered the gesture for a moment, then put down his mobile phone and shook hands with Mason. As he did Singh allowed a rush of telepathic energy to flow through him, through the connection with Mason, through Mason, and into Harris. He felt the unfamiliar tone of Harris's mind, the gentle and ineffective pushback from Harris's mind. Singh allowed the energy to flow more strongly, and Harris's resistance faded a degree. Singh focused on simply pushing waves of calming energy through Mason and towards Harris, feelings of safety and familiarity. He'd never tried to establish a connection with one person via another. It had been a gamble and a very interesting learning experience.

Mason and Harris let go of each other's hands. Singh smiled at Harris, and offered his own hand, the real test. Harris didn't hesitate, he took Singh's hand in what outwardly looked like a friendly handshake, and in that moment Singh established complete telepathic control over the man.

'I'd like to see your office,' said Singh, letting go of Harris's hand.

'Certainly,' said Harris, a smile forming on his face. 'Any friend of Jason is welcome.'

'There's no problem organising visitors' passes for us, now, is there? Just to go into a meeting room for a conversation?'

'No, none at all. I'll sign for the passes.'

'And the Head of Security?' Singh asked, pushing suggestions into the man's mind.

'I'll make sure he sees them tomorrow,' said Harris.

It was enough. He'd need to establish an even stronger control to overcome Harris's hesitation about allowing visitors into the more sensitive areas of the exVoxx facility, but he could do that in the privacy of a meeting room. From there, he'd have access to their network, but not the server rooms, not the high-security areas which housed all their main servers. Singh, though, had a plan to get around that little problem.

***

The three men walked the short distance from the cafe to the exVoxx office building. It was the largest building in the park, a hyper-modern glass structure. The only thing missing was any kind of corporate name or logo on the outside, nothing suggested who occupied the building. This was not a company that chose to advertise its presence.

The entrance foyer was relatively small with room for a few chairs and a couple of tables. There was no reception desk, no receptionist, no piped music. Harris asked Singh and Mason to sit while he presented his ID badge to the scanner by the large smoked-glass door. There was an audible clunk as the door unlocked, and Harris disappeared into the offices beyond. Singh could still sense Harris through the psychic link. Mason was no longer a problem, he was so controlled that he would sit there until directed to do something specific.

For Singh it was still a slightly strange sensation. He could see/imagine Harris returning to his desk even though he'd never seen Harris's desk. The thoughts were somehow more real, more solid than imagined thoughts. He could sense Harris's disquiet. The man was not entirely subdued, and Singh suspected that if someone senior challenged Harris strongly enough the psychic link might be broken. He had no choice but to wait as Harris logged on to the relevant program and entered the appropriate details for two visitors' passes.

A short while later the heavy glass door unlocked, and Harris emerged, holding two identity badges on lanyards.

'Please wear these at all times,' he said. Mason and Singh took a badge each and looped the lanyards around their necks. 'You'll need to scan through the door one at a time.'

Harris watched as Mason scanned his badge, waited for the door to unlock and then entered. Once the door had closed and locked, Singh followed him with Harris next. Singh looked around. He suspected there were cameras and sensors which would detect anyone entering through the door without having scanned their badge, but he couldn't see them.

A frosted glass wall faced them, with doors which presumably led into various office areas. Harris led them a short way down the corridor and into a meeting room. It was large enough for half a dozen people seated around the table, windowless and impersonal, it could have been in almost any office block anywhere in the world.

Singh wasted no time. He put his hands on either side of Harris's head. For what he needed to do next, he needed complete and total control over the man. He also had the layout of the building, and enough (he hoped) information about how to access one particular room.

It took him longer than he had anticipated, but he was satisfied he had established the control he needed, The next step almost felt like a step too far. Singh was acutely aware that much of this was unplanned, or at least not planned to the degree of detail he was used to. This was far more like making it up as he went along.

As instructed, Harris got up and left the room. Singh took his mobile phone and checked it. As expected there was no signal. The entire building was probably shielded against mobile communications from outside. He relaxed and let his mind reach out to Marshall. He needed Marshall to be ready to do something, something technical, and Marshall was not the best person to have to coach through a technical procedure at short notice. The easiest way would be for Singh to take control of Marshall and direct him at the computer, but Marshall was not a man to let anyone control him. Their telepathic communication, however, was impervious to the electronic communication jamming.

Before long Harris returned, accompanied by a woman. She was much shorter than Harris, smartly dressed, well presented, business-like in every way. Harris closed the door.

'This is the gentleman I was telling you about,' said Harris, smiling and gesturing to Singh. Harris turned to Singh. 'This is Marjory Fleming, she's one of the network specialists,' he said.

Singh shook hands with the unsuspecting woman and began his psychic domination. She was soon seated, quiet, staring into space, and Singh was exerting his control. Within minutes he and the woman made their way further along the corridor to a solid wooden looking door. It wasn't wooden; it was reinforced steel, no doubt with an embedded electronic mesh to protect further against unwanted communications. At his silent command, she presented her ID card to the scanner and tapped a security code into the keypad by the door. When the relevant light glowed yellow, she leant forward and looked closely at the small screen, a retinal scanner. The light glowed green and there was a metallic buzz. He heard the door unlock, and he pulled it open.

He looked inside. No-one else was in the room. It was dim and cold, lit mainly by the blinking green and red lights from the racks of servers. The rush of the cooling fans and the air-conditioning was loud and filled the room. The woman followed him inside and pulled the door closed. She seemed to hesitate for a moment. Singh wondered if he needed to increase the strength of his control over her, but then she walked slowly into the room, past racks of humming servers, and turned left into an aisle between two sets of racks. She pressed her thumb onto the scanner set into the handle of the door to one of the racks and pulled it open.

Singh turned around sharply when he heard the buzz of the lock on the outer door. There was the swish of the door being opened. He put his hand on the back of Marjory's neck and sent a wave of telepathic energy through his hand and into her mind. She shuddered as her mind reeled under the psychic onslaught, but he needed total control of her, and he needed it now.

Marjory walked back into the main aisle and faced the man who had just entered.

Although he struggled to hear their voices over the noise of all the cooling fans, he could hear her words in his mind.

'I wondered where you'd got to,' said the man.

'I needed to reboot one of the comms servers,' said Marjory.

'Why not do it remotely?' asked the man.

Singh telepathically urged her to remain calm, give a reason, and get rid of the man.

'It didn't respond remotely, easier to pop in and do it by hand,' she said. 'What brings you in here? I thought you were running all those simulations.'

'I am,' said the man. 'But I need one of the library servers patching into the development environment.'

'Oh I'll do that,' said Marjory, 'tell me which one and I'll have it done in a minute. You can get back to playing your games.' They both laughed a little, obviously an "in joke." The man gave her the details of what he wanted and left the room. Marjory returned to Singh.

He pointed to the server rack, and mentally asked her "which one?" Marjory Fleming indicated one of the servers in the rack. Singh slipped his USB memory stick into the port in the front of the server. The well-crafted virus program had soon installed itself on the server and had begun to configure itself. Singh would have liked to spend longer with the machine making sure that his code had loaded correctly, but time was of the essence. He finished up, and they left the room as quickly as possible.

As soon as he was back in the meeting room, he had Harris, Fleming and Mason sit and stay still. He opened his mind and linked with Marshall. Singh gave him his final instructions.

Marshall carried out Singh's instructions, but couldn't resist asking.

'No, I don't know if it's worked,' said Singh, mentally. 'I'll only be sure once I get back.'

Marshall took a few minutes to carry out Singh's instructions, using details that Singh took directly from Marjory Fleming's mind, the details flying through the company's electronic defences.

'I'm almost done here,' said Singh silently. 'I just need to make sure that everyone here thinks they've had a trouble free afternoon and hasn't met anyone of interest.'

It didn't take him long to make sure that Fleming and Harris were left with the lasting impression that their afternoon had been uneventful, that they had talked only with the people they usually talked with in the afternoon, and that their day had been like most other days. The woman left them and Harris escorted him and Mason from the building. Not before time, Singh was back in the car, with Mason, and the driver was taking them away from the exVoxx offices.

It was only then that Singh felt confident enough to reach out again to Marshall.

'It all went according to plan,' he said, in the mind-to-mind connection. 'But I won't know if it's worked until I get back.'

'You've got a laptop in the car?' said Marshall, half statement, half question.

'I daren't use a wireless connection from here, it's not secure enough,' said Singh.

'So what was all that stuff you had me do?' asked Marshall.

Singh was about to explain what he'd done and how it was a clever solution to a tricky problem. But he thought better of it. Marshall was rarely impressed with other people's achievements, even less so when it had to do with computers unless it directly resulted in making him money or killing someone.

'I'd love to explain, but I'll save you that pleasure for later. Suffice to say as soon as I'm back we'll see if our Chinese friends really did engineer code that gives us the keys to the kingdom.'

His original plan had been very straightforward. Gain access to the main server room, plant his code in the server that automatically distributed updates to all exVoxx servers everywhere, and in moments his code (engineered for him by some very capable and very expensive Chinese programmers) would be running on every exVoxx machine in the world.

But things had not gone according to plan. He'd only been able to plant the code in some of the communications servers. Whether that was sufficient, whether his improvised plan had worked, was yet to be seen.

He had also yet to see whether any surveillance cameras had caught him or Mason. He'd not yet seen any police or heard any sirens, but he wouldn't feel safe until he'd been back at the farmhouse, undisturbed for an hour.

He looked back at Mason sitting silently in the back of the car. If all had gone according to plan, then Mr Mason was coming to the end of his useful life.

***

Anna found it hard to concentrate. She was supposed to do the work Cho had assigned her, she was supposed to be hunting for the Three, and she was supposed to be tracing the mysterious call the Head had received. It was the last item that taxed her the most. This was quite possibly a call connected with the decision to send in the soldiers who killed the Three's mercenaries, and came close to killing Michael and Eric. The call had come through a secret and protected channel, hidden even from the security services. This was dangerous territory. She had several programs set up and ready to run, to try and trace the call, but it would be a delicate operation. People who ran dark communications channels generally didn't like people snooping around them. She would need to be careful to dig deep enough to uncover useful information but without making her activities noticeable. All that would take time and concentration, and at the moment she had neither. Cho had assigned Anna to the firewall configuration project, and following the first meeting Anna had a presentation to prepare for the following day. Cho had also made it clear that Anna would not now be working on any more activity related to the search for the three criminals (as Cho called them.) Maria Cho was still wandering around the office. Anna hadn't dared set her programs running, not yet.

There had been no word from the Head, no feedback on Anna's request to move to London, and she had to admit to herself that a little bit of her was beginning to hope that her request was denied. At least then she could say honestly that she'd tried but would, not entirely reluctantly, have to stay within the safety of GCHQ. Each time she caught herself following this line of thinking she reminded herself that Jason Mason probably wasn't where he wanted to be either, but he would have much less choice about his immediate future.

Anna had the presentation open on one screen, making it obvious that she was working on the project she had been assigned to. It wouldn't fool Cho, but it was better than nothing. She did have one ace up her sleeve, so to speak. Kingston had set a program running to do some tracing. As far as Anna knew, Cho didn't suspect Kingston of actively helping Anna. Kingston had been reluctant at first. He was happy to help run searches on people who might have directly helped the Three, but digging into the private communications of a senior MI5 officer, without reason or explanation took an extra degree of trust.

She looked around the office again and satisfied herself that Cho wasn't in the immediate vicinity. Anna opened up another window and set another sniffer program running, digging into various corners of the Internet, burrowing its way into various servers, looking for what Anna hoped were the telltale signatures of one of the Three's servers.

'I'm sorry Anna,' came Cho's voice from behind her. Anna jumped and almost yelped. Cho must have appeared out of thin air. 'I did say that you weren't to do any more work on searching for the criminals, and that doesn't look like it's anything to do with the firewall presentation.'

Anna swivelled her chair around to face Cho. Her surprise had almost escaped from her as anger, but it cooled, and Anna found herself more composed. She looked at Cho.

'Maria,' said Anna, mirroring Cho's faux-empathy. 'While spending some time on the firewall project, I do still have some work to do to find the three who are holding Jason Mason.'

Cho was obviously about to explain how Mason should be considered the fourth criminal, but Anna continued. 'Further to my experiences in London there are certain leads I have that have not been shared with the police, and it is essential I follow these leads as best I can.'

Cho took a sharp intake of breath ready to object, but Anna didn't give her chance. 'I can give you the details of a senior MI5 officer who will confirm this, and also confirm the importance of allowing me to spend just some of my time on this activity. I know you believe Jason Mason is a co-conspirator of the three criminals, but I believe he is, in fact, a kidnap victim and that his life is in imminent danger.'

Cho finally got a word in, and her voice had taken on a sharper edge. 'Miss Hendrickson, you do not work for MI5, you work for GCHQ. You work for me, and I decide what work you are allocated to. You will please devote all your attention to the firewall presentation, the project you have been assigned to, by me.'

Anna felt her shoulders starting to slump. She wasn't good at confrontation, and her bravado was starting to wane. Cho continued, 'I need to consult with someone more senior to decide how best to manage your situation. In the meantime, I am explicitly forbidding you from working on anything to do with finding the criminals. Contradict my instructions again and I will arrange for you to be suspended.' She turned around and walked away.

Kingston looked up, having diplomatically kept his head down while Anna and Maria had their conversation.

'That went well,' he said.

'I don't like her,' Anna said.

'No, I didn't think you did. But you might like this.' Kingston gestured to a window on one of his screens. It showed several lines of technical information. Anna trundled her chair to Kingston's desk and looked at the information.

'So, that's where her mysterious call came from,' said Anna.

'That shows us the route,' said Kingston, 'and that,' (he pointed to one particular item of code on the screen) 'shows us the location it came from.'

'I don't recognise it,' said Anna.

'No, it's a pointer to a particular location, but the location is held here,' he pointed to another item of information on the screen.

'Ah, that's unfortunate,' said Anna, 'that's going to be very difficult to access.' She had a sense of so near and yet so far.

'However,' said Kingston, sounding a little more upbeat. 'This little beauty,' (he pointed to yet another item of information on the screen) 'does show us the routing-server the call came through.'

'And do we know where that server is?' asked Anna.

'Yes, we do.' Kingston beamed at her. 'The Ministry of Defence headquarters in Whitehall.' Kingston looked up and across the office, and with a mouse click, he closed the window. Anna turned to see Cho walking back in their direction.

'It seems you have friends in high places,' said Maria Cho to Anna. 'I've been told to tell you that your request has been granted, you're to move to the London office with immediate effect.'

Anna beamed, a broad smile stretching across her face.

'I hope you know what you're doing Miss Hendrickson,' said Maria. 'You were nearly killed the last time you were there.'

***

Singh sat on the bar stool in the farmhouse kitchen, Marshall and Bullock looked over his shoulder at the laptop screen. Outside, the afternoon sun had faded to the grey of twilight and the occasional shadow moved as their puppet minders patrolled the grounds.

'So has it worked?' asked Bullock.

'This is the moment of truth,' said Singh. 'If you did your bit right,' he said, looking back at Marshall, 'you launched a hack of an exVoxx protected site. That would have told the exVoxx main servers about a new threat, and in response, they would have broadcast an update to all exVoxx servers around the world, an update which would include the code I'd put onto their system.'

'And that code gives you access to their system?' asked Marshall.

'That code should give us access to every system,' said Singh, tapping some commands into the laptop.

A window opened up, green text on a black background. Singh typed in more commands and the green text changed, the screen updating every now and again. Finally, Singh sighed and folded his arms, smiling, watching lines of information scroll up the screen.

'So? What's that?' asked Bullock.

'That, my friends,' said Singh, sounding immensely proud, 'is a list of all the items of evidence the Metropolitan Police have on us, as stored in their HOLMES2 system.'

'So you can see that?' asked Marshall.

'I can see it, I can remove bits of evidence, I can create new items of evidence, I can see all their CCTV feeds, I can go and have a rummage around MI5 or GCHQ or MI6 and see what they're up to.'

'So you can get into any system?' asked Bullock, still trying to make sure exactly what it was Singh had achieved.

'With the help Mr Mason gave, we can now get access to almost every government or military system in the world, no matter how secure. No-one will know we're there, they can't see us, but we can see and hear everything,' said Singh.

'So we can see where she is?' asked Marshall, emphasising the "she".

'We can see where she is, who she's talking to, what's in her diary. We can start to have some fun.'

Marshall walked away, pacing, thinking.

'So we can start to lead them astray?' he asked.

'I'll start now. I'll put evidence records into HOLMES2 to make them think we've been seen in Bristol, Leeds, Glasgow, phones detected in Edinburgh, emails discovered in computers in Belfast, all over the place. They'll start to spread themselves so thinly running down all the leads that we'll be able to move about without worrying. Their CCTV won't pick us up. I'll make sure it's always looking the other way.'

'Can we get access to the company yet?' asked Bullock sounding a little impatient.

'Soon, we need to be careful, but we can start working on that. Bit by bit we'll get all the right people into all the right places, and when the time comes we'll just walk in through the front door and take what we came for,' said Singh.

'What about Sanders?' asked Marshall. They both looked at Singh.

'We need to be careful. He's annoying, but he's not stupid. He won't just go rushing after the first breadcrumb we put down, we'll need to create something that he can't resist. Even if he suspects anything he'll be compelled to follow the lead, and I think I know what will do the trick.'

'What about him?' asked Marshall, nodding towards the lounge where Mason sat in one of the chairs, looking like he was asleep.

'Mr Mason has been very helpful and very useful, but his work is done, he's now just a liability.'

'I'll take care of him,' said Bullock.

'No,' said Singh, sharply. 'He's mine to take care of.'

He closed the lid of the laptop and stood up. He opened one of the drawers, thought for a moment, and then picked out a six-inch long carving knife.

'I'll take him down to the cellar,' said Singh, 'the freezer's down there, it'll keep him tidied away until we're finished here.'

'Well take the steaks out of the freezer,' said Marshall, 'I fancy steak tonight, and I don't want him lying on them first.'

'Oh don't worry,' said Singh, 'I'll rescue your steaks first, before Mr Mason and I have some fun together.'

'Don't make too much noise,' said Bullock.

Singh said nothing as he walked towards the lounge, the knife held loosely in his hand, his telepathic control reaching out to Mason. Mason opened his eyes and stood, he turned towards the door leading down to the cellar. Singh held the door open for him, and Mason went through, with Singh following, whistling quietly.

Ten

London - Tuesday morning

The London rush hour was as slow moving as always. Eric sat at the wheel of the Ford Focus, Michael in the passenger seat. Inch by inch they crawled along, heading for the GCHQ London office. Michael had been relieved to hear that Anna was being transferred, but he was also slightly apprehensive. She had been through a lot over the past few days, and she was an analyst, not a trained field agent. He wasn't sure that being in the field was the best place for her. It was also possible that Marshall and the others would get to know that she was now much closer to them, and it remained a possibility that they would try again to kidnap her. Michael had no intention of using Anna as bait, but he couldn't be sure that Marshall would be so obliging.

His mobile phone rang, the Head was calling him.

'Good morning,' he said in his most cheering voice. Eric shot him a look.

The Head, of course, did not use a cheery voice. 'There have been more sitings,' she said.

'I doubt any of them are genuine,' said Michael, dropping the cheerful disposition.

'So do I, the police are having local forces checking out each lead.'

'They've probably got people set up in different towns to look like each of them, let themselves be seen, then disappear,' said Michael, 'make sure the police can't be certain where to focus their efforts.'

'There are some leads you should check out, Miss Hendrickson has the details,' said the Head.

'On my way there now.' He looked at Eric.

Eric frowned, and mouthed 'fifteen minutes.'

'Good, she'll tell you about the possible mobile phone activity by Heathrow, I want you to check that out,' said the Head. Michael considered this for a moment. He didn't want to refuse her, but equally, he didn't think it was a good idea to go rushing off, particularly too far out of town.

'I'll have a look,' he said. He paused for a moment, waiting for her next comment, but the call ended.

Eventually Eric turned the car into a narrow side street. Michael could see the familiar sign of a London Underground station at the far end of the road. The road was the usual odd mix of architecture. On the right was a three storey brick office building, beyond that were coffee shops and sandwich shops. At the far end on the left was the Underground station, and closer to them on the left was a 1960s office block, with grey metal window frames, grey windows, grey panels, grey in every respect. GCHQ knew how to pick some ugly buildings.

Michael was pleased to see a parking space was available, and it didn't take them long to leave the car and get through the security checks and enter the building. Having called the lift and then waited for what seemed like an age (during which they could hear disturbing clanging sounds from the lift shaft) they decided to take the stairs to the second floor.

As they entered the office area, it was like stepping back in time. The carpet was from the 1960s, as was the office furniture, the dark green filing cabinets, the bare strip lights, and the cream window blinds. Michael half expected to hear the Beatles on a transistor radio. What struck him was the contradiction of the computer equipment. Every desk was equipped with several large flat panel computer screens, curved black keyboards, sleek wireless mice. Anna sat at one of the desks, staring intently at the screens, fingers in full flight across the keyboard, a large suitcase parked next to her.

'Hello Anna,' said Michael as they approached the desk.

She looked up and grinned. 'Hi,' she said getting up. There was the awkward and very British do-we-hug-or-do-we-just-shake-hands moment. They opted for the shake-hands approach.

'Hello Mr Chauffeur,' said Anna smiling warmly at Eric.

'Hello, Mrs Chaufess.' Michael assumed it was a private joke since neither made any attempt to explain it.

'Well, how's it going?' asked Michael. He and Eric found unoccupied chairs at nearby desks and wheeled them over to sit next to Anna.

'Well,' she said, clearly enjoying what she was doing. 'They've certainly been busy. Sitings have been cropping up all over the place.'

'All a bit sudden, isn't it?' asked Eric.

'Yes, it is,' said Anna, as though she were Miss Marple about to explain how she had deduced the identity of the killer. 'I'm not convinced that these sitings are genuine because there's one place in which no siting has been recorded.'

Michael's and Eric's raised eyebrows both suggested the same question: "Which is where?"

'London,' said Anna, 'not a single siting in London, which is just a little bit suspicious. That's leaving aside, of course, their gun fight at the Canary Wharf police station.'

'Of course,' said Michael.

'So I think they're still in town,' said Anna. 'They have Mason, they need him for something. They're trying to keep the police distracted while they infiltrate whatever system or organisation is their target.'

'Any idea what that is?' asked Eric.

'No, sorry,' said Anna. 'Mason knows almost everything there is to know about the Bank of England's IT systems, but I doubt they'll attack that again. Every weakness they could exploit has been armour plated. But Mason is also very knowledgeable about the exVoxx system, and that's used to protect most government and military installations, so I think they're going after something like that, rather than a corporate target.'

'What about the siting at Heathrow?' asked Michael.

'It's not a siting, it's an intercept of a text message, but there's something odd about that one,' said Anna, peering again at the screen. Michael and Eric looked at the screen, but there were many windows open, each showing lines of cryptic data. 'Not sure what, but I get the suspicion that one's not a genuine lead either.'

Michael was about to ask something terribly relevant when there was a low beep from Anna's computer, and a message flashed on her screen.

With an 'oh, really?' Anna clicked with the mouse, and a window opened on one of the screens. 'It's one of the sniffers I've got running,' said Anna.

Michael and Eric each suppressed the temptation for some school-boy humour. 'The programs sweep CCTV video and social media sites and run facial recognition, sniffing out any direct visual siting of any of the Three,' she explained.

The three of them leant in closer to look at the image which now occupied the whole of one screen.

It was a family photo, probably taken on a smartphone; male and female adults and two pre-teen children, all smiling. The setting looked to be some inner-city park, trees behind them, railings between the footpath and the trees. Other people either side of the family, passers-by, public, just ordinary people, yet one of them stood out, his face all too familiar. The boyish looks and blond hair of Evan Bullock were clear in the background, not looking at the family in the photograph, looking to the side, at someone or something out of the frame.

'Where is that?' asked Michael.

'When is it?' asked Eric.

Anna tapped more keys.

'Hyde Park, posted on a social media site this morning, the date and time data says yesterday evening. I'm running a deep scan on everyone in the photo, but no-one's showing as significant,' said Anna.

'Not significant?' asked Michael.

'Meaning none of them works for the military or security services, no-one in this photo has Security Clearance or is registered on any MI5 or GCHQ watch-list. Whatever he's doing he was unlucky, someone snapped his picture, but whatever he's doing it's not about anyone in the photo.'

'What's he doing?' asked Michael, leaning closer to the screen.

'We can't tell,' said Anna, 'whatever it is it's…'

'No, there,' said Michael, pointing, pointing at where Bullock was leaning with one hand on the railing, specifically on a notice tied to the railing.

'What's that notice?' asked Michael. Anna clicked with the mouse and had a program analyse the text on the notice.

'Can't see enough of the text to be sure, it looks like a notice about the fence being painted. What's significant about that?' asked Anna.

'It's one of my woo-woo powers,' said Michael, avoiding Eric's stare. 'I need to get there as soon as possible.' He stood up and headed for the door, Eric following close behind.

'Michael,' said Anna, 'a word?'

Michael stopped and turned. He gestured for Eric to carry on to the car and he walked back to Anna's desk.

'I traced that call the Head had. It came from the Ministry of Defence building in Whitehall, through an MI5 secure channel.'

'Where in the building?' asked Michael.

'I can't tell. The only way to find out is to get the SIM card from her phone.'

Michael considered this for a moment. Covert surveillance was his occupation, being clandestine and undetected was what he did, but stealing the SIM card from the Head's phone was "challenging" to say the least.

'That could be rather difficult to do,' he said slowly, 'but not impossible.'

***

It took another quarter of an hour for Eric to drive to the far side of Hyde Park. With no comms link via the car Michael used his mobile phone to stay in touch with Anna. She directed him into Hyde Park and along the footpath to where it looked like the picture had been taken. There were fewer people now than when the picture had been taken, now the occasional dog walker wandered past, joggers jogged at various speeds. Michael saw the notice, still strapped to the railings, a council notice about the fences being painted in the coming week. Eric had stayed with the car. Michael felt it was easier to get on with things rather than have to explain.

He walked off the path and over to the fence. He gently laid his fingers on the laminated surface of the notice, and at once recognised the sense of Evan Bullock's mind. Bullock's thoughts could sometimes be jumbled, but here his thoughts were focused. He was on a mission, a surveillance mission. Michael had the impression of Bullock being focused on someone. He'd been following someone, a very specific someone, but the image was hazy. Bullock had been gazing idly when the picture had been taken, he hadn't been staring at whoever he had been following, that would have made him too obvious. He had also been careless and made contact with the notice, a contact Michael could now pick up telepathically.

He took his fingers off the notice and looked around. The path stretched away left and right, the tail end of the Serpentine ornamental lake was in front of him. He looked up and down the path. Further along was a lamp post, and as is common in London, on the lamppost was a CCTV camera.

'Anna?' he asked into the phone.

'Yes, still here,' she said.

'There's a CCTV camera on a lamppost here, can you access it?'

There was a pause. 'Yes, and GCHQ keep a week's worth of recordings from it, I'm just bringing it up now.'

'Why a week?' asked Michael.

'It's close to Kensington Palace, lots of security around there. Right, got the video, what are you after?'

'Don't know, but Bullock was here, and he was very interested in someone. Can you look at everyone who walked up and down here in the minute or two before and after that picture was taken?'

'Yep,' said Anna, and Michael could hear the clatter of the keyboard, then there was a long pause. 'Right,' she said. 'I've got faces of everyone who was there five minutes before and after when we believe that picture was taken. I'm running facial recognition on them, see if there's anyone significant.'

While he waited, Michael took a few moments to enjoy the peace. The last week had gone quickly, a lot had happened, a lot of it bad, and the bad probably wasn't going to stop anytime soon.

'Oh,' said Anna. Michael recognised it as Anna's expression of "I've found something, and I don't think it's good." 'There was one man who does stand out. Jeremy Susskind. He's an engineer, a physicist actually.'

'What makes him stand out?' asked Michael.

'He works for AWE, at their site in Burghfield.'

Michael and Anna were both silent. 'The Burghfield site of the Atomic Weapons Establishment is where they assemble and maintain the Trident nuclear warheads,' said Anna.

There was no need to speculate out loud as to why Bullock might have had an interest in Jeremy Susskind. If the Three had Mason then they had access to knowledge about the IT system which almost certainly protected the AWE facility. Michael had seen the exVoxx servers in the data centre, Singh no doubt had more, so they had the hardware to attack a site protected by exVoxx, and now they were tailing a physicist who worked there.

'When they ambushed the police at Edmonton there were traces of uranium dust,' said Anna, 'could that be connected?'

'It's possible,' said Michael, 'we don't know if they're after technology, nuclear material, or an entire warhead.'

'I can't see how they'd steal a warhead from that site,' said Anna.

'No, but then a week ago I wouldn't have seen how they could steal fifty billion pounds from the Bank of England, but they very nearly did.'

Michael paused. He knew there was always the possibility that this was another fake lead, but the potential implications were too serious to ignore. 'I think I need to go and have a word with this Mr Susskind,' said Michael. 'He probably has no idea they have an interest in him, but if we know a bit more about him and what he does that might help.'

'I'll do some digging and find out what his job is,' said Anna.

'Dig as deep as you can,' said Michael, 'Susskind might just be their way to someone else, the real target. Get into his social media and everyone he knows and works with.'

'Do we tell the police?' said Anna.

'And tell them what?' said Michael. 'No, for the moment we'll keep this to ourselves and see what else we can find out.'

Michael hung up. His next job was to contact the Head and get her official support to visit Susskind at work. For this, he really would need her help. The AWE facility at Burghfield was a heavily guarded site and there was no way in without an official invitation, so somehow he would have to persuade her that for this they needed to be very definitely on the radar.

***

The morning sun glinted off the line of beer bottles on the kitchen window ledge, the only evidence of the previous evening's celebrations. Marshall stood at the counter, stirring a cup of coffee, resplendent in only his dark green boxer shorts. He tapped the spoon on the edge of the mug and then tossed it clattering into the sink. The only other sounds were birdsong from the garden and gentle sloshing from the dishwasher as it cleaned the glasses, plates, knives and forks of the evening meal, and one large and bloody carving knife.

Bullock wandered in, belched, and proceeded to make a mug of tea. He wore jeans and a grin and little else. It wasn't long before Singh joined them, smart jeans and a dark polo shirt, he was always smart. He carried a laptop computer under his arm and started setting it up on the counter top.

'So,' said Marshall, 'you've got access to the exVoxx network, does that get us what we came for?'

Singh waited for the laptop to start up, then typed commands into the keyboard, windows opening at his command. The other two watched him, waiting.

'Probably not,' he said. 'Even with exVoxx access we'll still have to be careful, I have no doubt that GCHQ will be looking for us, I don't want to rush things and leave a great big electronic fingerprint somewhere.'

'So be careful then,' said Bullock, 'but why can't we just go and get what we came for?'

'Three reasons. First, the company's network is very well protected. I can do a lot but I can't fake a security entry in their personnel database, I'll need a genuine one to work with. Second, I'll need a genuine company ID badge, it would take too long to forge one, and third, most important, I have no idea where in the building I need to go.'

'So find out,' said Bullock, as though it would be easy.

'There's one person we need to ask, but I don't think she's too keen to tell us,' said Singh.

'Maybe not,' said Marshall, 'but I'm going to enjoy persuading her.'

'Yes,' said Singh, 'and she also has security clearance to enter the site, two birds and one stone and all that.'

'So what about the ID badge?' asked Bullock.

'I was rather hoping you could take care of that. We'll find a suitable donor. Then you can go and persuade them to give you their badge.' Singh put an ominous emphasis on "persuade."

'Getting access to her could be difficult if Sanders is still sniffing around,' said Marshall, taking a swig of his coffee.

Singh looked at the laptop screen. 'No, he's easily diverted. He's following that lead you had our man plant. He's currently off chasing Susskind.'

'You mean he fell for it?' asked Bullock with a laugh.

'Oh yes,' said Singh. 'One faked image dropped on a social media site, one sign tied to a fence and off he goes chasing ghosts.'

'The man's more stupid than I thought,' said Marshall. 'So we can keep him running around for as long as we need. How do we get her?'

'Same trick,' said Singh, 'it seems to work. I've an idea for something that she wouldn't be able to resist. It'll get her out in the open.'

'Risks?' asked Marshall.

'Plenty,' said Singh. 'As always this is rushed, we've not got enough time to plan all the details, we'll be out in the open, another armed contact, in the city, so again it's the getting in and out that's the trick. Our friends can provide the vehicles, can keep us out of sight, but if there's a camera we've missed or they've one police patrol we've not anticipated then they can close the net very quickly.'

'So we get in, hit hard and fast, and get out faster,' said Marshall. 'Once we're out, they'll be in such a panic they won't know what they're doing, and if Sanders is out of the picture then it'll be all the simpler.'

'If he gets in the way then we can kill him,' said Bullock.

'Yes, but it's not our primary objective,' said Marshall, 'I'm not going to waste any time on him if we don't need to. Once we've done this he'll be exposed and isolated. We can pick him off any time we choose.'

'I need time to get the bait ready,' said Singh, 'this has to be a bit more subtle that the come-and-get-me ruse we used for Sanders, she'll be more suspicious, less quick to act.'

'You got something in mind?' asked Marshall.

'I have a plan,' said Singh, grinning.

Eleven

The latter part of the journey was through the open green countryside. The London traffic had quickly given way to the motorway and from there to the Berkshire landscape.

As they cruised through the ever more green scenery Michael started looking around the inside of the vehicle. There was little to occupy his thoughts, so he opened the glove box. He pulled out a rolled-up magazine. As he unrolled it he saw it was a comic book titled Never Tomorrow. The artwork on the front was dark, showing hooded figures striding out of what looked like a burning castle, while lightening forked in the sky overhead, very dark, very Gothic. He looked at Eric with a quizzical look.

'Yours?' he asked.

'Yes,' said Eric, not quite voicing the "what of it?"

Michael started flicking through the comic. 'I didn't know you were into comics.'

Eric rolled his eyes. 'It's not a comic, it's a graphic novel,' said Eric, as though explaining something obvious. 'And before you ask, yes, there is a difference.'

As Michael flicked through the pages a pen fell out. Michael saw that on the page where the pen had been wedged were thick black pen-strokes, adding to the artwork on the page. It seemed reasonable, doodling in a comic (sorry, graphic novel) would be one way for Eric to pass the time when he had to sit and wait for Michael. As he flicked through the book, though, he saw the pen-strokes were more than just idle doodling or scribbling. Here and there a stroke or a line or a shading added an extra quality to the pictures. In some it highlighted a character, in others it made the mood darker.

'This is good,' said Michael idly, flicking further through the book.

'Thanks,' said Eric, not sounding like he particularly valued the feedback.

'Do you do your own work?' asked Michel. 'Or, is this your work?' He suddenly realised that maybe Eric was the original artist of this book.

'No, that's not mine,' said Eric, 'but I do publish some stuff, under a pseudonym, of course.'

Michael closed the book and looked up. 'Well, the things you never know about people. Never had you pegged as an artist.'

Eric smiled, just slightly.

'So how come you ended up at MI5? Doesn't seem a natural progression.'

'Not sure my dad ever saw being a graphic artist as a suitable occupation for his son,' said Eric, 'not manly enough.'

'Ah,' said Michael, recognising a familiar tale. Parental pressure, it seemed, had a lot to do with several of the people he'd met in the armed services. 'So he marched you down to the army recruiting office?'

'Not quite, he enjoyed the art I did,' said Eric, 'but he couldn't see how it would ever be a respectable occupation, so he just gently nudged me in the direction of the navy, he was navy man.'

'I didn't know you were navy.'

'I wasn't, I joined the army, that really pissed him off.' Eric smirked, perhaps enjoying reliving a small victory over parental pressure.

'And you do the cartooning for fun now?' asked Michael. As soon as he'd said it he thought perhaps "cartoon" wasn't the right word.

'Sometimes,' said Eric. 'I also work in a volunteer group, we use art to help ex-service personnel deal with post traumatic stress.'

Michael had no response to that. He thought perhaps he'd seriously underestimated Eric, that there was more to the man than he'd realised.

'You know,' said Michael, 'if I pushed hard, telepathically, to get something out of someone, post traumatic stress is the least of the damage I'd do.'

Eric glanced at him, but turned his attention back to the road.

'We've both done damage to people,' said Eric, 'probably not for the last time. But the sooner you can stop these three the less damage is going to get done.'

'The ends justify the means?'

'Sometimes, I can't tell the difference between the ends and the means. We're at war with these three, and they're not going to be all sensitive over other people. If you have a way of finding them and stopping them, then that's what you need to do.'

Michael took a deep breath. 'Then let's hope Mr Susskind can lead us in the right direction.'

The AWE site didn't become visible until they were much closer. The site was big in terms of area, and the main buildings were large, but not tall, little of it stood up from the surrounding landscape. As they turned off one minor road and onto another, they started following the outer fence. Many places are bordered by fences, but few have two layers of high fencing, patrolled by men with guns and dogs, with notices about the use of lethal force to deter intruders. Nothing said what the site was or who occupied it or why it was so heavily guarded, but then if it needed such security, the owners would hardly advertise their activities. The site itself wasn't secret. Many people knew its location, particularly the anti-nuclear campaigners who had staged protests around the outer perimeter. Year after year, one generation of protester after another had vocalised their opposition to the site's activities, had expressed their disapproval of what went on here.

This was the second of two main sites run by the Atomic Weapons Establishment, and this was where they assembled and serviced and disassembled the nuclear warheads for the Trident submarines. For the anti-nuclear lobby, this was Ground Zero, so to speak. Michael had in fact been inside once before. For one particular operation during his time in Special Forces he and his team needed briefing on the appearance and handling of smaller nuclear warheads. They hadn't seen an actual warhead, only a mock-up, and pictures, and lots of explanations, but Michael remembered how much of an ordeal it was to get into the site.

Finally, they turned into the approach road and stopped at the gatehouse on the outer perimeter. Armed soldiers stood watching as names and ID badges were checked against visitor logs by official looking security guards, dogs sniffed the car (inside and out), and sniffed the occupants. Finally, the huge metal gate trundled aside, and they drove down the driveway to the main car park. Eric stayed with the car (only one visitor's pass had been arranged) and Michael walked to the main building. As he approached he heard the distinctive click of the door unlocking, he pushed open the heavy glass door and walked into the reception lobby. Another armed guard (police, army, civilian - it was hard to say) stood watching as Michael announced himself at the reception desk. More checking of name and ID badge and visitor forms. A phone call confirmed that he was expected and that his escort would arrive shortly and would he like to sit while he waited? No, Michael chose to stand.

Michael was almost considering asking the receptionist if there was a reason for the delay when the door to the inner area opened, and Jeremy Susskind walked in. Michael recognised him from the pictures Anna had retrieved, but other than the fact he was an engineer or physicist Michael knew little about the man.

They shook hands briefly, Susskind not giving the impression he welcomed the interruption at work.

'Mr Sanders?' said Susskind. Michael didn't as a rule divulge his name when interviewing people, but in such a secure building he had no choice but to be open about his identity and his role. 'I'm not sure what MI5 are doing here?'

'I'll explain everything,' said Michael, 'is there somewhere we can go?'

Susskind looked for a moment like the question caught him off guard. Surely he didn't expect to have a discussion in the reception area?

'Er, yes, we can go to my office. You're cleared into the building, aren't you?'

'Yes,' said Michael, tapping the visitor's ID badge hanging around his neck, 'accompanied visitor access.'

Susskind led Michael out of the reception lobby, along a short corridor and into an office area. It looked much like any other office suite Michael had seen, modern desks and chairs, large computer monitors, frosted glass obscuring the view into certain rooms, every door protected by a security lock which

Susskind unlocked with this badge. Finally, they arrived at a small work area, six desks in the centre, all facing inwards. Windows gave a pleasing view out onto the fields and beyond them the fence and guards and dogs. Michael noticed that as they arrived the three other occupants of the room all locked their computers, hiding whatever had been on their screens.

'I'm sorry,' said Michael, looking at the others who were watching him and Susskind. 'Is there somewhere private we can go?'

'Why? What is this about?' asked Susskind, sounding a touch irritated.

'It's a security matter, something MI5 are assisting the police with, I believe you may be able to offer some background information,' said Michael, keen to give away as little as possible.

'I think perhaps I might need my line manager to sit in with us,' said Susskind, and looked like he was about to turn and go to the phone on the desk.

'I don't think that's necessary,' said Michael, 'I only need a few minutes of your time, but there are some things I'm hoping you can help us with.'

Susskind paused, and Michael wondered if this was all about to fall apart. He really needed to find out if Susskind had any connection to Marshall, or ideally what reason Marshall had for being so interested in Susskind, but he was unlikely to discover that standing in an open office space with other people watching.

After a few moments, Susskind grunted his acceptance and led Michael to a small meeting room further down the corridor. Once the door was closed they sat down.

'Mr Susskind,' Michael said, not fancying his chances of the man responding well to Michael calling him Jeremy. What to tell Susskind? Some kind of half-truth and hope that Susskind would fill in the rest, or trust that he'd respond better to the truth, or at least part of the truth? Michael went for the truth.

'We're part of the operation searching for the people who attacked the police at Edmonton and were also part of the armed incidents in Croydon. What is not public knowledge, and still considered confidential information, is that the men were also part of a cyber-attack on the Bank of England.'

'And what does that have to do with me?' asked Susskind, in a way that made it clear he didn't believe it had anything to do with him.

'Yesterday we intercepted a photograph posted on social media which showed one of the men in Hyde Park, only a few yards from you, and the indications are that he was tailing you.'

Susskind said nothing. He stared into Michael's eyes. He might be a scientist, but Michael got the suspicion that he had a strong personality, and either through verbal questioning or other means he would not easily give up information.

'Naturally, given where you work, we are interested in establishing if this is coincidence or if the man had a genuine interest in you,' said Michael. 'Can I ask what you were doing in Hyde Park? Who you were with?'

'We went to see my brother. He lives in London. We had a long weekend with him and his family. We went for a walk in the park. That's about it,' said Susskind.

'So nothing connected with your work here?'

'I'm not discussing any aspect of my work.'

'Mr Susskind, this man is part of a team who are heavily armed, well resourced and who have no compunction about killing anyone they choose to, and now they've taken an interest in someone who works at the facility that builds the country's nuclear warheads. You can understand that we're more than a little concerned that there might be a problem here?'

'Mr Sanders,' said Susskind, speaking slowly to make his point. 'If you need to know anything about my work you will have to gain the appropriate clearance, at Ministerial level and with the Managing Director of AWE. Until then I am not saying a single thing about what I do here.'

Michael took a breath, considering his next move.

'Are we finished?' asked Susskind.

'Yes, of course, thank you for your time,' said Michael, smiling and extending his hand to Susskind, who of course accepted the gesture and shook Michael's hand.

Michael was quick to extend his thoughts through the handshake, calm and relaxing thoughts, ideas of being peaceful, friendly. The mind he met was prickly and sharp. Like a rose, it looked nice but it wasn't something you wanted to take a tight grip of. Michael increased the flow, allowing a surge of calming telepathic energy to flow through the handshake. He could feel Susskind relaxing, but equally, he could feel the man's reluctance. Even though Susskind couldn't know what was happening, and even though the experience was pleasant, he was still able to resist, almost like side-stepping someone walking towards him. Michael held in his mind the idea of the energy spreading out, covering Susskind like a warming blanket on a cold day.

He felt Susskind relax more and his defences eased, no more side-stepping, but equally, he wasn't yet fully compliant. Michael had the sense that if he started probing into the thoughts about his work Susskind might react strongly, enough that he might break the psychic link, and Michael doubted he'd be able to regain it. He needed a stronger connection, he needed to use more telepathic force.

It took a few more moments for Michael to sense that Susskind was deep enough under his control before he had Susskind lean forwards. Michael reached up and put one hand on either side of the man's head. He let a stronger pulse of telepathic energy flow into the man's mind, and he began to feel the resistance lessen. He started to sense ideas about metals and heat and equations, no doubt thoughts about Susskind's work.

Michael was, for a moment, oblivious to the door opening sharply and man standing there shouting 'what on earth are you doing?' It took him a second or two to realise that they had been interrupted and that someone new was standing watching them and talking to them. Michael disengaged from Susskind, but his own mind was still disengaged from the real world, it took him a concerted effort to refocus.

'What are you doing?' demanded the man, 'what is going on here.'

Michael stepped forward, about to explain, but the man stepped back and shouted down the corridor, 'security! Get security! There's a man being assaulted.'

Michael started to mouth explanations, vague and meaningless attempts to defuse the situation, but the man—perhaps Susskind's manager, perhaps Susskind's co-workers had summoned him after all—was having none of it. He ordered Michael to stay where he was. Before he knew it two armed guards had arrived at the door, submachine guns held against their chests, Michael noting that each had their trigger finger not on the body of the weapon but on the side of the trigger. This was not going according to plan.

***

Anna stared at the screen. Multiple windows showed slowly scrolling lists of information, the results of several dozen search programs running. Like independent life forms they each had a purpose, a skill, something that each of them did uniquely well. Some were burrowing into social media accounts, some comparing mobile phone records with bank account activity, others trawled through the contents of emails and text messages, still more scanned images from social media and compared them to the live video feeds from hundreds of CCTV cameras. Others were quieter, sitting watching, like a shepherd tending the flock, just keeping a watchful eye on things, waiting patiently, ready to respond should anything untoward be seen.

She had set up a variety of search parameters. It was a difficult balancing act. Make the parameters too narrow and the programs would look for only very specific things and potentially miss something obvious. Make the parameters too broad and the programs would be overwhelmed with the amount of work and would again potentially miss something significant. Having completed the clever work, the interesting work, it was now a case of sitting and watching and waiting, and hoping.

A beep and a line of red caught her attention, as it was designed to. Anna clicked on the red message and an image opened in a new window. Of all the search parameters this was one she never expected to yield a result. In fact, she had nearly dismissed it as being too much of a long shot.

The image was from a CCTV camera covering a public area, not one that Anna recognised. The camera was above head height, looking down on people, but not too high that it couldn't see faces and details. It was a street scene, busy, people walking towards the camera and away from it. What caught her eye was one man. Medium height, average build, wearing a smart business coat and from the visible length of trouser leg and the shoes probably a business suit. The image was black and white and slightly grained. The key feature of the image was tucked under the man's arm, visible to the camera, although the lettering was slightly pixelated. A light coloured folder, and across the top of the folder were two words: Psiclone Project.

Anna checked the time and date, checked the location, checked the metadata giving the route by which her systems had acquired the image, which system had identified the text as being a keyword or phrase to be red-flagged. She looked back at the image. There it was, as clear as day (apart from the pixelation,) a man carrying in public and in plain view a folder clearly showing the name of a top-secret military project. Anna made sure that the image and all the relevant data were saved and logged, and then closed the image. She started clicking at things on the screen, typing commands into the keyboard. She pulled up a map of the area. Red camera icons showed the locations of all the cameras she had access to. She started selecting cameras, retrieving images from a few moments before the image of the folder-carrying man was taken and a few moments after. She brought up each image, one after the other, looking for the man. He couldn't have simply appeared in the middle of the street and then vanished again, he had to have walked into the view of the first camera, and then walked out, walking in and out of the view of each camera along the street. There had to be some record of his progress along the road. She could pick out any number of people and track them as they moved up or down the road, into or out of shops. Each had a journey with a starting point and an end point, except this man. He was as clear as day on the first image, but only on the first image.

This troubled Anna. With two data points, she could plot a direction, predict possible starting points, possible destinations, perhaps identify anyone the man might have spoken to. But she had only one item of data, and you can't draw a line with only one point, and this left her with a dilemma; should she tell Michael?

She was fairly sure that he would want to rush off and investigate, no doubt having Eric drive him at high speed to the location. But where should she tell him to go? The man had appeared at only one location, and had since vanished.

Anna put on the telephone headset and selected Michael's mobile number, then pressed the dial button. The phone rang, and rang, and rang, and then went through to voicemail. She hung up, not sure what she'd say as a message. It was likely that Michael, and probably Eric, were interviewing Susskind, and weren't able to talk. She reasoned that she'd call him soon and talk to him once he had finished at AWE.

There was, of course, one other person she could tell, one other person who knew about the Psiclone Project and would no doubt be very keen to know of anyone being seen in public with relevant documents. The Head was not someone that Anna was desperate to talk to. True, she'd helped get Anna out of Cheltenham and away from Maria Cho, but telling the Head about the man and the folder would be irreversible. The Head might well instigate actions, with or without Michael.

'Sod it,' she said, to herself. She looked around. No-one else had heard her say it. She selected the Head's number and dialled.

'Miss Hendrickson, again,' said the Head as she answered.

'Yes, hello,' said Anna, unsure how to begin. 'I thought you should know. I found something, but it's odd. I tried to get hold of Michael, but he's not answering.'

The Head interjected. 'Why don't you tell me what you found?'

'I was running a job, watching video feeds and running facial recognition, but I'd also added some semantic filters…'

The Head interrupted. 'I don't need the detail, just the outcome.'

'A CCTV feed, one image of a man carrying a document, it clearly says "Psiclone Project" on the cover.'

'Where?'

'He was carrying it under his arm?'

'No,' said the Head, still calm and measured, 'where was he geographically?'

'Oh. Sorry. Woking,' said Anna. There was a moment's silence.

'Where did he go?'

'I don't know, there was just one image, he was in the one image, none before and none after.'

There was another moment's silence.

'We need to find that man and retrieve that document. Apply any resource you need to finding him. Keep trying Sanders, if you can't get hold of him let me know and I'll get hold of him, and alert me if this man is seen again.'

The Head hung up. Anna felt both a thrill of excitement and a pang of fear, but most of all she kept thinking of Sherlock Holmes' catch-phrase: "The game is afoot."

***

Singh had been sitting at the kitchen counter working on the laptop for an hour. Every so often Marshall or Bullock, or sometimes both, would wander in, watch him for a while then walk out. No doubt they each wanted to ask what he was doing, but equally, they didn't want to delay him. They had a lot to do and little time in which to do it.

They had agreed between themselves the broad outline of their next action, and Marshall and Bullock had worked out the details. There was a lot to get through. They needed to be sure they could get in, avoid police or security services moving in too quickly, and then be sure they could all get out again, without being followed. It was a tall order, given that GCHQ and the police were very keen to find them.

Finally Singh sat upright, stretched his arms, and said, 'right, let's find our badge.'

Marshall and Bullock came into the kitchen, and each looked over Singh's shoulders, as though they were going to understand what was on the screen. Singh looked at each of them, and they retreated a pace or two.

'What about getting her into place?' asked Marshall.

'All in good time,' said Singh. 'It's like fishing, we need to get her interested in the bait, then curious enough to move closer, then close enough to bite.'

'What's wrong with fishing with dynamite?' asked Bullock.

Singh sighed, deeply. 'Because it tends to attract attention, and it kills the fish, and we don't want dead fish,' he said, as though explaining to a five-year-old.

Marshall cut the interaction short. 'Enough about fish,' he said. 'Carry on setting the bait, she'll be ready soon enough. What about location?'

'Ah,' said Singh in triumph, 'I've found just the place.' He swung the laptop round so that Marshall and Bullock could see the screen.

'Why there?' asked Bullock in surprise.

'Because,' said Singh, 'it's got enough cameras that I can access, so I can keep an eye on things, but not too many around it that GCHQ can cause problems. There's an easy exit from the rear of the service area, there's a nice little ambush trap inside, it's close enough to the capital that she'll only be slightly suspicious, but far enough that the police can't descend quickly.'

'Make sure everything's ready,' said Marshall. 'What about getting an ID badge? Why not just make a fake one?

'Can't,' said Singh. 'Their security's too good. I can hack into their personnel database, almost, thanks to Mr Mason, and I can tinker with an existing personnel record, make someone's badge work for us, but I can't create a personnel record from scratch, we need to use a genuine one.'

'So, can you find a suitable donor?' asked Bullock.

'Yes,' said Singh. 'I can have a look through their personnel files. We need someone who can be absent from work for a while and whose absence wouldn't be a problem.'

'So we get their badge, get rid of them, make it work for us, and we're in.'

'Sorry to disappoint,' said Singh, 'but we can't kill them.' Bullock looked disappointed. 'Whoever we choose would almost certainly be missed if they just disappeared, and another dead body's going to be hard to hide. We need someone who could ring in sick for a day or two. I'm sure you could persuade them to feel sick for a day or two.'

Bullock grinned. 'Not a problem,' he said.

'And we borrow their badge,' said Singh. 'Then comes the tricky part.'

'Which is?' asked Marshall.

'We need a security access code,' said Singh, 'a genuine one, associated with a genuine personnel record. I need to link the code to the ID badge. The two together is what gets us into the site.'

'Gets you in,' said Marshall, making it clear who would be the one and only person on that particular mission.

'Yes,' said Singh, 'gets me in. We need her. We need her access code, I can't fake it.'

'So,' said Marshall, 'that brings us back to getting her where we want her, when we want.'

'We know where and when. We'll be ready. Any chance we can get rid of Sanders at the same time?' said Bullock.

There was a moment's silence, each of them mulling over the possibility of killing two birds with one stone. Marshall spoke. 'No. We take care of him later, let's focus on getting her.'

Bullock again looked disappointed. 'Oh I don't think Sanders is a problem,' said Singh. 'From what I can see he went out to AWE and got himself arrested.'

They laughed, and took a moment to enjoy Sanders' misfortune.

'Okay,' said Singh, 'half an hour to get into their personnel database…'

'I thought you said you could get in?' said Marshall, sharply.

'I can get in, but I'll leave digital fingerprints all over the place, I need to find someone else's Internet router I can go through. I need to find a hub I can hijack.'

'Any problem with that?'

'No, just one more thing on the to-do list,' said Singh, 'then another half hour to look through and find a suitable card donor, then it'll be time to drop the next breadcrumb to get her attention.'

'Okay,' said Marshall, heading for the door, 'get to it, tell me when it's playtime.' He turned to Bullock. 'Let's make sure we're ready to go.'

Twelve

The farmhouse - Tuesday, early afternoon

The three of them stood in the kitchen of the farmhouse. A silver Ford Mondeo sat in the yard outside, sitting in the driver's seat was the ginger haired man, and on the passenger seat was a document folder, the word "Psiclone" clear on the top. Singh kept an eye on the screen of the laptop, various windows of information showed him Anna's access to CCTV systems, her analysis of the image he'd manufactured of the man walking down the street holding the folder.

'If we're ready, gentlemen,' said Singh, 'I'll plant another image and no doubt the Head will come running.'

Marshall and Bullock looked at each other.

'We're not having second thoughts, are we?' asked Singh, in a slightly mocking voice. The other two turned to him, none of them smiled.

'Whoever sent those freelancers to kill us,' said Marshall, 'will certainly try again. If we do this then we succeed or we die, there's no half-way.'

'We can take the money and run,' said Bullock, 'they'll never find us.'

'They'll never stop looking,' said Singh.

'We didn't come this far to give up now,' said Marshall. 'We came to get something, and when we get it they'll never be able to stop us, all we need is that badge, and her.'

'Then let's stop talking and go and get her,' said Singh.

'Okay,' said Bullock, 'what the hell? It's just us versus the world.'

'Once we have what we came for,' said Marshall, 'the world will be ours, so will she, so will Sanders.'

'One last thought,' said Singh, and the other two looked at him, wondering what he was about to propose. 'If this does all goes tits-up, then I'll be going on one last mission. Rest assured, whatever happens, her time and Sanders' time is almost at an end.'

No-one spoke. No-one needed to. Soldiers, about to go over the top, needn't speak, not even telepathically.

Singh tapped a few keys on the laptop and watched for the response.

'Okay,' he said, 'I've planted another image of our man wandering around waving the file.'

There was a few moments more of silence, moments which stretched into minutes perhaps, they just waited. Before long, Singh raised an eyebrow as he read information from the laptop. The laptop connected to the exVoxx servers in the adjoining room, which connected to the exVoxx servers in GCHQ, which granted them access, and allowed Singh to wander around the security services' data systems without a care in the world.

'It seems Miss Hendrickson has picked up the latest breadcrumb, and so has the Head.' He grinned, continuing to watch the laptop. He laughed. 'Ha. It seems she's on the move. Gentlemen, start your engines.'

A final check that weapons were loaded and ready, and concealed, and Marshall and Bullock left the kitchen. They got into the rear of the car, and the ginger-haired man drove them away. Singh was left at the kitchen counter, watching the security services' own systems giving him a real-time update of who was where and what they were doing.

All was going to plan, but then that was always the case, until the shooting started.

***

Michael sat alone in the small interview room. He could see the outline of the armed guard through the frosted glass of the door. The Military Police soldier stood there, motionless. Michael had considered whether he could subdue the man telepathically before he had a chance to use his weapon, but decided it probably wasn't worth the risk. He drummed his fingers on the desk, then stopped, but couldn't resist the urge to carry on. Sitting still, waiting, was not something that Michael found easy to do. Time was slipping away while he sat here, opportunities were being lost. He didn't know who had alerted Susskind's line manager. Perhaps his colleagues in the office, maybe Susskind had himself before meeting Michael. It was irrelevant now. This was going to be difficult to explain, and the more explaining he did, the worse things could get.

He tried to control himself enough to consider his options. This was a secure government/military establishment, so there was little chance of using bluster and bravado to bluff his way out. Worse than that, other people were now likely to be informed. If the Head was informed then things would get worse, much worse. She would no doubt be angry, but Michael could deal with that. The biggest dangers were either that she denied all knowledge of him and threw him to the wolves, or that she would do enough to get him released but then deny him any further support. Even worse than the Head being involved was the prospect of Commander Halbern being informed. If the security officials at the site decided that Michael should be treated as a potential terrorist threat then, given recent events, it was possible that Halbern would be dragged in, and Michael had no doubt that Halbern would simply hang him out to dry.

A movement outside caught his eye. The guard moved to one side, and the door opened. It was Susskind's manager, or whoever he was.

'Mr Sanders,' said the man. 'I've spoken with your Head of Section at Thames House.' This sounded like the opening statement a judge would make before handing down a severe sentence. 'She did, grudgingly I have to say, confirm your identity and that you were here in connection with an ongoing operation. What you were doing with Mr Susskind has not been established, I need to...'

'I don't care what you need, I need to leave here,' said Michael, rising out of the seat. He needed to do something, anything to find out what the Three wanted with Susskind. Debating things with this man was not going to achieve anything.

'Yes, you do,' said the man, 'but don't think this is the end of the matter, you were assaulting a member of my team and I...'

'There was no assault. Has he accused me of assaulting him?'

'Mr Susskind has said very little about his time with you, but I will be talking to Mr Susskind again about the incident, and in the meantime, you will leave this site. This gentleman,' the man gestured to the armed guard, 'will escort you back to your car, and will ensure that you and your colleague leave this site immediately. I hope you have no intention of returning here.'

Michael said nothing and the man left without further explanation.

The Military Policeman took Michael back to the entrance foyer where he was relieved of his visitor's pass. The guard then walked with Michael back to the car, where Eric was standing, leaning up against the car, a look of thunder on his face. Parked behind their car was a Military Police Land Rover, which followed them to the main gate. As they drove away, Michael looked in the wing mirror and saw the gates closing behind them. Whatever the Three wanted with Susskind, Michael was going to have to find another way of discovering it.

Eric spoke very little as they drove away.

'I take it that didn't go as planned?' Eric finally asked.

Michael said nothing.

'Just for the record,' said Eric, 'I don't like being shot at or arrested. Is this likely to happen again?'

'Very probably,' said Michael.

'Oh great.'

***

Anna stared at the image. Another image of the man walking through a busy street, but just a single image, no trace of the man in the moments before or after, as though he had simply appeared there long enough to be seen by the camera and then disappeared again. His face was slightly blurred in one image, partly obscured in another. The various facial recognition programs she had running would narrow down possible identities, but so far the man remained an enigma.

What was quite clear was the document he was holding. A tan coloured document folder with the word "Psiclone" clearly visible on the top. He may as well have walked down the street waving a banner saying "come and get me." It was a set-up, that much was completely clear. That it was a trap was a very strong possibility, but a trap for whom: The Head? Michael? Anna?

Anna had tried Michael's phone, but it again went straight through to voicemail. She considered calling the Head again, but decided she wanted to talk it through with Michael first. She dialled his number again, it rang a few times (promising) and finally he answered (relief.)

'Please tell me you have some good news,' said Michael.

Anna was slightly taken aback by this. 'I have some interesting news,' she said, and explained about the images of the man and the folder.

'What did the Head say about this latest image?' asked Michael.

'I haven't told her yet,' said Anna, 'I wondered if you were anywhere close to Woking.' She heard Michael confer with Eric.

'About forty minutes away,' said Michael, 'but my concern is this isn't about me, I need to know what the Head's doing.'

'Wait a moment,' said Anna. She used her mobile phone and rang the Head's mobile. It too went straight to voicemail. Anna opened up an instant-messenger window on her computer. She picked from the address book an MI5 analyst she knew, he'd been part of the surveillance operations looking for Crossley and then for the Three. The man was online and available, and yes he was in Thames House. Anna asked him if he knew where the Head was. The answer was concerning. She ended the conversation and spoke to Michael.

'According to someone in Thames House,' she said, 'it seems the Head got some sort of message or alert on her phone, then she called for her driver and left.'

'Oh shit,' said Michael, 'two guesses where she's going.'

'But it could be a trap,' said Anna.

'Of course it's a trap,' said Michael, 'it's got "trap" written all over it. I bet she's thinking that because it's a shopping centre it's public and therefore it's safe. How long will it take her to get there.'

Anna referenced her map software and plotted various routes. 'About forty minutes, but she's got a head start on you, pun not intended.'

'What?' said Michael, having missed the pun. 'Keep trying her, I don't care how public that shopping centre is, I'll bet anything that Marshall's got a plan, and it's going to end badly.' He hung up.

***

The black Jaguar XF swept down the main road without fuss. The driver looked in keeping with the car, dark suit and dark sunglasses. His passenger, in the front seat for once, was a middle-aged woman with steely grey hair and an even more steely look. The Head kept her eyes on the road, noting their location from the road signs. There was a reason she wasn't a field agent, this was not her natural territory. In her world, she was fierce and dominating, but she made sure that she kept to her world. She sent others out into the world of streets and danger and conflict. This was not a world she knew. Out here she was exposed, vulnerable, but out here was someone wandering around publicly displaying a file about the Psiclone project.

She had, very briefly, considered that this might be a trap, but had almost instantly concluded that of course it was a trap. Marshall knew that maintaining complete secrecy around the Psiclone project was paramount and that she couldn't take any risk of any detail becoming known by others. He knew that if he waved this particular red rag in public that she would come running, she had no choice.

It had taken an effort to convince the Military Police at AWE that Sanders was a bona fide MI5 field agent, and that no matter what they thought they saw him doing he was there on official business. She hoped that Sanders had been released from custody, that would at least allow her the opportunity to discipline him herself. Whether she'd keep him on the case was no longer certain, there was now too much doubt, but she would have to deal with that later.

It was unfortunate about Sanders because he would have been useful, one of the very few she could have trusted to retrieve the document. The only observation that gave her any sense of safety was that they were in a very public place, and that Marshall and the others (if they were here) would be in a very precarious position. It was like fighting on a tightrope, don't look down. She tried to focus on the situation ahead, pushing thoughts of Sanders to the back of her mind.

'How long?' she asked.

'Five minutes,' replied the driver.

The Head took her mobile phone and dialled a pre-programmed number. It rang once, a younger woman answered.

'Miss Hendrickson?' said the Head, hardly a question. 'Any other sitings of the folder?'

'Not since the last one,' was the reply, rather stating the obvious. The Head stifled the temptation to rebuke Hendrickson for her lazy use of language, but the analyst was good, better than the rest, and she needed her skills.

'Where's he heading?'

There was a pause, no doubt the analyst was analysing things. 'All I can say is that a line from the first image to the second points to Woking shopping centre.' Another pause. 'There's no sign of him on CCTV in or around the centre, not that I can access. I spoke to Michael,' Anna said.

The Head ignored the reference to Sanders. She mulled over various theories about what the man with the folder was doing. He was obviously making himself visible to the cameras, making it clear where he was heading. But why somewhere so public? If Marshall and the others meant to attack her personally it would be more likely they'd lure her somewhere quiet, secluded, with fewer eyes. It seemed more likely that the man with the folder might do something to make the contents of his folder more public. If he stood in the middle of a public place and began reading a description of the Psiclone project, of what it was and what it did, no-one would believe him. She had no doubt, though, that it would be only minutes before foreign security services became aware of it, and they would take a very much more active interest.

The Head's thoughts were interrupted by Miss Hendrickson's voice on the phone. 'No, wait, I see him.'

'Who? Sanders?'

'No, the man, he's appeared again,' said Anna.

'Another image?' asked the Head.

'No, this is real-time video, he's walking across the car park, three hundred yards north of your position.'

201

The car turned off the main road and into the expanse of car parking adjacent to the shopping centre. The Head pointed in the direction of the far side, and the driver obliged. Driving as quickly as he dared, being mindful of parents with pushchairs, shoppers with trolleys, the ever-present hazard of drivers pulling out without looking, they were quickly becoming fish in a barrel, with the danger that someone else would do the shooting.

They turned around at the end of a line of parked cars and started driving back towards one of the main entrances to the shopping centre. There, clear as day, walking slowly, was a man in a dark blue coat, carrying a buff coloured folder, with the word "Psiclone" emblazoned on the top edge.

'I see him,' said the Head into the phone, 'he's going into the shopping centre. We're following him.'

'Do you have a comms set?' asked Anna.

'I'm not a field agent, Miss Hendrickson, stay on the phone.' The driver swung the car into the nearest parking space, he and the Head left the car and walked quickly towards the entrance to the shopping centre.

'I got hold of Michael,' she heard Anna say as they walked across the pedestrian approach to the shopping centre entrance. It was too late to worry about Sanders now. This was becoming like a chess game where each move was unavoidable but an obvious step closer to checkmate. The only positive was that they were in public, surrounded by CCTV cameras, in a heavily populated area, and Marshall and the others had to avoid detection at all costs.

'I'm following the man inside on the internal cameras,' said Anna. 'He's walking towards the public staircase, centre of the main shopping arcade.'

Inside was a typical shopping centre: bright and open spaces bounded by all the usual high-street brands. It wasn't busy, but not empty either, a moderate number of shoppers milled around, wandering from shop to shop. The Head looked around, but their target must have gone further into the centre.

'He's heading to the internal stairwell,' came Anna's voice over the phone, 'it leads back up to the upper-level car park. No, he's gone through the door into the lower service area.'

"Come into my parlour, said the spider to the fly" went through the Head's mind. And the fly, even knowing the fate that awaited it, knew it had no choice but to accept the invitation.

'Follow us as long as you can,' said the Head to Anna. She and her driver headed down the escalators to the lower shopping level. At the far end were the glass doors leading to the car park pay-on-foot machines, lifts to all levels, and a heavy grey door.

"Service Areas - Upper and Lower - Admittance to Authorised Personnel Only" was the official looking sign on the door.

'If you go in we'll probably lose the mobile phone signal,' said Anna.

'My driver is armed, we have to get that folder back. Is there any CCTV coverage in the service areas?'

'Minimal, but I can see he's gone down to the lower level,' said Anna.

Without another word the Head hung up the phone. The driver pulled the door open, his hand inside his jacket, resting on the grip of his concealed firearm. He slipped through the door, and the Head followed.

Inside was what she expected, dimly lit, thick pipes clad in silver coloured insulation suspended from the ceiling, heavy cables ran along conduits lining the walls. There was a faint hum from the electrical supply to the building, and which would no doubt defeat any mobile phone communication. The corridor led away to the right and in front of them were bare concrete stairs leading down into the service area. Their footsteps crunched slightly on the concrete as they descended one careful step at a time. At the bottom the corridor stretched to the left and the right, the right option led to another door, the left led around a corner. The driver led the way, his pistol now held out in front of him. The Head followed. This was snake versus mongoose, but which was which?

They rounded the corner into a more open space, a trolley of cardboard boxes sat in one corner, abandoned, another corner occupied by a stack of metal components for shop display shelves. The corridor continued into the dimness beyond the open area, and a heavy door was set into the wall on the right. The man with the folder had disappeared, again. The place was quiet apart from the hum of the power supply. For one moment the Head thought of backing up, calling in the police to secure the area and have the man arrested. She could contain the folder quickly enough, or was that what Marshall planned for her to do?

As they took a step forwards, a shape emerged from the shadows in front of them. Tall, broad shouldered, pistol raised, the smug grin of Vince Marshall unmistakable even in the gloom.

'Nice of you to join us,' he said.

The Head almost jumped as another voice came from behind them, she turned sharply to face the blond haired buffoon that was Evan Bullock.

'I'm impressed, I didn't think you'd fall for it that easily,' said Bullock. He took a step forward and pushed the driver ahead of him with a sharp one-handed shove to the back of the neck, the man staggered, obviously unable to decide if he should comply or fight back. The Head tried to indicate with a stare: do not fire. She felt the anger rising. The trap was sprung, it was to be an execution, a simple act of revenge. The only thought that consoled her was that Marshall and Bullock had no chance of escape.

'You have me,' said the Head, 'you can let him go.' She didn't for one moment believe that Marshall or Bullock would agree, but it had to be said. Her eyes darted around, expecting Singh to appear from somewhere. His absence was almost troubling, surely they would all be in it together.

'No, I don't think we'll do that,' said Marshall. 'You're coming with us, but he's going to stay here.'

There was a heavy metallic clunking sound and the door to the right started to open, perhaps Singh was here after all. Almost in the same motion Marshall and Bullock swung their guns around to cover the door, but it closed again. Before anyone could speak another figure appeared from the corridor from where Bullock, and previously the Head, had appeared.

Michael Sanders stood there, gun raised, pointing at the back of Bullock's head, Marshall only a few degrees to the left. The door moved again and in swift action it opened fully and in stepped Eric, pistol raised, clearly indicating he had a clear shot at Marshall and Bullock. The Head forced herself to be calm. She felt like cheering, but now things were critical. The advantage here could be psychological as much as tactical, her self control could be a critical factor.

'Well this is interesting,' said Michael 'Hello boys; Ma'am.'

The Head breathed deeply. Now they would find out if things had just got better, or worse.

***

For a moment they stood there, Michael and Eric behind the Head and her driver, Marshall and Bullock on the far side of them. Michael and Eric aimed past the Head at Marshall and Bullock, the Head's driver had a clear shot of Marshall. Michael dared to hope that the game had turned in their favour.

'Three against two,' said Michael, 'not sure the odds are in your favour.'

'Oh the odds are always in my favour,' said Bullock. He looked at the driver, who turned slowly, aiming his gun at the Head. 'Very useful all this mind control stuff.' The driver turned again slightly, his gun now aimed clearly at Eric.

'Walk towards me,' said Marshall to the Head. She stared at him but did not move. 'Walk, or I'll shoot you in the foot and then drag you.'

'Don't move,' said Michael, sharply. He had no doubt that Marshall would shoot the Head in the foot, but to drag her he'd have to lower his weapon, which would even the odds, making his threat more likely to be a bluff.

Marshall lowered his gun, aiming at the Head's left foot. Michael watched as the Head took a first, tentative step towards Marshall. If they got the Head out of the room then the chances of getting her back would fall dramatically. Somehow, Michael had to contain the situation.

What happened next took them all by surprise. The lights went out. In an instant the entire room went completely dark. Instinctively Michael dropped to the floor and rolled to one side, shots rang out, he judged from the location that Eric and the driver were both firing, no doubt both firing at where the other had been, then firing at where they thought the other might be. There was a loud crash as someone collided with a stack of shelving, then two more shots, one each from two different weapons as far as Michael could tell. Useful though the mind control power was (and that was a huge understatement) it gave Michael no ability to see in the dark. He scurried forward, pistol in one hand the other held out to stop him running blindly into a wall, he fired twice, in the direction of where he thought the corridor was down which Marshall and Bullock had no doubt retreated, the Head in tow. By now they'd have achieved psychic control of her, she'd follow them without resistance.

Two white lights came on, one on either side wall of the room, the emergency lighting. Michael blinked, the driver was only inches from him, gun pointed in the direction of the far corner, desperately close to Eric's position. Michael leapt and grabbed the driver by the back of the neck, pouring telepathic energy into the man, driving him down to the floor both physically and mentally. Bullock had achieved control of the man in only a brief time, an impressive achievement, but the control was weak and Michael overwhelmed it with an outpouring of his own thoughts.

'That way,' he said to Eric, gesturing with his gun towards the corridor, now also bathed in the lurid white light from the emergency lighting system.

'So who's the Lighting Fairy?' asked Eric.

'I can only guess that Anna's been keeping an eye on things,' said Michael. He willed the driver to stand and walk in front of them. He didn't like the idea of compelling a man to walk into the line of fire, but if Bullock retained any measure of the control over the man then Michael didn't want him behind them. Guns raised they inched forward into the corridor, mindful that all the time Marshall and Bullock would be retreating far more quickly, no doubt towards a pre-planned exit and escape.

Michael stepped forward, and something cracked and crunched under his foot. He looked down at the shattered face of a mobile phone. He had no time for that now, they continued forward, knowing that Marshall and Bullock could just as easily be laying in wait for them, waiting to kill him and Eric before they made their escape.

The corridor was short, and at the end was an opening on the left into what might be a larger goods-inward area, a perfect ambush situation. Michael thought for a moment of compelling the driver to walk through into the open and draw any fire that may be waiting. He wasn't sure, but he thought he saw the driver hesitate in his next step. He let go of the idea. Eric leapt across the opening to take up position on the other side. Michael looked at him, an unspoken question in his eyes. Eric shrugged, he hadn't caught sight of anything.

The lights went out again, all of them, even the emergency lights. Without hesitation Michael, Eric and the driver (as instructed telepathically) rushed through the opening, each firing a couple of times, Michael stepped sharply to his left as soon as he was through, the driver stepping with him. There were shots fired in response, Michael heard the sharp snapping and cracking of the bullets hitting the walls and shelves of boxes, all very close to them, too close, almost as if Marshall and Bullock could sense where he was. More shots, landing further ahead of him, no doubt aimed at Eric.

As the emergency lights came back on there was the sound of the panic-bar on a fire door being pushed open, sunlight glared from the side of the cargo area where the fire door had opened. Michael and Eric (the driver stayed behind, Michael was finding it too distracting trying to direct the man as well as plan his own actions) moved forward, guns raised ahead of them, heading for the shaft of sunlight and the open door. Before they reached the door, they heard a car engine and the sound of a car driving away. They reached the door and stepped out into the daylight, swinging the guns around to cover themselves, just in case. The concrete expanse of the goods inward area was empty, the entrance and exit driveways stretched left and right, lorries were parked at the far side having unloaded their cargo (or waiting to unload.) They caught a brief glimpse of the tail of a car disappearing round the bend at the top of the exit driveway. Michael and Eric aimed but it was too late. Michael fought back the temptation to fire, knowing that all shots fired would have to be accounted for, and he couldn't risk firing in anger.

'Fuck,' he screamed, and kicked the ground, hard. There was a crash and the splintering of glass. He looked up, Eric had punched the wing mirror of a van parked close to them. The mirror now hung broken from the side of the vehicle.

Michael pulled out his phone and dialled Anna.

She spoke before he did. 'I'm following them as best I can,' she said as soon as she answered the call, 'but they've picked a good spot, there aren't many cameras I can access.'

Of course they had, thought Michael, as he would have expected from them, this was all very well planned. In the distance came the sound of sirens, police cars no doubt, probably armed police. Michael's shoulders sank at the prospect of yet again having to explain who they were and what they were doing.

'I've lost them,' said Anna with a note of defeat. 'They've gone into a residential area. If they change vehicles there are too many ways out to cover them all.' Michael had no doubt that a change of vehicle was exactly what they had planned, probably

209

more than one, vehicles all lost in the swarm of traffic on the maze of roads.

'Talk to Anna,' Michael said handing the phone to Eric. He walked back into the cargo area. A thought had occurred, a slim possibility of being able to pull some small measure of success out of a whole heap of defeat. He retraced their steps back into the service area of the shopping centre, finally finding what he wanted. He quickly rejoined Eric outside as the first police cars came sweeping down the drive towards the cargo area, red and blue lights flashing powerfully, sirens wailing and squealing. Michael and Eric both pushed their pistols back into the underarm holsters. It wouldn't be good to be seen waving firearms around when the armed police turned up.

He let Eric catch a glimpse of the bent and cracked mobile phone as he slipped out the SIM card and the battery and pushed them all into his pocket. Michael was fairly sure he recognised it as the Head's phone.

'Solves the problem of how we were ever going to steal her SIM card,' said Eric.

'Sorry,' said Eric into the phone, still talking to Anna, 'have to go now, need to talk to some policemen, again.' He glowered at Michael.

Thirteen

Woking - Tuesday, late afternoon

It hadn't taken long for the local police to secure the area, and Michael was slightly surprised they decided not to evacuate the shopping centre. Surprised but pleased, evacuating it would have made it a much bigger news story and Michael was very keen to avoid any publicity. Having kept their firearms out of sight, to begin with, the Officer In Charge had been relatively cooperative and had verified their identities quickly. They'd avoided all that nonsense of being held at gunpoint and being threatened with arrest for possession of an illegal firearm while calls were made and senior MI5 officers verified identities, which could all get very tedious.

No doubt news would filter through the channels back to MI5, but Michael needed to take the lead. As soon as the police OIC had finished talking to them, Michael called the Duty Operations Director.

'Sanders,' said the DOD, 'you're to stay there and cooperate with the local police. They'll want your firearms for forensics examinations, from all of you.'

'Yes sir,' said Michael.

'We've already got GCHQ tasked with sweeping the area with electronic surveillance. I'll liaise with the police and inform them that this is a kidnapping. For the moment your task is to do nothing. Is that clear?'

'Yes sir, clear,' said Michael. Clear, but not necessarily something Michael could live with. He called Anna.

'I don't know what they think they can do,' said Anna, 'I was following them on live video feeds from the moment they left, and I can't find them.'

'Does she have her squealer on her?' Michael asked. The squealer was a panic device, press the button and it would send multiple radio transmissions calling for help, connecting to short wave radio as well as mobile phone networks. Even if not activated, the squealer acted as a homing beacon. As a key MI5 officer the Head would have carried a squealer as a matter of course.

'Probably,' said Anna, 'but they'd expect it. I can't find any trace of it, so I expect they'll have put it in a shielded box, or destroyed it. I can't trace her mobile phone signal either.'

Michael smirked, unseen by Anna. 'Yes, there's a good reason for that, she dropped her phone and it got trodden on, so now I have it for safe keeping.'

'Ah, how useful,' said Anna, implying that she understood the significance.

Michael put his phone away. Police vehicles now filled the concrete space. Ambulances hovered on the outskirts, armed police milled around the usual uniformed officers. No-one, it seemed, was quite sure what to do, except the Scene of Crime forensics technicians, they always knew what to do at a crime scene. Everything else had happened and finished, the party was over, the shooting had stopped (literally.)

Michael and Eric stood together, both feeling the need to do something, to be somewhere else where they could do something to follow Marshall and Bullock. Michael was beginning to doubt that they'd find Mason alive, and now the Head's life was in danger. Marshall would surely kill her when he'd finished with her, whatever it was he had planned.

'Where's the Head's driver?' asked Michael.

'Over there,' said Eric, gesturing towards one of the ambulances. 'He seemed very confused by what happened. The paramedic told him it was probably PTSD.'

'Good explanation,' said Michael, 'should avoid some awkward questions.'

'So what's the plan?' asked Eric. 'I assume you have plan.'

Michael looked at him, never sure when Eric was joking and when he was serious. 'At the moment, no. No plan,' said Michael.

'So why not go and talk to her driver? Read his mind, or whatever you do.'

Michael was starting to get frustrated at Eric's sniping. 'Because he doesn't know anything,' snapped Michael. 'I could read his mind, or I could just ask him. Either way, he doesn't know anything. And before you ask, no, I can't see the future or just magic up some vision of where they've taken her.'

'Some superhero you are,' said Eric, the sarcasm obvious in his voice. 'I assume they got control of him, that's why he started waving his gun at me.'

'Yes, they did, then I got control of him.'

'So why didn't you have him charge ahead of us, he could have drawn their fire, we'd have got a clear shot at them, we could have stopped them,' said Eric, with a barely suppressed anger Michael hadn't seen before.

'You want me to force a man, against his will, to walk into the line of fire?'

'If that's what it takes, yes,' said Eric. 'He's an MI5 field agent, he knows the risks, if you could give him some kind of mental push then yes, why not?'

'I'll kill people if I need to,' said Michael, 'I'll order people into battle, even if it means they'll die, but they have to go willingly, I won't use telepathic control to force them into being killed.'

'How far are you willing to go?' asked Eric. The question left Michael speechless. 'How very high and mighty of you,' said Eric, 'you just gave the Head to them. I hope it was worth it.'

Michael drew breath ready to answer but was interrupted by the ringing of his phone. It was the Duty Operations Director.

'They planned this well,' said the DOD. 'Do you know if the Head of Section had her phone or comms device, or squealer?'

'No comms,' said Michael, 'but yes she probably had a squealer, I guess they'd have destroyed it quickly. Don't know about her phone.'

The DOD paused for a moment. Michael had no doubt that at some point they'd have someone in GCHQ analyse the signal from the Head's phone and determine exactly where it was when it was deactivated. Michael could only hope they'd conclude that Marshall or Bullock quickly deactivated it and took the phone with them.

'Okay, continue there as long as the police need you, I'm sure they'll want you back for statementing,' said the DOD. He ended the call.

Eric obviously hadn't finished. 'They've got Mason, they've got the Head, they've been leading us on a merry dance all the way. Whatever they're planning we haven't done anything to stop them. How about if they do get hold of a nuke, what do you think they'll do then?'

Michael didn't have an answer to this. He looked at Eric. A shouting match wasn't going to help anyone.

'There are three of them, and one of me,' said Michael. 'Even though we've got GCHQ and all their technical power, Marshall still has a huge advantage.'

'Then we need to find a way of using that power to neutralise their advantage,' said Eric. 'And quickly.'

***

Michael and Eric sat in the front of the police patrol car while police and Scenes of Crime technicians milled around them. Nobody was rushing, and Michael felt it was all a little too calm, they should be doing more, putting in more effort into finding the Head. Time had been running out from the moment she had been taken. Eric's mobile phone rested on the top of the dashboard, Anna's voice coming through the phone's loudspeaker.

'Okay,' said Eric, 'since Captain Woo-Woo here can't use his magic powers...' Michael coughed and spluttered and tried to argue.

'Now now boys,' said Anna, 'if you can't play nicely together. Did you see the car they got away in?'

'No,' said Eric.

'Okay, I only saw one car, if you didn't see any other cars let's assume they used just the one. Have the police mentioned anything about the third man?'

'What third man?' asked Eric.

'The one with the folder,' said Anna, 'the bait.'

'I'd assume once his baiting duties were over he was the getaway driver,' said Michael. 'Are there any CCTV images of him?'

'None that are good enough to give an immediate ID,' said Anna. 'The facial recognition systems are narrowing it down, but none of the possible suspects so far could have been near the shopping centre when the images were taken.'

'So what do we know?' asked Michael.

Eric shrugged.

'We do know that they took Mason,' said Anna, 'and probably because of his knowledge of exVoxx.'

'So they're possibly aiming to hack, attack or penetrate somewhere protected by exVoxx,' said Michael.

'Yes, although that doesn't narrow it down much. I've got details of servers they might be using, but I've not found any evidence of Internet traffic from those servers, there are too many places to look.'

'And now they've got the Head,' said Eric.

'And she knows about exVoxx protected sites, including nuclear sites, and we know they've got an interest in Jeremy Susskind,' said Anna.

'Well,' said Michael, 'we only think they have, there's still the possibility that's a diversion, a distraction.'

'Anna?' said Eric, his voice lightening. 'Can you run any kind of check on the Head? Where she's worked, what she's done, any possible targets.'

'I can, but it will be a big list, so far we've nothing that will narrow it down.'

'Except her SIM card,' said Michel.

'So how does that help?' asked Eric.

'The Head communicated with someone, through a secure MI5 channel, someone who ordered the squad of soldiers to kill Marshall and the others. I doubt this person knows where they're holding the Head, but I bet anything that this person knows a lot of things we don't.'

'They might know something that will narrow down the search,' said Anna.

'There's another problem,' said Michael. He paused, but nobody asked him what the other problem might be. Perhaps it was too obvious a question. 'The Head has always acted as a protection against this other person. If she's gone…'

'Then there's no-one to stop this other person ordering in their assassins,' said Anna, completing Michael's sentence.

'Exactly. The Head was always paranoid about any detail of the Psiclone Project leaking out. This other person wanted to take a more direct approach and kill the project and almost everyone involved. This man wandering around with a banner saying Psiclone was just too much for her to ignore, it might be too much for this other person to ignore. We have to find them.'

'So bring me the SIM card,' said Anna. Before Michael or Eric could speak, Anna continued. 'There's another problem. Well, it might not be a problem, but it's a big coincidence.'

'Which is?' asked Michael.

'When you went to see Joanna Crossley, the car's camera caught an image of another car leaving. That same car was in the public car park of the shopping centre this morning.'

'Whose car?' asked Eric.

'Grant Bray,' said Anna. Michael and Eric looked at each other, and both shrugged their shoulders. 'He's a journalist,' added Anna.

There was a silence while they each contemplated what this might mean.

'Maybe we need to have a word with Mr Bray,' suggested Eric.

'It's possible the man with the folder really did have something on him about the project and was going to give it to this journalist,' said Anna.

'I think our first priority has to be to get the SIM card to you,' said Michael.

'Okay,' said Anna. 'I've dug a bit into Mr Bray's profile, he's not on any watch lists, he's never been seen as any kind of security threat, in fact, there's no evidence that this is anything other than coincidence.'

'I don't believe in coincidences,' said Eric, 'not like this.'

'I agree,' said Michael, 'but for the moment he's not a threat and we have higher priorities. Anna, let us know if this Bray does anything or goes anywhere that suggests he's actively involved in what's happening.'

'Will do,' said Anna.

The conversation was again interrupted by Michael's mobile phone ringing. He recognised the name of the caller, and answered.

'Yes sir,' he said.

'I need you and your driver back at The Office as soon as possible,' said the Duty Operations Director. 'Everyone's being assigned roles in searching for the Head of Section. I need you included.' He hung up.

'They want us back at The Office,' Michael said to the other two. The Office, Thames House, the headquarters of MI5, was in the centre of London, and all major operations were directed from there. Michael had no doubt that a major operation to find the Head was already being mobilised.

'This could complicate things,' said Eric.

'It could. I suggest we get back there, but we'll drop the SIM card off on the way. Anna, see you in about an hour.'

***

Anna couldn't stop staring at the single image frozen on her screen. The image was a low-quality still from a CCTV camera, taken in a low light setting. It showed three people, two men and a woman, walking out of the door, obviously moving from inside to outside. It was the last image of the Head that Anna had acquired, a frozen record of the Head's last moments of freedom as she was being taken by Marshall and Bullock. Or perhaps she had already lost her freedom by this moment. The phrase Anna couldn't let go of was "dead man walking." Somehow "dead woman walking" just didn't sound right, or she didn't want it to sound right.

There was activity in the office around her, people moving from desk to desk, comparing notes, looking at data on each other's screens, discussing items of information and their potential significance. Anna, for the moment, took no part in this. She had watched as a spectator as Vince Marshall deprived yet another person of their freedom. Was he also going to deprive her of her life? Anna forced herself to think about something else.

A flashing light distracted her, indicating an incoming call on her desk phone. She put on the headset and answered the call, the phone showing the name of the caller.

'Hello Anna, it's Maria Cho,' said the caller, almost certainly knowing that Anna would have seen who was calling. 'I imagine things are quite busy there at the moment.'

'Yes, they are,' said Anna, not really in the mood for small talk or casual conversation.

'You know why I'm calling,' said Cho, making a statement rather than asking a question. 'You're being assigned to the search operation for the MI5 Head of Section.'

'Yes, of course,' said Anna.

'Anna, this means full involvement and cooperation,' said Cho. 'Anything else you may have been working on, even for the Head, is now stopped. Your only involvement is with the search operation. Is that clear?'

'Yes, yes it's clear.'

'Good. Were you working on anything with the Head when she was kidnapped?'

Anna stopped. She hadn't expected such a direct question, even though it was probably the most obvious question anyone could have asked.

'Yes, yes I was,' she said, still sounding like she was half asleep.

'I need you to share all the information and data you have,' said Cho. 'I want you to put everything into the common data pool.'

'But,' Anna started, hardly knowing how to respond. 'But most of this is highly classified, some of it's "eyes only," I can't put it in the pool.'

'You can now, and I need you to, quickly.' Cho hung up.

Anna considered the implications of what Cho had asked her to do. The common data pool was where files were placed for everyone to access. It was the quickest and easiest way of sharing files with anyone and everyone. As such only low grade or unclassified material was ever placed in the pool. Classified files and above couldn't be placed in there, never mind anything that was secret or top secret or above. Anna had no doubt that Cho would be watching, she'd be waiting to see files loaded into the pool by Anna, and Anna had no doubt Cho would come chasing her if she ignored the request.

Anna lined up various files, the images of the man with the folder, video files from CCTV cameras, information from when Anna had tried to follow them after they'd left the shopping centre, logs of her hacking into the shopping centre's power systems to turn the lights off. She knew she should do as instructed and upload it all to the common data pool.

She looked at the files with the images of the man carrying the folder. She enlarged one of the images, and the word "Psiclone" was clear for all to see. If she uploaded this to the common data pool then everyone would see it, the word Psiclone would become common knowledge, and Cho and others would all come banging on Anna's (and Michael's) door demanding to know what it meant and what was the Head's connection to it.

Perhaps some things were best kept secret, even from the secret service. Anna selected the images, and deleted them. No doubt there would be a price to pay for doing that.

Fourteen

The Head became aware of sitting in a chair. She wasn't sure what had happened before sitting in the chair, memories swam around her mind, but always stayed out of reach. She remembered being somewhere, then somewhere else, and there were people, and things happened, but she wasn't sure what had happened, or when, and now she was here. The chair was wooden and solid, and for one horrid moment it reminded her of an electric chair. She moved her head but felt nothing pressing down on her scalp. She looked down, and sure enough, her wrists were clamped to the arms of the chairs by thick leather straps. She could feel similar restraints holding her ankles, but she felt no electrodes, nothing else attached.

The room looked as old as the chair, or perhaps older. It had a floor of dark grey flagstones, stone walls, a heavy iron and wood door on big rusting hinges. It could have been a medieval dungeon if not for the single electric light bulb hanging from the ceiling. Perhaps it was a medieval dungeon, re-purposed. She wracked her brain trying to think of old and ancient buildings she knew that might feature a dungeon such as this, but her memories continued to come and go. She remembered her name, yes she remembered who she was, or at least she could

223

remember the name she called herself. Another part of her mind started to take over, a more analytical and calculating part. She hadn't yet considered why she was in this room, or why she was restrained, and therefore hadn't yet considered whether she was in danger. Her first thought was that she was probably not in the company of friends. She didn't think people tended to strap their friends into chairs like this, at least none of her friends. Yes, she had friends. Blurred faces came to mind but then faded. She let them go, there was no point chasing them.

Was she in danger? Yes, came the answer. Someone obviously wanted to keep her from leaving. Yet this also meant that whoever this someone was, they wanted to keep her, and since this someone was so far not present in the room she judged that she was not in imminent danger, but the situation could change at any time. There was no sound, but perhaps the door was heavy enough to insulate her from any sound. Marshall might come through the door at any moment. She shuddered and tensed as the memory of that man came into her mind. Without meaning to she pulled her arms up, testing the restraints, but they were strong, much stronger than she was. She forced herself to remain still, to breathe in deep and even breaths. Yes, Vince Marshall, she remembered. Then more memories came back. She remembered the shopping centre, shots being fired. Sanders, she remembered seeing Michael Sanders, but then the time between those events and this room faded into darkness. The only logical conclusion was that Vince Marshall and at least one other of his gang had kidnapped her and that Michael Sanders had yet again proved inadequate and had failed to prevent it.

There was a deep metallic clanging sound from the door, the sound of a large key being turned in the lock. It was all very melodramatic, the locked door was unnecessary, given the restraints holding her in the chair. She expected the door hinges to creak and echo when the door opened, and sure enough the door swung open, the creaking echoing around the stone room. Vince Marshall stepped into the room. He looked taller than she remembered, solidly built, dark jeans, a dark sweatshirt, combat jacket. All he needed to complete the stereotype would be sunglasses.

'Well,' said Marshall, 'I have to say I've been waiting for this.' He walked closer to her.

'Is this one of your psychic hallucinations?' she asked.

'Oh no,' he replied, 'sorry, but this is very real, so be careful.'

He stood in front of her, arms folded, looking down, the cat ready to play with the mouse. She remembered a line from a TV programme, something about there being only one way to win this game; don't be the mouse.

'So what now?' she asked.

'To begin with, I have something to show you.' Marshall turned to look behind him, at the door.

Two big men, she didn't recognise them, entered the room, holding between them the slumped figure of her driver. Despite herself, she took a sharp intake of breath. The two men dropped the man to the floor. He knelt there, obviously still conscious, but she could see the blood running down his face from head wounds. She couldn't see much of his face, but she could see enough to glimpse the bruising and swelling. There were many things she thought of saying, but she remained silent. She had found silence to be very effective, in all sorts of situations.

Marshall stared down at her. She held his gaze for as long as she could, as long as she dared, then she had to look down, to look at her colleague, kneeling on the floor, semi-comatose. She willed herself not to imagine what they had done to him. She thought only that she knew he was strong, he'd been beaten before and survived, that they wouldn't break him just through kicks and punches.

'I've brought you here,' said Marshall, 'because I need some things from you.'

'You'll get nothing from me,' she said before she could stop herself.

'I think we both know I'll get whatever I want from you. But for now, I just wanted to show you something.' He turned around, stepping slightly to one side so that he and the Head both faced the kneeling man. She didn't see the signal he must have given, but in a single movement one of the big men pulled out a gun and pushed the barrel into the side of the man's head. The shot was deafening in the small stone room. It caused dust to leap off the walls and drop dramatically from the ceiling. Blood and brains sprayed and spilt onto the stone floor and the lifeless body fell sideways, one foot twitching, then still.

The Head realised she was shaking, but at least she'd remained silent, she hadn't screamed, she still had some control, they hadn't taken that from her, yet. She watched, transfixed, as the two men dragged the body from the room.

'You didn't need to do that,' she said.

'No, but I wanted to,' said Marshall. 'I'm sure you see me as the villain of the piece, and as all good villains do I want to stand here and boast about how much I've achieved and how you'll never stop me.'

'You haven't achieved anything,' said the Head. She wanted so much to stay silent, to ignore Marshall, let him say his piece and get no reaction, but it was so much easier to want it than to do it.

'Haven't I? I got Mason. You thought you had us on the run, that you were the hunter, again, but then

I took Mason right from under your nose.' Marshall sneered, exaggerating every moment of his boasting.

'What could you possibly want with him?' she asked, already knowing the answer.

'exVoxx,' Marshall said, 'he has some very particular contacts when it comes to the exVoxx system.'

The Head's mind raced, thinking through possibilities, playing out scenarios. 'Even with him, you won't find exVoxx so easy to hack.'

Marshall laughed, a single dismissive laugh. 'Hack it? We don't want to hack it. Mason helped us get inside it. We've got access to the entire exVoxx network, we can get into any exVoxx protected site we want.'

He bent down close to her. 'Ever stopped to think why those images of my man and the Psiclone file just "popped" into your surveillance feeds? Because I put them there. I just walked into your system and put the images in and you just couldn't resist it.'

'You didn't put them in,' said the Head, 'you wouldn't know which way up a keyboard goes.' She stared him in the eyes, tensing slightly, bracing herself for the punch or kick that might result.

Marshall stood up. 'You're right, Julian is the real technical guru, so credit where it's due, Singh fed you those images, and you came running, and now we have you.'

'I won't help you,' she said.

'I don't want your help, I only want your memories, and I can just walk in and take those whenever I want, and we both know you can't do anything to stop me.'

'What are you after, Marshall?' she asked, trying to get any kind of information that might help, if not now then perhaps later, if she had a later.

'We came back for a reason. We came back for something. We're going to take something that will make us even more powerful. Not even you could imagine how powerful this is going to make us.'

She just stared at him, unsure if he was exaggerating or if he really did have a plan, but she remembered that Marshall was very skilled at what he did, and he rarely did anything without a plan.

'I'm going to be so powerful that you won't be able to stop me,' Marshall said, bending down again, his nose point-to-point with hers. 'I'll be so powerful I could walk into 10 Downing Street and piss on the Prime Minister's desk and no-one could stop me. I could even piss on the Prime Minister.' Marshall sounded like he was enjoying the bravado, 'Fuck, I would walk into the White House and piss on the President, and there is no-one who could stop me.'

'Nothing's going to give you that much power,' she said.

He touched his finger to her forehead, and an image came into her mind. She saw the building, she saw what Marshall was thinking of. She gasped, she tried not to but she couldn't help it, she gasped as she understood what he was planning. Not that. Anything but that. She had to get out, she had to warn Sanders, she had to call someone, something had to be done to stop these people.

'Why?' The question escaped from her mouth before she could stop herself.

'Why what?' asked Marshall. 'Why come back? Why take it? Why kill you? Why do you think?'

'Revenge? Is that what this is about?'

'I'm a simple man,' said Marshall, folding his arms again and standing over her, looking down. 'I only need simple motivations. Once it was following orders, being a good soldier, completing the mission. But then someone turned me into their pet lab' rat and made me psychic. You knew, didn't you? You knew what the drug would do?'

The Head was silent. She had the idea it was like negotiating with a drunk. Ration and reason would play no part in this conversation, her skills were of little use. All she could do was maintain a modicum of self-control. 'Yes. I knew,' she said. She thought there was little point in denying it, not now.

'You changed us,' said Marshall. 'You changed everything. Then you decided we weren't what you needed, so you tried to kill us.'

'No,' she snapped, 'you changed everything. You decided you didn't need us. You decided you didn't need orders or superior officers. You decided you'd go freelance. You went rogue.'

'We could have worked together,' Marshall said, bending lower towards her. 'You crossed the line when you decided to have us killed.'

'I'd…' she began.

'I don't care who gave the order or who said what,' Marshall shouted down at her. 'You were a part of it. You were a part of the chain of command. You were a part of deciding to kill us. And do you know what?' Marshall let the silence hang in the air, one moment stretching into the next. 'I have a very anti-social reaction to people who try to kill me.'

The Head considered several things she could say in response to that, but chose silence instead. There was no prospect of reasoning with this man, there never had been.

'So we took charge of our own destiny, and now we're back to take what we need,' said Marshall. He crouched down, his face level with hers. 'You let the genie out of the bottle. You tried to kill the genie. But now the genie is back, and believe me, I'm one really pissed off genie. But now I like being a genie, I like the magic you gave us, and we want more of it, much more.'

She willed herself not to meet his gaze, not to look him in the eyes. Escape seemed impossible, but somehow she had to find a way of stopping the man, of stopping the Three of them. Someone had to find a way of stopping them.

'Don't worry,' said Marshall, standing up again. 'That's not all we want. Once we've got what we want from you, then we're going to have a little fun.'

The Head felt cold, very cold. Marshall was never about fun, but what Marshall did enjoy usually involved pain.

'Once we've done I'm going to enjoy killing you,' he said, 'slowly, bit by bit. Singh's a whizz with a scalpel, but me, I just prefer cutting off fingers, one at a time, then other bits, one at a time, and we have all the time we want.'

She pulled hard at the leather straps holding her arms, but they were far too strong for her. The mouse was caught securely in the trap.

***

Marshall looked down at the Head, sitting in one of the easy chairs in the farmhouse lounge. He had his finger resting lightly on the top of her head. Her eyes were closed and she looked like she was sleeping. Her arms twitched slightly. He took his finger away.

'So how's our guest?' asked Singh, standing next to Marshall and watching.

'Very unhappy,' said Marshall.

'Glad to hear it. What did you show her?'

'She saw us execute her driver,' said Marshall.

'Why not show her Sanders being killed?' asked Bullock as he walked into the room.

'She might not believe it, she's very suspicious of everything, but for the moment she's shocked and scared and totally uncertain of what she can believe and what she can't.'

'Perfect,' said Singh. 'Leave it a while and she'll be ready for our little sightseeing tour.'

***

Anna watched the sun disappear from the London skyline. She listened on her headset to the conference call being run from the MI5 Operations Directorate in Thames House. The new, temporary, Head of Section was taking the lead in the search for the Head. Multiple agencies and forces were represented on the call, including various teams from GCHQ, and she knew some of the analysts and team leaders who were on the call.

Anna had been slightly surprised that she had been invited to join the call, given that Maria Cho was also on the call. She'd expected Cho to give her orders after the call. The police had interviewed potential witnesses to Marshall and Bullock's escape, giving a range of descriptions of the possible getaway vehicles and drivers. Anna was tasked with a deep and intrusive social media probe for all the possible vehicles and drivers and anyone connected with them, cross-referenced with analyses of traffic surveillance video from the potential escape routes. In short, she was to do anything and everything to try and identify the car and the driver based on almost no evidence.

Her ears pricked up when she heard that a GCHQ tech' services team had arrived at the shopping centre. She went straight to her keyboard and looked up the team and their equipment. They were, in fact, fully equipped. She could imagine the anonymous looking van or lorry turning up at the shopping centre, passers-by blissfully unaware of the amount of hi-tech surveillance equipment packed into the vehicle. She knew that the technicians would be plugging their equipment directly into local mobile phone masts, telephone junction boxes, and every local CCTV system they could find and more.

There was a short discussion about whether they had anyone free to pilot the Remote Surveillance Units.

'I can fly them,' said Anna, but no-one responded, she was ignored. Anna looked at her phone, at the red light showing her microphone was muted. She pressed the button and spoke again. 'I can fly the RSUs,' she said.

'Sorry, who is this?' asked the Acting Head of Section.

Anna heard Cho explain who Anna was, and why she was on the call. Anna wasn't sure she liked being described as "an analyst who'd offered some low-level technical support to the Head of Section."

'I think it's probably better if someone on the ground pilots the units,' said the Acting Head, 'they'll have visual sight of the drones.'

'Sir,' said Anna, quickly. 'I was working with the Head on surveillance and analysis when she was taken.' There was silence from everyone on the call. 'I'm qualified to pilot the Units and I can directly link their data feeds to the data we were analysing at the time of the kidnapping.' She stopped talking. She felt a desperate urge to say more, to explain why she would do a better job than anyone else, but she also had to take the awful gamble that sometimes, less is more.

'Very well,' said the Acting Head. 'Co-ordinate with the lead technician in the field. I'll want a summary of your results as soon as you've done. Get to it, there won't be much daylight left.'

Anna didn't wait for any further discussion, and she certainly didn't wait to give Cho a chance to object. She pressed the button on her desk phone and left the call.

It took Anna only a few minutes to contact the lead technician at the shopping centre, a man called Dave, and it only took Dave a few moments to confirm that Anna had clearance (and qualification) to pilot the RSUs. While Dave was getting his confirmation, Anna closed all the programs on her computer and brought up the flight and data control programs for the Remote Surveillance Units.

Each RSU looked like a middle-of-the-range, four-rotor drone that hobbyists and would-be voyeurs could buy from any high street (or online) retailer, except these were also fitted with two hi-def' cameras and a range of radio surveillance devices that few hobbyists would recognise. Each RSU (almost everyone called them drones, it was hard not to) was linked by radio to the tech' services vehicle and from there to the GCHQ computer network, allowing them to be piloted from almost any geographic location.

Within minutes the two drones were airborne, Anna piloting them both using a program which allowed her to specify a search area and the program then took care of the moment-by-moment manoeuvring of the machines. Anna checked that the drones' video feeds were coming through to her screens, as were the data feeds from the machines. As they flew they could pick up mobile phone traffic, without needing to hack the relevant network, identify the individual people the cameras were looking at, identify all vehicles and their drivers. From there other programs would search all manner of databases and would flag anyone of potential interest.

Anna had to assume that anyone actually involved in the kidnapping was long gone, but there might still be physical or electronic clues she could pick up. She had the drones fly to the road leaving the cargo area of the shopping centre. This was where Marshall's escape route started, this was where her hunt began.

Anna had the system station the drones one either side of the road leading away from the shopping centre. On the screen she watched the four windows, each showing the feed from one of the onboard cameras. She could see the adjacent railway line. They almost certainly didn't go that way. She checked the online maps. One way would have taken the fleeing kidnappers North, but would have gone through more and more retail and commercial areas, and the maps showed increasing numbers of CCTV cameras. The other way would have taken them South, out through more residential areas (fewer cameras,) past the golf course, and ultimately towards the A427 and other main routes. One or two vehicle changes in secluded areas and by the time they past a CCTV camera they would be just one of the swarm of vehicles in the evening commuter traffic.

She programmed the computer, and the drones followed the road out towards the residential area. Adjacent windows showed logs of calls made to and from mobile phones in the area at the time of the escape, and who owned the phones. A line of information appeared in red, an unregistered phone. One call, short, the phone's ID had never been logged before and had never been logged since. Anna smiled, it might indicate a call from a one-time phone to alert an accomplice to be ready with a change of vehicle. Anna set one of the drones' cameras to its infra-red setting. An abandoned vehicle might be hidden from sight, but its heat signature might still be visible.

After half an hour's work Anna sat back, grinning from ear to ear. The drones were returning on automatic pilot to the tech' services vehicle, and the police were on their way to investigate a BMW Mini hidden on a dirt track, covered by a tarpaulin sheet. It was unlikely, she had to admit, that Marshall or Bullock would have left any clues that Michael could use, in whatever way he used clues, but at least it would vindicate her insistence on piloting the drones, and it would be one in the eye for Maria Cho. It also meant that Anna would have more ammunition if it ever came to a fight about whether she should remain in London or return to Cheltenham.

Anna looked at the clock on the wall. Michael and Eric should arrive soon, with the Head's SIM card. Then, perhaps, they would make some real progress.

Fifteen

The farmhouse - Tuesday, late afternoon

Marshall and Singh walked into the lounge. They stood and looked at the Head who was still sitting in her chair, eyes closed, motionless. Darkness was falling outside, and the only movement in the garden beyond was the occasional security consultant walking around the building on guard duty.

'Is she ready?' Singh asked.

'As ready as she'll ever be. Let's go,' said Marshall.

The two men each sat in a chair and closed their eyes. It looked as though each of the three was snoozing, none moved, none spoke, but a huge surge of mental energy was taking place.

Marshall looked around the dungeon. He didn't remember the transition from the outside world to the inside of the Head's mind, it happened outside a moment of conscious awareness. Yet here they were. He and Singh stood in front of the Head, still strapped into the solid wooden chair.

The Head looked up at them. She said nothing.

'Good evening,' said Marshall, in mock politeness.

Singh grinned at the Head. 'Rosalind Garvey,' he said, 'how wonderful to see you again.' Still she said nothing. She had no reaction to him calling her by name. Marshall was impressed, perhaps she was stronger than he'd first thought, they'd soon find out.

'It's time to go for a walk,' said Marshall.

Something happened. The walls moved, they shimmered in the way that water on a lake shimmered in sun and wind, a rippling that moved through the walls and floor of the dungeon. The shimmering stopped.

Singh looked at Marshall. 'Problem?' he asked.

Marshall looked down at the Head. 'What are you doing?' he asked, as though addressing a misbehaving child.

'I like it here,' she said, 'I thought I'd stay.'

'Well I don't want to stay,' said Marshall, more firmly.

'This is my hallucination, my delusion, and I choose to stay in it,' said the Head, matching his firmness.

'Can we get out of here?' said Singh.

The walls shimmered again, stronger this time. The single light bulb remained bright and yet the light in the room changed, taking on an unreal intensity. The floors and walls and ceiling shifted and swayed, and yet the Head and chair remained unchanged. The light and walls stopped their disturbing dance.

'She's fighting me,' said Marshall.

'Of course I'm fighting you,' said the Head, without moving her lips or using her voice.

'Need a hand?' asked Singh. Marshall looked at him. This was no time for playing games, they had things to do. Marshall nodded. Singh and Marshall both looked down at the Head. She had her eyes closed, perhaps summoning her energy to resist whatever came next.

The room shattered, the entire fabric of dungeon disintegrated into fragments as though made of glass and struck by a hammer. The sound of it was unreal and almost deafening, felt as much as heard. In place of the dungeon the three of them were now standing in sunlight, by the side of a road. On the opposite side of the road was a building. It was wide, six storeys tall, made of deep blue glass and dark metal. The entire building was surrounded by a high and solid looking fence. Between the fence and the building was a car park, separated from the road by a heavy metal gate which secured the driveway in and out of the site. The strangest aspect of the scene was the second building, smaller and to the right, surrounded by its own fence, but with no gate and no car park and no road in or out. The only visible connection was an enclosed bridge connecting the two buildings.

'Where is it?' asked Marshall. The Head turned slightly to face the smaller building.

Her voice came to them in an unspoken, unverbalised form. 'It's in there,' she thought/said.

'How do we get in?' asked Singh.

Neither Singh nor Marshall was aware of the change, yet they were now standing outside the main entrance to the larger building. Large glass doors slid aside as people entered and exited the building. The people entering the building pressed their ID badges to a scanner and the inner doors slid open.

The world around them flickered and changed as though they were stepping in and out of life-sized pictures. A wide corridor, the inside of a lift (badge presented to another scanner,) the fourth floor (no-one spoke, Singh and Marshall just knew it was the fourth floor.) Another door, a laboratory, glassware, smells of chemicals. The scene changed quickly, images coming and going, their journey through the imagined landscape happening to them in staccato moments. The far side of the room, another door, badge and numeric code entered into a keypad. Marshall had the sense of trying to enter the code into the keypad, yet it felt like he was dipping his fingers in water.

'She's resisting again,' he said. There was a wash of telepathic energy. If it had been physical it would have felt warm. Singh and Marshall both sensed the Head stagger, psychically speaking, her resistance was weakening.

Through the door, and into the corridor. Marshall wasn't sure if they walked down the corridor or glided down it, or if he was simply aware of the idea of moving. They knew, without knowing how they knew, that they were moving along the corridor from the main building and into the smaller, secure building. At the end of the corridor was another door, it slid open automatically.

Another laboratory, fewer people, none of them noticed them in this vision/hallucination.

Another door. Badge, numeric key code, a small keyboard with shapes and symbols, another code. Inside, dark and cool, a laboratory from the future it seemed. Marshall tensed. They were close. She knew where it was, he could tell.

They didn't move. He looked at Singh. She was resisting again. They were close, they couldn't afford to allow her to dig in her psychic heels and build up resistance. Marshall pushed hard and in a blink, they were standing in front of a work bench. On the bench was a small refrigerator, and next to that was an instrument case. Here it was, simply sitting on the desk, almost as though it was waiting for them.

Without being aware of the moment, it was over. The dream had faded. Marshall blinked, and saw

Singh sitting forward in the chair, also blinking, re-orientating himself. The Head was still motionless, eyes still closed. Marshall looked around the living room, making sure he really was back in the real world, back in the farmhouse.

'That was it?' asked Marshall.

'That was it,' said Singh, 'that's where it is, and that's how we go and take it.'

'You got all that?'

'I got the codes, I've got access to her personnel record, all I need is a badge and I can get in.' Singh stood up, slowly. 'We're close, we're very close.'

Marshall looked at his watch. 'Bullock should be back with the badge soon.' He looked at the Head. 'Something's not right,' he said. 'She was resisting too much, it didn't feel right.'

'Miss Garvey is a strong woman. Not strong enough. She put up a decent fight, but we've almost done with her.'

Marshall stood up. He waved to the man patrolling the garden. 'I'll have her put in one of the bedrooms, she'll be okay in there.'

'Just don't let Bullock get at her,' said Singh. 'Just in case we need anything else, I need her in one piece until I know we've got it.'

'Don't worry,' said Marshall. 'She'll be asleep all night and still intact until we've finished.' He looked down at her. 'Then, I'm afraid, our Miss Garvey is going to meet with a really unpleasant end.'

***

The road wound through the woods, long shadows fell from the trees and lay across the tarmac as the sun set. It was a still and peaceful scene, a long way (spiritually) from the commuter routes on nearby main roads. Here just the occasional car passed by, once in a while a dog walker or rambler would saunter past.

A car rounded the bend, and the driver slowed, peering at the road ahead, slowing more. A dark shape lay across the road, with something moving. The driver slowed to a crawl, and she could see the shape was a motorbike lying on its side, the movement was the rider pulling himself out from under the bike. She stopped the car and watched for a moment. The rider stood up, slowly, shaking his head, the movement exaggerated by the helmet. He bent down to grasp the handlebars of the bike. It looked to be an effort as he pulled the bike upright, and started to walk it to the side of the road. She noticed that he was limping. A glance in the rear view mirror showed that there was no-one else nearby.

She pulled the car over to the side of the road, stopped the engine and got out.

'Are you alright?' she said, approaching the rider.

The man looked up. She judged from his eyes that he smiled. 'Yes, thanks, just a silly mistake.' He kicked the prop down and pulled the bike back onto its stand.

'Do you need a hand?' she asked.

The man started to pull his helmet off, uncovering a mess of blond hair. 'No, thanks, I'm fine, probably just bruised.' He stepped forward but staggered as his leg gave way, he nearly dropped the helmet. She held out her hand almost instinctively in an offer of help or support.

'Thanks,' he said in a calm voice, he took her hand to steady himself. The woman made a slight gasping sound. Her shoulders sagged and she almost staggered, at the same time he stood upright, grinning, all trace of his "injury" gone. They stood there for several moments, a bizarre instance of him holding her hand, her eyes closing, his burning brightly.

'Now then, Yvonne,' he said, still holding her hand. 'You're going to go home, just an ordinary journey home, nothing remarkable at all.'

The woman nodded her head, slowly.

'But tomorrow you're not going to feel very well,' he said with an almost theatrical sadness, still grinning. 'You'll ring in sick, won't you?'

Again the woman nodded, slowly, looking to be half asleep.

'Good stuff,' he said. 'You'll ring in sick for a couple of days. Now, give me your ID badge.' Slowly she pulled the lanyard from around her neck, the attached plastic identity card swinging on the end. She held it out, and he took it. 'Thank you very much.'

He looked at her, up and down, his grin fading slightly, his expression changing, his eyes rested on her breasts. She seemed unaware of his attention, ignorant of his staring which, had she been properly conscious, she would have found immediately offensive.

He was distracted by the sound of a car, not yet in sight but it was approaching.

'On your way, Yvonne,' he said. 'Forget about this, forget about the badge, who cares about a badge? Sorry about the headache you'll have tomorrow.' He let go of her hand. She started to walk slowly back to her car. He swung his leg over the bike and started the engine. He pulled the helmet back on.

She was back in the car and had started the engine by the time the approaching car came into view. As it passed them the sound of the driver having a conversation on the car phone could be heard clearly from the roadside. The driver didn't even look at the car and the motorbike.

Yvonne's car pulled away and within a moment had disappeared around the next bend. Evan Bullock looked at the ID badge, the company name and logo next to her name, job title and department. He pushed the ID badge into an inside pocket of his jacket, and with a shower of dirt the bike took off in the opposite direction, and soon the woods were peaceful again.

***

Anna looked up at the clock, again. She didn't particularly look forward to going back to the hotel, but neither did she want to stay in the office much longer. She had half a suspicion that if the Acting Head or Maria Cho knew she was still here they'd find something for her to work on and she'd be there all night. But she couldn't risk missing Michael and Eric. She'd got herself into this situation, she had to make the most of it. She started to think about her flat in Cheltenham. It felt inviting, just her, cooking her own tea, settling down in front of the television. Maybe it was a mistake coming back out into the field. Was this really where she was meant to be?

She was brought back to the present moment, and breathed a sigh of relief and smiled as the doors opened and the two men marched in. Before she could stop herself, Anna was out of her seat and dashed towards them. She hugged Eric first, lingering longer than she thought. Then she hugged Michael, the three of them each grinning.

'Sorry,' said Anna, letting go. 'I was so worried. I was watching, in the shopping centre, but I couldn't…. I couldn't communicate, not with any of you.'

'It's okay,' said Michael, 'we knew you were watching.'

'I take it you turned the lights out?' said Eric.

'Yes, the only thing I could think of.'

'It worked,' said Eric.

'It worked well,' said Michael.

Their smiles faded, relief fading as attention came back to more urgent matters.

'But they still got her, we didn't stop them,' said Anna.

'It's okay,' said Michael. 'They were ahead of us all along, they've always been ahead of us.' Anna sat back down at her desk, Eric and Michael pulled over chairs from adjacent desks and sat with her.

'So how do we get ahead of them?' said Eric.

'I did find one of their getaway cars, hidden not far from the shopping centre.'

'They must have swapped,' said Eric.

'Yes, but we've no surveillance of the swap, so whatever vehicle they used after that was lost in the rush hour. Sorry. Are you going to look at the vehicle we found?' she asked.

'No,' said Michael. 'No point. They knew the vehicle would be found, they won't have left any usable imprint there.'

'So what do we do?' asked Eric. 'They've got Mason, they've got the Head, they can't be far from doing whatever they're planning to do. Clock's ticking.'

'We've got the SIM card from her phone,' said Michael, putting the SIM card down on the desk next to Anna's keyboard.

Anna looked at it. 'I know it's important,' she said, 'but it's not going to help find her, is it?'

'It's more than important,' said Michael, 'it might be the only thing that keeps those soldiers from storming in and killing us.'

'Anna's right,' said Eric, 'we need to find the Head. We can look at her phone bill later.'

Michael looked at each of them, his face impassive. 'Please understand,' he said, slowly. 'Whoever ordered in those soldiers could decide to get rid of the whole Psiclone problem at any time. They could just decide to get rid of everyone who's got any connection with the project, and that includes both of you.' He let the message sink in for a few moments. 'Whoever she spoke to is a key player, and we don't have any idea who they are or what their agenda is. They're as dangerous as Marshall and friends, more so…'

'How can they be more dangerous?' asked Anna.

'Because they don't have to worry about staying safe, they don't have to worry about avoiding detection, they have armed forces they can call on at any time, Marshall doesn't.'

'I'm not convinced of that,' said Eric.

'I am,' said Michael. 'It was Marshall and Bullock at the shopping centre, and at Canary Wharf. They've been taking huge risks coming out in public to do their own shooting and kidnapping. They might have other people driving for them, but they've no-one else they can order out into the field to shoot people. Whoever this mystery person is definitely does have armed forces to call on.'

Eric and Anna looked at each other, and then at Michael.

Michael continued. 'Imagine we find the Three, we rescue the Head, we rescue Mason, we still wouldn't be safe from this person, not even with the Head back and able to argue we should be kept alive.'

'We need to get back to The Office,' said Eric. 'If we go AWOL now they might take us off the case, then we're completely screwed.'

'Agreed,' said Michael, 'but I need to know who the Head spoke to.' He looked at Anna. 'Can you find out.' He tapped the desk next to the SIM card.

'Yes,' she said.

Michael and Eric stood, but Anna stopped them. 'No, wait, this will only take a moment,' she said. They sat back down.

Anna picked up the SIM card and slipped it into a slot in the front of the desktop PC. She tapped some keys, worked for a few moments flicking between different windows on one of the screens. Eric and Michael watched as she copied data into another window, and then into another.

'Oh,' she said, sitting back and staring at the result the computer had presented to her.

'What?' Michael and Eric both said together.

'I found it,' said Anna, 'the source of the call she received.'

They both looked at her, eyes widening, waiting for an explanation.

She said, 'it came from the office of Major Liam Turner.' She tapped a few more keys, and frowned. 'Who apparently has an office in the Ministry of Defence building in Whitehall, but who doesn't have a job title, or department, or anything.'

'So who is he?' asked Eric.

'Well that's the problem,' said Anna, 'I can't tell. The internal phone directory has almost no information about him.'

'Can you do some digging?' asked Michael.

Anna frowned. 'I'm not sure. I can't guarantee that if I go digging into the records of someone like this that it won't set off an alarm somewhere.'

'Is he in his office?' asked Michael.

Anna checked with another window on the screen. 'No, looks like he's gone for the day. But his diary shows he's got meetings tomorrow, eight o'clock onwards.'

'Then tomorrow,' said Michael, 'I need to go and have a word with Major Turner.'

'You're going to get us all into trouble,' said Eric, 'again.'

Sixteen

London - Wednesday morning

Michael and Eric left Thames House and walked out into the chilly grey of the London morning. The 7 am briefing had been quick and perfunctory, the Acting Head of Section had reviewed overnight progress (none to report) and assigned analysts and field agents to various tasks. Michael and Eric were to return to the shopping centre and attempt to trace the route taken by Marshall and Bullock. They suspected this was a nonsense assignment intended more to keep them out of harm's way than to yield any useful results. Neither, however, had any intention of travelling directly to Woking.

The Ministry of Defence building in Whitehall, the so-called Main Building, was barely ten minutes from Thames House. Already the streets were busy with people walking to work. Most had their heads down and collars pulled up against the chill.

'Only two questions,' said Eric. 'What's the plan, and does it involve us getting arrested or shot at?'

Michael wasn't in the mood for Eric's sarcasm. 'We just need to talk to this Major Turner, and no, I don't expect he'll start shooting at us.'

Eric grunted his lack of conviction. 'Can't you just mind-meld with him or whatever?' he asked.

'I could, if I can get close enough,' said Michael. 'The first thing is to get into his office and get close enough without him objecting or setting of an alarm.'

'Yes, alarms bad,' said Eric, 'alarms likely to mean getting arrested again.'

Michael said nothing. He mulled over the various things he'd like to say to Eric, few of them polite or complimentary. They carried on along Millbank, heading towards Westminster, the (misnamed) tower of Big Ben rising up before them.

'So what exactly are we hoping to achieve?' Eric asked. Michael heard the sarcasm in the question. He knew exactly what he needed to achieve and was starting to get annoyed that Anna and Eric didn't appreciate, or didn't understand the danger they were in. Michael felt this unknown person and their propensity to order in armed soldiers hanging over him like a sword of Damocles, a single strand of hair holding it in place.

'I need to make sure they're going to leave us alone to find Marshall and the others and aren't going to order in the exterminators,' said Michael.

They walked past the Palace of Westminster, oblivious to the two or three famous politicians they almost walked into, ignoring the television camera crews on the lawn on the opposite side of the road.

'And assuming this person talks to you and agrees to play nice, then do we go and find the Head?' asked Eric.

Michael stopped and turned to face Eric, his face inches away. His voice became sharp.

'I know you didn't ask to be involved,' Michael hissed, 'and I'm sorry you got dragged into it, but I didn't ask for it either, and right now there's someone, out there, who very probably wants us all dead and who has a large team of very well trained killers he can send to make sure that happens.' Michael paused to let a passer-by walk out of range. 'I know Marshall has the Head, and I'm fully aware of what he'll do to her, probably very soon, but we need to make sure that we're safe. Even if we find her, we need to make sure this mystery man isn't going to have us all shot the same day.'

Eric maintained Michael's gaze, not blinking, not betraying any emotion on his face. Michael looked into Eric's eyes. 'Now I need you,' Michael continued, 'I can't do this alone, but I can't do it if you're not a hundred per cent with me.'

'I'm with you,' said Eric, 'I'm just not sure I like being with you.'

Michael hesitated, but then turned and carried on walking. Eric fell in behind him. It took them only another few minutes to reach the so-called "Main Building," the white edifice of the Ministry of Defence building in Whitehall. They made sure their identity badges were hung around their necks and visible as they walked through the main door and into the entrance foyer. The security procedures were much the same as at Thames House, their MI5 credentials allowed them quick access, and within minutes they were walking up the grand staircase to the first floor.

Anna had located Major Liam Turner's office, towards the end of a corridor on the first floor. She hadn't been able to find out any detail about him. As a serving officer in the British Army, she should have been able to find at least his regiment, who his commanding officer was. All she had been able to establish was that he had been with the Light Infantry, but after that, he had been seconded to an Intelligence unit and from there his record went blank.

As they walked down the corridor, footsteps almost silent on the heavy blood-red carpet, Michael felt a growing unease. He'd considered various strategies for getting past Turner's assistant (he almost certainly had an assistant or secretary who would be the jealous keeper of his diary,) and various explanations as to why Turner should give him time and not call security at the first opportunity. Michael had thought about various ways of playing the encounter, but no option seemed workable, all sounded false and an obvious cover for some ulterior motive.

They arrived at the door, dark panelled with a large brass door handle, in keeping with the dark panelled corridor, dark carpets and an altogether sombre mood.

Michael and Eric looked at each other. Eric shrugged, he obviously had no workable plan either. Michael knocked twice on the door and marched in.

The office was a moderate size, well appointed, and would have looked in keeping in a country mansion. The central feature of the room was a grand but not overly large desk facing the door, and behind the desk sat a woman wearing a stern and serious look. She had been writing something when they entered. She put her pen down as she looked up at them. Michael noticed that behind and to one side of the desk was the door through to Turner's office. There would be no getting into the office without her permission, and no chance of forcing control or access before she could raise the alarm.

'Good morning,' she said, in a manner that did not invite small talk. 'Can I help?' Michael thought she might as well have asked: "How can I dismiss you?"

'Good morning,' said Michael, trying to sound professional but not aggressive. 'I'd like to see Major Turner, please.' He smiled, to mask the tension, as he readied his arsenal of explanations and cover stories.

'And you are?' she asked.

Michael hesitated, it wasn't quite the question he'd expected. 'Michael Sanders.' He willed himself to keep looking at the woman and not glance across at Eric.

The woman picked up the phone and pressed a button. Whoever had answered spoke first, she listened, then answered a question. 'Michael Sanders,' she said into the phone. Another pause and she put the phone down.

She looked at Michael. 'Captain Sanders,' she said, 'Major Turner will see you.'

Michael wasn't sure if his mouth was hanging open, but he felt it should be. This was perhaps the one scenario he hadn't planned for and suddenly felt very unprepared.

The woman glanced at the door, to indicate that Michael should go in. He couldn't stop himself, he glanced back at Eric, then walked to the door, grasped the handle and twisted. He walked into the office as though walking onto the parade ground, or into the field to face the enemy.

***

Turner's office was larger, large enough to accommodate a more impressive desk, two chairs facing the desk, and four easy chairs around a low, antique looking coffee table. Turner himself was seated at the desk and rose as Michael entered. The man was ordinary in every respect, a smart but plain business suit, average height and weight, average brown hair, the kind of man who would disappear into a crowd and be invisible in plain sight. As Turner rose to stand, Michael stood to attention, standing tall, arms straight and by his side. He didn't salute the senior officer, neither was wearing a cap or beret. Turner returned the gesture, standing to attention, then both men relaxed.

'Captain Sanders, I'm not sure I can say this is a surprise,' said Turner.

'I think you have me at a disadvantage,' said Michael. He stepped forward and offered his hand to shake.

Turner looked down at the hand, then at Michael. 'I should hope I do,' he said, 'but I don't think that shaking hands would be a good idea, do you?' Michael thought that under the circumstances it would be a very good idea, and he really wished Major Turner would shake hands, but had to accept that it was unlikely.

'Please sit,' said Turner, gesturing to one of the two chairs positioned facing the desk. Turner sat back down behind the desk. Slowly, still trying to assess the situation and whether he had any advantage here at all, Michael sat in one of the chairs facing the desk. Turner picked up the phone and pressed a button.

'Miss Harrow, would you bring in a tea and a coffee? And please look after Captain Sander's associate.' He put the phone down. 'Now, Captain, what can I do for you?'

'You're not surprised I'm here?' asked Michael.

'Surprised that it's today, surprised that it's now given everything else that's going on, but not surprised that sooner or later you would come here.'

'I want to know about the Psiclone project,' said Michael.

'I'm sorry, Captain, but that's not something I can discuss, not even with you.'

Michael eyed the man. 'Sir, I'm sure you know that the Head of Section has been kidnapped. I'm also sure you are one of the few people who know what Marshall, Bullock and Singh are truly capable of doing.'

'Of course I do,' said Turner, 'but even though you were part of the same project doesn't mean I can discuss any of it with you.'

'We're running out of time, Sir.' Michael stressed the "sir," keen to give the impression that rank only meant so much, and no more. 'We're well past the point where there's any value in keeping secrets.'

'I don't mean to be evasive, Captain, but unless you know the secrets how do you know there's no value in keeping them?'

'I'm the only one who can get the Head back alive, and I'm the only one who has a chance of stopping Marshall.'

'Do you know what he's planning to do?' asked Turner. There was a silence between them. Michael knew that he had to avoid admitting that he had no real idea what Marshall was planning.

'It doesn't matter what he's planning, I'll find him and I'm the only one who can stop him, but I'm working in the dark, unless you tell me about the Psiclone Project.'

'Really? I'd have thought you'd want to know who sent the soldiers to kill you.'

Michael looked at the man. More questions formed in his mind, but he had no sense of certainty that any would prompt a useful answer. He was still too far away to touch the man, to impose telepathic control.

'Is that a part of the project? To close it down and remove all evidence?'

Turner hesitated, perhaps deciding what (if anything) to divulge. 'When Marshall and his friends became too ambitious, it was decided that the project presented too many risks,' said Turner, 'that their activities would almost certainly draw the attention of foreign powers, attention we didn't want. There were those who decided that, as you put it, the project should be closed down and all evidence removed. Those who made that decision still believe it is the best course of action.'

'Then why am I still alive?'

'Because they're not quite sure if you really can stop Marshall, Bullock and Singh. They're not quite convinced that if they kill you they could still find and stop the others, they're not quite convinced whether you are still useful to them or not.'

'And what if I do find and stop the others?'

'I don't know, Captain Sanders, I do not know what their decision would be.'

'Who is "they"?'

Turner was silent. Michael let the silence hang. This was the one question he truly wanted an answer to, he wanted Turner to fill the silence.

The door behind Michael opened and Turner's assistant, Miss Harrow entered carrying a small tray with two china cups. She placed the tea close to Turner and the coffee at the edge of the desk nearest Michael. Without a word she turned and left the office, closing the door behind her.

'There are various parties who contributed to the project,' said Turner, choosing each word with care. 'I can't exactly give you their names and addresses, I can't identify them at all. You know some of them. You knew Lieutenant Conway, you know the MI5 Head of Section, beyond that, all I can say is that there were others.'

A muscle tightened in Michael's jaw. It was an answer, but it wasn't enough, it wasn't anything he couldn't have guessed already.

'So if I do your jobs for you and stop Marshall and the others, how do I know you won't then kill me anyway?'

'I don't want to kill you at all,' said Turner, emphasising the "I." 'But I admit that I don't speak for others. But there again, if we killed everyone who was involved in every secret military project, we'd hardly have anybody left.'

'Who's running this project?' asked Michael, sharply, feeling his patience ebbing away.

Turner levelled his gaze at Michael. 'Does it matter, Captain?'

Michael considered his next question but felt a sinking feeling about whichever question he might ask.

'I think your priority should be to find Marshall, find the Head of Section, stop whatever plan Marshall and the others have, show that you can be trusted.' Turner paused. 'There's nothing else to know about the project that would help you. I think our conversation is at an end.'

Michael's shoulders slumped as he gave up wanting to ask anymore. Turner reached for the phone. In a swift and sudden movement Michael lurched forward, arm outstretched, and took hold of Turner's hand before he could reach the phone. Summoning all the energy he had Michael poured a torrent of psychic energy through his hand and into Turner's. Turner gasped, his hand trembled as his armed tensed. Michael felt a heat come over him as though they'd stepped into a sauna, there was a power here he'd not met before, a resistance he'd not encountered. Finally Turner slumped back down into his chair, but his eyes were still wide open as Michael continued to pour his thoughts into the man, thoughts of domination and submission, of control and surrender. He could feel Turner starting to relax, the heat started to ease, but there was still a feeling of swimming through mud, and something else. If it was a physical sense it would have been a taste or a scent, it was a tone that characterised an individual mind, but it was different to Turner, and it wasn't Marshall or Bullock or Singh.

Michael realised that Turner had been under telepathic control, but someone else, someone he didn't recognise, someone very powerful. Who? He poured the question into the man's mind. He felt the resistance, the feeling of pushing against glass, but he simply powered through. Who? Images flashed before him, fleeting glimpses of something, a bird, snatches of something familiar, like catching sight of something underwater, looking down through waves seeing it shimmer and fade.

There was a beep from the phone and a light flashed, most likely the secretary calling. Michael focused, he needed Turner to be calm, to return to a passive state of mind, as though none of this had happened. He let go of Turner's hand.

The man leaned forward and answered the phone. Michael could hear the woman's voice. 'Your next appointment is here, sir,' she said.

'Thank you, I'll be ready in a moment,' Turner said and replaced the phone, as though nothing untoward had happened at all. He turned to Michael, who was standing in front of the desk. 'I'm sorry Captain, where were we?'

'I was about to leave Sir, thank you for your time,' said Michael. He stood to attention. Turner just looked up at him.

Michael and Eric left the building as quickly as they could without drawing attention. Michael wasn't sure what he'd say if (when?) Eric asked him what happened with Turner. He just hoped that somehow Anna could do some searching based on the vague images and impressions he'd got from Turner's mind. He hoped it would be enough, but as the Head had reminded him, hope was not a strategy.

***

As Michael and Eric walked back towards Westminster Michael called Anna, hoping she'd be in work by now. She was. He explained quickly that he'd spoken to Turner, and had some leads she needed to follow.

'I had a quiet word with him,' said Michael, giving Eric and Anna a moment to understand the meaning of the phrase. 'I got images, not much, a bird, possibly a bird of prey, something about France, some connection between Turner and whatever this is.'

'So what am I looking for?' asked Anna. 'Is this a person, a place, what?'

'I was asking him who runs the Psiclone project, this is what I got, so I assume it's something relating to a person or an organisation, something connected to the British military, possibly to MI5, but that's all I've got.' Michael didn't look at Eric, he didn't need to, he could imagine the raised eyebrows.

'Okay,' said Anna, 'I'll get the systems looking for semantic connections, cross-derivational relationships…'

'That's great,' said Michael, 'let me know if you find anything.'

'Don't hold your breath,' said Anna before Michael could hang up. 'I found so little about Turner, there's very little to go on. I'll try.' She hung up.

Before either of them could speak Michael's phone rang. He looked at the caller ID, and his heart sank. It was the Acting Head of Section. This was unlikely to be a social call.

'Yes sir,' said Michael as he answered the call.

'Are you at the shopping centre yet?' the Acting Head asked, no polite "good morning" to begin the call and a hint of an unfriendly tone in his voice.

'Not yet sir, there was a related lead here I wanted to check out first.'

'Let me make this perfectly clear, Sanders,' said the Acting Head, the rising anger in his voice now unmistakable. 'You've been given an assignment as part of this search and rescue operation, you've deliberately disobeyed a direct order. Not only that, I've just had a call from the Head of Security at AWE asking about your assault on a member of their staff.'

Michael said nothing. He considered nothing to be the best thing he could say, under the circumstances.

'I don't know what you were doing at AWE,' said the Acting Head, 'but you understand how sensitive an installation that is, and that an assault on a member of their staff, on their site, is a very serious affair. You and your driver will return to The Office immediately. If you're not back in this office within the hour, I'll have you suspended from duty.' The call ended.

'I guess we're not in anyone's good books today?' said Eric.

'No, I don't think we are,' said Michael.

'Where next?'

'I think we better go back to The Office, and for whatever happens there, I'm sorry.'

Seventeen

Anna turned the pen over and over in her fingers as she stared at the screen. Michael hadn't set her a difficult challenge, he had set her an impossible one. She enjoyed challenges, but there was usually a way into a challenge, some starting point. She couldn't find a way into this challenge. How to identify someone or something (couldn't say what) linked to a man about whom she could find almost nothing, using only a couple of vague clues which could be symbolic instead of literal. The vast power of the GCHQ computer systems lay waiting for her to press buttons and engage them, but the search parameters were too vague, they would likely return billions of possible results. There again, given that almost nothing was known about Major Liam Turner perhaps there was just as little known about the target, in which case the search might turn up no results at all.

She needed something else, some other vector, some other point on the graph. She couldn't just hope to get lucky like they had with the image of Bullock in Hyde Park. Something nudged at her consciousness, an idea floating in her mind, just out of reach. What was it? Something about Bullock, which led them to Susskind at AWE. No, that wasn't it. It was something about finding the image, and a plan started to coalesce. She didn't have a picture of Turner, but she could probably find one. If nothing else, anyone who worked in Whitehall would walk past security cameras, there would be an image of him somewhere. She could then start the systems running searches for his likeness in published media, social media, surveillance cameras and the like. All the time she could have other systems scanning and analysing anyone and everyone else in any found images, looking for anything that related to anything French and anything to do with a bird. All of which was fine if they were looking for a person. If they were looking for a company or a project code name, then the search could be a lot more difficult.

What would help would be some indication of the time frame. When was the Psiclone project running? How far back should she be looking? She picked up her phone and dialled Michael's number. It didn't even ring but went straight to voicemail. Frustrated, she put the phone back down, hard. She got up and marched over to the nearest vending machine and selected a cup of the filth it labelled as coffee. She sat back down and stared at the screen, uncertain what to do next. She had an idea, which in hindsight was a really obvious thing to try.

Anna picked up the phone again and called Eric.

'Well good morning,' he said, in an overly cheery voice.

'Hello soldier,' she said, matching his cheeriness.

'Is this a social call, or are we just going to talk business?'

Anna paused, feeling a sudden and giddy urge just to talk about anything other than work, just talk to someone as a friend, to have a laugh, to forget everything that was going on. 'Depends what you're in the mood for,' she said, and realised she was blushing as soon as she'd said it.

'Anything other than work would be a welcome relief,' said Eric.

Anna sighed. 'I'm afraid my social life is fairly limited, and being in London has made it non-existent. So unless you want me to talk about the room service in the hotel, I'm not sure I've got anything to talk about.'

'That's too bad.' Eric paused, almost like he was about to say something. 'Not sure I've got much to chat about either.'

'Poor us,' said Anna. She was about to say something about having to do something worth chatting about, but bit her tongue, uncertain if that would be a step too far. 'Looks like it's just business this morning then,' she said. 'I'm trying to search for Michael's clues.'

'Good luck with that,' said Eric, sounding a touch dismissive.

'It does feel a bit like a needle-in-a-haystack job,' she said.

'First find the right haystack,' said Eric.

'I think I need to find the right field first. Do you know when the Psiclone project was running? I'm trying to set some kind of time frame for this searching.'

Eric paused. 'I'd say go back no more than four years. It's possible that whoever's running the project was running it before Sanders was involved, but try between one and four years ago.'

'Right,' said Anna, 'I'll do that.' She waited, not sure what she should say next.

'Anything else?' asked Eric.

Anna was about to try a bit of chit-chat, but a question popped into her mind, and she couldn't help asking it. 'I tried to get hold of Michael, but it just went through to voicemail. Do you know where he is?'

'No, I don't,' said Eric. His voice changed, more serious. 'I've been reassigned, I'm not working with Michael at the moment.'

'What? Why not? What are you doing?' Anna suddenly had a lot more questions.

'It's a long story. Short version is, the Acting Head of Section wants to have a long chat with Michael about recent events, and I don't think he's going to be sending Michael back out anytime soon.' There was a noise in the background on Eric's side of the call. 'Sorry, got to go.' He hung up.

Anna went straight to her keyboard. There was nothing she could do about Michael at the moment, she wasn't sure what she'd be able to do at all, but she could start searching for the clues he'd given her. She typed the final few parameters into the search programmes. The clues were minimal, the search was broad, but the search programmes used artificial intelligence and fuzzy logical and simulated cognitive reasoning. If anyone had the brains and the tools to find the missing piece of the jigsaw she did.

The desk phone rang, and Anna almost stopped breathing when she saw the identity of caller. She almost had to force her hand to reach out and pick up the phone.

'Hello Maria,' she said, trying to sound friendly.

'Hello Anna,' said Maria, as though they were the best of friends. 'How are you?'

'Fine, busy, lots to do, you know.'

'Of course. Look, Anna, I just wanted to give you a heads-up. There's a lot of activity supporting the search for the kidnapped Head of Section, I'm sure you know that.' Anna had to stifle a sarcastic reply.

Cho continued. 'We need all hands on deck for this, so it's likely that you'll have to come back to Cheltenham.'

Anna was speechless. It was true, she didn't need to be in London to run the search programs or to access any of the surveillance systems. She could even have piloted the drones from Cheltenham. But if she left London she'd lose touch with Michael and with Eric. It was only because she'd been close that she'd been able to get the Head's SIM card so quickly. It took her a moment to realise that despite all her misgivings, she was now thinking how much she wanted to stay in the field and not return to the Doughnut.

'I, er, well, yes, um…' was all she could manage to say.

'Nothing's decided,' said Cho, 'just wanted to let you know. Bye.' The line went dead.

Anna stared at the screen, at the window showing the set-up of the search programs. Was it a wild goose chase? Even Michael admitted that searching for this mystery person wouldn't help find the Head. Anna had found the other mystery man, Major Turner, but now he wasn't mystery-enough, there was someone even more mysterious. Turtles all the way down. Perhaps Maria Cho had a point. Perhaps she would be better focusing her efforts on finding the Head. Which would be better, being a key player in helping Michael find his mystery man, or being a small cog in the big machine that found the Head? If they found the Head, they might be in time to save her life, maybe even two lives if they could find Jason Mason as well.

Anna clicked the button on the screen and set the search programs running, then turned her attention to looking for any trace of Julian Singh's servers. At least she had a tangible thread of evidence she could look for, one more needle in one more haystack in a slightly different field.

**

The image of the man stared out of the screen at her. The window on the screen showed the image of a formal photograph of a group of people, but one, in particular, stared out at Anna. She stared back at him. The computers said there was only a thirty-seven per cent probability that this man had any real-world connection with Major Liam Turner, who was also in the photograph but on the other side of the group. Anna stared at the man. He was the only result the computers had found. They may be only thirty-seven per cent sure, but he was a hundred per cent of the results found.

She looked at another window of information, at the few lines of data that summarised how and why the search algorithms had identified this man, the computer equivalent of "why him."

Anna looked at the phone, and then at the cursor on the screen, hovering over the Delete option. She knew that Michael had reasons for wanting to find this man, but even if he did it still wouldn't help find the Head or Mason, and their lives were in real danger. Surely if the man she was looking at wanted to send assassins after her and Eric, then he would have done so already. If this man posed a threat then surely it was a potential threat? Or a low probability of a threat? The Head and Mason were in real, mortal danger. The Three would almost certainly kill them, and soon, if they hadn't already.

She looked again at the phone. She knew that as soon as she told Michael he would go after the man, he would even ignore orders to find the Head in order to go after this man, and so she looked again at the cursor on the screen and the Delete button.

Another window on the screen was still largely blank. The programs running searches for evidence of the computer server that Singh had (probably) acquired had still not found anything. Looking for the digital footprint of that machine was like looking for one specific fish in the Atlantic ocean. It was there, but finding it was more than a little challenging. If she could search a little more specifically she might be able to find something. Trying to monitor all Internet traffic was beyond the capacity of the GCHQ computer systems, or at least beyond the capacity that she was able to draw on.

The desk phone rang. It was Michael. She put on the headset and answered the call.

'Any news?' he asked, making no attempt at courtesy or politeness. Her hand moved a little towards the mouse.

She sighed. 'I found someone,' she said.

'Who?'

'The computers show only a thirty-seven per cent chance that this man actually has a real connection with Turner.'

'What about the other results?' Michael asked.

'There are no other results, this is the only one the systems found.'

'So who is he?' From the sound of it, Michael was having a bad day.

'Yves Falcone,' said Anna. 'Falcone, French for falcon, it's the only connection the system could locate.'

'So how is he connected?' asked Michael.

'He's a non-executive director of three companies.'

'Any connection to the military?'

'He's a non-executive director of a specialist engineering company which supplies the nuclear industry and has done some work for AWE. He's also on the board of a drug company and on the board of an investment bank.'

There was a pause, no doubt as Michael thought through each of the three possible connections.

'Can you dig into the AWE connection?' asked Michael, a little more softly than before. 'Any connection to Susskind. And, has the investment bank been involved in any nuclear-related deals, arms deals, anything like that?'

'I'll search. Much of this is going to be classified, so if it's there, I'll find references to it, probably not the detail itself.'

'Okay. Where do I find this Yves Falcone?'

'Today he's at the London office of the drug company he works for. I'll text you the address.' Anna paused, knowing what the answer would be to her next question. 'You're going to see him, aren't you?'

'Have you found anything else? Any other leads to chase down?'

'No,' she had to admit

'Then I have to go and see him,' said Michael, and hung up.

***

The pedestrian traffic was slightly less dense than at rush hour, but there was still a tide of people to battle against. Michael always felt they were going the opposite way to him, no matter which way he was walking. It was very tempting to shoulder-barge as they pushed past him, but he also knew that would invite trouble, and he could hardly afford any more trouble.

He and Eric had returned to Thames House, The Office, but as soon as they arrived, Eric had been summoned to a meeting in a different department. Michael had, perhaps naively, expected to join the next mission briefing, but instead had been taken into a side room by the Acting Head of Section. The Acting Head had remained quite calm as he detailed Michael's recent "issues," and there seemed to be more than Michael remembered. It had been made quite clear that Michael was now assigned to desk duties only, and was forbidden from undertaking any field activities. In short, he'd been grounded. Michael doubted that he'd heard the end of this, but he hoped that he could find who was directing the Psiclone project and maybe even locate the Head before they finally threw the book at him.

Anna had given him the name and location of the mystery man, or the man who might be the mystery man, she hadn't guaranteed it, but this was a chance to discover who was behind the Psiclone project, and who was so keen to close it down, terminally. This was not a chance he could pass up.

He felt a vibration from the inside pocket of his jacket, and he knew who was calling him even before he looked at the phone. He had thought the Acting Head would have noticed his absence sooner, not that it made any difference. Once you've jumped out of the aeroplane, it doesn't matter how soon you notice you've not got a parachute.

'Yes Sir,' Michael said, answering the call.

'Since you're not at your desk, and no-one here can explain where you are,' said the Acting Head, 'I have to ask you, where are you?'

'I'm sorry Sir, but there's a lead I have to pursue, a chance of finding the Head, while there's still time.'

'We have an army of people in The Office, in the Doughnut and in the field all pursuing leads, Mr Sanders. Please tell me what is so special about your lead that it warrants you disobeying my explicit instructions.'

'I'm sorry Sir, but I can't tell you,' said Michael.

'Mr Sanders,' said the Head, more sternly, 'as your superior officer I am privilege to all information you are. There is no evidence you have that is secret from me.' It was evident from his voice that the Acting Head was finding it harder to remain calm.

'This relates to a military activity from some years ago, it is something I am not at liberty to discuss with you, Sir.'

'If it involved the Head of Section then it is something you are at liberty to discuss. Now, what is this lead?'

'Sir, I have a real chance to find her and maybe even find Jason Mason, and since not a single one of your army has made any progress whatsoever, I cannot, in all conscience, not follow this lead.' Michael was disappointed with himself at the anger that had become so apparent in his voice, his patience too was almost exhausted.

'Let me make this completely clear, Mr Sanders,' said the Acting Head, speaking more slowly. 'As of this moment, you are suspended. You are to return to Thames House immediately to face disciplinary proceedings.'

'I will return Sir, but not immediately,' said Michael.

'If you continue to disobey me I will have a warrant issued for your arrest.' The Acting Head hung up.

Michael stood still, and another pedestrian almost walked into the back of him. The young man barked an obscenity at Michael as he pushed past, but Michael didn't hear him. He stared at the red traffic light facing him. The crossroads was a major junction, cars and buses whisked past, pedestrians marched across the road, some skipped in between moving vehicles. The road extending away to the left led towards Piccadilly and Knightsbridge and to the offices of PanMedic. Michael looked right. He could walk back to Thames House. He doubted the Acting Head could actually have him arrested. He wasn't carrying a firearm and other than his mobile phone didn't have any MI5 equipment with him, so in the absence of Michael committing a criminal offence the Acting Head's threat was just an empty gesture.

He looked again at the crossroads. The age old decision; left or right? If he didn't find the Head then his career in MI5, such as it was, would probably be over, and with it any protection he ever had from the forces behind the Psiclone project. If he did succeed in finding whoever was behind the project he had no certainty they would talk to him, or answer any questions, or change his situation in any way. This was a messy situation. The fight was unclear, the enemy uncertain, the dangers unseen. He'd led his men into this mess, was there any way to make things right again? Or at least make other people safe from being killed?

His musing was shattered by a double decker bus that appeared from the right and rushed past, almost clipping the kerb and coming uncomfortably close. As the red menace belched a cloud of diesel fumes at him. Michael looked up at the advertisement on the back. Set against a stylised graphic of a cloud and sunbeams was a Biblical quote:

"Ask, and it shall be given you; seek, and ye shall find; knock, and it shall be opened unto you."

The bus grunted its way down the road. Michael sighed. 'Okay, I get the hint, I'm asking,' he said to no-one in particular. He turned left and walked, walking like a man on a mission.

Eighteen

London - Wednesday, early afternoon

As Michael neared Centurion House, PanMedic's London office, he wondered how he was going to get inside, and realised that he hadn't planned his approach at all. All his training and experience had suddenly seemed irrelevant. He had no idea how he would explain his presence or what he wanted or why anyone should let him in.

The building looked to be of dark brick with dark windows, an office building like any other office building, but as he got closer, he saw that it was marble, not brick. This was a building for tenants with money, lots of it, who needed a prestigious office in the centre of London. The front doors were heavy with glass panels and brass-like fittings, and he could see into the marble floored foyer. A marble lined desk was placed to face visitors and a smartly dressed individual sat behind the smart desk.

He had half expected the door to be locked, with entry requested via an intercom, but when he pulled on the door it swung smoothly open, and he walked inside. The young lady behind the desk stood and smiled at him.

'Good morning Mr Sanders,' she said, 'welcome to Centurion House.'

This was turning out to be a day of surprises.

'Good morning,' said Michael, portraying as much of an air of confidence as he could manage.

'Mr Falcone has asked that you go straight up to his office,' said the young lady, gesturing to the lifts on the far side of the foyer. 'Please go up to the fifth floor and you will be escorted from there.'

Michael walked towards the lifts, and as he past it, he read the list of the building's occupants. Floors five and six were PanMedic, presumably the drug company of which Yves Falcone was a non-executive director. The lift door opened as he approached. Had the spider ever spun a more inviting web for the fly? He entered the lift and pressed the button for the fifth floor.

The lift glided almost noiselessly upwards, and the doors swished open at the fifth floor. The decor of the corridor was sombre but expensive. A heavy wool carpet, wallpaper that may as well have been woven from banknotes, heavy brass light fittings. Dark wood panelled doors led no doubt to offices occupied by rich and powerful people. A man in a dark yet immaculate business suit stood waiting to greet Michael. The man made no attempt to shake hands but bowed his head ever so slightly.

'Good afternoon, Mr Sanders,' said the man. 'Mr Falcone is ready to receive you now.' He gestured with one hand to the door at the end of the corridor. Michael contemplated the door, but when he turned around the man was already walking away from him and then disappeared into one of the offices.

To enter, or not to enter? That is the choice. He'd come this far, and perhaps the only man who could give him answers might be in that office. Michael had considered whether it might be a trap, but had fairly quickly concluded that if whoever was behind all this wanted Michael out of the way then they would just do that, they had no need of elaborate traps. He drew his shoulders back, took a breath, and walked to the office door. He grasped the handle, turned, and entered.

The office was as plush as the corridor. It might have been part of a stately home, and for a moment it reminded him of a darker more sombre version of Liam Turner's office in Whitehall. The carpet was a deep, heavy red. Cabinets adorned one wall, paintings on another. The office was only lifted by the light from the window and the view of the almost stereotypical London skyline. Yves Falcone had been sitting behind the desk but was now standing to greet Michael. He was an older gentleman, thinning grey hair, smartly dressed, small but undoubtedly expensive cufflinks. He gestured to the chair facing the desk.

'Good morning Captain Sanders, please sit,' said Falcone. 'I'm sure you'll understand if I don't offer to shake hands.' Falcone sat in his grandiose chair behind the desk.

Michael sat down, still wondering which question to open with, or whether he need ask any questions at all.

Falcone continued. 'I'm sure you have many questions, and I'll answer some of them, but I doubt it will be a surprise when I tell you that I won't answer all of your questions.'

Michael smiled and waited for Falcone to continue.

'Once you'd been to see Major Turner it was only a matter of time before you arrived here,' said Falcone, 'so I assume that you're starting to understand some of the players involved in our little game.'

'Game?' said Michael, almost as an accusation, 'this "game" has already cost a lot of people their lives.' Michael struggled to bring himself back under control. This was an encounter he was going to have to manage through intelligence, not force.

'People have been killed only because of Mr Marshall and his associates,' said Falcone. 'They were never supposed to leave the project and go freelance, but once they did, they threatened everyone with exposure. Do you think their activities have gone unnoticed by foreign intelligence services?'

'I doubt anyone's missed their activities,' said Michael, 'but so far no-one's tried to abduct me or my team.'

'And your attitude to this makes we wonder if you understand just how real that threat is. We don't believe that as yet any foreign power has put the pieces together and concluded that Mr Marshall and his associates have advanced telepathic powers. After all, any intelligence analyst taking such a conclusion to their superiors would need a very convincing case to be taken seriously. But what do you think it would take to make someone suspicious enough to start keeping a very close eye on them, and on you?'

Michael hadn't expected this and had to admit (to himself) that it was a question he hadn't considered. He knew the threat of exposure was real, but he'd only believed it a theoretical risk, he'd never thought what might give them away.

'Imagine a scenario where a senior Bank of England IT manager suddenly starts co-operating with Marshall and friends, to the point of helping them commit major theft. An insurance company effectively hands them the keys of a brand new data centre. A scenario where Julian Singh simply walks in through the front doors of the exVoxx company, despite being one of the most wanted men in the country. Might this perhaps come to the attention of the CIA? Or the Russian SVR? Or the Chinese MSS? Might they become curious about how three individuals were able to carry out such activities? What would happen if they interviewed any of the people who were a part, or a victim, of these activities? How quickly do you think they would conclude that there was something going on worth finding out about?'

'I imagine they would come to that conclusion quite quickly,' said Michael, not wanting to play too easily into Falcone's game.

'Yes, we believe at least one of them already has come to that conclusion,' said Falcone.

Michael considered this. Trying to find the Three was proving difficult enough, trying to fend off doubters on his own side was simply making things even more difficult. If he also had to avoid agents of a foreign security service then finding the Head might just become impossible. He felt more and more like an ant watching elephants fight, and in that scenario the ant was at a disadvantage.

'We'd like this whole mess wrapped up as quickly as possible,' said Falcone, 'before anyone has a chance to go digging any deeper into the shit pile. I still believe you have a chance of sorting all this out for us, am I right to put my trust in you?'

'Are you the person whose trust I need to worry about?' asked Michael.

'Your MI5 Head of Section trusted you, at least enough to fight your corner. So far I've believed in her judgement, but I'm not the only person involved in this project. Major Turner has his own opinions about how problems should be sorted, as I think you've already discovered.'

'So Turner sent the soldiers after us?'

'You can't trust anyone these days, I'm afraid,' said Falcone.

'So what's your role in this?' asked Michael.

'Mr Sanders,' said Falcone, feigning disappointment, 'you haven't worked it out yet? Who the key players are?'

'Turner's obvious, he's the senior officer behind the recruitment of soldiers into the original programme. The MI5 Head of Section is part of the project either to maintain its security or because it's actually an MI5 project not a military project. And you, perhaps you financed the project?'

'I'm afraid you're wrong on almost every count, Captain,' said Falcone, leaning back in his chair. 'I thought you were brighter than that. Perhaps you're not worthy of our trust after all.'

Michael stared at Falcone for a long moment. 'How high does this go?' Michael asked. 'How high up the chain of command does this go?'

'I'm sorry to disappoint you, Captain,' said Falcone. 'This isn't some huge government conspiracy. In fact, we've worked very hard to make sure no-one anywhere near the government knows anything about this. Anonymity is our protection, and we can only maintain that if we stay as small as possible. Security through obscurity, you might say.' Falcone allowed himself a slight grin.

Michael shot out of his chair, hands on the desk and leaning over towards Falcone. Falcone pushed his chair backwards smoothly, just a few inches, enough to stay out of Michael's reach. Michael had wondered if Falcone was telepathic, and if he was how powerful he was. Was this the man who'd exerted such a degree of control over Turner? Or was this another puppet? Was there still someone else pulling all the strings?

'Why don't you stop playing games and just tell me straight what's going on,' he hissed, 'or maybe I'll come to the conclusion that actually you're supporting Marshall and the others and that you're the one I need to get rid of.'

'Sit down, Captain Sanders,' said Falcone, not flustered in the slightest by Michael's aggression. 'As with any operation of this nature, information is given on a need-to-know basis, and frankly you don't need to know. I don't care if you know who has what role, I do care if you're able to stop Marshall, Bullock and Singh before they achieve their plan, whatever it is. Please consider, they've gone to a very great deal of trouble and are still going to a very great deal of trouble, to execute a plan. I hope you have some insight into what that plan is because I have absolutely no doubt that if you fail and they succeed that we will all very much regret it. I have no doubt that they did not come here just to rob a bank, they are after something much more damaging than that.'

'They're possibly after nuclear material, even a nuclear device,' said Michael, not wanting to divulge too much of what he knew, or how little he knew.

'There are much worse things that they could get their hands on,' said Falcone.

'Like what?' asked Michael.

'I think it's time you turned your attention to stopping them, and stop trying to dig any further into this project. Stop them first, then perhaps I'll answer more of your questions, but I think it is now time for you to leave.'

'No,' said Michael, 'I think it's time you answered a few more of my questions. What exactly is the Head of Section's role in this? You know why Marshall wants her, don't you?'

Falcone eyed Michael, staring into him. Michael considered how he could get close to Falcone, close enough to make physical contact and establish a telepathic link. He also considered that Falcone had no doubt thought about this and was being self-assured simply because he was confident that Michael could not reach him.

'I think perhaps,' said Falcone, 'that you ought to take a look at this.' He picked up a dark leather document folder. It had a design embossed into the leather, and was tied closed with a black ribbon, all very theatrical. 'This might answer the question that drove you here.' Falcone reached forward and offered the folder to Michael. Michael leant forward and took the folder.

The world around him exploded as telepathic energy poured out of the folder and into his mind. All he could feel was that he was being washed away, helpless to fight against an almighty tide, a huge and overwhelming torrent of energy. He tried to breathe but couldn't, his head pounded as the world around him went black. He had a sense of falling, of being lost, and wanting to escape this nightmare. The blackness swelled over him and through him, sweeping away his thoughts, leaving only a primitive and desperate desire to survive, until even that faded out and there was nothing.

***

Anna put the phone down and stared at it. Maria Cho had been unusually short and abrupt. Her message had been clear. Anna was expected back in Cheltenham in two days. Tomorrow was to be her last day in London and she would be expected to wind down all her activities there before rejoining the team in the Doughnut. Anna didn't know whether to cry or celebrate. She had no more clues to finding the Head, no more ideas about where to look. She had one lead to look for, the identifier for the server Singh might be using, but she had the whole of the Internet to look in. She'd found Michael's mystery man, but she had no faith that this individual would point the way to finding the Head, or Jason Mason. Was Mason still alive? Was the Head still alive?

She looked out at the window, at the building opposite. The GCHQ office had no majestic London skyline to look at, just the brown bricks of the office block opposite them. Anna had the thought that she wasn't going to spend another day just looking at the office block across the street, she would at least do something to try and make a contribution. She picked up the phone and dialled Kingston's extension.

'Long time no hear,' he said. 'How's life in the smoke?'

'Horrid,' she said, not meaning it, not completely. 'Not making much progress. You?'

'Same old same old,' he said. 'I'm now on analysing mobile phone traffic from around the kidnapping. Can't say I'm holding out hope of finding anything.'

'I don't even know where to start,' said Anna, realising how much her voice betrayed the low ebb of her feelings.

'What, don't know which bit of evidence to look at, or don't know where to follow it?'

'I don't think we've even got any evidence.'

'Then what have you been doing?'

It was a very good question. Anna wondered, what had they been doing? Chasing ghosts? Every lead they had chased had been a ghost. Most of her thinking had been around chasing digital ghosts, the footprints of servers and Internet messages.

'They set her up,' Anna said. 'Marshall and the others, they set a trap for her.' She realised she had spoken quietly, either to hide her confession from the others in the office or because it felt like she was admitting failure.

'If they set a trap, there must have been bait,' said Kingston. 'Bait is evidence. Always start with the evidence.' There was a pause. 'It's Cho. Got to go.' He hung up.

Evidence. Kingston was right, he always was. Start with the evidence. What evidence? Anna tapped at the keyboard and brought up the image of the man in the street holding the folder which said "Psiclone." That was evidence. It was the bait the Head had followed straight into the trap. So where to follow this piece of evidence? It didn't lead anywhere, nowhere obvious. A thought tickled the outer edges of Anna's consciousness. No, it didn't lead anywhere, and it didn't come from anywhere. It had just appeared, as had the other image. If the evidence didn't point to any obvious direction to follow, then examine the evidence in more detail. Perhaps this digital ghost had left a real footprint, a real and tangible clue as to where it came from.

It took Anna a few moments to dig around, electronically, and bring up the various logs of activity from servers and communications routers and the like. Everything that happened inside the GCHQ computer network was recorded; which computer sent which message to where and when. She looked at the logs relating to the image. Most of the information was just lists of numbers, identifying each of the servers the image had passed through, and various identifiers on the message as it had made its way through the GCHQ network.

Anna realised, slowly, that it was staring her in the face. She was looking at the image on the screen, the image of the man carrying the folder, in the street. Next to the image was the window of computer information. It was there, right in front of her, but it only dawned on her slowly that she was looking directly at it. Like most CCTV images, the picture had the small black box in the bottom corner. White numbers showed the date and time and frame number of the video image. In the window on the computer were the dates and times the image had been logged on each of the different servers. Anna stared at the date and time the image had entered the GCHQ network, when the message containing the image had passed through the GCHQ firewall. It was two seconds before the image on the screen. How could an image have appeared in their network two seconds before it had been taken?

It was possible, probable, even likely, that the clock in the CCTV system was wrong, that this was a simple case of a clock being two seconds slow or fast, but it was still very curious. Anna started digging. She looked at the other image of the man, it too had appeared in their system two seconds before the image had been taken, supposedly. Anna carried on digging through the screens of information. Where had the image come from? Even messages entering the network had identifying information, the IP address of the server it had come from, the encryption certificate, the entry in the routing-table which had forwarded the message to its destination. There it was, on her screen, the logical equivalent of a smoking gun. The message had come directly through the GCHQ firewall, with an exVoxx security certificate, and the identifier number of the server she suspected Singh of using. The evidence led her directly to their own front door, real and meaningful evidence of what their enemy had been doing.

But then she froze, she realised she'd stopped breathing as she came to understand the meaning of what she was looking at. The evidence led to their own front door, but the evidence told her more than that, and what it told her was terrifying. They hadn't kidnapped Mason to hack a site protected by exVoxx, they'd kidnapped him so they could hack the exVoxx network itself, and they had succeeded. They could reach inside the GCHQ network, they could pass through its front doors without worrying about all the defence mechanisms in place. The image had appeared from nowhere because Singh had been able to reach inside their network and simply place it there. And if he could do it there, he could do it to any site protected by exVoxx, potentially almost any military or government system in the world.

She started thinking, what other evidence did they have? She ran through all the conversations she'd had with Michael, and with the Head. She replayed the kidnapping in her mind, thinking through what she'd seen, what evidence had been logged. She thought about what Michael had been doing, about his concern that the project would be discovered by foreign forces, about how this mystery man was hiding in the shadows, able to order their deaths if they became too much of a risk. She knew the man's name, Yves Falcone, but what was his connection? He had to have a connection. He was involved in a drug company, a nuclear engineering company and an investment bank. Two, potentially all three, would have computer systems protected by exVoxx.

Anna picked up the phone and called Kingston. She spoke before he'd had chance to even say 'hello.'

'I'm following the evidence,' she said, 'but I need help. I need to find out more about someone. I can't tell you who, but he's involved in various companies. I haven't got time to monitor all the sites of all the companies, how do I find…' She realised that with Falcone she didn't know what she was looking for.

'How do you find what?' asked Kingston.

'I don't know,' said Anna, 'I'm not sure I even know what I'm looking for.'

'Do I need to tell you again?' said Kingston, teasing. 'Start with the evidence. Is there any connection between this person and any evidence that you have currently?'

'Thanks,' said Anna, 'I'll look.' She hung up and stared again out of the window. What connection could there be between Falcone and the image of the man? It's not like she could phone him and ask him.

This time, the idea hit her like a bolt out of the blue. It appeared in her mind in a flash, a huge surge of realisation, and a big wave of relief that something so obvious had occurred. She couldn't phone Falcone, but perhaps someone else could have. She could access a lot of communications data on Michael's calls, Eric's, various MI5 field agents and vehicles, and the Head. She had the SIM card from the Head's phone. All she had to do was search the communications logs of all these people and see if any of them had made or received any calls anywhere near any of the sites run by any of the companies with which Falcone had a connection. At least it would keep her busy.

***

Yves Falcone hadn't meant to fall asleep, but sitting back in his chair his mind had wandered as he went over and over what had been said with Sanders. No-one would disturb him, his secretary would screen any calls and he had no more visitors planned. He wondered if he'd said too much, or had he not said enough and would Sanders be back? Without being aware of it his thoughts had started to drift and soon he was in a light sleep. He wasn't aware of dreaming, but he was aware of a feeling, and then a voice. He was aware of the voice and it sounded familiar.

He woke suddenly as he realised the voice was all too familiar.

'Yves,' said the voice. He didn't hear the voice so much as just know what the voice was saying. He stared into the empty room, convincing himself that the room was empty, and that the voice really was coming directly into his mind. He tried to suppress the thought that he wished the voice would stop, but perhaps the speaker of the voice could hear that thought. If it could, it said nothing about it. The voice, His voice, came directly into Yves' mind, and Yves could do nothing to stop it.

'Yves,' said the voice again. 'You did well with Sanders.' No doubt He had been aware of the encounter with Sanders. Was there anything He wasn't aware of?

'He'll be back,' Yves said out loud, knowing He would hear/sense the words.

'No, I don't think he will,' He said.

'He doesn't know what Marshall is doing,' said Yves.

'No, I don't think he does, which is unfortunate.'

'Will he find her before they kill her?' Yves had tried not to think of what Marshall and the others might do to their captives, or what they might have done already.

'I'm not sure that he will, but if he doesn't that will take care of a problem for us,' He said.

'Why? Why does there have to be more killing?' pined Falcone.

'This is a terrible situation,' He said, in an almost soothing manner. 'And we both know that some terrible things must be done to make sure we keep it all under control.'

'You could find them, you could reach out and find Marshall and the others, couldn't you?'

'Yes, Yves, I could. And if I did they would sense me, and we both know that they must remain completely ignorant of my role in this,' said the voice.

'But you could find them, you could know what they're doing, then you could just have Turner's men move in and just get rid of Marshall and the others, then all this would be over.' It sounded so reasonable to Falcone, it was simple, it could all be made to go away so easily, this whole mess. He tried to close his mind to it, to all the killing, to how it had all gone so wrong.

'No, Yves. I couldn't. Marshall and the others have become too powerful. If I found them I'm not sure that Turner's men could defeat Marshall on their own, and how would you explain to Sanders how you suddenly knew the location of Marshall? Sanders is just as ignorant of my role. He too must stay ignorant, until this is all cleaned up.'

'You mean until you've had them all killed,' shouted Falcone. He hadn't meant to shout but the anger just burst out of him. There was a silence. Perhaps He was waiting for Falcone to calm down. Falcone stood up and walked around the desk, taking care to walk around the document folder which still lay on the floor where Sanders had dropped it when he fled the office. Falcone stared down at it for a moment, and then began pacing round the office.

'If we knew what Marshall was doing we'd find a way of tipping off Sanders, just enough to let him find Marshall and take care of things,' said Falcone. He was sure he could see how this could be done.

'No, Yves,' said the voice, in a stronger tone. 'I will not make contact with Marshall, I will not allow them to become aware of me, even if that means I do not know their specific plans. Sanders will find them, he will engage them in battle, and when he does

Turner will send in his men and this will all be taken care of.'

Falcone completed a circuit of the office and stood facing the window, looking out over London.

'Be strong, Yves,' He said. 'This will all be over soon.' Falcone felt the surge of energy, of His mind connecting directly with his own. He wanted to resist, to argue, but it was simpler, easier, just to give in, to allow His mind to make everything clearer. Falcone soon forgot about arguing, and it all became so clear and simple, and he could see how He was right, how He was always right.

***

It kept her busy for three minutes. The flashing red indicator on the screen showed that one of the search algorithms had found a match, and it was the algorithm she'd started only moments before. The SIM card from the Head's phone had registered a call made from the same cell tower that covered the PanMedic research facility in Hampshire.

So the Head had some connection with PanMedic, the drug company of which Yves Falcone was a non-executive director. Falcone was, possibly, connected to Major Liam Turner, who had made a covert call of his own to the Head using an MI5 dark channel. All of this was a series of tenuous links, the chance of one possibility being connected with another possibility. Michael had yet to confirm that Yves Falcone was in fact related to any of this, but the series of connections was becoming too consistent for it all to be just random chance or coincidence.

Anna got to work. She now had a target. She knew that Singh had used the server supplied by Roger Foreman to hack into the GCHQ network, perhaps he'd used the same server to access the PanMedic facility. She started accessing Internet routers and hubs in the area of the PanMedic facility, looking for the tell-tale signature of the server. She brought more and more search systems and surveillance systems online. No doubt Cho would have a very stern telling-off to deliver when she found out that Anna was not winding down her activities, but was, in fact, using more and more GCHQ resource to pursue her wild goose chase. But the goose was almost found, Anna had the growing sense that she was nearing her target, and realised that she was getting excited. This was more than a game, it had become more than a rewarding intellectual activity, she might actually be getting closer to saving someone's life.

The information presented on the screen was both rewarding and disappointing. There was the signature of Singh's server, on packets of encrypted Internet traffic directed at the PanMedic network, along with security certificates and authentication messages from the exVoxx network. Singh was using exVoxx to enter the PanMedic computer system. There was only one thing Anna couldn't determine, and that was where the messages had come from. She knew they came from a data hub only a few miles from the PanMedic facility, but she had no way of knowing where they came from before they got to the hub, not without being able to access the routing-table from the hub. Each hub acted like a telephone exchange for Internet messages, directing them to the right recipient, often the next hub in the chain, before they reached their final destination. The routing tables were temporary records of where messages had come from and where they had been sent. Anna knew there was only a limited opportunity to access the table and trace Singh's messages. Her problem was, the hubs were extremely well secured, and not even GCHQ could just tap into them and read the tables. Perhaps, with time, she could find a way in, but time was not on her side. She needed someone who could effect a more direct entry.

She rang Michael's phone, but it went straight through to voicemail. She didn't leave him a message.

She rang Eric's phone, and after a couple of rings he answered.

'Well this is a pleasant surprise,' said Eric.

'Hello,' said Anna, in a more cheery voice than she'd intended. 'How are you?' She suddenly thought what a lame way that was to start the conversation.

'My day's going from dull to disappointing,' said Eric, 'I'm working with someone else now, and she's not exactly Miss Charisma.'

'I'm sorry to hear that,' said Anna. 'Eric, I need a favour,' she said, dropping into a more serious tone of voice, and explained what she'd found and what she needed.

'Wow,' said Eric, 'that's not a small favour.'

'Sorry. I know it's a big ask,' said Anna.

'Yes, breaking and entering, ranks along some of the bigger favours you could ask.' Anna resisted the temptation to make a flippant comment about what kind of favour he'd like her to ask. This wasn't the time.

'I know,' said Anna, 'but it's the only way to find out where Singh's Internet traffic came from, it will tell us where they are, where the Head is.'

'Will it?' asked Eric, and Anna's heart sank a little. She knew she couldn't say for definite, it might point back to just another hub. 'As it happens, that hub is not far from where I am,' said Eric. 'But there's no way I can leave this operation. If I get chance I'll see what I can do.'

'Please,' said Anna, 'it's the only chance I've got, and I can't tell anyone else, they'll just ask too much about all the stuff we can't talk about.'

'I have to go,' said Eric, and Anna could hear voices approaching him in the background. 'You're going to owe me big time for this.' The line went dead.

Anna hoped this wasn't going to be a case of so-close-yet-so-far. She had to find a way of getting that routing-table, it was now their only chance of finding where Marshall, Bullock and Singh were currently holding the Head, whose time must now be running out.

***

Julian Singh was relieved that there was little traffic on the main road running past the PanMedic research facility. The big blue glass construction was in ugly contrast to the green fields, and for a moment Singh wondered how anyone had achieved planning permission for such a thing. The driver slowed to give Singh a better view of the building on the opposite side of the road. He could see the occasional person walking in or out of the main doors, the entrance to the lion's den.

The driver pulled up only a short way past the building, and Singh got out. As arranged the car drove away and would soon be lost in the traffic. He pulled his cap down to cover as much of his face as he could, without looking like he was hiding. He knew that there were no public CCTV cameras in range of the building, but the facility itself was bristling with surveillance. He checked the road and crossed over, fiddling with the ID badge that hung around his neck.

Bullock and Marshall were at the farmhouse, no doubt waiting for him to communicate with them, to either tell them telepathically that he'd been successful or to warn them they needed to escape. He drew a deep breath, it was his neck on the line for this operation. Unlike Marshall's abduction of Mason, if things went wrong he would have nowhere to run, he would likely be trapped inside the building, cornered like a rat. No, like a tiger, and like a tiger, he'd tear apart anyone who tried to capture him.

He looked ahead and focused on the front door. Now was the time to put aside any concerns about what might happen and to focus solely on the task at hand. As he walked towards the front doors, he was joined by a couple of people from the car park. They were deep in discussion with each other and seemed to pay him no attention.

The pair walked ahead of him, and in turn, they presented their ID badges to the scanner and the doors slid open to allow them entry. Singh stepped forward. He held out his ID badge to the scanner, and there was a muted beep to confirm his badge had been read. A green light flickered on the scanner, and the doors slid open. He walked inside.

There were fewer people inside than he expected, and no reception desk, no receptionist. This was a building where the only people who gained entry were those who were supposed to be there and who knew where they were going. He looked to one side and saw the lifts. He walked over and pressed the lift call button. The doors slid open, and he entered. He pressed the button for the fourth floor and again presented his ID badge to the scanner. Beep, flicker, the doors closed and the lift began its journey up to the fourth floor. Now he was in, and now he was trapped if anything went wrong. If anyone suspected him, they could cancel his ID badge, and he'd lose all ability to leave the building.

The doors slid open, and he stepped out into the fourth floor. It was almost familiar, the laboratory space, the smell of chemicals, the muted rush of the air extractors inside the fume cabinets. People worked at the various benches, hunched over racks of test tubes or computer terminals. No-one looked up, no-one noticed him.

On the far side of the laboratory space, he could see the doors, and he walked to them. Set into the wall beside the doors were a keypad and a badge scanner. He presented his badge and the green light flickered. He entered his code. This was where he would find if his exVoxx access really had allowed him to set up his own code against this "borrowed" badge. A red light blinked and a muted buzz told him the code had not worked. He tried again with the code, red blink, buzz. He looked at the keypad, and somehow it looked strange, the keys were wrong.

Then it dawned on him. In her imagined/hallucinated guided tour of the facility the Head had been clever, she'd been strong, she'd tried to mislead them. She had shown him the keypad upside down, and here it was the right way up, the keys in the opposite orientation. He typed in the code, paying attention to each numbered key. Green light, beep, the doors swept open.

Beyond the doors was a long corridor, the bridge from the main building across to the separate building, a secure facility inside a secure facility, walls within walls. All this security was impressive, but it simply screamed that here lay something extremely precious. He looked behind him. All the laboratory workers were still focused on their work. No-one was looking at him. He settled himself. He'd told Marshall and Bullock to avoid any telepathic contact while he was in the building, he needed to be free of any distractions, yet he couldn't help feeling that someone was with him, close but unseen. He walked into the corridor. If he wanted to, now was the time to turn back. The other two would never know. He could say that what he came for wasn't here, or it had been moved, or too many people were in the way, or the code didn't work. He could invent any excuse, and they'd never know. If he wanted to avoid almost certain detection and capture he could turn around now.

He started to walk, and after only a few steps the doors slid closed. Step by step, one foot in front of the other. It felt like he was wading through water, his steps so slow and forced, and he realised that he was shaking slightly. He never shook, he was always calm and controlled, yet his stomach quivered, and his jaw rattled.

It wasn't worth it. It wasn't worth the risk. No matter what he was here for, it couldn't be worth the risk he was running. And only him, no-one else was running this risk, he was the only one here, the only one in danger, and for what? Some grand prize that Marshall had fixated on. He was risking his liberty, possibly his life, just to please Marshall?

He took a deep breath and calmed himself. No. He was here because what he was after was for him and for the others and was worth all the risks he had taken, and the risks the others had taken. He walked on.

Twice he stopped and looked behind him. Something wasn't right. He felt it. Not in any way he could explain, not even to himself, but he'd trusted his instincts often enough to learn when they were right. He continued to the end of the corridor, and another set of doors slid open automatically, and he entered the second building.

Just as he remembered it from the imagined/hallucinated guided tour it was another laboratory area, but with no people. It smelled the same. It sounded the same, but it didn't feel the same. He felt unsafe. Off to one side was the door that led to the inner laboratory area. He moved as quickly as he could, but it didn't feel quickly enough.

He pressed his badge to the scanner and entered the code of numbers and symbols. The doors slid open and he walked into the futuristic laboratory area. It was darker, most of the light coming from various computer screens and automated devices. This room too was uninhabited, but now Singh had the distinct impression that there was someone standing behind him. He turned around, knowing in his mind that he was alone, but unable to shake the feeling that someone was lurking in shadows, behind him, unseen.

He could see the workbench in front of him. It was so close. On the bench next to it was the equipment case, all exactly as the Head had shown them in her own mind. He willed his legs to move, but he was rooted to the spot. He tried one foot, then the other, but they were stuck to the floor. He became aware of a growing tightness around his chest. For a brief moment, he had the insane idea that he was having a heart attack, but heart attacks didn't (he believed) include paranoid delusions or hallucinations of being glued to the floor.

He shook his head and then shook himself from one side to the next, then projected his mind outwards into the empty space around him. In an instant he felt lighter, his feet came easily up from the floor, and he took a deep relaxing breath.

Singh marched over to the workbench and pulled open the door of the refrigerator. The sound of the alarm was unmistakable, it was distant, coming from the corridor and perhaps the main building, but he could hear it nonetheless. His time was now short, perilously short, but he was so close he wasn't going to stop now. He took out of the refrigerator the black case and put it and the equipment case into the lightweight backpack he'd carried in a jacket pocket.

From under his opposite arm, he pulled his pistol. Whoever he encountered first was going to be his shield and his guide to the nearest fire exit. No matter how secure the building was it was still visible from the road, visible to health and safety and fire inspectors, and so somewhere or other there had to be a fire evacuation route. On his own or in the wake of a large body count he didn't care, but he was leaving.

Nineteen

The gentle breeze blew the empty plastic back down the street, sending it sliding down the pavement as though free of any friction with the ground. The handle of the bag caught on the man's foot and hung there for a moment before a turn in the gentle wind picked it up again and sent it on its way.

The man stared at the bag as it wandered away down the street, and slowly started to realise that it was his foot the bag had caught on. How curious that the bag should choose him to catch itself on, to choose his foot. It was only then that he started to realise that he had another foot, and quickly noticed that he had a complete body, sitting on the cold hard concrete. He blinked a few times as though waking from a nap.

He looked around, and saw he was sitting in the doorway of a closed shop. The insides of the windows were covered with paper, a heavy wooden board had been screwed over the glass of the door, and a solid padlock secured the door shut. He looked at the street, none of it was familiar. He had no idea where he was. As he thought about it, he realised that he wasn't sure who he was, but he did know that his head hurt. He pulled his legs in and braced himself ready to stand, but realised that for the moment standing was beyond him.

For the moment the only thing he could think to do was look at his feet, which he found funny. He giggled to himself, which drew a curious look from a couple of the Londoners who passed him by, just another down-and-out in a shop doorway. His head still hurt, like someone had punched him. But they hadn't, had they? He stopped giggling as he remembered that he hadn't been punched. He remembered a leather folio, and a powerful psychic force the moment he touched it. It had been a more powerful telepathic assault than he'd ever experienced before, because he'd experienced telepathy before. He was Michael Sanders. The knowledge sort of floated back into his mind. More and more of the pieces of the jigsaw came together. He remembered the man's face as he handed over the leather document folder, and he remembered taking it, not suspecting that the object might have been infused with an enormous charge of telepathic energy.

That hadn't been the start of it. Things had happened before. He remembered walking to the office, but the time before that was hazy. He looked at his feet again, the feet that had got him to the office, but from where? Where had he been before that? And where was he going next? Because he needed to go somewhere, that much came back, the knowledge that he needed to go somewhere and do something, something important. But what? Anna would know. Anna! He remembered Anna, her voice, her face, her smile. Yes, he needed to see Anna, and he needed to tell her that he'd seen Falcone. The name came into his mind suddenly. Yves Falcone, and the name brought back more memories; the Psiclone project, Vince Marshall, the search for... Some of it was still hazy, but he knew he needed to tell Anna that he'd seen Falcone. Seen Falcone, and achieved what? He slumped back in the doorway.

He had to admit to himself that as far as he could remember (which at the moment was not far) he hadn't achieved anything. He'd spoken with Falcone, but without actually discovering much of importance. Overall he'd forgotten far more as a result of the psychic blast than he'd learnt in his chat with Falcone. Not only that, he'd wasted time. There was something else he needed to be doing, something urgent, something important. He had the feeling of a clock ticking, counting down, time running out. Time for what he wasn't sure, but whatever it was he'd wasted time learning nothing from Falcone. Which meant only one thing: he'd have to go back.

The thought brought with it a tidal wave of despair, of disorientation, the world around him starting to swim and turn. He focused on his feet, he stared at them, willing them to be still. He looked up and looked around him, up and down the street, forcing his brain to be aware of anything but the idea of going back to Falcone. It was clear that he couldn't go back and see Falcone. Whether Falcone was himself a telepath, Michael couldn't be sure, but he knew that Falcone was protected by an enormously powerful telepathic force. Michael knew in his bones that he couldn't go back.

If he couldn't see Anna and he couldn't see Falcone, what could he do? He could call Anna, he thought, so he took his phone from his pocket. It showed lots of missed calls, most from Anna and several from the Acting Head of Section. The Head. Everything about the kidnapping, the Head, the Three all came crashing back into his awareness. He felt dizzy and sick and leant to one side, ready to vomit. He breathed deeply and tried to keep himself calm until the feeling passed. He remembered everything now, as far as he could tell. He sat back and stretched out his legs.

Michael's awareness was jarred as someone walked past and, perhaps by accident, kicked Michael's foot.

'Bloody druggies,' muttered the passer-by without even looking down at Michael.

Michael was amused to find that he felt not a jot of anger or even annoyance at the kick, possibly because an idea had started to form in his mind. The comment, being called a druggie, had sparked something, the germ of an idea.

Drugs. Drug companies. PanMedic. It was no accident that Falcone had been in the office of PanMedic. True, he was also the non-executive director of a nuclear engineering company, but it was the drug company that was the significant factor. The idea, the understanding grew in Michael's mind, as did the realisation of why PanMedic was so significant.

Now he really did have to talk to Anna. He looked at his phone, but the screen was blank, and the phone unresponsive when he tapped the screen. He couldn't remember the last time he'd thought to charge it.

Michael looked at his feet.

'Sorry guys, but we're off again,' he said, to his feet.

***

The Audi Q7 was parked by the side of the road. It looked out of place in this part of town. It was too big, too flash. The people around here didn't drive cars like that. The driver sat in the car while the passenger stood on the pavement, leaning against the car, talking on her phone. The seven-seat SUV was dark, the windows were slightly tinted, and a keen observer would have noticed the wider than standard tyres, perhaps suggesting a more powerful than standard engine.

There were houses on each side of the roads which led away from this main road, houses with old furniture on the sad patches of grass in front. The cars parked along each road were all ten years old or more. The Audi was brand new. Most of the houses had satellite dishes, some no doubt had cable, almost all would boast two or three smartphones, and the occupants of all the houses would be astounded if they knew what equipment was packed into the Audi. Eric smiled when he thought what they'd think if they knew how much weaponry and firepower was on board.

Eric sat in the driver's seat and smiled very slightly. He liked the vehicle. He liked all the toys and equipment that came with the car. Unlike the Focus this car had almost every piece of equipment he could wish for. It also had more bullet-resistant Kevlar lining the body panels. (No-one in the Service ever thought of them as bullet "proof," nothing was ever completely proof against bullets.)

The front windows were both open slightly, allowing a pleasant breeze to blow into the car. He could have had the air conditioning on, but Eric often preferred to feel fresh air, even if it was heavy with vehicle fumes from the main road. He could hear part of the conversation his field agent was having on her phone. He hadn't decided if this was an improvement over working with Michael, or not. Michael Sanders was a very strange man, with a very strange past. Eric wasn't so sure what Sanders' future might be. A lot of bad things had happened in the short time he'd worked with Michael, but he had to concede that the man had achieved a lot as well. Marshall, Bullock and Singh were formidable, and Michael had defeated them once, with Eric's help.

However, Eric hadn't appreciated the reprimands and temporary demotion that had resulted from working with Sanders, and now he was working with a different field agent. Dominique Solas was tall, long legged, dark hair, and far too smartly dressed for this part of town. Her designer sunglasses sat on top of her well-styled hair. She and Eric were supposed to be locating someone who might have provided a mobile phone that could have been used somewhere close to the route the kidnappers might have taken after they'd abducted the Head of Section. Eric sighed when he thought how tenuous the lead was, and how desperate MI5 was getting in its so-far fruitless search for the Head. Was Anna's lead any more solid? Certainly Anna believed it was, and he'd come to appreciate her abilities, and her personality. His daydreaming was interrupted by Dominique Solas' voice.

'I have to say,' Eric heard Dominique say, 'she may be dead already.' Solas was discussing the lack of progress with a fellow field agent. 'She's been missing nearly twenty-four hours, no ransom demand, no contact.' Solas started pacing down the pavement.

There was a pause as Solas listened to the other agent speak, then she continued. 'I agree, they took her for a reason, and they've either got what they want or they haven't. Either way, I don't like her chances.'

Another pause and Solas blurted out a single laugh in response. 'No, no, there's no chance of rescuing her, not unless some superhero just flies in and saves her at the last moment.'

Eric tuned out of the conversation. He'd never had much time for people who took the negative line in thinking. For him, the Head was alive, and there was still a chance of finding her, and he'd keep on believing that until (no, unless) there was proof to the contrary. He sighed. His chances of making any positive contribution to the search-and-rescue seemed to be slipping away. Miss Stylish (that's how he'd come to think of Solas) seemed more focused on following orders and believing it to be pointless than in thinking of something useful and productive to do.

He took out his phone, tapped the screen a few times and brought up the message from Anna.

She'd sent him details of the data hub, where it was, what it did, floor plans, outlines of security measures, almost everything he'd need to get in, if he chose to. It was likely that Miss Stylish would soon want to get back to The Office, she was always keen to join the scheduled briefings and report her activities. Eric wasn't sure what progress they'd have to report, but no doubt she'd have lots of activity to talk about. He looked again at his phone. There wasn't going to be any time in her schedule to take a detour via the data hub, and certainly not without Eric going into a lot of detail about why it was important, which he had no intention of doing.

He picked a number from the phone's contact list and dialled.

'Hello,' said Anna, in a bright and cheery voice. 'Don't suppose you've got into the data hub yet?'

'Not yet,' said Eric. He paused, not quite sure how to confess that he wasn't entirely sold on the idea of breaking into the building. 'Remind me again why you need this thing from this hub.'

'It's the only tangible lead I've got,' she said. 'Someone's been using exVoxx to access the PanMedic facility, and whoever it is they're using a server supplied by the same person who sold servers to Singh for the data centre, someone who's managed to get into the exVoxx network, almost certainly with Jason Mason's help.'

'So where is this person? In this data hub?'

'No. Their Internet traffic is coming through the hub, but I can't tell where it's coming from before it gets to the hub. I need access to the hub's routing table. That will tell us where this person is.'

'Which is where they're holding the Head?'

'Probably. Possibly. I can't be sure, but it is the only real physical lead we've got.' Anna was starting to sound desperate, Eric thought.

'So all I need to do is get in and plug your magic USB device into any computer in the building?'

'Not quite,' said Anna. No, Eric thought it couldn't have been that simple. Anna continued, 'you need to plug it into any computer inside the secure area in the building. The computer on the reception desk won't work, but any computer inside the office area.'

'Then you take it from there?'

'If you leave it plugged in long enough I can find the routing tables and get a copy of the one I need.'

'Simples,' said Eric.

'Pardon?'

'Never mind. I'll see what I can do.'

He put his phone away and focused again on Solas, who was still on her phone. Eric was never sure how much of her phone use was agent-to-agent updates and how much was just social chat.

'It's simple,' he heard Solas saying, 'if we all just do our jobs and follow procedure we'll get the job done.'

Eric tuned out again. There was only so much of that he could stand listening to. His choice was simple. Not easy, but simple. If he did the hard thing, would he be doing it for himself? Or for the Head? Or Michael? Or Anna? Perhaps he was thinking too much about it. He took a deep breath. 'Once more unto the breach,' he said to himself. He pressed the buttons to wind up the windows, then started the engine. Solas turned to look at him, raising her eyebrows to question what he was doing, while still talking on the phone. She took a first step back towards the vehicle.

'Fortune favours the bold, or the foolish,' he said, again to himself. He put the Audi in gear and set off. He accelerated hard down the road, watching Solas shrink in the rear view mirror. Before she could do anything he'd turned the corner and she was out of sight.

The in-car phone rang, a muted warbling. Eric looked at the display. He was slightly surprised Solas had managed to call him so quickly, but he pressed the red phone icon and rejected the call. He didn't have the enthusiasm to try and explain to her what he was doing, he wasn't sure he even wanted to try and explain it to himself. He just hoped this was going to be a productive course of action. As he drove, he programmed the address of the data centre into the Audi's sat' nav'.

***

Bullock paced into the kitchen, again, and looked at the wall clock. He checked it against his watch, again, as though there was any chance either had lost track of time. Singh was late. Marshall sat on one of the bar stools, staring out of the window. Both wore lightweight casual jackets, each concealing an underarm holster. One of the puppet security consultants sat in the car outside, ready to take them away at the first sign of danger. Other plans were in place, other arrangements had been made. People were on standby to whisk them away at a moment's notice, should the need arise. So far there had been no sign of danger, or of Singh. He'd not made telepathic contact either. Both had expected a telepathic message once Singh left the PanMedic facility, to indicate success or failure. The facility was a civilian establishment, so it was unlikely that Singh would have run into armed guards, and certainly not run into trouble which would lead to his instant death, before he could warn them. Bullock walked out of the kitchen and back towards the lounge. Marshall continued to stare out of the window. He strained to hear the noise of any traffic from the road. If things had gone badly, he doubted any police or military force would advertise itself by using sirens. So far all he heard was nothing.

Their waiting was interrupted by the sound of car tyres on the gravel of the drive approaching the house. Marshall sensed the reaction of the man sitting in their waiting car; it was a sense of familiarity, a recognition of his own colleague and of Singh. Bullock marched into the kitchen, his hands loose by his side. They heard the car doors open and close, and in moments Singh walked in through the door, carrying the holdall.

'Where the fuck have you been?' asked Marshall, his voice measured but firm.

'Exactly where I needed to be,' said Singh. He lifted the holdall up onto the counter top.

'Were you followed?' asked Bullock, as though it were the most important question in the world.

'No, I wasn't followed,' said Singh, his tone indicating how stupid he thought the question was.

'So why no contact?' asked Marshall.

Singh looked at Marshall, just holding his gaze. Then he turned to look at Bullock. He pulled out one of the bar stools and sat down. 'She showed us how to get in alright, although she had tried to mislead us in a couple of ways,' said Singh.

'So why the silence?' asked Bullock, his nervousness still evident in his tone.

'Because something else happened,' said Singh.

'What else happened?' asked Marshall. 'No-one had any reason to suspect you. What happened?'

'There was someone else there.'

'What do you mean, someone else?' asked Bullock. Marshall shot him a glance, wishing he'd be quiet.

'There was another presence there, someone else was in that building, someone telepathic.'

No-one spoke. After a moment Singh continued. 'I could feel him, or her, not sure. They were strong, very strong. They knew I was there, they tried to scare me off. I could feel them hiding, trying to make me just give up, without any direct contact, but I knew they were there.'

'But you got the drug?' asked Bullock.

'Yes, I got it, but they knew that's what I was there for. When I got it, they triggered the alarm. That made getting out…interesting.'

'But you got out?' asked Bullock. Marshall and Singh both looked at him as he realised how stupid the question had been.

'It took some doing, but yes I got out, and yes I got back without being followed.'

'This other mind didn't stay connected?' Marshall asked.

'No. I think whoever it was, they were trying to hide, they didn't want me to know they were there, and certainly didn't want me knowing anything about them. But they were so powerful, it was a force I've never felt before. Being in that laboratory, it was like being in a dream, they were twisting reality.' Singh looked at the holdall. With slow and deliberate movements he pulled the zipper open and took out the two small black cases.

He opened one case. Set into the moulded foam were six hypodermic syringes complete with a supply of needles.

All attention turned to the second case. Twelve inches square, the solid plastic equipment case had the PanMedic logo embossed on the front. Singh opened the clips and swung open the top. They looked at the contents of the case.

Set into the foam were two rows of six glass phials, each containing a colourless liquid. They all stared at the phials. All their planning, all their work, all the risk and the danger had been for this. Their prize sat in twelve little glass containers. Marshall thought that at least one of them should have a label on saying "drink me," but he knew the drug had to be injected. Would it work? Had it all been worth it? Did they now have the drug which had made them all telepathic, and could now make them even more powerful?

'Do we take it?' asked Bullock. 'Is it safe?' Finally, he voiced the one question they were all thinking. 'It could be a trick.' They'd all thought it. Perhaps this was a trick, a trap. Perhaps this was a drug that would kill them, or rob them of their telepathic powers.

'We don't have a choice,' said Marshall, firmly.

'I think you'll find we do have a choice,' said Singh.

'No, we don't,' said Marshall. 'The game has changed. Sanders and the others aren't our concern anymore. What you found at PanMedic changes everything. If we take this, and it's a trap, we die. If we don't take it then we can't stop whoever was at PanMedic. They'll come for us. Sooner or later they'll come. We can kill Sanders any time, but not this new one. They almost got you.' Marshall looked at Singh.

For a moment Singh held his gaze, but then dropped his eyes back to the phials.

'Well I'm not going first,' said Bullock, taking a half step back away from the case and away from the phials and syringes.

'He's right,' said Singh. 'What I felt was a mind so powerful we've got no chance against them, not at the moment, and they don't want to be friends with us.'

'Then use your computer access, get Sanders to go in and kill them,' urged Bullock. Marshall and Singh almost looked at each other again, but didn't.

'I'll go first,' said Marshall. No-one argued with him. Singh reached for the first hypodermic. He attached a needle, picked up the first phial and drew a measure of the clear liquid into the syringe. Marshall rolled up his sleeve.

'They say fortune favours the bold,' said Singh.

'Just get on with it,' said Marshall. 'We do this, then we take care of her, then we go and deal with Sanders.'

Twenty

From the pocket of the very smart and very expensive coat hanging on the hat stand, Yves Falcone took a pair of leather gloves and put them on. With just his finger tips he picked up the leather document folder from where Michael Sanders had dropped it on the floor. He looked at the object, and then looked around the room, uncertain where best to place it. He walked around the desk, pulled open one of the drawers and put the case in the drawer. He pushed the drawer shut.

Unsatisfied, he opened the drawer again, and just as delicately took out the folder. He placed it on the desk. Falcone walked over to the drinks cabinet in the corner of the room. He opened the door of the cabinet and revealed the dark green of a solid metal safe. An old-style combination wheel was set into the front door of the safe. Falcone spun the wheel one way and then the other, and then twisted the handle and pulled the door open. He picked up the document folder from the desk, placed it inside the safe and shut the door, spinning the combination wheel. He slumped down in the chair behind the desk.

He felt it before he heard it. He was never sure whether he truly heard the voice. The words appeared in his mind, so it was as though he was hearing them, but he knew the voice had no physical presence, the words came to him, from one mind and into his.

'Yves,' said the voice, always calm and polite. 'There has been a development.'

Falcone wasn't sure what He meant, but he suspected that this development was not going to be good news.

The voice continued. 'Julian Singh broke into the facility.'

Falcone almost stopped breathing. He tried to think of all the things this might mean, but of course it meant only one thing.

'Couldn't you stop him?' Falcone asked.

'He is powerful, I wasn't aware of him until he was inside the building. I couldn't confront him directly,' said the voice.

'You could have had security stop him,' said Falcone.

'They tried to stop him leaving, but he was armed, he would have killed people…'

Falcone interrupted, sharply. 'That doesn't normally worry you,' he snapped, and then regretted it.

'It does, Yves, you know it does. But if Singh had killed people inside the facility it would have drawn the attention of the authorities, it would have risked exposure.'

'What was he after?' asked Falcone. The voice didn't answer, it didn't need to. Falcone knew only too well what Julian Singh had been after.

'He took a significant quantity of the drug. Soon they will use it and their telepathic powers will grow, they will become too powerful for anyone to stop. This cannot be allowed to happen.'

'No,' said Falcone, 'there must be another way.'

'There is no other way. You know what I want you to do. It is time we put an end to this. We must be decisive.'

'No, this has to stop, we can't go on killing people,' said Falcone.

'We will, and this will be the end of it. One last time, we must take firm action, we must be rid of this problem,' said the voice.

'But we don't know where Singh and the others are hiding,' said Falcone. 'If Sanders knew, he wouldn't have come here.'

'Michael Sanders does not know where they are, but I do. I connected with Julian Singh when he was inside the facility. I sensed his desire to return to where they are hiding. They will not be there for much longer, but for the moment I can tell you where they are and where to send the soldiers.'

'Please,' said Falcone, almost begging. 'No more, there must be another way.'

'This is the last time, Yves,' said the voice. 'We must take care of this, we must tie up all the loose ends. Michael Sanders, Vince Marshall, Evan Bullock, Julian Singh, Rosalind Garvey, and anyone else who has come into contact with the project. They must all be taken care of. Then there will be no more.'

'I can't do it,' moaned Falcone, sounding like a child not wanting to follow a parental directive, 'I'm tired of this, too tired.'

'I can help you, Yves,' said the voice. 'I can help you call Major Turner. I can tell you where to have him send the soldiers. I can help you tell him the people who need to be taken care of, and when we've done that there will be no more of it.'

Yves Falcone picked up his phone and dialled a long series of numbers. The numbers connected him with one secure communications system and then another, routing his call through a myriad of connections, and finally to an office in Whitehall.

***

Anna hadn't asked how Eric had got into the data hub, nor how he managed to get past security and into the main office area, nor how he had sneaked the USB device into a computer and then kept people occupied. She was, however, grateful that he had managed it. She had had time to access their file servers, locate the routing tables, and copy them onto her own system. She was about to pinch a copy of their activity logs when the connection was lost. Whatever Eric was doing had been interrupted.

With the information safely filed she got to work cross-referencing logs of activity to and from PanMedic's systems with the Internet traffic to and from the hub, looking for the telltale signature of the server Singh might be using. She was glad that the others in the London office had largely left her to get on with her own work. They'd been friendly enough, but also professional enough not to ask too many questions. The odd phone call from Maria Cho had been easy enough to dodge. Anna got the impression that Cho had much bigger problems to contend with. It did seem, however, that unless they had a breakthrough by the end of the day, Anna would soon be back in Cheltenham and would become one of Cho's bigger problems.

Cross referencing the logs was a time-consuming activity, laboriously comparing various spreadsheets, looking up values, having programs run pattern matching algorithms against huge files of data. She jumped and almost yelped when she realised Eric was standing next to her.

'What are you doing here?' she asked in a light-hearted way, glad that he was there. 'I thought you were off on some other assignment.'

'I am, and I'll need to get back,' he said. 'I don't suppose you've heard from Captain Fantastic, have you?'

'No,' said Anna. She wondered how much of her concern she should voice. After Michael had been gone an hour, she'd tried calling him every few minutes, but it always went straight through to voicemail. She hadn't left a message, knowing he'd see the missed calls. After that, she tried occasionally, but still without result.

'No, nor me,' said Eric. 'Was that stuff from the data hub useful?'

She tried to smile, but could see from his face that he knew she hadn't got far with the information. She didn't want him to think that the effort he'd gone to had been wasted, that perhaps he might also face disciplinary action because he'd done a favour for her. She nodded at one of the screens.

'The programs are still analysing the data,' she said, trying to give some encouragement.

'Okay. I need to go now,' he said. He hesitated for a moment, but Anna couldn't think of anything else to say. Eric turned and walked towards the door.

***

The walk back to the GCHQ London office had been a bit of a blur for Michael. At one point he did consider going back to The Office, but then thought the reception he'd get from the Acting Head of Section would likely be hostile, and unproductive. When he put his hand in his pocket, he was relieved that he still had his ID badge, and had no problem entering the building.

He pushed the doors open and walked into the office area, and almost walked into Eric who was coming towards him. Eric stopped in his tracks.

'You look like shit,' said Eric.

'Nice to see you too,' said Michael, and couldn't help but grin. Eric grinned back.

'No offence, but you look like you've been drinking for a week,' said Eric.

'No, no drink, I promise,' said Michael. The two of them walked over to Anna, who was standing and beaming a huge smile at him. She hesitated, arms reaching forwards, slightly, not sure if she should hug him. She did.

'You do look rough,' she said.

Eric pulled up a couple of chairs. He sat on one and Michael collapsed onto the other. Anna fetched a cup of water from the machine. Michael gulped it down like he'd been lost in the desert for a month. He gulped down another three cups.

'Please tell me you didn't run into Marshall or one of the others,' said Eric.

'No, not Marshall,' said Michael. He told them about Falcone, as much as he could remember about the visit to Falcone's office. He told them about the psychic assault, that it was so powerful he didn't remember leaving the office or how he got to the shop doorway. They had to gesture several times to Michael to keep his voice down, some of his explanation attracted inquisitive looks from others in the office.

'So this Falcone character's also got woo-woo powers?' said Eric, keeping his voice low.

'I'm not sure if it was Falcone,' said Michael. 'I'm not sure who it was. I don't think it was one of the Three, but I can't be sure it was Falcone.'

'If it wasn't Falcone,' said Anna, 'then logically it was someone else, there's someone else with,' she paused and looked around, 'special abilities.'

'There's something else,' said Michael. 'PanMedic is the key.'

'Yes, I know,' said Anna, in a triumphant voice. She explained about locating a call made by the Head very close to the PanMedic facility, and tracing the Internet traffic, and the data hub, and she was still waiting for the programs to find where the traffic had come from.

'It's more than that,' said Michael. 'PanMedic is what the Three are after.'

'Why? What do they want with a drug company? asked Eric.

'Oh no,' said Anna, a sudden look of worry falling across her face. She's obviously realised the significance of Michael's statement. 'They want the drug, don't they?'

'Yes,' said Michael. 'All that nuclear stuff was a feint. They're after the drug that made us all telepathic. If they get more of the drug, they'll get more powerful.'

'Then I think it's time we stop them,' said Eric.

'It's probably too late for that,' said Michael. 'If they haven't got it yet then they very soon will have. No, we need to find where they are, because as soon as they get it, they'll kill the Head.'

With timing that couldn't have been better, there was a beep from Anna's computer. She checked the screen, clicked with a mouse, tapped some keys, and sighed. Whatever the news was, it wasn't particularly good.

'Any news?' asked Eric.

'Yes, and no,' said Anna. 'I've traced the traffic from Singh's server. I can trace it back from the data hub, but only so far as the hub before it.'

'I'm not sure I can get into two in one day,' said Eric. 'That's more than my job's worth.'

'I don't know if we can pin it down any further. The hub's in Kent, there are about fifteen locations which could connect to the hub.'

'We've no time to investigate each one,' said Michael. 'Is there any way of narrowing it down?'

'I have narrowed it down,' said Anna. 'I've ruled out the hundreds of houses on the housing estate, the office block which is next to the police station. Just looking at individual properties, there are fifteen possibilities. It's on the outskirts of Sevenoaks. If it had been a hub in Sevenoaks then there'd be thousands of locations, but this one's out in the sticks.'

Something occurred to Michael. A thought came back to him. It seemed so long ago, yet in reality, it was very recent.

'A church,' said Michael.

'Why? You suddenly getting religious?' asked Eric, his usual sarcasm coming through again.

'No. When we went to see Joanna Crossley, I connected with something in their house. I got a brief connection with Singh. I got a sense of where they were fleeing to. All I got was the image of a church, in the countryside, an old church.'

Anna was already clicking away on the computer, bringing up maps, locations of churches, cross referencing with listed locations.

'There's only one,' she said. 'There's only one property connected to this hub in sight of a church.' She giggled a little. 'It's Saint Michael's church.' More tapping on the keys. 'It's an old farmhouse,' she said, talking as she typed. 'The owners live in Portugal, they rent it out through a letting agency. It's currently let to a company, which seems to have remarkably few details recorded for it.'

'Bingo,' said Eric. 'Let's saddle up.'

'What?' exclaimed Anna. 'You can't just go barging in.'

'No, you're right,' said Eric, 'we'd have to knock first.'

'Eric's right,' said Michael. 'I'm currently suspended, it would take time for anyone to verify your investigations, time we don't have.'

'But there are three of them,' said Anna, not adding the very obvious "and only two of you."

'Can't deny it, they've got every advantage,' said Eric. 'Numbers, firepower, they know the location and we don't, they're prepared and we're not, it might be dusk when we get there but it won't be dark. Time to be brave.'

'So let's call in the cavalry,' said Anna, trying not to sound desperate. 'Call the Acting Head, he'll have to listen to you.'

'Sorry,' said Michael, 'but we don't have time. It's now or never.' He turned to Eric. 'Can that Focus of yours get us there in time?'

'Well, it's funny you should ask,' said Eric, grinning, 'but I've managed to get an upgrade.' He told them about the Audi Q7, particularly about the equipment and armaments that came with it. Anna seemed very slightly reassured but was still certain they should tell someone, anyone.

It was Anna who sounded the cautionary note. 'Do we really have enough evidence to start shooting people?' she asked. 'None of what we've got would ever stand up in court.'

Michael and Eric looked at each other. Anna was right, the evidence they had was circumstantial, it all fitted together very neatly, but none of it was physical proof. It was a very shaky basis on which to start shooting people, to start killing people. If they were wrong, about any of it, and killed an innocent individual, they're almost certainly be guilty of manslaughter, if not murder.

'We won't get to see any more unless we get out there,' said Michael. 'If we have visual confirmation of the Three or the Head then we'll have enough to engage them.'

'If we see even one of them,' said Eric, 'we'll have to decide to commit, no half measures.'

'Anna,' said Michael, in a steady and calming voice. 'It's now or never. If we don't act now then the Head has no chance. I need you to get as much intelligence on this farmhouse as you can, especially anything from any live cameras in the area. Route it through to the car. We'll plan en route.'

There was a moment when none of them quite knew what to say. They knew what they wanted to say, they each had something they wanted to give voice to, but were shy or now was not the time.

Michael turned and marched towards the door, Eric following him. Anna turned back to her screens.

Twenty One

Kent - Wednesday, early evening

The Audi was a vast improvement over the Focus. For the journey out of town and towards Kent, the flashing blue lights and the sirens were a Godsend. They cut through the traffic and roared down the motorway. As Eric drove, weaving in and out of the traffic, Michael was in constant contact with Anna. They looked over the ariel photographs of the house, the grounds, and surrounding countryside. They looked over the floor plans of the building, estimating how he and Eric might enter, where they would be in danger of getting trapped and, perhaps most importantly, where the Three might be holding the Head. Eric kept glancing at the video display in the vehicle's centre console, making suggestions and observations. Michael and Eric were both keenly aware that their usual method of operation would be to practise and to prepare, but that was something they wouldn't be able to do. If they went in, they would have to be fast and violent, it would be the only way of evening the odds.

Once off the main roads and onto the smaller country roads Eric turned off the siren, they didn't want the sound carrying across the fields and alerting the Three. Two miles from the target he turned off the blue lights and dropped the speed. By the time they reached the outskirts of the village they were just another City worker driving an overly big car through the countryside. Eric turned off the road and onto a farm track and drove to the edge of a wooded area. Thick trees and bushes separated them from the field beyond, and at the other side of the field was the boundary of the farmhouse property. They each pushed in their communications earpiece, these linked to the comms system in the Audi which connected via a secure link to the mobile phone network, and from there to Anna's workstation in the GCHQ London office. and then opened the boot and worked quickly to pull out the equipment they'd need first; two holdalls of clothing and a large black equipment case. As Michael pulled the clothes out of the holdalls, Eric opened the case.

The two drones were small, no more than twelve inches across, black and hi-tech looking. Small propellers were mounted around the edge and a hi-def' camera on the underside of each. Eric switched on each of the drones, and almost without a sound they each lifted into the air and hovered. There was a slight hum and vague sound of moving air, but the little pieces of very expensive high-technology were almost silent.

'I'll pilot the drones into place,' said Anna over their earpieces, 'while you get ready.' Almost magically the drones lifted higher into the air and floated away over the tops of the trees. In moments they had disappeared from hearing and from sight. Eric and Michael got to work, quickly pulling on the one-piece black combat outfits. Pockets and clips accommodated grenades, side-arms and knives. It was always a balance between carrying enough equipment for any eventuality and not too much to be slowed down by excess weight. They had submachine guns, helmets, gloves and face-masks ready. They climbed back into the front seats of the car, and Michael connected the video display to Anna's video feed from the drones. Two moving images in the top and bottom halves of the video display. They could see the images from the drones as they skimmed the field, approaching at almost knee height. No-one in the farmhouse would be able to see the small black objects, not in the fading light of the approaching evening.

Moments later the video feeds showed the two drones splitting up. One headed away from the farmhouse and towards the edge of the field where it bounded the road so that it could approach the property from the other side. The other slowed and hovered slightly higher. The video zoomed in and panned slowly from left to right. They could see the rear of the house beyond the stone wall marking the boundary of the property. They could see a car, seemingly with someone sitting at the wheel, motionless. Dim lights showed from the ground floor windows of the farmhouse. A couple of minutes later the second drone skirted the opposite side of the property. They could see one man walking around. He looked almost casual, but the hand held inside his jacket betrayed the presence of a weapon.

'We're going to have to hit them hard and fast,' said Eric. 'They're just civilians.' He nodded to the image of the man patrolling around the house.

'They're armed and they're under the control of the Three,' said Michael, 'in which case they're enemy combatants. As soon as we hit the first one of them, no matter how quiet we are, Marshall and the others will know about it, and civilian or not they'll starting shooting at us.'

'We'll need to hit the car first,' said Eric.

Michael studied the video. 'One of us hits the car and one of us hits the man on the other side of the house.'

They watched as the image zoomed in, and they could see one of the windows of the lounge. They strained to see. It looked like someone was sitting in one of the chairs in the lounge.

'Anna, can you get a better view of that room from drone two?' asked Michael.

Without replying the drone moved slowly closer and zoomed in further. Although still slightly grainy from the digital magnification they could see three men, each sitting in one of the lounge chairs. It wasn't clear if they were talking or sleeping, but the three figures had three unmistakable appearances. The Three were in the farmhouse, in one room, with no heavy weapons apparent, but they were soldiers, their weapons would be close to hand.

Eric could see that Michael was frowning. 'Problem?' he asked.

'I doubt they're asleep,' he said. 'The drug makes you drowsy for an hour after taking it.' They watched for a few more moments. There was no movement.

'That's our way in,' said Eric, pointing at the other image. 'It's got to be across the field, over the wall and hit the car first.'

'I agree,' said Michael. 'Anna, can you get drone one to see into any of the upstairs windows?'

'I'll try,' she said. The drone was on the move again, and rising slightly higher into the air. Still staying as far away as possible and using as much of the optical and digital zooms as possible, the nearest of the first-floor windows expanded in the image. As far as any of them could see, the room was empty. The drone glided sideways, and the window of the next room came into view. Mentally Eric and Michael related the window to the floor plan of the building. It was hard to make out the detail, but the room had one occupant, sitting in a chair up against the wall. The colour of hair, what they could see of the clothes, it was far too similar to the Head to be coincidence.

'Time to go,' said Michael. They had their proof. Michael no longer felt any doubt, they'd found the Three and the time to strike had come. Eric turned off the ignition of the car, and they got out. He left the keys under the driver's seat and they shut the doors. Anna locked the doors. Eric was amused at the idea of just how 'remote' her control was. They pulled on their helmets and masks and gloves and set off into the trees.

The light was fading quickly, which worked to their advantage. Keeping low they kept to the side of the field, the trees behind them and the farmhouse on the far side of the field in front of them. They skirted the field as quickly as they dare, but maintaining an element of surprise was vital. The odds were not in their favour, so anything they could do to tip the odds their way the better.

They were soon at the top end of the wall, shuffling along it towards the back of the farmhouse. Anna guided them, telling them how close they were from the back yard of the house. When they were level with the parked car, they halted. She gave them a progress report on the man circling the house, waiting until he was on the far side of the building. Eric shuffled further along the wall, and Anna told him when he'd moved level with the edge of the house.

Michael pulled off his gloves and stuffed them into a pocket. The grip of the weapon was cool in his hands. It felt reassuring.

In a whisper, Michael said, 'three, two, one, go.'

***

Anna stared intently at her screens, oblivious to the others in the office, who paid her scant attention anyway. She heard Michael's countdown, and before he reached one, she pressed the key on her keyboard.

As planned her system initiated a series of pre-programmed events. The programmes she'd set up hacked instantly into the mobile phone network and broadcast a stream of messages, mimicking the effect of the Head's squealer. The squealer was a simple idea. A small device that an agent could trigger which would broadcast their location on a variety of radio frequencies and mobile phone channels. The monitoring systems of CGHQ were primed to respond to a squealer and were set up to respond instantly to any that had been flagged as a priority. The Head's squealer had been flagged with the highest priority. Within a second, messages started appearing on Anna's screen showing that the monitoring and surveillance systems had detected the Head's squealer and had pinpointed her location. Without needing to do anything Anna knew that police and MI5 would already be responding. Armed agents would be moments away from streaming out of Thames House and on their way to the Kent countryside. Phone calls would already be underway. The nearest armed response units would be mobilised and all local police would be alerted to the presence of armed and hostile hostage takers - their role would be to secure the surrounding roads and impede anyone trying to flee the area.

She turned her attention immediately to her screens and watched the first shots of the battle. Part of her was very glad that she was so far from the action. There was nothing she could do to help when soldiers started shooting, but she quickly reminded herself that there was an immense amount she could do to help. The soldiers on the ground could live or die by the quality of the information they had on the movements of the enemy, and information was what Anna did best. She watched them for only a moment, thinking that the soldiers on the ground were her friends, and she was to watch over them.

She selected the next pre-programmed sequence for the drones and sent them into their close-range surveillance mode.

***

As Michael said 'Go' he stood up and fired a burst of machine gun fire into the car. Although his gun was silenced the bullets hitting the car made a deafening banging and cracking as the glass of the windows exploded and the bullets tore into the bonnet and the bodywork of the car. The man inside was dead instantly. Simultaneously Eric had vaulted the wall and crouched at the side of the house. As Michael ceased firing and ducked back down behind the wall, Eric rolled a grenade under the car and shuffled back along the side of the house, using the building to shield him from the explosion.

The exploding grenade made a noise that would be heard three counties away. Pieces of the car ricocheted off the wall and the building, one chunk narrowly missing Eric's legs. The force and noise of the explosion were disorientating, even though they had been expecting it. Eric waited a moment, to make sure no more debris was going to fall on him, then he leapt forwards. He and Michael crossed paths, working to the plan they'd agreed. Michael kicked hard at what was left of the back door to the house and fired a burst of gunfire into the house. As he stepped forward bullets exploded into the door frame, he ducked back instinctively, escaping the barrage of small arms' fire coming his way. The Three were supposed to have been stunned by the explosion, but obviously somehow they had been forewarned. Michael poked his gun around the corner of the door and fired again, then ducked into the house firing bursts of machine gun fire into the kitchen as he entered.

Eric moved around the burning wreckage of the car, looking for the second man who had been patrolling the grounds. The yellow flames from the car threw dancing shadows across the yard and the garden, the smoke for a moment reduced his visibility to nothing. A curl of smoke blew across him and the moment it cleared he saw the patrolling man getting up off the ground, the explosion having blown him off his feet but perhaps saved by the protection of the building. The man had seen Eric and in a deft moment had pulled out his gun and fired. Eric rolled to one side and as his gun came to bear he fired a burst at the man. The bullets disappeared into the evening sky as the man rolled to the other side. They both came to their feet at the same moment, lunging towards each other and aiming at each other, but Eric was quicker on the trigger and fired two bursts of two shots into the man. Eric had a moment of surprise when it seemed to have no effect, the man continued to approach at an almost frightening speed. Eric fired again, a sustained burst directly into the man's chest. For a moment the man staggered forward and Eric had the unsettling thought that perhaps the man had been made impervious to gunfire, but then he crumpled to the ground and stopped moving.

Flames were coming from the open mouth of what used to be the kitchen windows, smoke billowing out and further blackening the outside of the house. Eric started to move towards the door but was stunned as another man cannoned into him from the side, appearing almost from nowhere. The two of them fell together almost onto the burning remains of the car, twisting at the last minute and crashing into the gravel driveway, Eric's gun falling away into the smoke and dark. Eric thrashed and writhed and twisted free from the man's grip, but as he turned to face the new assailant he was met with a flurry of punches. The man was fast and strong, his punches snapping hard, fast and accurate at Eric, who slapped each away with a hard blocking action. He'd avoided letting any of the punches land but he couldn't risk trading blows for long, this man was too dangerous for that. He pushed hard and the man staggered backwards, ducking suddenly to avoid catching his ginger hair in the flames jetting from the kitchen window.

Eric reached for his knife but the man was on him in a moment with another series of punches and strikes, one of them stunned Eric's wrist and weakened his grasp of the knife. Eric let the man hold his knife hand, knowing the man's hand was occupied allowed Eric to punch hard with his other hand, and as the man blocked the attack, Eric brought his knee up hard into the man's stomach. The man hardly seemed to notice the blow and in one almost invisible movement let go of Eric's knife hand and put his hand across Eric's forehead.

The feeling was the strangest and most deeply unpleasant experience Eric had ever had, a sudden sense of being drained of strength, his legs becoming heavy and his arms unresponsive. The air left his lungs as he exhaled, but he couldn't summon the strength to inhale, and he had the sudden awful feeling that this must be the experience of the fly at the mercy of the spider. Eric looked up and for a moment saw an enormous man, tall and black, staring down as Eric's knees buckled and he sank to the floor. He fought to draw a breath, not understanding what was happening.

The man he was fighting had ginger hair, but now he didn't, he'd changed. What kind of magic was this? He could have sworn he was now looking into the eyes of Vince Marshall, eyes that seemed to expand and become his whole world, burning into him, spreading pain throughout his being. Eric felt his grip on life starting to slip away.

***

Michael had entered the kitchen with as much noise and violence as possible. He sprayed machine gun fire around the room, not expecting to hit anyone but making sure that no-one could stand and shoot back, forcing Marshall and the others to retreat. He moved as quickly as he dared, flames were already spreading from behind him, and he heard shouting from the lounge ahead of him. He fired again and again as he advanced into the lounge. He doubted that anyone would have made a move for the cellar, there was no other exit from there. As he advanced into the room he could see the front door was open and a figure was disappearing through it, the slim and lithe figure of Julian Singh, with a black bag slung across his back. Another movement caught his eye, feet disappearing up the stairs. He fired at the stairs and dashed in pursuit. He fired again just missing the feet as they reached the top stair and turned onto the landing. Michael leapt three stairs at a time, reaching the top stair as fast as he could. The moment before he reached the top he heard a sustained burst of machine gun fire, and as he turned onto the landing he saw Bullock had strafed the wall and the door to the second room, aiming to kill whoever was inside, sending a shower of wood and plaster debris across the landing. As Michael fired, Bullock lunged at the

330

bullet riddled door and crashed through into the room, Michael only one step behind him.

Around the room bullet holes lined the wall at chest height and the room's spartan furniture had been reduced to splinters, but Bullock had paused for a moment as he realised the Head had tipped her chair over and was lying on the floor. Michael was about to fire into Bullock's back when he whirled round, knocking Michael's gun aside. Bullock was on him, now too close for guns, trading blows too rapidly to reach for a knife. Each punched at the other, blocking punches, attacking and counter attacking. Knee kicks flashed out from each. Punches turned into palm edge strikes to throats. Bullock's strikes were too fast for Michael to trap and turn into any kind of wrist lock, and he dared not try and grapple the man to the ground, that would give up too much stability and offer an advantage to Bullock. The room spun as Michael stepped to avoid a kick, he punched but his punch was slow, or it felt slow, it felt like he was fighting in water, punching through a dense and viscous liquid. Bullock punched again and again, and Michael could see only the mad eyes and blond hair of Evan Bullock. The world was disappearing into blackness around him. He had the desperate thought that Bullock wasn't just telepathic, he was now almost magical. He could make the world disappear.

'I can,' said Bullock, 'I can make your world disappear.' He punched again and again, and one punch caught Michael in the ribs, and he collapsed to the floor. Bullock stood over him, a victorious gladiator standing over his defeated opponent, waiting for the signal from Caesar; let him live, or make him die. There was no Caesar, there was no signal, there would be only death.

Bullock screamed, not in victory but in pain. The world came back to Michael almost hitting him in the face like an express train. He saw Bullock staggering back as the Head had stabbed him in the back of the knee with a large wooden splinter. Hardly a mortal wound, but it had broken Bullock's concentration. Michael rolled to one side and reached for his gun, but Bullock lunged forwards and kicked Michael in the ribs. Michael rolled away, the wind knocked out of him and pain shooting through his body. As quickly as he could, he forced himself up into a kneeling position only to see Bullock picking up the submachine gun and swinging it round to point at Michael.

For a moment, Bullock's eyes widened. For one insane instant, Bullock realised, too late, what had happened. Michael felt the connection, the telepathic link through the imprint he'd left on the grip of the weapon. He felt the psychic link open, and Michael forced all the mental energy he could muster into one violent telepathic assault. Bullock screamed like he'd been showered in boiling water, he convulsed and staggered backwards. The effect lasted only a moment, and in that moment Michael pulled the pistol from his side holster and fired into Bullock's chest, then fired again, and again, and kept on firing, blood splashed out of Bullock's dying body as he collapsed backwards and fell to the floor. In one bound Michael was on his feet and stood over the fallen man, and fired a single shot into Bullock's head, the blond hair turning forever red in a spray of blood.

The effect was disorientating. It was as though the world had suddenly fallen silent. Like every voice in the world had ceased. Michael, all of them, had wondered what it would be like to be mentally connected to someone at the moment of death. It felt like nothing he'd ever experienced before. He had to force himself to turn and look at the Head. She was still lying on the floor, wide-eyed, shaking.

'I hope he's dead,' she said, weakly.

'I bloody well hope he is,' said Michael. He went to her and used his knife to cut her bindings.

'We have to get you out of here,' he said, lifting her to her feet.

'You have to go and stop the others,' she said.

'No, we have to get you out, the building's on fire.' He holstered his pistol and picked up the submachine gun, then pulled her towards the door. Half way to the door something pulled him sideways. The Head had taken a step towards Bullock and delivered a powerful kick to the lifeless body's ribs. Michael was sure he heard at least a couple of ribs crack, and had to suppress a smile, the woman had spirit. He pulled her towards the door, holding his gun ready to shoot anyone in front of them.

'Please tell me you're not alone,' she said.

'No,' he said, 'I have some help.'

***

Eric's world was fading into blackness, and the man towered over him. Was it Marshall, or was it the other one? It really didn't matter, his strength had almost left him.

There was a loud crack as a large black object hit the man on the side of the head. The man staggered and let go of Eric. The telepathic link was broken and Eric saw the ginger haired man again, the mirage of Marshall had gone. The man looked around for a moment to see what had hit him, not noticing Anna's drone circling around behind him. The single moment was all that Eric needed. He reached for his knife and lunged at the man, burying the knife in the man's chest. He fell instantly to the ground and moved no more.

'Thank you,' said Eric.

'You're welcome,' came Anna's voice through his earpiece, as casually as if she'd just passed him the sugar.

'Where's Michael?' he asked.

'In the house,' said Anna. Eric looked, the fire was now consuming the ground floor, preventing any entry via the kitchen. 'No, he's behind you,' came Anna's voice in his ear. Eric turned and saw Michael and the Head coming around the corner of the house.

'Where are they?' asked Michael.

There was a pause and Eric saw the drone which had saved him float away.

'Take cover,' shouted Anna over their earpieces. Michael pushed the Head back into the cover of the side of the house, Eric dashing after them as bullets smacked into the house and the gravel and the wall and the remains of the car. Gunfire crackled from a short distance away, muzzle flashes betraying the position of their attackers.

'Okay, there they are,' said Michael.

'Two of them,' said Anna, 'behind the wall on the west side. Can't locate the third.'

'Bullock's dead,' said Michael. He saw Eric grin, and he was sure he heard a barely suppressed cheer in his earpiece.

At least now it was becoming a more even fight, two against two. Michael and Eric probably had more guns and ammunition, and Singh and Marshall were together, no opportunity to set up any pincer movement. No doubt their focus would now be on escape.

Over the growing sound of the fire came the unmistakable sound of a helicopter. It was low, and getting closer.

'Oh no, them again?' Michael heard Eric say, probably not meaning his comment to be heard.

'We have to get out of here,' said Michael.

'You have to stop them,' said the Head. 'You can't let them get away.'

Michael turned to her, his masked face close to hers. 'If it's your little band of soldiers come to finish the job then I've no doubt they'll kill everyone here, we have to leave, now.' He pulled her towards the wall.

They'd taken barely half a step when bullets blew up gravel and stone chips. There was no sound of gunfire, but Michael could hear the bullets landing near them and on the other side of the garden. This was someone new, someone with a lot of guns, firing at all of them.

'Shit,' he said, sharply. 'They're already here.' He thought for a moment that night-vision goggles would help, but the dazzling light from the fire would have made them ineffective. The assassins were here. Michael couldn't see where they'd appeared from, but they'd approached unseen and unheard. Now they were caught in a pincer movement, by gunfire from Marshall and Singh behind the wall and from the four new soldiers in the garden.

More gunfire, the cracks of the guns fired by Marshall, and Singh. More snaps and twangs as the bullets landed from silenced weapons firing back. For the moment the battle seemed to be between the newcomers and Marshall and Singh.

'Anna, who's firing?' Michael asked.

'Marshall and Singh behind the wall on the west, four unidentified soldiers, moving from the north side of the garden, they're moving towards the wall on the west side. They're going for Marshall and Singh.'

'Then why are they shooting at us?' asked the Head.

'That's the question I've been wanting an answer to,' shouted Michael, perhaps louder than he intended.

It became harder to hear Anna's voice as the noise of the helicopter got louder and louder. There was suddenly the deafening roar of the helicopter's engines and the blast of the wind from its rotors as it swung directly overhead, clearing farmhouse property from one side to the other in a moment and sinking to ground beyond the far wall. There was more gunfire from that side, audible even above the roar of the helicopter. And then the gunfire stopped. In the dancing light from the fire, flickering across the garden, Michael and the others watched as four soldiers moved slowly across the garden towards the far wall. They held their silenced submachine guns in front of them.

Everyone's attention was taken by a small black object flitting across the garden just over head height. As the scream of the helicopter's engines grew, the drone headed straight for it in a kamikaze attempt to stop the aircraft. It was a bold move, and Michael applauded Anna's ingenuity, but the drone was small, and the helicopter was very large, and the moment the drone came into the path of the tips of the rotor blades it was smashed into a cloud of fragments. The helicopter leapt into the sky and moved away. The soldiers in the garden raised their weapons and fired, but the helicopter was already moving out of range, its noise receding into the night sky.

Michael, Eric and the Head huddled down at the side of the burning farmhouse, looking at the four soldiers crouched in the garden. The soldiers faced them, not moving but weapons pointing directly at them. This was where the odds had shifted very definitely in favour of the opposing force, Michael thought. The moment seemed to stretch out forever.

Michael and Eric resisted the urge to fire, four against two was not a fight either of them wanted to join. Perhaps the four newcomers were receiving orders, perhaps considering their best course of action. Perhaps someone was again deciding if Michael and the others should be allowed to live or if they had out-lived their usefulness.

Without warning, the four soldiers started to move backwards. Keeping their focus on Michael and the others, the soldiers retreated into the darkness of the far side of the garden and were gone. The sound of the helicopter was disappearing into the distance, the night now fractured by the noise and light and heat of the burning farmhouse.

'That was weird,' said Eric.

'Looks like someone decided in your favour, again,' said the Head.

'Yep,' said Michael, 'and I still want to know who.'

In the distance, they could hear the wail of the sirens of police cars, and flashing blue lights started to light up the countryside.

Michael and Eric pulled off their masks and helmets.

'Is everyone okay?' came Anna's voice in their earpieces.

'Yes, by and large,' said Eric, 'I think we're doing okay.'

'Anna,' said Michael, 'contact the Head of Operations and tell them the Head's alive, Bullock's dead, Marshall and Singh have escaped. Someone needs to track that helicopter and shoot it down.'

'Will do,' said Anna, and her channel went quiet.

'This is going to take so much explaining,' said Michael.

'You have no idea how much paperwork this is going to generate,' said the Head.

Twenty Two

London - Wednesday, evening

Yves Falcone stood at the window and looked out over the London skyline. He never tired of looking at it. In fact, of all the cities in the world, this was his favourite. He always felt at home here. He could almost lose himself in the vista, watching each of the twinkling lights, wondering what life-stories were being played out behind each door and window, what successes people had enjoyed that day, what failures people had endured. This was a city of life, a city for living in. It was that thought that brought him back to the heaviness in his heart. Where had it gone wrong? Where had the success become such a failure? Where had the quest for life turned into a mission to kill and destroy? He had never wanted to be a part of killing, and yet here he was, at the centre of a conspiracy to keep a secret, by murder if necessary, when necessary. It seemed to have become more and more necessary. He had played this game for too long, and now he had had enough.

He bent down to the safe, turned the tumbler left and right, and pulled the door open. Wearing his favourite leather gloves he took out the leather document case and put it on the desk. He knew that he if he touched the object it would create an instant connection with Him. But he didn't need to touch the object. He was so powerful He could enter Falcone's mind at any time. Only minutes before, He had come into Falcone's mind. The voice had been urgent, aggressive. Marshall and one of the others had escaped. Turner needed to be told, to tell his men to withdraw, to leave Sanders alive, for now. That could mean only one thing. Despite all the promises, the killing would go on. There would be other demands to send in troops, to give orders to have people killed.

Holding it so gently, he slipped the leather case into the thick yellow envelope and pressed the flap shut, the adhesive binding the envelope closed. He placed it neatly in the centre of this desk. The label on the envelope was large and simple and clear. They had an established procedure for this. As a company that dealt with much confidential material, there was often a need to ensure that documents were taken out of harm's way. He had left instructions, the envelope would be taken and dealt with. The label read: FOR IMMEDIATE DESTRUCTION.

There was a sensation that preceded the voice, only by a moment, but it was enough for Falcone to know that the voice was about to appear in his mind. He felt it now. He braced himself.

'Yves,' said the voice, so calm and soothing. 'What are you doing?'

Why did the voice come now? Could He sense what Falcone was doing? Was He aware of Falcone at every single moment? Was he ever alone, and if not, for how long had he never been apart from this man?

'I don't think I want to talk to you at the moment,' said Falcone, out loud. He stood up and buttoned up his suit jacket.

'Yves, I sense that you are troubled,' said the voice. 'Talk to me.'

Yves Falcone said nothing. He'd said everything he wanted to say. He had nothing more to say, certainly nothing more to say to Him.

Falcone left the office and walked down the corridor. He pushed through the door and into the stairwell. He walked up the stairs to the top floor, then through the door into the maintenance area. It was a dimly lit space where the water tanks sat. One door led to the lift machinery, another to the air-conditioning plant.

'Yves, please stop and talk to me,' said the voice. He expected the voice to get louder, to make him stop. The voice had done that before, made him do things, against his will, but this time it felt different. He'd decided not to play this game anymore, and it seemed that He had no control anymore.

'I've had enough,' said Falcone, against his better judgement. 'I've had enough of the killing. You said it would stop, you said there would be no more, but there will be, won't there?'

'No, Yves,' said the voice. 'No more killing, I promise.'

'I don't believe you,' said Falcone loudly into the dimness of the room. He walked quickly to the other side, to a heavy door. He took a key from his pocket and unlocked the door. He pushed open the door and stepped out onto the roof.

The air was fresh, a breeze blew his hair, and he breathed in the London air, car fumes and all. In its own way, it smelled so good. Perhaps he should have come up here before to enjoy the view. No matter. Such things did not matter now.

'Yves, stay where you are,' said the voice in a strong and commanding tone. Falcone felt the voice as much as heard it. The voice rattled through his body, and he found it hard to move. He took a moment, took another breath, and relaxed. This was not a battle he could win, and he reminded himself that this is why he had decided not to fight, to withdraw from the field of battle.

'I'm just going for a short walk,' said Falcone, and smiled. He walked across the roof to the edge. A waist-high barrier circled the roof of the building. As he took hold, he felt the barrier was too high to climb, but then he told himself that wasn't his thought, it was His thought, a distraction, a diversion. He held the barrier firmly and swung one leg over and then the other.

As he stood on the edge he could see the side of the building stretching down to the pavement. He thought that we would be afraid. If he was going to feel fear he thought it would have been here, but he didn't. He felt a little sad, this wasn't how he wanted to end things.

'Then don't,' said the voice. 'Keep going, work with me. We've done good things together, Yves, don't throw it away now.'

'We've done some evil things together,' said Falcone. 'You've done evil things, and you've made me carry out your bidding. I never wanted to be a part of this.'

'Yes you did,' said the voice. 'When you realised the power of the drug you wanted to be a part of it. You were a full and willing participant in what we did.'

'Not in the killing, that was your choice, not mine.'

'Did we have a choice, Yves?' asked the voice, more softly. 'Tell me, what would you have done? What other way would you have taken? Or would you have brought disaster down upon us all?'

Falcone hesitated. He had no answer to the question. He never did have an alternative. Perhaps there had never been an alternative. Perhaps what they had done had been the only thing that could be done, but that didn't mean they had to keep on doing it. And despite the promises, there was always more killing. It never ended. It had to end. He had to make it end.

As he stepped forward, he had a sudden feeling of being free. For the few brief moments it took him to fall he felt alone, a peaceful kind of alone, where his thoughts were his own, where he was free of the guilt of what he'd been a part of, where he felt whole and himself, only himself.

***

There had been a lot of activity in Thames House. Michael, Eric and Anna had been interviewed several times by several different departments, and there would be police interviews in the morning. They hadn't had much time together since they got to The Office. Anna had gone straight from the GCHQ London office to Thames House. Michael and Eric had been interviewed briefly at the scene by the local police. Their vehicle had been impounded, much to Eric's annoyance, their weapons taken for forensic examination. They had at least been able to retrieve their civilian clothes. Another MI5 driver had driven them back to London.

The Head had stayed out of sight. Most people knew that she'd been rescued and that she was back in the building, but few saw her. More teams were put on the search for her abductors, but Michael, Eric and Anna knew that their search would be fruitless. The Three (now Two) had had the helicopter on standby and had an escape route planned, there would be no tracing them tonight, not by any of the regular MI5 or GCHQ teams.

Michael found Eric at the drink vending machine, grimacing as he sipped from the cup of so-called tea.

'Good day at the office?' Eric asked, smirking.

'Oh, had its ups and downs,' said Michael, grinning back at him.

'So what do we call them now? The Two? The Twins?' asked Eric with an even broader smirk.

'Let's not underestimate them,' said Michael.

Eric looked past Michael, and Michael turned. Anna walked over to join them. They hugged without saying much. There was so much they wanted to say to each other, but none felt any great need to put it into words.

Michael noticed, Anna wasn't smiling like he and Eric were.

'What's up?' he asked.

'I had alerts set up, in case anyone involved in any of this appears in the media or any official reports,' said Anna. She paused, perhaps searching for the right words. 'Yves Falcone committed suicide a short while ago.'

None of them said anything. At this news, none of them knew what to say. This was unexpected, and brought more questions, more concerns.

A mobile phone beeped. They each checked their phone. Michael's phone showed a message.

'The Head wants to see us in her office,' he said.

'I don't suppose she's going to say thank you, is she?' asked Eric.

'Don't be silly,' said Michael.

'Well, if you're busy on company business, I'll head off,' said Anna.

'No,' said Michael, 'she wants to see all three of us.'

They made their way to the Head's office. It wasn't a big office but big enough for her desk and two two-seater sofas for visitors. They closed the door and stood, waiting for her to speak first.

'Please, have a seat,' she said, gesturing to the sofas. The gesture was unexpected, the Head wasn't known for her congeniality. 'The first thing I want to say,' she said, 'is thank you. It doesn't really seem enough, just saying thank you, when you saved my life.'

The three of them exchanged glances, not quite sure how to respond.

'However,' she continued, 'there is unfinished business to take care of. Miss Hendrickson, I don't suppose there's any trace of that helicopter?'

'No ma'am,' said Anna. 'We know where it came from, but the helicopter and its pilot are still missing, and so are they.'

'Yes,' said the Head, 'they are.' She looked at Michael. 'Close, but not close enough. At least one of them has been taken care of.' There was a silent, collective cheer. A small but significant victory. Anna knew that many in GCHQ would cheer when they heard the news. Some would be vocal, some would cheer in their own silent way, some would cry, but they'd all feel some small measure of justice had been served.

'They found Mason,' said the Head. 'They had killed him, probably as soon as they had access to the exVoxx system.' This was not a surprise, but it was a blow. He hadn't deserved what had happened to him.

'Did they get into PanMedic?' asked Michael, 'did they get any of the drug?'

'From Miss Hendrickson's analysis of their Internet activity and from what CCTV coverage has been examined, I think we have to conclude that they did, and this makes them even more dangerous. Even if there are only two of them, I think it's the more dangerous two who survived.'

'With respect,' said Michael, 'this makes our job even more impossible. They're acting to a plan, they're working together, they're now more powerful.' Before anyone could interrupt him, he went on. 'We're operating in the dark, alone, with no resources, and there's still someone else out there who can order in a bunch of assassins any time they want. Someone who is also powerfully telepathic, maybe even powerful enough to compel someone to take their own life.' Michael stopped short of confessing his knowledge of Falcone. He still wasn't sure of the relationship between the Head and this man. Did she know he was dead? Did they work together? Who reported to whom?

Anna updated everyone on what had happened to Yves Falcone. The Head stared out of the window for a few moments, her face implacable. None of them could read her expression. She looked back at them.

'They also still have access to the exVoxx network,' said Anna. 'The computer servers at the farmhouse were destroyed by fire, but all Singh will need is a laptop and his access codes and a bit of hardware, and he can access and control exVoxx. Don't we have to tell someone about that?'

'And who do you suggest we tell?' said the Head. 'We could tell the exVoxx company, but then we'd have to explain how they got control and how we know, and then we're having to answer a lot of questions I really don't want to have to talk about in public.'

'We can't tell anyone,' said Michael. 'We still have to keep this to ourselves. But with a supply of Batch four-two-seven, there's no telling how powerful they'll become.'

'What's Batch four-two-seven?' asked Eric.

'The drug that made them telepathic,' said the Head, 'the drug manufactured by PanMedic. An increased dose of the drug makes the recipient's telepathic abilities more powerful.'

'Why don't we all take some?' asked Eric, 'even things up a bit.'

'It's not that simple,' said the Head.

'With respect, Ma'am,' said Michael, the frustration becoming more evident in his voice, 'we have to do something to make it simple. We have to do something to even things up. You're setting us up to fail, and to be brutally honest, that nearly cost you your life.'

The Head drew a breath to speak, but Michael spoke first. 'Yes, I know we have to keep this secret, but enough's enough, we need to know the whole story. We at least need to know who we're fighting, or there's no point. We may as well pack up and go home.' Michael braced himself to stand, angling towards the door.

'Wait,' said the Head, sharply. Michael sat back into the sofa.

Without warning, she stood up and walked out of the office, leaving the others to exchange nervous glances. There were so many questions, so many unknowns. They started to speculate what they were going to do next, what they could do next, what Marshall and Singh might be about to do next, and then the Head came back into the office, followed by a catering assistant pushing a tray of cups and saucers and tea and coffee and biscuits. The catering assistant left, and the Head sat back down behind her desk.

'I assume you can serve yourselves?' she said, nodding at the trolley.

As they started to pour the drinks, the Head continued. 'I can tell you about the project, how it started, who was involved, what happened. Some of it I know from my own involvement, but Michael, you'll need to fill in some of the story from your side.'

'Yes,' said Michael, cautiously.

'Some of it I can only tell you from what I've heard from others or from supposition,' said the Head, 'and Miss Hendrickson, you'll have to tell us your part of the story.'

'Me?' said Anna with extreme surprise.

'Oh yes,' said the Head, 'although you didn't know it at the time, you were involved in the project.'

Before Anna could ask anything more, the Head began to tell them the story of the Psiclone project.

The Psiclone Project
the third book in the series...

The End

The Psiclone Project

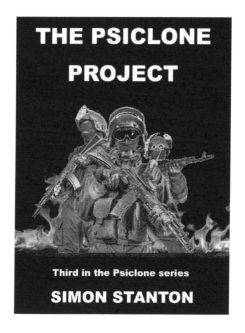

THE PSICLONE
PROJECT

Third in the Psiclone series

SIMON STANTON

The third book in the Psiclone series - the
story of how a unit of Special Forces soldiers—
Captain Michael Sanders, Lieutenant Julian Singh,
Sergeant Vince Marshall, Corporal Evan Bullock—
were recruited into a secret military experiment they
believed would boost their stamina and resilience, but
the experiment had an unexpected outcome and the
soldiers became powerfully telepathic.

Their telepathic skills gave them a unique
advantage in their mission, but some of the soldiers

start to see other, more profitable uses for their new-found skills. Shadowy figures behind the project begin to suspect that the soldiers and their new talents have become more of a threat than an asset.

Secrets are exposed and identities are revealed as the story of the Psiclone project is told. Loyalties are tested, and broken, as the events leading to the fateful operation in the freezing desert of Afghanistan are retold, an operation where betrayal and murder would lead to comrades becoming mortal enemies.

To find out more, go to:

www.simonstanton.com/

Simon Stanton

Simon Stanton fell in love with stories at an early age, reading and writing science fiction. Despite the best efforts of parents and teachers to broaden his horizons, Simon remained obsessed with sci-fi. Teaching himself to touch type so he could get his thoughts on paper quicker, Simon wrote shorts stories, ideas for bigger works, and finally his first novel length work - a piece which remains safely locked away. Then he stopped writing, and after a thirty year hiatus (which not even he can adequately explain) he began writing again, first short stories and then his first proper novel, A Mind To Kill, the first in The Psiclone Series, published on Amazon. This was followed by Force Of Mind, and now the third (The Psiclone Project) is well under way.

Simon lives in West Yorkshire, UK, and balances his writing with home life, a job in project management, and his practise of Aikido (a Japanese martial art.)

To find out more about Simon, his (free) short stories, and the Psiclone novels (but, to be fair, not much about Yorkshire), visit his website at:

www.simonstanton.com

or follow him on Twitter at:

@TheSimonStanton

or on Facebook at:

www.facebook.com/simonstantonwriter

Printed in Great Britain
by Amazon